PENGUIN BOOKS

Chasing the Fire

Paisley Hope is a *USA Today* and *Sunday Times* bestselling author of spicy contemporary romance. She loves to write found family, dreamy settings, happily-ever-afters and the occasional dark romance that will keep your pulse racing. Paisley spends all her free time with her husband and children. She loves to bake, garden and travel.

Praise for Paisley Hope

'Paisley Hope. . . I'm your biggest fan!!'

'Perfect in every way'

'Loving this series and can't wait for the next one'

'Paisley Hope has me in a chokehold with the Silver Pines series!'

'This book is everything I dreamed of and more'

'I'm telling you this is going to be the next big cowboy series'

'If you haven't started your cowboy era yet, please saddle up and read Silver Pines!'

'I giggled, sweated, kicked my feet and had my jaw on the floor throughout this read'

Also by Paisley Hope

Silver Pines Series:
Holding the Reins
Training the Heart
Riding the High
Freeing the Wild
Chasing the Fire

Soldiers of Bedlam Series:
Wolf.e
Dove
Foxx

Chasing the Fire

PAISLEY HOPE

PENGUIN BOOKS

PENGUIN BOOKS

UK | USA | Canada | Ireland | Australia
India | New Zealand | South Africa

Penguin Books is part of the Penguin Random House group of companies
whose addresses can be found at global.penguinrandomhouse.com

Penguin Random House UK,
One Embassy Gardens, 8 Viaduct Gardens, London SW11 7BW

penguin.co.uk

First published in the US by Dell, an imprint of Random House,
a division of Penguin Random House LLC, 2026
First published in the UK by Penguin Books 2026

001

Copyright © Paisley Hope, 2026

The moral right of the author has been asserted

Penguin Random House values and supports copyright. Copyright fuels creativity, encourages diverse voices, promotes freedom of expression and supports a vibrant culture. Thank you for purchasing an authorised edition of this book and for respecting intellectual property laws by not reproducing, scanning or distributing any part of it by any means without permission. You are supporting authors and enabling Penguin Random House to continue to publish books for everyone. No part of this book may be used or reproduced in any manner for the purpose of training artificial intelligence technologies or systems. In accordance with Article 4(3) of the DSM Directive 2019/790, Penguin Random House expressly reserves this work from the text and data mining exception.

Chapter page stock art by Plawarn and MEM/Adobe Stock
Ornament stock art by fendy/Adobe Stock

Printed and bound in Great Britain by Clays Ltd, Elcograf S.p.A.

The authorised representative in the EEA is Penguin Random House Ireland,
Morrison Chambers, 32 Nassau Street, Dublin D02 YH68

A CIP catalogue record for this book is available from the British Library

ISBN: 978–1–804–95627–4

Penguin Random House is committed to a sustainable future
for our business, our readers and our planet. This book is made
from Forest Stewardship Council® certified paper.

*To the Ashby family for changing my life the way two pink lines changed Asher and Olivia's: unexpectedly and permanently. And to every one of you who fell in love with each character alongside me.
Silver Pines forever*

TW:

Talk of violence associated with organized crime, past tense, not detailed, mild
Talk of loss of parents
FMC is adopted, talk of birth parents, adoptive parents, and all that goes along with it
Open-door sex scenes, mild degradation
Mild alcohol use
Death by fire, flashback not detailed
Unplanned pregnancy, labor and delivery, descriptive, on page
Talk of death of a beloved pet, not on page

Chasing the Fire

CHAPTER 1
Olivia
APRIL

MOM
> Are you okay, sweetheart? You seemed a little sad today when we left the airport.

Adding a cup of flour to the bowl of dry ingredients on my kitchen island, I can almost see my mom nervously tucking her blond hair behind her ear while she waits for an answer to her text. She knows me better than anyone, but since I don't want to talk about my self-proclaimed hot girl slump right now, I take another big sip of my wine, right from the bottle, and lie.

ME
> I'm fine, it was a great weekend. And so nice to see the whole family.

MOM
> It really was, wasn't it? Aunt Lena sent me the photos.

My phone pings as, one by one, the photos come through: my cousin in her perfect wedding dress, with her perfectly handsome groom—who also happens to be a doctor—in the beautiful Florida sunshine where we spent the weekend.

Down the hatch goes another big swig.

> DAD
> Since we're sending photos *Side eye emoji*

His message is followed by a shot of my uncle Bobby passed out drunk in his piece of cake at the reception. I laugh as I continue sifting my ingredients. My dad is always trying to make me feel better. I know he could tell something was off with me, but he's always been there to balance my mom. Everyone knows Lynn Sutton is a hopeless romantic, and even though she's my adoptive mom we're a lot alike, because I too am usually ga-ga for a good love story. Though not lately.

Yes, my cousin's wedding was beautiful. Just like my best friend CeCe's wedding was last year, and how I'm certain my other best friend Ginger's will be in a few weeks.

Everyone I know is either already married or getting married, having babies, or both, while I'm still coming home alone, *extra* alone since the death of my fifteen-year-old orange tabby cat Biscuit. My best furry friend went peacefully in his sleep almost two weeks ago. It feels crazy to have cried over a cat as much as I did, but I spent two days with swollen eyes and tissues after that chunky little ball of fluff left me. Now, I push the brimming tears down, just as a private message from my mom comes through.

> MOM
> Your Prince Charming is out there.

MOM

> Remember, I didn't meet your dad until I was thirty-two.

She might be a worrywart, but she's bang on. I *have* been feeling like my time to meet my soulmate has passed, or like my biological clock is ticking, though I'm not even thirty yet. A flash of one of my favorite movies, *27 Dresses*, runs through my head as I crack two eggs into a dish. *Always a bridesmaid, never a bride.*

I'm still envisioning my very own James Marsden showing up out of nowhere to sweep me off my feet as I mix my banana bread batter. Nine-thirty P.M. isn't the time I'd normally bake, but when I'm sad I reach for wine, sweet treats, and a good rom-com. Which is exactly my plan for tonight.

Just as I go to turn up the volume of my country playlist, my phone starts ringing and my best friend Ginger's pretty smiling face pops up on the screen.

She probably wants to talk about wedding plans and I know if I don't answer now, she'll just call again.

"Babe, you're back?" she asks animatedly into the phone.

"Yep." I look around my all-too-quiet space.

"Wedding conference! I can't wait to tell you both what I found today." She's already adding our other best friend CeCe to the call before I can respond. Ginger is always energetic, but as a bride? She's over-the-top giddy. The funny thing is, she's already married, but you'd never know it as she plans her formal wedding to one of CeCe's older brothers, Cole. They eloped "accidentally" one drunken night in Vegas last summer and, somehow, *that* was what pushed them to realize they've been in love since they were teenagers.

A half hour later, most of my rosé is gone. I'm more than a little drunk, and still listening to the two of them chatter, while I line a pan with parchment paper, pour in the batter, and put my bread in the oven.

". . . And we're gonna have a photo booth and props," Ginger continues.

I've barely said anything since she called. Taking what's left of my rosé with me, I move outside into my dark and chilly backyard, my fuzzy sherpa sweater wrapped around my floral silk pajamas, my cow slippers snuggled on my feet.

". . . And oh my God, we got that videographer we wanted too," Ginger continues.

I can't tell Ginger how much I envy her finding Mr. Right. I also can't tell CeCe I feel light-years behind her, watching her baby bump grow while she and her husband Nash prepare for the arrival of their daughter.

I can't tell either of them how lonely I feel every time I glance at Biscuit's cat bed in the corner. He'd been my companion since I was fourteen, right around the time I started feeling the loss of my birth parents. That's when I started asking more questions. What did I get from each of them? What were their personalities like? What were their dreams, their aspirations? Questions that will go forever unanswered. My adoptive mom was my birth mother's second cousin and her closest living relative. Some old newspaper articles about their car crash and a few photos my mom salvaged from my family's home are all I have left of them.

Since I can't bring all *that* baggage to my two friends right now, who are experiencing the best time of their lives, I simply gush with them and say all the right things from my end of the phone, like the dutiful bridesmaid I am.

After we say goodbye, I wrap my sweater tighter around my body, my head swirling. It's still cool, although spring is almost here and the sugar maples in my yard are starting to bloom. They frame the outdoor space and remind me why I've loved this house since the moment I viewed it with my parents after college. It's historic to this part of Laurel Creek, and it was cheap, because it needed a lot of cosmetic work. Which I loved. Design is my passion: clothing, interior, landscape, even baking fancy desserts. You name it, when it comes to being creative, I'm in.

I hit play on my country playlist as I wait for my bread to bake and a sappy love song by Kacey Musgraves plays as I pull up the photos of my cousin's wedding. I scroll through them quickly before making the mistake of moving back into my own camera roll. Photos of me, CeCe, and Ginger a few years ago, just after CeCe moved home from living in Seattle. We were almost always together back then, and seeing our smiling faces fuels a sense of nostalgia.

What I fail to notice during my drunken stroll down memory lane is the smoke filling my kitchen. It isn't until I hear the smoke alarm that I jerk up and bolt into the house. The moment I see flames through my oven door, I scream and run through fire safety 101 in my head. Ripping flowers out of a vase on my island and tossing them to the floor, I make it to the oven armed with just a touch of water and yank the door open.

Big mistake.

The flames escape as I toss the vase water onto the burning bread. I'm not accurate, so half of it lands on the floor as the towel hanging beside the stove lights up. I try to grab it and toss it into my sink with another scream, but it lands on my counter instead and I watch in horror as my kitchen curtains catch fire. It feels like I'm having an out-of-body experience as the flames start to move—to my well-lacquered wooden range hood, the stack of bills on my counter, my cookbooks. The fuel is abundant in my small kitchen. It's been mere moments but this is well beyond my drunken realm of management.

Pulling my phone, which is ironically blaring "Burning House" by Cam, from my sweater pocket, I call for the fire department.

"Nine-one-one, state your emergency," the voice answers as I back out of the kitchen and into my living room.

"Everything is on fire! Oh my *God!* . . ." I stammer, the heat following me. I give the woman on the end of the line my address, trying to explain what happened in a tipsy sort of word vomit.

"Ma'am, you need to go outside," she says calmly, though I'm already pulling open the front door. "Don't stop to take anything with you, understand?"

"Yes. I—" I start coughing.

"Okay, ma'am. Are you outside?"

"Yes."

"Okay, good, stay there. LCFD are already on their way. I'm going to stay on the line. Don't go back into the premises."

I cough again as I do what she says, shifting from one slipper-clad foot to the other on my front lawn, shivering and sobbing as I wait for the fire department to arrive. Fresh panic falls over me as I watch the flames continue to blaze in my kitchen.

Finally, flashing red lights round the corner of my street. A cruiser truck hurtles toward me, followed by a full-sized firetruck.

My throat is hoarse and I'm shaking as I move toward the truck, which pulls up in front of my house. The moment the door opens I freeze, because the *last* man on earth I'd choose to see me like this exits the truck. He's dressed in full fire gear, helmet pulled low over intense gray eyes and what I'm almost certain will be an annoyed furrow in his dark brows. Our mysterious and dangerously hot fire chief, Asher fucking Reed.

CHAPTER 2
Olivia

My stomach drops and I'm suddenly all too aware of my slightly drunk, very frazzled state. One that isn't equipped to handle Asher. Because this man is not *just* good-looking. That's much too boring of a description for him. At six foot five, he's big *everywhere*; his jaw is wide and chiseled, covered by a full dark beard. Every angle of his face is symmetrical, straight and strong, and his skin is laden with ink, intricate tattoos that run from his neck all the way down to his knuckles. The mysterious burn scars that creep up his hands, only add to his allure.

He's powerful and commanding, and as he leans into the truck and pulls out a thermal blanket, my mouth goes dry and my vision blurs. Asher calls orders over his shoulder to the rest of his crew as they start pulling a thick hose out of the truck. One of them is familiar: Walker Black, the middle son from the Grosvenor Cattle Ranch just outside of town and, if I remember correctly, Asher's volunteer assistant captain.

Asher doesn't waste any time approaching me. His woodsy and clean scent, one I'd know anywhere, smells like oak and bergamot. Right now it's mixed with a hint of smoke from his gear, and somehow even that is enticing.

Of course Asher would be on call tonight. Of course he'd be here smelling delicious and peering down at me like I'm the biggest pain in his ass.

"Liv," he greets curtly as he wraps the blanket around my shoulders. His voice is a deep timbre with a slight Irish accent. It's a voice that has always felt like the promise of something darker, born from the most suppressed part of my dreams. The kind of dreams I've pushed down for as long as I can remember.

God I'm drunk.

"I need to assess you," he says, as I rearrange the idiotic stare I'm sure I'm wearing while I watch his face, his throat, his lips.

He doesn't seem to notice; his gray eyes are devoid of emotion as he checks me over.

"Anyone else on the premises? Pets?"

Grief steals my words as I shake my head, a fresh set of tears filling my eyes for my little Biscuit as Asher's men work to put out the flames inside my house. My front door is wide open and the hose lays across my threshold. I look around and see it took only a few minutes for almost every neighbor on my street to take up residence on their front porch to watch my world crumble.

"Come with me." Asher nods to the back of the fire cruiser, pulling his helmet off as he lowers the tailgate and I step off the curb. I misjudge its depth and almost fall until he steadies me.

I'm accident-prone, which Asher has witnessed more than most. I can't count how many nights he's stopped me from stumbling out the door at the Horse and Barrel, the local bar where he sometimes works. As he helps me up onto the tailgate now, his hands circle my waist to steady me. The skin he's touching immediately breaks out in goosebumps.

"I'm not hurt. I'm sorta drunk . . ." I croak out, nearly choking on a sob.

"Aye," he mutters as he pulls out a medical bag.

As I look at my house and see the damage, I try not to hyperventilate.

"How *drunk*?" Asher asks, trying to catch my gaze with his own.

"A couple glasses of wine?" I answer, but he waits, staring at me until I look up at him with the truth. "Most of the bottle."

"*Christ sakes* . . ." he mutters under his breath, so softly it's almost inaudible.

"How long were you in there? Try to remember. This is *important*."

"M-maybe two minutes," I tell him as he moves robotically, popping an oxygen mask on me.

"Deep breath in," he orders. He's always been a man of few words, which makes him unapproachable on its own, but, in his fire gear, he seems even more intimidating.

I inhale, thinking of the way I must look right now: pajamas, tears, a mask, and to top it all off, my overstuffed cow slippers. Thankfully Asher doesn't seem fazed by my appearance as he spends a few minutes taking my blood pressure. His warm, calloused grip grazes the underside of my arm, and everything buzzes under my skin when I watch his strong jaw tense.

"Again," he orders as he watches his meter.

Smoke catches my eye again. *Oh my God, my house . . .*

"*Olivia*." Asher's voice is deep and commanding. The sound of it normally sends what feels like a live wire through me, but right now it's oddly the only thing stopping me from spiraling out of control.

"It'll be okay, understand?"

"Okay..." I say, my voice breaking. A few moments pass as Asher removes the blood pressure cuff and pulls off the oxygen mask, his finger lifting my chin as his scent washes over me again. God, he smells so good.

"Eyes here." He points with two fingers to his own gray pools. I almost get lost in them before a light blinds me. I squint, and his frown deepens before he removes the light. He clips something onto my finger before glancing over his shoulder, assessing. "It's nearly out now."

His calm assurance allows me to take a deep, settling breath, and I realize I shouldn't be so surprised he's the one who's able to calm me.

Asher Reed is somehow never far when I'm in need. At least I *think* it's him who watches over me; I've never built up the courage to ask.

I think back to the time a handsy cowboy spent the night hitting on me at the Horse and Barrel. I escaped to the bathroom to hide from him, and when I came back he was gone. His friend told me he got kicked out, and when I looked over to Asher standing behind the bar, he just nodded. I knew it was him.

A few weeks later, I worked a series of late nights at my clothing store running inventory. When I arrived at the store on the last morning, there were muffins and coffee from Spicer's, our local bakery, resting on the step of my storefront. That was about a year and a half ago. Now, when I find myself in need of something, it seems to appear out of nowhere. The snow brushed off my car when I leave my shop on a cold night, or my driveway shoveled in the morning. My front porch light was replaced once, and my dad denied it was him. I know on instinct that it's Asher and, although I know it's not normal, it doesn't scare me. It fascinates me. If I ever told anyone, they'd probably tell me I had some sort of stalker fetish. But what they don't know is that I've always been drawn to dark and mysterious men, and Asher Reed *definitely* fits that bill.

"You have to be more . . . aware," he scolds me now, bringing my attention back to the present. "Especially when you live alone."

His comment stings, but I cover it with a laugh. "Are you saying I need a *man* to take care of me?"

"Fuck no, and you'd probably find a way to take out the poor bastard anyway." His eyes briefly flit to mine, but they don't linger. "I'm suggesting you fuckin' drink less while you're alone, seeing as you tend to be . . ."

"Accident-prone?" I chide.

"To say the goddamn least."

"What if he's an everyday superhero, like you? Mr. Right Place, Right Time," I fire back jokingly. Sober me is gonna hate this tomorrow. "Seems tonight you're my knight in shining red truck." I pat his solid upper arm.

"You've had way too much to drink," Asher grits out.

I snort in response. "Don't go getting your dalmatian-covered knickers in a twist. I'm joking. And, for the record, it's not that I don't *want* a man."

Now would be a great time to stop talking, drunk Liv.

"But I wouldn't hit on *you*, so don't worry," I try to recover. "For one, you grimace way too much. Like Oscar the Grouch."

Asher just peers down at me with those damn hypnotizing eyes, very Oscar like.

"Tough crowd," I whisper under my breath.

"My job is to make sure you aren't suffering from smoke inhalation, not to entertain you."

"You're the one who brought up marriage," I quip. *Didn't he?*

"Fucking alcohol," he mumbles. "The last thing I'd be talking about is marriage. *You* need to sleep." Asher's voice trails off as he puts his oxygen meter away.

"Why?" I ask.

"Why what?" Asher's eyes drop to my mouth as I lick my lips. He swallows slowly, and the way his throat works sends a thrill through me. Suddenly I'm hyperaware that I'm sitting here in very thin pajamas and no bra.

"Why wouldn't you be talking about marriage?" I tighten the sweater around me.

"Because it's a ridiculous institution."

"What do you mean? You never want to get married?" I push.

His jaw tics again. "No."

My eyes widen. "*Never*? I mean, no partner, no companion? Isn't that what everyone wants?"

"No."

I narrow my eyes at him. "Why not?"

"Take this off." Asher tugs at the bottom of my sweater and my stomach drops with his commanding tone, though I do what he says as he moves around to my back. I hold my breath as he gently brushes my thick hair over my shoulder before pressing his stethoscope to my back through my tank. As his warm fingers connect with my skin, little sparks race through my chest and my nipples harden. The mortification sets in when I realize he'll be able to hear how fast my heart is beating. A moment passes as he listens. If he does notice, he doesn't let on.

"Getting married is a sham for people who want to feel secure. Nothing lasts forever. Including romantic love. Now, give me a deep breath," he orders.

I want to dig deeper into his thoughts as he finishes listening to my lungs, but I don't get the chance to ask him what made him so cynical because a county police cruiser pulls up beside us and I see that it's Wayne, Laurel Creek's deputy sheriff. Asher quickly repacks his medical bag and walks over to meet him.

"Her vitals are normal but she's three sheets to the wind."

Asher looks down at my cow slippers over his shoulder. "Maybe four."

"Hi, Wayne," I say, waving from my place at the back of the cruiser.

"Hey, Olivia." He tips his hat. I went to school with Wayne, and it's nice to see a friendly face in this moment.

Wayne takes a look at my house, hands on his hips, as the last of the smoke dissipates out the now open kitchen window.

"Do you have somewhere to go tonight?" he asks me as he comes closer, Asher beside him.

The realization that I can't go inside my own home hits me with a force I'm not prepared for and, suddenly, the wine in my stomach starts to churn. All my belongings, my clothes, mementos, photos. Everything I own . . .

"A friend? Your parents?" Wayne pushes softly.

I shake my head. CeCe and Nash have an early doctor's appointment. And CeCe's hardly sleeping as it is. Cole and Ginger's spare room has turned into wedding central, plus I wouldn't want to wake Mabel on a school night, and I'm *not* dealing with my parents right now. My mother's worried energy would send me over the edge.

"I'll just . . . I can stay at the Motor Court Inn and call my parents in the morning."

Asher looks me over, and I can almost see those mysterious gears grinding behind his eyes.

"Walker," he calls over toward one of his crew. "Quick report?"

Walker Black pulls off his helmet as he starts to fill us in. He's tall and broad with a thick, dark beard. His face is covered in soot from being inside the house, and the color contrasts with his deep blue eyes.

"The fire was contained to the kitchen, but I'm afraid the house is uninhabitable." He turns to me. "I'd say everything in your house *should* be salvageable, aside from . . . anything in the kitchen."

"Thank you," I all but whisper as I hold back another wave of tears.

"Ma'am." He nods. Walker turns to go as Asher pats him on the back, then glances toward me.

"Where are your keys? And some proper shoes?" He looks at Wayne. "I'll take her."

Wayne seems satisfied as he shakes Asher's hand before following in Walker's footsteps.

"In the basket in the entryway and . . . my sandals are at the front door," I answer. "Thank you. I obviously . . . can't drive."

Asher's jaw tics.

"Obviously." He pulls his cellphone out of his pocket as his stormy eyes rake over me. "But I'm not taking you to a hotel."

CHAPTER 3
Asher

It's a goddamn miracle Olivia Sutton makes it through each day alive. She's the most oblivious to danger and accident-prone woman I've ever met in my life. So much so I've privately dubbed her *Oblivia*.

The call to her house came in right at the end of a double shift where I just left a family of four, including two toddlers, at the local hospital after they flipped their minivan to avoid crashing into a deer. There are days since I began my firefighting career on Staten Island a decade ago, and especially since taking over in Laurel Creek as battalion chief, that this job shows me horrors. And those horrors are hard to forget. Today was one of those days. Made even worse by *Oblivia's* antics.

Something to trip over? She'll find it. A bar fight breaks out? She'll be caught in the middle. Any chaos and Olivia is always there. She's like a moth to a goddamn flame. And yet, I couldn't fucking get to her fast enough tonight.

My radio continues to sound as I cruise through the quiet streets of Laurel Creek in my truck. Olivia sits beside me in the front seat as the sound of soft country music fills the space.

Before tonight, I hadn't seen Olivia for over a week. I know she's been away because she hasn't been at her clothing boutique downtown in days. I know because watching her, making sure she's safe and hasn't accidentally fallen asleep on a train track, has become a bit of a shameless ritual for me since I met her. One that fucking pisses me off.

Because I've never watched *any* woman before. I've tried to figure out why, but I can't. She just compels me. Outwardly, Olivia is an illusion. *Always* wearing a smile, even though I know it hides hurt. I know that there's a truer version of Olivia behind the sunshine mask, and learning what makes her tick has become a habit I can't fucking break. Those deep blue eyes both haunt and tether me. I've told myself it's because she *needs* watching over, and because watching people from the shadows is second nature to me. I was trained to watch by my father since I was very young. And I'm good at it. So good that locating people and keeping eyes on them became my job in my past life.

Shit is hard to let go of, especially when watching Olivia means I could potentially keep her from choking to death or getting kidnapped on her way home from work. Or, in tonight's case, burning to death.

Keeping my gaze trained to the dark road ahead, I push away the thought that she could have been another set of screams added to my haunting memories. Instead, as Olivia's eyes flutter closed from exhaustion beside me, I think back to the first time I met her.

"Are you fucking trying to die?" I ask, scowling down at the woman who just about offered herself up as a sacrifice to the old gray truck passing us now. Zach Bryan blares out its open windows as she turns to look at it. It takes her about two seconds to realize she was almost a redheaded pancake, then she straightens out and looks up at me, big

blue eyes peeking out from under copper bangs. She's clearly terrified of me—an inked, leather-clad, unfamiliar man. I can see her fear, but another emotion also lingers there. Intrigue maybe?

"I-I would've seen it before I crossed." Her sweet voice is tinged with a hint of attitude.

"Aye. Doubtful. You were oblivious," I counter, letting go of her soft arm, noticing the way my tight grip marked her pale skin. She rubs at it with the back of her hand.

It wasn't the gold necklace dipping lower into her cleavage, or those full hips that lead to a round, plump ass barely covered by her little white sundress, bouncing perfectly as she walked. It wasn't her small waist and full tits or her smooth, shiny-looking hair tied back with a silk scarf that caught my attention. It was that I couldn't figure her the fuck out. This woman was a blend of way too much confidence with way too little self-awareness, about to step right out into traffic, texting on her phone, like all the traffic would stop for her.

I let my eyes move to her face now, taking in her features. I knew she was pretty as soon as I saw her. But close up, the details of how pretty are breathtaking. There's a dusting of freckles across her nose that I imagine gets darker with the sun. Her lips are full and luscious, glossed in candy apple red, and thick black lashes frame big ocean-colored eyes. Her smooth skin contrasts perfectly with thick copper hair, the color of which I can tell is one hundred percent natural. I suppose that explains the sass.

She straightens out her dress and looks up at me quizzically.

"You're new here? Tourist?"

"What makes you think that?" I ask, surprisingly invested in her response. Talking with a stranger is rarely something I'm interested in.

"That isn't exactly a Kentucky accent. And . . . everyone knows everyone in Laurel Creek. Though I don't know you."

Her tone is sharp, but the way she looks at me? The way those blue eyes heat for just a second? She's judging my appearance, and if

I didn't know any better, I'd say she likes it. I stare her down, my eyes drifting to the paper cup she's holding. Olivia *is scrawled on it in Sharpie. I allow myself to breathe her in for a beat, inhaling her scent of cinnamon and sugar. It's fucking mouthwatering.*

She backs up slightly and I let my gaze drift to her throat. Pink creeps up her pale skin and she swallows, licking her lips. The sight causes blood to rush to my cock. Christ, what is wrong with me?

Turning, I toss a "remember to look both ways before you cross the street" at her as I pop my sunglasses back on and head toward the realty offices down the street.

"Hey!" Olivia calls out from behind me. "In case you're staying for any length of time, men around here don't just grab women they don't know like that. Even if they are trying to be heroic!"

I turn to face her and, walking backward, give her the two-finger salute. "Noted. I'm here to stay. But, next time, I'll just let you walk into traffic, Liv." I turn back toward my destination, not waiting for her response.

"How did you—" She pauses, until the realization dawns on her that her name is on the cup. I'm already pulling open the door to the realty office when I hear her call out from behind me, "It's Olivia."

My radio buzzes on the dash now, pulling my attention back to the present.

"LCFD Green back at base." The voice is Walker Black's, my captain, arriving back from Olivia's house.

"I'm not far behind," I add quickly, casting a glance to the woman beside me. I know she's close with her parents—I've seen them at her shop multiple times—so I wonder why she didn't want to call them. Finding out from Nash when I first moved to Laurel Creek that she was adopted only made me more curious about her. Where she came from, how she ended up with Ken and Lynn Sutton. It only took a small amount of digging to find out her birth parents died in a car accident when she was four. Ken and Lynn were in their early forties, Lynn a distant cousin, but they didn't hesitate to take her in, and they made it official the following year. They seem like really good people.

Olivia stirs beside me but doesn't wake up. Her movement only serves to push her sugary scent through my truck, only tonight it isn't quite right. It's mixed with smoke, which kind of makes her smell a little like me.

She's still wrapped in the thermal blanket, her eyes closed in the dark as I drive. A thin pink tank top with flowers on it clings to her, and the matching shorts barely cover her full, perky ass. Soot marks her pretty tear-stained face, and her feet are still in her ridiculous cow slippers, even though I grabbed her sandals. As the lights from Silver Pines Ranch come into view, her eyes shoot open, filling with a hint of fear that sends a thrill through me.

"So hot . . ." she whispers, her words slurring. Somehow, she still manages to look fucking sinful even in this decrepit state.

Her nipples are hardened to points as she shrugs off the blanket. Then she looks down. *No bra.*

A hint of pink travels up her neck as she folds her arms over her chest. The fabric of her pajama top is so thin, I wonder if she'd blush even deeper if I wrapped my lips around one of those pebbled little buds and sucked it into my mouth. I wonder if she'd soak through those silk shorts for me if I touched her in all the right places. I wonder if she'd *beg* me—

"Thank you for thinking of this," she offers as I turn my gaze back to the gravel driveway of Silver Pines, pushing Olivia's perfect curves from my mind. Fuck, I need to get it together. I'm supposed to be getting her to a safe space, not fantasizing about her.

I pull up to the cabin my friend Wade Ashby directed me to

bring Olivia to. His mother, Jolene, stands on the porch. But I can't get out of my fucking truck yet, because after letting my thoughts run wild, I'm still half hard beside this oblivious little minx.

"Oh God, I feel nauseous," she groans, cracking the door for fresh air.

This fucking night just keeps getting better and better.

CHAPTER 4
Olivia

"There's not much space here, darlin', but it's all yours. And tomorrow we'll go to your place and get anything that makes you feel more comfortable."

CeCe's mother, Jolene Ashby, though we all call her Mama Jo, smiles at me as she tucks a piece of rogue hair behind my ear. She's still a pretty woman at almost sixty, just an older version of CeCe. She wears her long blond hair in a braid down her back most days, and the weather of six decades shines through the soft crinkles at the corners of her kind eyes.

Asher was on the phone with Wade for only a few moments before he hung up and told me I could stay here tonight, which sounded much better than calling my parents.

"This ranch is your home as long as you need it to be. You know that. I have everything you need at the big house," she continues as she leans in for a hug. I hold on to her but it only causes more tears to well up.

I nod as I back up and swipe at the water pooling in my eyes. Looking around the small space, I'm grateful to be here. This cabin is called Stardust, one of the four on the ranch named for Willie Nelson albums. The others are Blue Eyes, Bluegrass, Spirit, and Legend.

"We'll know more about the damage after I do my walk-through," Asher says now, as if reading my thoughts. He's leaning on the doorframe of the cabin, still in his standard uniform. The deep tan of his face is accented by the soft light in the room, and his dark hair sticks to his forehead as he stares at me through thick lashes. He's dirty and obviously tired, but how he still looks *this* good after tonight is beyond me.

"Oh! I'll grab you some coffee for the morning," Mama Jo says as she tosses on her boots. "Be right back. Anything else you might need?"

"A good contractor?" I pull my hair out of its clip and let it fall around my shoulders before running my fingers through it in exasperation.

Jo crosses the space quickly and pulls me in for another hug.

"We can start sorting these things out tomorrow, darlin'. I'll help you make the bed up when I get back, then you have a nice shower and get some sleep. Things have a way of looking easier in the light of day, okay?"

I nod as Jo smiles up at Asher. He moves swiftly out of the way to let her exit as I drop down onto the overstuffed brown leather sofa. I know no one has been here since Wade's pseudo sister-in-law Cassie Spencer left last month. She's a bluegrass singer and was staying on the ranch to recover from a traumatic event that occurred at one of her concerts. She's doing much better and is back on the road, at least for now.

Asher fidgets with his suspender buckle as he watches me. The intense look has returned, and he seems as though he's trying hard not to lecture me, which pisses me off.

My eyes snap to his. "What?"

His dark brows shoot up as he studies me but doesn't say anything.

"You've obviously got something to say," I press.

"You've been through enough tonight. We'll talk another time."

I stand and stalk toward him, folding my arms over my chest as I look up at him. Normally, I don't come this close to him on purpose, but I must still be just tipsy enough, because there are no warning bells going off telling me not to antagonize him further.

"No, let's have the lecture now, *Dad*," I coax.

Those gray eyes darken as he watches me before moving to close the gap between us. I scoff and roll my eyes at the same time he uses his thumb and forefinger to tilt my face to his. My breath hitches at the contact and, this close, I can see the fight in him to stay calm. I have no idea why, but it's obvious he isn't my biggest fan. He drops his hand when my eyes meet his, but I can still feel the heat from his touch coursing through me.

"It's time you start . . ." He searches for the words to say. "Just try to be a little more cautious. Self-preservation is a thing, yeah. Like, tonight, if you get the hankering for food, don't fucking cook anything. Maybe order a pizza?"

He backs toward the door and, as he swings it open, Jo climbs the steps to my cabin.

"Night, Jo," he says gruffly. "Thanks again."

She pats his arm. "'Course. Get some sleep, kid. You look exhausted."

He squeezes her hand sweetly. "Aye. No rest for the wicked, eh?"

"Hell, that must be why I don't sleep!" She laughs as she heads in and sets my coffee pods on the counter. "Right, girl. Let's get you settled. We'll sort everything else out tomorrow; have you got someone to cover for you at work?"

I nod as I think about my clothing boutique: Lavender Grove, named after my favorite flower. We're getting into the busy months here in our hometown of Laurel Creek, Kentucky.

The spring and summer are when the streets are flooded with tourists wanting to visit Sugarland Mountain or to get outside on our nature trails and beaches near Cave Run Lake. We carry fine lingerie, swimsuits, designer dresses, and accessories, all handpicked by me. Opening the store was a dream come true. A dream I've had since I was young and my mom and I would thrift fabric for me to practice making clothes with. I had a whole rack of Olivia Sutton designs, and my mom would come and pretend to shop at my store. It's my pride and joy, and I truly miss it when I'm not there.

"Yeah, short term but I have a huge shipment coming in this week."

"I think that's a good thing. It will do you good to keep busy . . ." Jo offers.

"Maybe it's just." I look up into Jo's kind eyes. "What am I gonna do?"

"You're gonna lean on all of us, that's what," Jo says surely, and something about her unwavering support causes me to break. Dropping back to the sofa, I can't help the emotion that pours out of me as I start to cry for what feels like the hundredth time tonight. Sobs rack through my chest as Jo settles beside me and wraps her arms around me, supportive but firm. I can't stop, but then again, she doesn't ask me to.

Instead, she simply holds me close and whispers into my hair. "Oh, darlin'. It's okay. Let it out, I've got you."

CHAPTER 5
Olivia

"Baking is a science." My nana's small, wrinkled fingers work carefully to knead her pie crust. I have no idea how it's perfect every time and she doesn't even measure. "Cooking is something you do with love."

I'm only twelve, but since she moved in with us a year ago, we've started a tradition of cooking together every week. She says it's important to learn to create food, that it's an art, a form of therapy. She says her best thinking is done when she's baking. She looks over my shoulder where I stir the lemon curd for her famous pie. Tomorrow is a big day. It's my grandpa's birthday, maybe his last one, and even though he's in a home now, we're still taking him his favorite dessert.

"Perfect, Livi," Nana says with a smile. "You're a natural."

I breathe in her rose scent as "Can't Help Falling in Love" by Elvis Presley starts to play through the radio. Nana grabs my hand, her diamond ring from my grandpa glints in the sunlight as she twirls me, singing as she does, and I've never felt so safe or so loved.

The commotion of voices through thin cabin walls wakes me from my sleep. A smile is spread across my face, though my eyes remain closed. It always feels as though my nana is visiting me when I dream of her.

I open one eye and take in my surroundings, realizing I am not at home.

Ugh. My head is pounding as I remember everything from the night before. It wasn't a nightmare. It was real. My eyes well with tears as I think of the damage to my kitchen. My dad and I spent hours sanding my hundred-year-old wood floors and painting the old cabinets in the kitchen white to brighten the space. We added new hardware and made my cozy little craftsman perfect for me with a mix of warm woods, soft comfortable fabrics, and décor. The old fireplace in the living room was restored to its original wood-burning status and the mantel is a pretty walnut color, home to family photos and trinkets I've collected over the years. My house was my safe space and now it's in shambles.

"Babe?" I hear CeCe call through the cabin wall now.

"Here," I croak, rubbing my eyes with the heels of my palms as Ginger's and CeCe's smiling faces appear at the bedroom door. CeCe is holding an extra-large latte from Spicer's. *Bless her damn soul.*

"Why didn't you call us?" Ginger asks, taking a seat on the edge of my bed and wrapping her arms around me. Her long, curly brown hair smells like coconut.

"Holy shit, you smell like a vineyard. What *happened* last night?" She wrinkles her nose and I flop back down. I can't tell them the reason I was drinking was because every time one of them talks about their glowing future it feels like a stab to the heart.

"I was just having some wine. Maybe too much wine," I admit. "I was feeling lonely, I guess. Ever since Biscuit died my house is so quiet." I look up to their faces full of pity and I hate it.

"Anyway, I thought I would bake some banana bread. Wayne said I must have used wax paper instead of parchment to line my pan. They're pretty sure that's what caught fire."

"You should've called. You could've stayed with us." CeCe sits at the foot of my bed, running a hand over her five-month baby bump. Her long blond hair is in a high messy bun and the navy Henley she wears is snug, making her look like she's ready to pop.

"As if I'm going to interrupt what little sleep you get right now," I say before turning to Ginger. "And your spare room is taken over by wedding props and gifts. Asher thought to ask your mom."

CeCe raises an eyebrow, her green eyes dancing with intrigue. "*Asher* thought? He mentioned he was on the scene, but finding you a space to stay, that's going above and beyond."

I only hear the first part of her sentence, not acknowledging that it is above and beyond for him to take care of me when he hardly knows me.

"He mentioned it? When?"

"This morning. He was at the big house."

I glance down, knowing the look CeCe is giving me. She and Ginger have always said that there was some kind of spark between us. Every time we're at the Horse and Barrel and he delivers our drinks, or side-eyes me, one of them nudges me. I'm not denying I'm drawn to Asher, but most of the time it feels as though it pains him to say more than two words to me.

"It was strictly professional. He brought me here after they put out the fire and he medically cleared me."

I remember the way his eyes dropped to my lips, before I push the vision from my mind. Instead, I glance at the clock on the wall, noting it's only seven-thirty in the morning. News travels fast.

"Don't you have an appointment?" I ask CeCe, attempting

to change the subject. She shakes her head immediately. "Uh-uh. You're not doing that, my appointment is hours away. What do you need? We're here for *you*."

I take a deep breath and look between my best friends.

"I need to call my insurance company. I need to call my parents. But first, I need coffee." I motion grabby hands at CeCe.

"He asked about you, you know," she says as she places the paper cup in my hand.

I shy away from her smug look. "Just doing his job," I mumble.

"We told him how grateful you were that he was there, and that we'd say hi for him," Ginger adds.

"Because you're shit disturbers," I deadpan.

Ginger pushes her dark curls off her shoulder with a giggle.

"He also said you'll need some water and Tylenol. He probably does that for everyone though. Strictly professional."

I feel myself blush. "Nothing is going on."

"We know, but the real question is *why not?*" she asks, waggling her eyebrows playfully. I look up at her. She doesn't understand; she met her soulmate when she was a teenager, even if it took them years to admit it.

"Look, I'll be honest. Seeing the two of you settled, happy, planning out your blissful futures, it's made me crave what you both have. But Asher Reed isn't the answer. We are total opposites in every way."

The two of them look at each other and try not to laugh.

"He doesn't need to be your future to be . . . *fun*," Ginger offers.

"The problem with you two"—I point to both of my best friends—"is that you've gone from baddies to married little biddies now and are just searching for juicy drama where there isn't any."

CeCe places her hand over mine. "Okay, so Asher isn't 'the one.'" She pauses for a beat, tapping her lips. "Ooh, I have an idea. What if we sign you up on eMatch? Maybe you'll find the one there."

"No way. I draw the line at dating apps." I mimic tracing an invisible line in the air.

"They aren't what they used to be," Ginger pipes up. "Lots of people meet their soulmate online now." Her tone is so convincing she could advertise for the damn app.

"You're incredible, Liv, and I bet you'll have so many matches you'll be handpicking them—"

"You know what? Fine," I give in, hoping they'll stop talking so I can sip my coffee in peace. "I'll *try* it. But if I get any weirdos, I'm out."

"Define weirdos . . ." Ginger grins. I shoot her a look that tells her I'm about to change my mind.

"Of course, no weirdos. Deal," CeCe says, clapping. "We'll help you set it up."

"This is gonna be so fun!" Ginger's excitement scares me. Cole has turned her into a blissful romantic who wants everyone else to be as starry-eyed as she is.

"And we're only doing this because you won't take advantage of what is right in front of you," CeCe adds, holding up her orange juice.

"Look, even if we weren't *extremely* different"—I remember our fire chief's words from last night—"Asher is not the type to settle down. He told me himself. Plus, he's the epitome of the bad boy I said I'd *never* date again. *And* he's a firefighter."

Ginger gasps and covers her mouth in mock horror. "Not an extremely hot, hands-on profession!"

I start to laugh in spite of myself. "Look, it's just the idea of being with any man with such a risky career is a hard no for me."

The fuzzy image of him getting out of his truck looking

like a small-town superhero last night enters my mind. I suppose Ginger has a point—it *was* hot.

"I'd just like to know the odds are on my future husband's side that he'll come home to me every night."

"I hate to break it to you, but your future boring husband could get hit by a bus walking across the street," Ginger fires back.

"We don't have buses in Laurel Creek," I answer dryly.

Ginger sticks out her tongue. "Semantics."

"And we're talking about it for nothing. All I'm looking for right now is a long-term, steady relationship. Asher Reed not only sorta, kinda scares the shit out of me, but he also has *zero* interest in that." I picture his face scowling down at me last night. *"Or me."*

Reaching for my phone, I almost moan as I take my first big sip of coffee, knowing it's time to face the music. I quietly dial my parents' number, take a deep breath, and brace for impact.

"What are you doing up here so early, darlin'?" a deep and kind voice asks as I pull in the fresh air and the view from the big house back porch.

"I didn't know you were here. I don't want to disturb you," I say to Jo's dad, Dean. We all call him Papa Dean. I've known him for almost my whole life; he's not just the Ashbys' granddad, he's everyone's granddad.

"There're plenty of chairs out here for a reason." He brings his coffee to his lips and takes a big sip, his white mustache twitching, his form of a grin.

"I just came to grab one of Jo's famous muffins and another coffee."

"Mm-hmm. Needed some breathing room?"

"Yep," I answer, settling into the moment as we look out over the peaceful property together.

"I was thinking about taking a walk through the trails, to clear my head," I admit. The early-morning sun is beaming down, evaporating the light dew in the grass.

"Spring is such a nice time, isn't it? Everything's so fresh and new . . ." Dean replies as he glances at the wide, flat yard. Jo's daffodils and the Virginia bluebell beds are in full bloom, meaning the property is alive with color as far as the eye can see.

I follow his gaze as the sun creeps over Sugarland Mountain in the distance.

"Normally I love spring," I tell him softly. "But this spring is a bit of a challenge for me." I have no idea why I'm saying this to him, aside from the fact he's always been easy to talk to.

"Heard about your place. You know you're welcome here as long as you need." Dean rocks in his chair, his eyes filled with the wisdom of almost eighty years of lessons learned.

"I know, and I'm grateful. But my home has always been *my* space and, without it, I feel unsteady. Like the rug has been pulled out from under me."

"Well, honey, the only constant in life is change." He keeps his eyes trained to the yard. "Especially when you least expect it."

"Ain't that the damn truth," I scoff.

"And sometimes, when you can't understand why something's happened, you find out later that it's because this big ol' universe has a whole new path for you."

"I kinda liked my old path." I take another sip of Jo's delicious coffee.

"Well, here's what I say." He side-eyes me. "When you have a stone in the road like this and you stumble, you just make that little misstep part of your big dance."

Dean turns his twinkling eyes to me as I face him.

"It's that simple?" I ask.

"It's that simple. No matter what path life decides to take you on, you just have to go with it. Always give a hundred percent is my motto." He lets out a little chuckle as if in afterthought. "Unless you're donating blood, of course."

I chuckle back. "Of course."

Feeling refreshed after my caffeine fix and chat with Dean, I decide a walk in the woods is exactly what I need. With my feet tucked into a pair of CeCe's worn-in cowboy boots, a pair of Jo's comfortable jeans, and a soft white sweater, I set out through the trails we all grew up on. CeCe, Ginger, and I used to camp out here, telling ghost stories, our tent loaded with snacks. More times than not, Cole and his friends would come out at some point to scare the shit out of us, and we'd all end up laughing and talking until the early hours of the morning.

I smile at the memories as I meander down the lazily mulched and narrow horse trails. They're flanked by woods on either side and the creek runs through the trees to the left of me. I'm not sure how far I've gone when I hear the echo of branches cracking behind me. Turning quickly, a sliver of fear runs up my spine as I realize how early it still is. I have no idea what could be out here at this time.

I've made it quite a way from the cabins on the Ashbys' vast property, but I'm pretty sure that if I keep going I'll soon come to the clearing where one of their maintenance cabins sits.

When I hear the crunching again, I freeze before spinning on my heel to search the space. There's no sound but my breath as my heart beats faster. When I hear it again, coming from the thick pines that line the path to my right, I suck in a breath and prepare to bolt just as I see a flash of gray. At first I think maybe it's a dog, but then I realize it has to be something bigger. I'm hoping it's just a coyote, but it could be a small black bear . . .

I scream and clap before breaking into a sprint, but I don't get very far before a thick, leaf-covered root trips me up and throws me into the dirt.

My breathing is erratic and panic engulfs me at the thought of the unknown chasing me. Just as I'm scrambling to stand, I hear the steady, even gallop of a horse and a long, sharp whistle. I manage to pull myself up onto my knees and, as I tilt my head to the sky, I find myself staring up into deep gray eyes. My mouth drops open as I curse my luck. Because sitting atop one of the Ashbys' deep chocolate Morgans, in fitted light jeans, a cream-colored long-sleeved Henley that hugs his muscular arms while he grips his reins tight, is Asher. In a cowboy hat. And he looks . . . just as pissed off as last night.

"The hell are you doing out here, woman?" he grunts out.

"R-running from a coyote . . . or something, who knows," I answer, moving to stand while swiping dirt and mulch from my sweater.

Asher extends a long, corded arm downward and his scarred and calloused hand feels smooth and warm over mine as I take it, allowing him to help me up. Angry or not, I'd rather face him than a wild animal.

"I meant, what are you doing in the damn woods alone so early?"

"I was trying to clear my head," I offer as a thought occurs to me. "What are *you* doing out here?"

His jaw tics as he watches me pull a twig from my hair.

"Same."

I don't say anything but, surprisingly, Asher goes to fill the silence. "I'm working on the cabins today with Wade. I like to ride. This ranch just feels . . ."

"Home?" I finish without thought, cocking my head as I

look up at him.

Asher just nods. "Come on then, I'll take you back."

"Oh . . . I can walk," I say. The idea of being that close to him . . .

Asher's eyebrow raises. "Aye," he half growls. "Looking to provoke a bear while you're out here too?"

I think I already did.

"So sweet to know how much you care," I mutter, but decide not to argue as I let him help me up onto the back of his large horse.

"We don't need to add a concussion to your injuries today," Asher growls as I wrap my arms around his chiseled waist and will my heart to calm as I breathe him in. I wonder briefly if this is what it would feel like to ride on the back of his Harley, the one I've seen him around town on.

When he reaches back to tug both my thighs, pulling me closer, an impossible thrill runs through me. Inhaling his delicious spicy scent, I feel safe pressed against his warm, muscled back and I hate it. He pats the horse's neck and mutters a command before we take off on a light, easy trot through the woods. Asher doesn't speak as we ride, so I take in the pretty scenery that surrounds us. Wild violet blankets the forest floor and silver pines—the towering trees this ranch was named for—sway in the spring breeze as my hair blows behind me. I take another deep breath in. The power emanating from this man calls to me, even though I know it shouldn't. Dark, controlling, broody, and fully closed off. Exactly the kind of man I keep telling myself I shouldn't want, the kind of man I have no future with. It's hard to tell if he's annoyed with me or if he's just committed to speaking fewer than five words at a time, yet I still fight the pull to him.

"Here we go," he says as we approach the cabins. I dismount first; once again Asher extends his hand to hold me steady. He's easy and comfortable on this horse, and on these trails, and it shows.

A moment of silence passes between us. But I don't have time to feel awkward because Asher is already tightening his grip on the reins, looking down at me.

"Stay out of the goddamn woods, yeah?" he warns before making a tight clicking sound with his jaw. And then he's gone, leaving me filthy, standing in the driveway of my cabin, before I even have a chance to say thank-you. Or tell him he's an asshole. I may not have a concussion, but I definitely have a good dose of whiplash from the man who just saved me for the second time in twenty-four hours.

CHAPTER 6
Asher

"*Asher! James! Please ... someone ... please!*"

My mother's screams the last time I ever heard her voice fill my head. They only haunt me when it's quiet like this. I turn up the Deftones in my ears. The slow, steady rise and fall of my breath quickens as I sink into an ice bath and the muscles of my body go rigid as I flex my aching fists under the water. I went hard in my weight session this morning. My daily workouts have been a routine I've kept up since I went to prison when I was younger.

There was nothing to do there but get stronger. Some men turn to drugs inside, some to sex, but I wanted to become as strong as possible to ensure I'd never end up in the type of situation that put me in that shithole in the first place. As a habit still, when I feel stress creeping in, I push my body to its limit. Like today. Physically, a harsh deadlift session was just what I needed. But mentally? My brain never shuts off, and over the last five days since Olivia's fire, I've been thinking about her *way* too much.

Something about how she looked up at me so helpless and

afraid outside her burning house. And then again when I found her in the dirt on the Silver Pines trails. It's like she can't help but put herself in dangerous situations and I can't help but interject. Even if it means bringing her closer to me in the process. Which is the last place she should be.

Fourteen long minutes pass as I soak in ice and my own fucked-up thoughts and feel the familiar needles creeping in under my skin. I stand and step out onto my deck. Wrapping a large towel around my hips, I take a deep breath of fresh mountain air. The only sound in my yard is the birds chirping. Just how I like it.

My property sits at the west side of Laurel Creek, almost out of town, on ten acres. The house itself is a smaller two-story farmhouse from the seventies, but I've remodeled it over the two years I've spent here. The expanse of land is what I always wanted. The fields ahead are shrouded by trees and, behind the main house, my deck faces out toward lush woods and the big red barn that I've turned half of into a state-of-the-art woodshop. The other half remains in its original, rough form and is where I store my yard equipment, guns, and feed for the chickens that roam freely here in the summer months. I spend most nights I'm not on duty, or at the bar, in the workshop. My hands always need to be busy, and I can turn my music up as loud as I like to drown out the demons that like to haunt me when it's quiet.

I shake my hair out, letting my body air-dry as I place my thumb and finger between my lips, whistling short and sharp just before I head inside my house. With the sound, my hundred-pound black cane corso Duke stands reluctantly from where he was snoozing in the sun to follow me. He's just shy of three and it's taken me almost two to fully train him. He's a beast—strong and fiercely obedient. He's also a big sucker, though only for me. He loves to run through the trails on my property with me, or snooze in his bed in the corner of my workshop at night while doubling to scare the shit out of any foxes or possums that linger around here.

Duke is at my heel as I enter the kitchen and close the door behind me. The space is clean but sparse, with deep stained-pine cabinets and a natural wood ceiling. It's decorated with iron accents and the walls on the main level are a light gray. A living room with a wood-burning fireplace, an office, and a flex space I haven't finished off just yet rounds out the area. My bedroom and a full bathroom are on this level and upstairs are two more bedrooms and another full bathroom. I glance over at the table where my phone is vibrating.

I pick it up immediately when I see it's Wayne.

"Got some news for me, deputy?" I ask, setting my phone to speaker on the counter then reaching down to scratch Duke behind the ears.

"We're meeting the insurance adjuster at Olivia's place in an hour. Can you make it? He'll need your official report." He pauses for a beat. "And, with it being a heritage house, the governing office from the county may come too."

In other words, this reno could take a while. "Fuck," I huff out, heading to my room to get dressed.

"Yeah. With the cabinetry and the floors, she's gonna have a lot of hoops to jump through with the repairs on this one."

"I swear to Christ, Laurel Creek is the only town in America where the heritage designation matters on the inside of the house," I say as I drop my towel and pat my arms dry.

"You're right about that one." Wayne chuckles.

Looking at the clock, I realize I could just stop by the department to give my report before I head to the Horse and Barrel for my shift. But, like anything that has to do with Olivia, before I can tell myself not to, I'm moving toward her instead of away from her.

"I'm on my way, Wayne."

CHAPTER 7
Olivia

"I've got this, babe," Lucy, my shop manager, says as I grab my purse to head to my house. My store is ready for the day. We just finished stocking some new crochet maxi dresses. I tend to curate the store based on what I like, which are soft color palettes and neutrals for everyday wear. My staple is what I'm wearing now: a soft floral skirt and a black tank paired with gladiator sandals. I stock lots of those and they always fly off the rack. So do the linen cover-ups in the summer months. Now we're heading into busy season, our inventory is looking great. The shop is the first project my dad and I ever took on, and I am so proud of the colorful space that welcomes locals and tourists alike. Unlike a lot of people, I love going into work every day. Don't get me wrong, running your own place is not without its challenges: leaky pipes, a pesky debit system that drops out at least once a week, late shipments. But it's *mine*, leased and stocked five years ago with the help of my parents and every penny I could save throughout college, where I earned my degree in fashion merchandising.

"Thanks for holding down the fort. I'll be back as soon as

I'm wrapped up at my house. Here's hoping the debit system holds up for you."

Lucy smiles at me, her half-light-brown, half-pink hair up in two cute little space buns today. She's young, only twenty-three, but she has an incredible eye and the customers love her. "Praying to the shady-as-hell debit gods," she quips as I head for the door.

The short drive between the shop and my house passes quickly. This will be the first time my parents are seeing my house since the fire. There's a sign in the window that gives notice of impending construction and abatement, the front door is wide open, and my parents are already here, along with Deputy Wayne. I see my insurance company's truck and a staunch-looking lady with white hair pulled back off her face carrying a clipboard as she exits the vehicle marked *Laurel Creek Heritage Society*.

I take a deep breath and move to get out of my car before I'm stopped dead in my tracks by the sound of a thunderous motorcycle. I glance up to see Asher cruising down my street; his matte-black custom bike is a beast and, though I've seen it many times at the firehall and the Horse and Barrel, I'm still transfixed as he gets closer. Worn-in, distressed jeans hug his thick thighs as they straddle the wide bike. His black T-shirt clings tightly to his inked arms, and, on his face, he wears his uniform black aviator sunglasses.

He cuts the engine as he pulls into the end of my driveway. I stand at my car, door still wide open as I watch him.

"Are you coming in, honey, or are you just going to stand there staring?" my mom calls from the porch.

Asher hangs his helmet from his grip and turns to face me,

catching me gaping at him. *Perfect*.

DAD

I haven't spoken to my wife in years.

DAD

I thought it would be rude to interrupt her.

I grin down at my dad's message; my mom hasn't stopped talking since I arrived at my house thirty minutes ago. I look up and meet his eyes across my living room. The tuft of white hair atop his head is askew from cleaning, but he's the picture of cool, calm, and collected. Nothing fazes my father—not my mother's constant chattering, her harebrained ideas for the house, my teen years of princess-like behavior, any random crisis at his job before he retired from thirty years as the manager of a busy marketing firm. Nothing. He's our family rock and the best man I've ever known.

"I have all I need." I turn to meet the voice and shake the hand of Arthur, my insurance inspector. "I'll be in touch."

"Thank you for coming." I breathe out a sigh. The good news is he's deeming the fire accidental, so everything will be covered. The bad news is the wiry little Heritage Committee member, Sheila Wilmington.

She's already told us all about five times since she arrived that she is an expert in legacy architecture, design, restoration, and history.

"What does this all mean?" I turn to face Wayne and Asher once she leaves me with her card and heads out the door, telling me she'll watch for my construction permit.

"It sounded expensive and time-consuming," my mother adds, looking for direction too, tucking her blond bob behind her ear the way she does when she's nervous. I place a reassuring hand on her shoulder.

"In short, it will be," my father pipes up, still calm but looking frustrated by seeing all our hard work in shambles. He busies himself pulling down what's left of my curtains—basically the rod—then he picks up a garbage bag and starts adding food from my fridge to it, hoping to get rid of anything that will spoil. Miraculously, the only appliance I'll need to replace is my stove.

Asher shakes Wayne's hand as the deputy fire officer places his hat on his head and bids us goodbye. I let my eyes trail over Asher when he's not looking as he claps Wayne on the shoulder and walks him out. The image of him looking down at me from his horse the other day, that veil of sweat covering him, powerful and commanding as he extended his heavy, scarred hand to me flashes through my head. I can't decide if it was his touch or the way he told me what to do that I liked most. Regardless, I can't fight the heat as it flushes my cheeks with the memory.

The buzz of my phone pulls me from my thoughts.

GINGER

All right, girls, I need a mental break from wedding planning. Liv, I'm sure you could use some girl time after the last few days too.

GINGER

Sangria?

CASSIE

I'm in. Haden is painting anyway.

Our little group used to be only myself, CeCe, and Ginger. But then Ivy moved onto the Ashby ranch and fell in love with CeCe's oldest brother, Wade. Then, most recently, Ivy's sister, Cassie, who just arrived home this weekend to profess her love to Wade's right hand, Haden. Even though she was on a hot track to becoming one of country's fastest-rising singers, she's chosen to pursue writing music full time and she and Haden are planning on fixing up his new horse rescue ranch together.

CECE

> Ugh. Sorry, guys, I'm there in spirit. I have the worst heartburn.

IVY

> 1/8 teaspoon of baking soda into a glass of room-temperature water. Saved my life more than once in the last trimester with Billi.

CECE

> And maybe cutting back on the Mexican?

GINGER

> Damn, now I feel like nachos.

IVY

> I'm in, at least for a couple of hours.

Once Wayne has left, silence descends as we tidy up. I'm just finished spraying down the window covered in soot when Asher pulls out a measuring tape and starts laying it across the floor of what was once my kitchen.

"You know your insurance company will send cleaners and abaters," he says gruffly, focused on his measurement.

"I know," I sigh. "But I feel like I need to do *something*."

"Just make sure the nozzle is facing the right way when you spray. Those are toxic chemicals."

I scoff, setting my sights on what to clean next. As I turn to examine the space, I slam my hip into the kitchen island. Asher grunts from behind me, not missing a beat.

"I'm fine, thanks for asking!" I mutter sarcastically, and I swear I hear him chuckle in response.

The truth is, even with his snarky comments and grumbling attitude, I'm glad Asher came today. His honest feedback and confirmation of everything I told the insurance adjuster helped deem my claim an accident. And, whether it should or not, its unavoidable. His presence makes me feel safe.

I look around the space. Everything east of the fridge— above the counters—is charred ruin and the whole south wall is black. I move closer to my counter and reach out to pick up my old cookbooks. Tears fill my eyes as I hold up the absolutely decimated first edition self-published copy of *The Joy of Cooking*. It belonged to my nana, and my great-grandmother before her.

It was the book my nana used to teach me and my mother how to cook. Images of us frosting cupcakes for birthdays and baking pies for holidays while we listened to Elvis come flooding back. It had all her handwritten notes, as well as her mother's, and was decorated in splatters and flour fingerprints. I might be able to find another book by some sort of miracle, but I'll never find one with those memories. Now, I open the charred pages, blackened and shriveled. Tears fall down my cheeks as I trace my finger over her chocolate cake recipe.

"Oh, honey . . ." My mom moves toward me from the living room to pull me in for a hug. I welcome her embrace, leaning into her for support.

"Of all the things to lose." I swipe the tears from my face and lay what's left of the book flat on the counter.

Asher's phone ringing brings me back to the present, though I don't look back as he picks it up and moves outside. His voice is muffled from my porch.

"He's a quiet man," my mother notes. "Kind of . . . what's the word you girls use? Broody?" She smiles at me, though it doesn't quite reach her eyes. She can't handle it when things go wrong, especially when it comes to me. She's a natural fixer. But my burnt-to-a-crisp kitchen is one thing she can't save.

"He's damn helpful too," my dad chimes in. "Had he not backed you up, the adjuster might not have believed it was all an accident."

"Saving my ass . . . yet *again*," I say under my breath as Asher comes back inside, his big hands resting on his narrow hips.

"The biggest problem you're gonna have are these floors, cabinets, and walls," he announces. "You don't see three-quarter-inch black walnut anymore, and that's what the Heritage Committee will want."

Asher crouches down and runs his big inked hand across the kitchen cabinets in appreciation before turning to me. I swallow hard as those gray eyes find mine.

"So you'll need to rip out everything from the entire kitchen," he tells me matter-of-factly as he stands. "Damn shame."

"What does this all mean?" I tighten my ponytail. "Every step of the way I have to get approval for the remodel from that Sheila lady?"

Asher sets his jaw and folds his arms over his chest. Even though every window is open in my house, the lingering smell of smoke is starting to give me a headache.

"Yes," he answers firmly. "And to be honest, heritage committees can be a pain in the arse. Everything that's ruined—the plaster, the floors, the cabinets—it all needs to come out."

I sigh and take a seat on my coffee table.

"I did a quick search this morning and found a local company. Shelford Restoration?" I mention, looking up at Asher, who's shaking his head.

"Your insurance company only approves them because they're cheap. In this case, you'd be better to get a specialty contractor."

I can see Asher warring with himself about whether he should get involved with my troubles. Why does this man, who I barely know anything about, get so frustrated with me?

"I know a good bloke," he says finally. "I was just talking to him. And I'll . . . make a few calls on the wood for your floors and cabinets. You need someone who does heritage builds to install them so they can mimic this inlay properly."

Relief I wasn't expecting washes over me. I have no idea how to handle any of this, and seeing Asher now, calm and prepared, it's obvious he does.

"Thank you," I tell him sincerely.

He nods curtly.

"After everything has been abated, you'll get your keys back and can come in and out freely. You won't be able to live here, or at least it would be hard to without a working kitchen." He runs a hand through his thick, wavy dark hair then tucks his pencil back behind his ear. "But you can visit during the restoration process as long as it's safe. My guy's named Shane. He owns Red Rock Restoration."

"I know them," my dad pipes up, tying a garbage bag. "They did our neighbor's house when her basement flooded. It was an excellent job."

"Aye." Asher comes closer and holds his phone out to me, unlocked. I gulp as he towers over my five-foot-seven frame. "Add your number and I'll pass it on. He owes me a favor."

I just stare up at him, speechless at his proximity. And shocked that he's willing to do this for me. Thankfully, my dad makes his way over to us and extends a hand. I blink and take his phone, adding my number quickly.

"Thank you for attesting to Olivia's statement," my dad says with a nod. Asher is at least five inches taller than my father and twice his size.

"Just doing my job, sir." Asher returns my dad's firm shake then looks back at me, taking his phone and placing it in his back pocket. "Even with the quicker restoration, with this being such a strict district, it could still take a few months. It won't be a quick process."

"Well, I suppose it's a good thing you were the fireman on the scene when it happened," my mother says as cheerfully as the situation allows. "A fireman who dabbles in construction—what are the odds?"

Asher nods. "Just a hobby."

He turns to me. "You can grab anything you'd like to bring with you now. I have someone to meet before heading to the Horse and Barrel."

He looks to my parents. "It isn't safe for you all to be in here alone, so I'll follow you all out."

My mother is grateful he was on the scene and, truthfully, so am I. But sometimes when I look into his eyes I get the sense he isn't choosing to help me. It's as though he feels he *has* to. Maybe it's because he was here the night it happened, but still. I want to tell him that he's under no obligation to help me, considering it seems to pain him to do so, but now is not the time to talk to him about it.

As my mom and I pack up some of my clothing and toiletries and a few personal items I don't want to be without, I text the girls to take Ginger up on her offer from earlier. A drink and some country music with my girls sounds damn good. Especially when it means I can find the chance to speak a little more freely with one scowling firefighter who also just happens to be the ladies' night bartender tonight.

CHAPTER 8
Asher

> **WADE**
> Good for the final fitting for suits next week?

> **ME**
> Yep.

> **WADE**
> Bring your pretty face and your good hair.

> **ME**
> I'm always fuckin' pretty.

I tuck my phone in my pocket with a grin. Wade Ashby and his brother Cole, along with his brother-in-law Nash and Wade's top hand Haden, were friends I didn't expect to find when I arrived in Laurel Creek. I knew when I left New York that I'd have to keep my circle small. It's been ingrained in me since I was a child to never trust anyone. Though I soon realized that the Ashbys are a different breed.

I've been working for Rocco, the owner of the local bar, the Horse and Barrel, for a couple years, which is how I got to know them all. Nash used to be a big-time hockey player but came back to his hometown a few years ago and took over most of Rocco's duties. He's now my pseudo boss, though he isn't in much anymore. It was the perfect job to introduce me to the town because, at one point or another, everyone ends up at the Horse and Barrel.

But tonight the bar is my base for watching Olivia find new ways to put herself in harm's way. Which she's been doing. *All fucking night.*

Drinking way too much sangria with Ginger and Cassie, which, for the second time in a week, is highly unlike her.

Toward the end of the night, Ginger, Cassie, and Olivia are the only women still here. They dance right through last call, and since Olivia has decided to wear the tightest, slinkiest lavender dress I've ever seen, she has the attention of every single man in the place. The front is high-necked with long sleeves but the back is wide open and looks incredible against all those copper waves.

Oblivia. Unaware of the way every man in here is itching to take her home.

I try to keep busy but every time she almost eats it in her four-inch heels on the way to the ladies' room or the dance floor, I fight the urge to cut her off, toss her into my truck, and take her back to the ranch.

"Barkeep, one more?" I hear less than an hour before close. I don't need to look up to know the voice from the end of the bar is Olivia's.

"You didn't hear last call fifteen minutes ago?" I ask, moving closer. The last thing she needs is one more of anything, except maybe water and her bed.

"Ugh . . ." She leans forward onto her forearms at the bar top, swaying her hips from one side to the other as I turn to face her. It's miraculous I don't pop a tendon, I'm gritting my jaw so hard. Matt, my bar help, chuckles and shakes his head.

I lean down on my side of the bar. "Stand up."

"Excuse-eh moi?" She lifts her head, her slender fingers flying to her chest.

She's fucking toasted.

"*Stand*. The fuck. Up," I repeat, as one of the cowboys behind her mimics the shape of her ass with his hands and bites his lower lip. My flexing fist balls up and then I'm moving without thought, to the other side of the bar, behind her, gripping her waist to block his view.

"*Now*," I order.

She laughs, standing up and turning to face me, but she doesn't shy away from my arms and suddenly I'm looking right down at her.

"You like to tell women what to do?" She breathes out, patting my jaw as her plush lips pop open. I don't even think she admits it to herself, but I see it clearly. There's a part of Olivia that feels the same pull I do when I look into those ocean eyes. Her breath hitches as I tighten my grip on her waist and her gaze heats just like I knew it would.

Back up, I tell myself. But those fucking lips—

"Y-you're not gonna kiss me . . . are you?" Her voice is breathless, tempting me to do just that. Goddamn this woman is frustrating.

"*Fuck* no," I say clearly, nodding to her cowboys behind her. "I'm trying to stop those two shitheads from getting a *real* good look at your arse."

She gulps and looks over my shoulder.

"No. Eyes here," I command, cupping her chin and forcing her face to mine. "Good girl. Now either you stop leaning over the bar, or I'll be forced to drive my fists through both their faces."

Her mouth pops open in shock. "You don't like me very much, do you?"

"Not right this moment, no . . ." I lie.

"Then why do you watch me? Why are you always doing things for me before I even ask?"

I grunt as I look away from her. I'm not ready to answer those questions right now. Hell, I don't even know the answer.

"That's right." She pats my chest with her small hand. "I know you're the one who cleans my car off, who delivered me coffee after an all-nighter, plus you slid me that chocolate last Christmas. I have no idea how you knew it was my favorite . . ." She leans in closer. "I haven't even told CeCe and Ginger these things. But what I don't understand is *why* you do it all."

Fuck it. She could use a little dose of reality.

"Behind this bar, I see *everything*." I speak just loud enough for her to hear over the buzz of the crowd. "You give all of yourself to your friends. You put on a happy face, plaster a fake smile across these pretty lips, and you go along with everything they ask, even if it means you're sacrificing your own needs. But not one of them notices it." I sound pissed off and I know it. But she's looking at me like what I'm saying has never even registered with her, so I continue. "Not to mention, since you're a walking incident report, for some goddamn reason I need to make sure you're safe."

Her face falls slightly with my confession, knowing I'm right, but she fights her emotion and reaches between us, tapping me on the chest. And like a complete rookie, I look down, allowing her to chuck a finger under my chin as she giggles.

"Listen, I'll save you the trouble," she offers, trying to appear unaffected with our proximity. "You don't have to help me find wood for my house. This scowling face will just put a bad aura in my space."

Now she's a rambling little brat.

"We can have this conversation when you're sober," I grit out.

Olivia waves a hand in front of herself and makes a *pshhhhh* sound before turning her eyes, now blazing blue, on me. "I'm capable of doing all things. In fact, I'm barely past the point of sober."

Her words string together, proving her wrong, but the cocky way she looks at me has me wanting to fuck with her. "Oh yeah?"

"Yeah," she says, but it sounds thready as she lifts her chin and places her hands on the bar behind her for stability.

Splaying my hand across her lower back, I tug her closer, until her hot little body is pressed right against mine. Her breath hitches in her throat and my cock fucking loves the sound. I bring my lips down to the soft column of her throat just under her ear.

"Does this smart little mouth ever fucking stop running, Liv? Maybe you need something to fill it, hmm?"

I have no idea why I'm taunting her like this, but I can't stop this need to be close to her, to test her.

"Well . . . I am kind of hungry," she whispers back sweetly, not missing a beat. "Is the big, bad bartender planning on feeding me?"

"If I was, what would you have to say to that?"

"I'd say . . . that I've never been a picky eater."

Fuck. I did not expect that, nor did I expect the hint of darkness lurking in her eyes.

My grip tightens reflexively before I force myself to let go of her and grit my teeth.

"You are definitely *not* fucking sober, woman." I force myself to let go of her waist and watch her eyes turn from feisty to sad.

"You're running from something tonight, drinking like this," I tell her. "And maybe no one else sees it, but *I* do. It isn't the answer. So *go home*, Liv."

I force myself to turn away and move back behind the bar, pushing the flash of need that filled her eyes from my mind.

"Look . . . it's been a rough few weeks, okay?" Olivia offers from behind me. "My cat died, and he was my best friend. I have no home and . . . I guess I'm just looking to forget everything for a few hours." She gives an exasperated shrug. "But you don't need to watch out for me, Asher. I'm a big girl."

Olivia turns to face one of the cowboys who was eyeing her ass. He's not paying attention to her anymore, but when she walks right up to him and pulls him toward the dance floor by his shirt, he's all hers. *Fuck me.* She looks too damn good, and I have no idea why she's affecting me so much *now*, or what's changed between us, but it's impossible to ignore the pull I'm feeling toward her. Olivia Sutton is fucking *gorgeous.*

I look back at Matt. He nods at me, letting me know he's got the bar and then I'm on the dance floor as the cowboy's hands drift dangerously close to Liv's ass. As I push through the crowd, I question why I can't just look the other way, and the only thing I can come up with is that it's ingrained in me to help people, especially when they're walking headfirst into danger. But I'm playing with fire here. I know she's too innocent for me, too sweet. I know the darkness of the life I've lived would dim her light, and yet here I am, bending to her like a weed to the sun.

I don't even slow my stride as I pluck Olivia by her waist, dropping her beside me.

"Nope," I bite out to the cowboy.

"Hey! Find your own woman!" he growls in response.

"His name is Ty . . ." Olivia says, trying to wrestle out of my grip and back toward him. Was this piece of shit actually planning on taking her home like this?

"Like *fuck*," I mutter as I lose my last thread of patience. Snagging a firm grip on her hand, I pull her to the door. She comes with me easily for a moment and then tugs to let go of my hand.

"Where are you taking me?" she asks as I double down, tightening my grip.

I pass Haden and his girlfriend, and then Ginger, who's laughing as she watches me cart Olivia through the bar.

"Where you belong. To bed."

She doesn't stop fighting my grip, but I'm not having it as Ginger hands me Olivia's purse on my way by. I'm not letting some prick take advantage of her like this.

"I'm taking her home," I tell Haden. "She was about to leave with that shithead."

"Liv! He's been with every woman but us in this town!" Ginger calls to her friend.

"Sounds good, brother," Haden adds. "I've got these two."

"Text me in the morning!" Ginger calls to Liv. "I'll be sleeping in, Mabel's at the ranch!"

"Cole's gonna love coming home from his shift to this . . ." I hear Haden's voice fade as I head outside.

"Let go," Olivia bites out. "I can get home myself."

"Now you care who's taking you home?" I retort as I push through the door and into the cool night air.

"I told you I'm not your problem!" she argues.

"You're right. You're not," I huff out as we reach my truck. "But I might be the only man in that place who will drive you home and *not* try to fuck you while you're in this state, which means you're stuck with me."

I crack the door, lifting her and dropping her right onto my front seat. I breathe in her sweet perfume, holding her in place as I reach across and buckle her seatbelt for her.

Her chest heaves, but out of nowhere she starts to giggle drunkenly as she pushes her auburn hair off her face. She doesn't stop laughing as she presses the pad of her first finger to the center of my chin. Her breath is still heavy from her over-the-shoulder rant and her eyes are wild.

"I was right," she says with alcohol-induced confidence.

Leaning in closer, I watch as her pink lips part expectantly. My gaze trails slowly over her face to her neck, where I see her pulse thrumming, blood rushing to paint her pretty cheeks pink. I allow myself a single moment to imagine what it'd feel like to let my teeth skate over her there, nipping and sucking at the delicate skin.

"I knew you liked to tell women what to do," she whispers.

I can't help it, I smirk at her.

"You have no idea, Livi girl. Now fucking behave or I'll be spanking that arse before I even get you home."

CHAPTER 9
Olivia

My head is swirling in the passenger seat of Asher's pickup truck after he yanked me away from that cowboy, then threatened to spank me.

He's right about me normally not drinking this much. But over the last few weeks, it's been either drink or cry whenever I feel like the proverbial rug has been pulled out from under me. And I'm damn sick of crying.

I lean my head against the seat, knowing I can't run from this reality any longer. I have to channel my inner Lynn Sutton and find the positive in these situations. The people I have in my life are one in a million and I *will* have my house back thanks in part to this pissed-off bartender driving me home.

I close my eyes, listening to Ty Myers sing "Ends of the Earth" as I breathe in the fresh clean scent of Asher's truck. The rustic, sultry sound of this song doesn't deter me from imagining just what that spanking would feel like, and how the thought sends a thrill through my body. Hell, I need to get it together. I'm almost thirty, and the time to play around with the town bad boy and live like I'm in college having one-night stands is over.

Asher clears his throat and turns up the song as he focuses on the road, and he leans back in his seat. The hum of the road seems to relax him as he drives, and I wonder just what is going on inside that head of his.

"You like this song?" I ask, turning my body toward his, tugging at my seatbelt to make some space.

"Yes," he answers.

"But it's about a man who's so in love with a woman he can't stand to be away from her," I push. "How he'd follow her to the ends of the earth."

His strong features flex. "And?"

"And you don't believe in love."

"You don't have to believe in love to appreciate the way others believe in it." Asher side-eyes me. "And you're welcome to get to know me better, Liv, when you're more . . . clear-headed."

His voice has an icy edge and he keeps his eyes focused on the road. But it hits me all the same as I watch him push his hair off his forehead with one large, inked hand. Asher Reed is gorgeous—a dripping with masculinity, rugged competence, and surety kind of gorgeous. My eyes drift over his angled cheekbones, the perfectly imperfect black hair, and his beard, thick but trimmed close over his wide jaw. It makes me imagine what his face would feel like drifting slowly over my stomach, then up between the valley of my breasts. The scruff counteracting his soft, full lips as they skate across my flesh. His arm is lined with veins as he grips the wheel tight, and from this position I get a closer look at the ink that spans his tanned skin. There's a crown with roses woven throughout the sleeve design, a clock stuck on one-twenty-five, numbers and writing in a language I don't know. I look away when my core starts to heat just from studying him.

"For the record, it's easier for me to ask about you with a few drinks under my . . . dress?" I say with a grin. "You're not always approachable."

Asher turns his dark eyes on mine for a split second. "That's *your* assumption of me."

I snort. "That's *everyone's* assumption of you."

"Aye, but *you* judged me the moment you met me."

I hum in admission.

"And what did you assume?" he asks, tapping his heavy thumb on the wheel.

"I assumed you were the same as the last man I knew like you," I blurt out.

"Assumptive, discriminatory bullshit? Surprising for you, Livi."

Livi? That's the second time he's called me that.

"Not discriminatory. Just similar. He was big like you. Well, not quite as big. He wasn't bearlike. Maybe more of a baby bear . . ." *What the hell am I saying?* "Lots of tattoos, always wearing a semi-scowl." I take a deep breath. "He was my boyfriend. We met the summer before college. WKU."

Normally, the warning voice in my head would appear and tell me to shut the fuck up, but she's sleeping off her sangria so *I* keep talking.

"Nathan Stokes. Nate. He was on the wrestling team, ran with a rough crowd, partied a lot." I watch Asher's gaze intensify on the road ahead as he grips the wheel tighter. "He was older than me, drove an Indian motorcycle, a Scout."

Asher scoffs. "So he's a wanker."

"Oh?" I laugh. "So you're a bike snob?"

"You wouldn't catch me dead on anything but a Harley, so your 'he was like you' shit doesn't fly."

"So, you *are* a snob," I reiterate before resuming my story. "Anyway, everyone told me he was bad news. He was a total flirt, dabbled in a lot of drinking and sometimes drugs. I couldn't stay away from him. He was gorgeous—"

"Aye. So maybe a little like me then."

A smirk plays on Asher's lips, which I try to ignore. Along with the sangria swirling in my stomach. Or is that butterflies?

"We had fun, for a while. But after Christmas break, I came back to my dorm early and found him in bed with my roommate, Tania. She had become a really good friend."

I glance out the window as a vivid memory pushes into my brain: his hands on her, kissing her, both of them naked.

"He didn't even stop fucking her. He just looked up at me, then back to her, and kept right on going like I meant nothing to him. I had to live with her for the next three months as they dated. I had to be there when he came over every day. It was... terrible. And completely humiliating." My voice trails off. "I knew then I was done with bad boys."

"Cheating makes weak men feel strong." He turns to look pointedly at me and my stomach somersaults again. "This Stokes? He's *nothing* like the man I am."

A rolling heat hits my core as I turn my gaze to the window. "Well, he taught me a lesson. The man I marry will be kind, he'll come from a good hardworking family, maybe he'll be a businessman, he'll be home every night like my dad was, and he'll be a real family man who wants all the same things I do."

"Which are?" Asher's jaw tics as he turns onto the Silver Pines drive.

"All the notes in my journal." I shrug.

"A journal about your made-up future husband?"

"Yes, a journal. I've had one since I was eleven. It's always made me feel more in control to put my goals in writing. I want a man who wants a family with me and our family will be more important to him than anything else in this world. A man who puts me first. Do you think that's too much to wait for?"

He pulls up to my cabin and cuts the engine. I'm reminded

when his gray eyes fix to mine that I'm with *Asher*. Talking to him like I would CeCe or Ginger.

"Whatever you want from any man is never too much." He pauses and I see that pinch of his brow as he considers his next words. "And whatever he gives you in return, it still won't be enough."

I'm speechless, but Asher doesn't give me a chance to respond as he gets out of his side of the truck and makes his way over to mine. He's right. Everything I think I know about him *is* an assumption. But he is mysterious, quiet, always seems to speak in riddles, and he definitely has an aura of danger. Which means I can't be *that* far off. To the world, Asher Reed is the epitome of *bad boy*.

"I shouldn't have compared you to Nate. But it does seem as though you have a past. At least, that's what I thought the first time I saw you," I offer as he opens my door.

"You don't want to know about my past, Olivia." It isn't something he's saying as a reflex. It's a warning.

"Did some girl do a number on you? Is that why you hate love now?" I ask as I step out to feel the earth rock under my feet. I'm dizzy with both the curiosity I feel about who he really is and all the alcohol in my system.

"Christ," he mutters under his breath as he scoops me up into his strong arms. I'm helpless to stop him when he looks down at me. "I don't hate love. I just don't believe in it."

He cradles me tight and I rest a hand to his hard chest as he carries me up the steps to my cabin. I try not to enjoy this, but I nuzzle my face against him and breathe him in. Maybe just for one night . . .

"Don't even fucking think about it," he remarks, as if he's reading my mind. My cabin is unlocked—there's no place at Silver Pines that isn't safe—and Asher makes his way in to set me down.

"You don't know what I'm thinking," I fire back, smoothing

my dress over my hips.

Asher tosses my purse down on the bench in the entry of the cabin and flicks on the lamp. Jo was definitely here today; there are new magazines on the table, candles, and throw pillows on the sofa.

"I know when a woman is getting comfortable in my arms. I'm not your drunken cowboy hookup, Olivia." He moves closer to me, the angry way he says my name sending a shiver up my spine.

"And whoever you assume I am, wherever you assume I come from, I can assure you that you're *wrong*." His voice is even lower now. "If getting comfortable in my arms is something you want, that's something you can tell me when you're sober. Do you understand?"

The weight of his eyes and the strange feeling that he sees *me*, what *I* might really want, makes the room spin even more, and suddenly I feel like I'm about to throw up. I cover my hand with my mouth and make a run for the bathroom, barely getting to the safety of the toilet before I empty my stomach.

Fucking sangria Sundays.

CHAPTER 10
Olivia

I upchuck everything I drank tonight as I tell myself I'll never touch alcohol again. Washing my face to remove every stitch of makeup makes me feel a bit better before I brush my teeth. Some small working part of my tipsy brain tells me I need water, so I make my way into the bedroom and pick up my reusable water bottle.

I'm expecting Asher to be gone when I come out into my living room in my fleece pajamas and cow slippers twenty minutes later. But he's not. In fact, he's sitting comfortably on my sofa, his long, thick legs relaxed as he types on his phone.

He doesn't look up at my arrival. "Everything but the kitchen sink?"

"Yes," I answer, heading to my fridge. "You didn't have to wait around for me, you know."

My balance is off and I don't know the space well yet, so I walk right into the corner of my kitchen counter and stub my toe, hard.

"*Son of a—!*" I cry out. Pain radiates up my ankle to my calf as I pull off my slipper to investigate the damage. "Fucking demon cabinet."

"Isn't that what you wear those ten-pound cow slippers for? Protection?" Asher deadpans as he moves to help me to the sofa, slinging my arm up over his muscled shoulder as his hand grips my waist. My pajama top is cropped so his fingers brush my skin just below my ribs, sending another jolt of heat to my core.

"You're like one of those people from that movie series. Certain injury and accidents follow you every fucking place you go," he mutters as we walk.

"*Final Destination*?" I ask, trying to focus on anything but the way his fingers feel on my skin.

"Aye. The logs and the highway . . ." he adds as he helps me sink into the sofa, then sits across from me on the sturdy wooden coffee table.

He lifts my foot, his hand circling my calf as he brings it up and bends my second toe.

"Christ, this isn't your cabinet's fault. Your second toe is longer than your biggest. It was practically begging to be destroyed."

My mouth falls open. "Are you making fun of my feet?"

"Fuck yes I am." As if he can't help himself, Asher smiles at me, a straight wide smile that is so genuine it both shocks and warms me.

"I'm glad my injured toe can help us prove you actually feel emotion," I grunt out as I flex my foot in his hands. My toe throbs. "And screw you. People with longer second toes are more intelligent, you know," I bite out, pulling my foot away. "I could make thousands selling pics of these feet, thank you very much!"

"Fuck . . . just what you need. Some foot-obsessed creeper wandering Laurel Creek looking for you," he says sarcastically as he stands.

The throb in my toe subsides, but the need to kick him

swells with the look on his smug face.

"Like you have perfect feet."

"Fucking right I do." He leans in "But this isn't a 'I'll show you mine if you show me yours' kinda night, Livi." My mind wanders somewhere else completely at the thought of there being another night . . . *Goddammit, Olivia.*

"Be a good girl, lock your door after I leave." His accent is thick as he assesses me. "And get some sleep."

My eyes drop to the ink on his neck, gray and black vines intertwined around an ornate cross. I force my eyes to flick back up to his.

I hate how good he looks right now.

"Okay . . ." I swallow as his jaw tenses and he backs away. He makes it to the door before turning back to look at me over his shoulder, just as I was checking out his perfect ass in those jeans.

"What was your cat's name?" he asks. If he caught me staring at him, he doesn't say.

"Um . . . Biscuit," I answer, swallowing down the pain of the loss again.

He nods. "Straight to bed, yeah?"

I can't help myself as I stick out my tongue. "Yes, *Daddy*."

A deep growl rumbles through him with words I can't quite hear before he opens the door and exits into the dark night.

I lean back against the sofa when I see his truck lights fade away and reflect on my evening with Asher Reed. The way he carted me out of the bar. The deadly look he gave the other man trying to talk to me. The way his eyes darkened when I called him Daddy. I definitely didn't miss *that*.

I glance down at my toes and fold my arms over my chest. *Fuck him, my feet are pretty.*

CHAPTER 11
Asher

MAY

> **OBLIVIA**
> www.vendellsreclaimedwood.com
>
> **OBLIVIA**
> It's a hard wood and paints really easy.
>
> **ME**
> Maple? Oak?
>
> **ME**
> Is this a random wood-guessing game?
>
> **OBLIVIA**
> Look at the picture, smartass.

I click the link and see a nice selection of maple from a local company and that it's in stock.

> **OBLIVIA**
> Would this work for my floors?

> **ME**
> Possibly.

> **OBLIVIA**
> Thank you for that insight, man of many words.

> **ME**
> Anyone ever tell you, your longer second toe makes you mean?

> **OBLIVIA**
> No, but it will do a real good job of gripping my four-inch heel while I kick you in the ass.

A photo comes through of her slender foot perfectly encased in a hunter-green stiletto with gold accents.

> **ME**
> All I see is a tripping hazard.

> **OBLIVIA**
> I'll be wearing them all night, so if you feel the need to make any sarcastic comments at the reception, I can't say I'll hold back.

I suppress a smirk as I tuck my phone into my pocket. The only thing I got from this conversation was maybe I'm into feet? Because fuck, even her feet turn me on. So goddamn pretty. Just like the rest of her.

"The fuck's up with you over there?" Wade asks, watching me as he straightens his tie and turns to enter the wedding chapel in Cave Run Park. Today is Cole and Ginger's wedding.

"A man can't have his privacy?" I retort, shaking my head and feigning a scowl.

"Just never seen you grin down at your phone like that before." Wade smirks as he pulls the heavy wooden door open.

"Or grin, period," Nash adds with a deep chuckle as he runs a hand through his disheveled hair, a regular look since he found out his wife was pregnant. Though I've never seen him happier.

Nash and Wade are right. I shouldn't be grinning at my phone, but this is the first time I've heard from Olivia since the night I took her home from the Horse and Barrel. *I shouldn't be happy to see her name light up my phone, especially when* for once it seems she's actually staying away from something dangerous.

Me.

Olivia

"Oh my God, that's incredible," CeCe says from behind me as I slip on my 1920s flapper headpiece.

"Thanks. So's yours," I say, trying to push down the flush creeping up my neck from Asher's text. It's the first time I've spoken to him in almost two weeks. I've been avoiding him like the plague, but texting him now was strategic. I had to do something to break the ice so it wouldn't be awkward as all hell today.

What I didn't expect was for those butterflies to resurface the moment he answered.

CeCe turns her head to the side. The lacy headband that

holds her feather and flower is similar to mine, though hers has little jewels that surround her face, whereas mine is just lace and feather.

I give myself one more glance and then back away, letting the other girls have the mirror.

Cole and Ginger's wedding is, of course, picture-perfect. The May sun is shining, the insects are buzzing, and the green space outside the wedding chapel is alive with laughter and chatter as I look out the window from our dressing room.

Ginger practices her vows in her own mirror. She looks incredible; her ivory lace dress fits perfectly, little pearls dot the back, and the long skirt drapes all the way to the floor. Our dresses are also long and flowy but keep with the flapper style, figure-hugging with a slit up to the thigh, which shows off CeCe's adorable six-month baby bump beautifully. The heart-shaped bodice is strapless and the whole dress is covered in a sheer beaded overlay. I added my own little flair with vintage earrings and dramatic eye makeup.

Our hair has been styled expertly by the girls at Bendall's Salon in town. We all have long loose waves down our backs and our makeup is dramatic and period perfect. It's definitely the most fun I've ever had with wedding attire, but I wouldn't expect anything less than fun from Ginger and Cole.

I take a deep breath, counting down the minutes until I see Asher again. I can't take back the fact that I blurted out everything I want and need in a man like a drunken prom queen. All I can do is make sure nothing like that happens again. I'll be drastically limiting my drinks tonight. Best behavior Liv reporting for bridesmaid duty.

"How are things going with your house?" CeCe asks now, fiddling with her hairpiece in the mirror.

"I'm hoping it will be fully demoed by the end of the month," I answer, based on the daily updates Shane's been giving me.

"And you've got Asher helping you source the wood for the

cabinets?" Ginger asks before applying a little more lip gloss. "Have you seen him since he took you home?"

Shit.

I wince and brace for it.

"He took you *home?*" CeCe's face is animated, like a surprised little mama cartoon character. "Why didn't I know this?"

"It was this one's fault." I hook a thumb in Ginger's direction. "Too many pitchers at the bar. Besides, it was no biggie. He was leaving anyway."

"He practically dragged her out," Ginger adds with her trademark smirk.

"It's nothing. It was just embarrassing. I haven't been back to the bar or had a drink since."

"The way he was holding you at the bar told a different story." Ginger grins.

"Holy shit, what am I missing staying home?" CeCe quips.

"Nothing, I promise." I look at both of them. "When I first met him I assumed he was just like Nathan. A bad boy, a player. But now I'm not so sure. He's . . . a mystery."

CeCe and Ginger know all about Nathan because it was them I called crying when I found him in bed with my best friend.

"Mysterious men are the hottest." CeCe giggles. "Nash was a mystery when we started um, hanging out."

"Code phrase for fucking like bunnies." Ginger laughs.

I trade my gaze between them. "Well, we're definitely not doing *that*. He's an acquaintance at best. One who keeps popping up to save my ass."

"And one you definitely think is hot as hell," Ginger adds with a snort. "Even though you refuse to admit it."

"Semantics," I retort in my best Ginger voice. "Look, Asher Reed isn't my Prince Charming. But I have faith my soulmate will come."

I've been feeling better the last couple weeks. Something about being on the ranch, breathing in the fresh air, my morning porch chats with Dean. It's been calming, peaceful.

"Until that prince comes, just thank the universe for vibrators." Ginger laughs just as Camilla, her mom, knocks on the door with Mabel in tow.

"It's time, ladies." She smiles widely as she starts fawning over her daughter.

CeCe points to me, trying to sound firm. "Now's not the time, but there's more here. You're definitely attracted to him."

"Okay, officer." I laugh. "If there's anything to tell you, I promise you'll be the first to know."

We shuffle out of the room, and I try hard to fight those butterflies in my stomach just thinking about laying eyes on my *acquaintance.*

CHAPTER 12
Olivia

I don't hate love. I just don't believe in it.

I repeat Asher's words over and over in my head because all the moments I've spent telling myself that I'm not attracted to this dark mystery of a man do nothing to prepare me for how devastatingly sinful he looks dressed in a perfectly fitted three-piece suit.

In keeping with the 1920s theme, each groomsman is wearing pin stripes, with a gold pocket watch chain draped elegantly over their vest. Asher's hair is a touch shorter than when I saw him last—though it's still wavy—and his beard is trimmed back but still thick. With the ink creeping up his neck out of his crisp white dress shirt, he's giving hot, rugged mobster. Which means that, no matter what I tell my body, she has other ideas tonight because holy hell, I'm heating up just looking at him. The thoughts that run through my mind come from that dark place I've tried to push down for years. I want to see him unravel, to witness his loss of control . . . to be the *cause* of it.

The way his eyes meet mine as I walk down the aisle ahead

of CeCe and Ivy makes me feel like I'm the only woman in the room. His focus is unashamedly on me, like it's his job to guide me safely to the front of the chapel.

Ivy follows me, smiling at Billi on her mama's lap in the third row, followed by CeCe, her big bouquet of flowers resting sweetly on her baby bump. A certain sort of magic hangs over the room when Ginger starts down the aisle with her father, just behind Mabel, who's scattering petals along the walkway.

Her eyes meet Cole's and he smiles so big both dimples in his clean-shaven face pop out. I look between them and that familiar pang of jealousy hits me. It's not born from malice. It's more like a wish that one day a man will look at me the way Cole looks at Ginger.

I do my best to keep my focus on them, fighting the nagging feeling that I'm going to end up the crazy cat lady while all my friends live happily ever after.

Ginger has tears streaming down her cheeks as Mabel presents her with a special bracelet with two hearts on it. One for each of them.

My heart swells as I watch my best friend say her vows to her new little family, a family she was destined to have, but my eyes can't keep from straying to Asher. Illicit thoughts of tearing open that suit coat and running my hands over his hard body fill my head as the officiant says the magic words and Cole and Ginger are announced husband and wife. The chapel cheers when they kiss.

Asher's eyes meet mine across the aisle, heating as they glide over my body. He isn't coy; he doesn't try to hide it. He looks at me like it's his right to do so, like nothing would pull those mercury eyes away. Call it the romance of the day or simply the fact that I haven't had sex in what feels like eons, but more than ever, that heated way he's been looking at me since the night of my fire is starting to feel less like coincidence and more like unfinished business.

CHASING THE FIRE

"Me and Mom want one picture with you, sweetheart, before you scamper off." My dad approaches with my mother, sweet smiles on both of their faces. They've known Ginger since she was a girl and they're so happy to be a part of her big day. We've been at photos for over an hour already and the photographer has every shot she's planned among the maple trees and honeysuckle bushes. Ivy is breaking off to feed Billi—with Wade close behind—and the rest of the wedding guests are milling about with champagne flutes in the early evening sun. There isn't a breath of wind, and the sky is a clear, duck-egg blue. It couldn't be any more perfect.

"Okay, but I'll take it," I tell my dad.

"Don't trust the old man's photography skills?" he chides, passing me his cellphone.

"We just want to have foreheads in the picture, Ken, and that might not be the case if you take it." My mother and I look at each other with knowing grins as my dad shrugs with a chuckle. It's been the three of us for so long that we know one another inside and out.

"Touché," my dad agrees, feigning a scowl.

I hug them before they congratulate Ginger one more time and head off to change before the reception.

"Do you guys mind heading over first to make sure everything is perfect for me?" Ginger asks me, Asher, CeCe, and Nash as we mill about, chatting.

"Of course, we can head over. Whatever you need," I answer right away.

"I really want to get out of this dress," CeCe says to me. "You're welcome to come with us, but I'm going to stop at home and change first."

"You can come with me, I'm heading straight there," Asher

says cooly from my left. My mouth falls open in surprise. It's not like he's asking. He's telling me in his trademark nonchalant, commanding way. Standing beside Nash, his inked hands are casually parked in the pockets of his suit pants as his intense eyes burn through me, and with that voice directed at me for the first time in weeks, even the tips of my fingers tingle.

CeCe shoots him a glance and then her eyes find mine. "That okay?"

"Of course," I answer way too quickly, avoiding Asher's heady gaze. "We'll make sure everything is hunky-dory."

Hunky-dory? My dad says that. *Why am I so awkward right now?*

"All right . . . I guess it's settled," she says with a smile as I give her the best hug I can around her baby bump. "We'll meet you two there."

"You kids behave now." Nash chuckles as he goes to shake Asher's hand.

"Aye," Asher answers at the exact same time I blurt out, "We're just friends."

Everyone in the vicinity stops and stares at me. *All right, well, time to crawl under a rock.*

"Of course," Nash croaks out, trying not to laugh.

I can almost feel my palms sweating. The thought of being alone with Asher is making me beyond antsy, yet I *want* it.

As the others start to head out, Asher raises a perfectly suit-clad arm, gesturing for me to go first.

"Thanks for letting me tag along," I say in an attempt to break the silence.

I can almost feel the heat of his gaze on me as we descend the chapel steps. His hand meets my lower back to guide me forward and my nipples instantly pebble at the touch.

When we reach the bottom of the steps, he stops and drops his hand to my arm. I turn to face him and find those gray eyes I've been avoiding for weeks searching mine.

"You don't need to avoid me, Liv."

"I'm not . . . honest." I look up into those eyes and almost forget my own name.

"Mm-hmm. Okay then. Well, since we're being honest, I say this in the *friendliest* way possible"—his eyes move slowly, hotly—"you look *really* fucking beautiful today."

He tilts my chin up and I breathe him in deeper, aching to touch him. The thought sends sparks through me, straight to my core.

He may not be Mr. Right, but as he backs up slowly and heads around to his side of his truck, I drink him in. Part of me is really wishing he could be Mr. Right Now.

CHAPTER 13
Olivia

"It's your best friend's wedding. Her dream day and all that. So, what's wrong?"

Asher is nothing but direct as I sit down on a thick padded leather stool across from him in Wade's wedding barn. He unloads bottles of Kentucky Owl behind the bar I know he helped build. I look up at his question, surprised he's starting a conversation with me. Guess there's a first for everything, even witnessing a more human side to Asher Reed.

After just fifteen minutes, I've finished checking on everything I was supposed to. Place cards are set, menus are out, and all the flameless candles are lit. This is the first time we've really talked since we drove over here in comfortable silence with The Highwaymen playing through his old truck.

"All I've done is smile today. Why do you ask like you think something is wrong?"

"Smiling doesn't mean all is well," he observes.

"Always the listener. Even when you're not on bartender duty, huh?" I prop my chin up onto my palm. We're the only ones here so he's removed his suit coat, and the way his dress shirt clings to his muscular arms, the sleeves rolled up to his elbows showcasing those veiny and rippled inked forearms just for me, feels like a reward.

"Eh," he grunts out. "I'm sort of on duty."

Cole and Ginger hired a server to run the bar, but Asher has offered to stock everything and relieve him when he needs a break. Asher decided to get the jump on making sure the bar was ready while I lit all the candles in the mason jar centerpieces. They're surrounded by vases filled with roses and adorned with greenery that match our dresses. Each one sits on a mirror to reflect the light. They twinkle, just like the ones woven into greenery along the heavy beams in the ceiling, to create a romantic, whimsical feel.

"Well, to answer your question, I'd say aside from always feeling like the friend who will end up the crazy cat lady, I'm good. The day has been beautiful."

"I wasn't asking how you felt about the day," Asher says, closing the cooler and turning to face me. His big hands spread out onto the bar and he tilts his body toward me. "I want to know how *you* are. How you're doing being away from home, feeling displaced?"

I blow out a sigh and bring my hands down to my lap. It makes me nervous when Asher asks these questions because, although I'm close with my friends, we don't talk about *me* all that much these days. I'd much rather hear what's going on with them, so I shrug off their questions and change the subject. Frankly, their lives are a lot more exciting, and I'm still confused about everything changing in my life.

I look up at him from my freshly painted red nails. "I'm all right." I shrug, pushing my hair off my shoulder. "Like my dad says, it is what it is. I just have to get through it. Plus, Jo has been amazing."

He nods. "Atta girl. Just focus on the progress. Shane and the guys are great."

"Uhhh. Enough about my misfortunes. Tell me about you," I say, tapping the bar top.

Asher remains where he is for a beat, studying my expression. Then he ducks down and grabs two glasses from under the bar.

"You don't always have to be the one who listens. It's okay to let someone listen to you," I tell him as he uncorks a bottle of bourbon. Cole and Ginger are graciously keeping an open bar for everyone to ensure they have the best time.

"Aye. What do you want to know?" He narrows his eyes.

"I don't really know anything about you, so surprise me." I watch as he pours a shot into a glass for me, then for himself. "Unless there is some sort of law that says I'm not allowed to ask the bartender questions."

"No law. I just rarely talk about me."

He passes me my glass and, as I reach out to take it, the tips of my fingers brush his calloused knuckles, causing electricity to spark in my blood at the contact. I pick up my glass and take a sip; the whiskey doesn't even burn it's so smooth.

"So you're just a hypocrite? Lecturing me, yet you clearly won't talk about yourself either." I prop my chin back up and grin at him. "I don't want your deep dark secrets. It just feels unfair that you've sorta seen me at my worst lately . . ."

I take another sip as Asher looks down at his glass, swirling his whiskey.

"I can ask you questions because it's my *job*." He pats the bar. "Your job doesn't qualify you to hear about my past, Liv."

Did Asher Reed just joke with me? I watch as he wraps his plush lips around the rim of his glass and takes a good-sized sip. When his thick, inked throat works into a swallow, I wish I was the whiskey.

I snap my eyes up. "I'm a lingerie store owner. You wouldn't believe the things people tell me. Whatever you have to say, I guarantee some of the women who shop with me have told me worse."

I pretend to button my lips. He smiles unexpectedly and fuck if it isn't a beautiful sight.

"Let's start simple. Tell me how you ended up in our fine little town," I say.

His brows dip in thought.

"My mother, she painted and always loved the mountains. Said they were a place to find peace. When I came for the interview here and saw that the firehall was basically at the base of the mountain, I figured it was a sign. And Laurel Creek"—he looks around—"seemed like the furthest place from my old reality possible."

"And that reality was?"

"A desolate one." His eyes darken. "One of arrogant insolence."

Asher looks at me in a way I've never seen before. Open, as if he's deciding whether or not he can trust me. The echo of danger that emanates from him slinks up my spine.

"Every day that goes by, I feel farther away from it," he adds carefully. "But the history is still there."

"And you weren't . . . happy? In your old life?" I swallow.

He stands and knocks back the rest of his shot. "It wasn't about happiness. With the . . . power I had, a man can grow a godlike complex. And that kind of man wasn't the man I wanted to be."

He sets his glass down, and that openness from earlier disappears. "I don't know why I'm telling you all of this."

"Because I'm easy to talk to," I tell him, matter-of-fact. "That's why everyone comes to me with their life problems. It's not your fault. I'm a magnet for those in need of sound advice."

He stares at me for a long moment. The barn around us is quiet and I swear I almost start to sweat under his gaze. "You can't drain your cup to fill others'."

"Deep," I joke in an attempt to cut the thick air between us. His eyes remain on mine. "Truth is, I'm sort of a mess. I've always had a plan for everything, yet lately I feel stuck. Like I'm behind on starting my life—"

"Fuck that," he says so passionately I flinch. "Everyone's journey looks different. Besides, you have a habit of tripping into things. Your time will come."

I can't help it, I laugh, and damn it feels good. I raise my glass.

"I'll drink to *fuck that*. Who needs a husband anyway? At this point I'd settle for some good sex," I blurt out, then instantly regret it. "Hypothetically.I mean."

I anxiously slide forward off my stool, hoping for breezy, but instead my heel jams in the rung and I almost fall. My palms slap to the bar top as I brace myself. I look up to see Asher's plush lips curve into a half smile as he shakes his head. Thankfully, he doesn't say anything as I round the bar to help him finish stocking. I watch with surprise as he adds one more swallow of whiskey to each of our glasses. He picks his up and slides mine to me. The sound of glass clinking fills the air as he knocks them together, swallowing his whiskey before leaning in so close, I swear my heart stops.

"Don't settle for good sex, Livi girl. Make sure it's fucking incredible, yeah?"

CHAPTER 14
Asher

"Not easy to find..." Olivia mutters back, licking her lips, completely unaware of how fucking perfect she is.

Her gaze is stunned, needy, in a way that instantly makes my dick stand to attention. A shallow inhale through her rosebud lips has me ready to bend her heart-shaped ass right over this bar and drive my cock deep while I fist those thick coppery waves.

It's been too long for me because, aside from Olivia, no one has interested me. I had my share of women before I came here, too many. All too willing to be with James Donovan's son, heir to the throne, a promise of wealth and power. But those women never realized they'd be selling their soul to the devil. They'd live at his beck and call only to escape when he was done with them.

"Asher?" Olivia whispers my name, her blue eyes simmering. The desire to make her scream it overwhelms me as my eyes drift to those pouty red lips. "How much time do we have before people start showing up?"

"Not long."

Olivia's pupils are blown wide as she takes a step toward me, forcing my cock to throb against my suit pants. Her ocean eyes trail my face, landing on my mouth.

"We're friends, right?" Her voice is raspy and full of want, enough to obliterate a man's resolve.

"Yes, friends," I agree, bringing my thumb up to test her, tucking a piece of hair behind her ear. I'm transfixed by this needy but somehow bold side of her. The side that *begs* for ruin.

"Friends . . . have each other's backs?" She fists the vest of my suit in her hands, inching me closer. I have no idea what is happening here, but if this is an invitation, I'm nowhere near strong enough to turn it down. Her eyes drift to my mouth.

"And maybe friends could have incredible sex. Just once. No strings attached?" Her voice is a whisper as her lashes flutter. The sexiest goddamn thing about Olivia is that she has no idea how she affects me. Hell, she doesn't even have to try. "And, Asher?"

"Hmm?" is all I can manage.

"I'm *very* sober right now," she says softly. "Just this once . . . ?" she pleads, looking up at me. Goddamn, she's asking so nicely, and the moment her tongue wets those pretty lips, I'm done for.

"Fuck it—" I barely get the words out before I'm crushing her curves to me as I claim those plush lips for my own. The electricity crackling between us has all my muscles rigid and pulsing. She pulls back, staring up at me, a question in her eyes I can't wait to answer as I pull her closer again.

"You asked for it, woman."

I growl as a desperate sort of hunger takes over; there's not a hope in hell of stopping now. Olivia surrenders to me as my tongue meets hers and everything else fades away. It's just us, this moment, and the taste of possibility. The feel of her plush lips on mine destroys any semblance of willpower I have, and I can't seem to get enough. In return, she's a little fireball, all-consuming as she pulls me flush to her. As always, she surprises me, kissing me in a way that has me trying to keep pace with *her*, and the little sounds she makes have me so damn hard. My hands roam across her back, then up through her hair, and I don't know how the fuck we move together so effortlessly but we do. I pull back slightly, just as breathless as she is, tipping my forehead to hers, my thumbs grazing her jaw. I'm out of my fucking mind.

"This is the only time I'll offer. Tell me to stop, Livi girl." I grip her face. "Tell me I shouldn't take you to my truck and make you scream my fucking name."

"Okay . . ." she breathes out. "Don't take me to your truck, Asher," she whispers in an almost breathless pant. My stomach drops.

"It's way too far away. Take me right *here*."

Olivia

"Christ, you smell so fucking good," Asher growls into my neck as he plants hungry open-mouthed kisses down it. I grip his strong shoulders as he grabs my ass tight through my satin dress, my curves spilling between his big palms.

"Asher, *please*," I beg. I need this: one hookup, no strings attached. And he knows it. Right now, it feels like he knows *everything* as he's hiking my skirt up and lifting my legs to wrap around his waist. I have no idea where we're going. Hell, I don't care where we're going. I only care that Asher doesn't stop kissing me as I feel him push us through a door and into the ladies' room.

Asher pulls open the heavy wooden door to the first stall and then we're inside, and I'm pinned up against the wall with my dress hiked up around my hips.

His hungry eyes roam mine, then trail down my throat. His thumb grazes my hardened and aching nipple through my dress and I moan with abandon.

"Tell me you want to be fucked," he demands.

I throw my head back and arch into him, whimpering as he swipes his thumb over me again.

His lips gently brush mine, and when he pulls away, I'm the one leaning in, desperate for more.

"Words, Liv."

"Fuck, Asher. *Yes...*" I murmur as he pulls my chin down, giving his mouth full access to mine. I rock my body against his, and he wastes no time as he pulls the top of my dress down.

"*Fuck...*" he breathes out, taking in the sight of me. My core throbs with the white-hot frenzy I see in his eyes. "*Show me you want it. Squeeze those perfect tits together for me.*"

His accent is thick now and he barely gets the words out before I'm doing just what he commands. I never understood until right this moment that this is what I needed to quench every want I've ever had, to settle every craving. A man who will take total and utter *control*.

Asher uses one arm to hold me up tight while he flicks his tongue over one of my nipples, toying with me to the point I feel like I might combust before he's moving to the other and giving it the same attention.

It's so fucking unbridled and brazen how he takes the time we don't have without care. I feel his teeth as he nips at my breast. I cry out but just as quickly he licks over the pain, and I'm a quivering mess. I rub against him, blazing, searching for friction against his huge cock.

His free hand slides down my waist, over my belly, and between my legs, pulling my thong aside. *Am I about to do this with Asher Reed?*

His thumb slides over my clit then through my soaking core as he takes his bottom lip between his teeth.

"Mmm . . . I knew you had this side to you . . ."

"What side?" I ask, breathless.

His eyes search mine. "A need for depravity."

"H-how did you know?" *I* didn't even know until now.

"Your eyes, Liv. I knew you'd be such a needy little slut for me . . ." He pinches my clit and I swear I stop breathing.

"Touch me . . . please," I beg as his finger slides through me.

"Touch you?" He adds more pressure to my clit. "I'm not gonna touch you, Liv . . . I'm gonna fucking ruin you."

"*Asher . . .*" I breathe as his finger slips inside me.

"Aye . . . say my name," he mutters as I bite my lip, and the familiar heat that slinks up my throat whenever he *really* looks at me creeps even higher. Right now, he's watching me like he'll never get enough. My eyes flutter closed as my pussy clenches around his thick, dominating finger.

"Eyes here, Olivia," he orders. "Now."

They flutter open, and I swallow hard as my walls pulse when he adds another finger, stretching me. I'm so close.

"Not yet," he whispers, sensing my reaction. "Don't you dare fucking come until I tell you to."

Holy fucking hell. This man will be my undoing as he expertly pumps his fingers in and out of me, keeping his heavy thumb over my clit.

I moan a strangled sound but, just before I fall apart, he slides out of me. The loss is so profound I whimper with it. Asher chuckles as he lifts his hand and sucks his first two fingers into his mouth. His eyes close on a groan and, when he opens them, they're wild as he reaches down again, bringing my arousal to my own lips. I shudder as he pushes his fingers into my own mouth. I keep my gaze locked on his as I take them deep.

"Taste how fucking sweet you are, Liv."

I let my tongue swirl between his fingers, moaning around them. There's an even darker side to Asher than I realized, and it's a world I want to stay in.

He reaches into his pocket, fishing for a condom. I shake my head.

"No . . . I want to feel you," I say. "I'm on birth control."

Asher hovers for a minute, and his expression turns almost crazed as he realizes what I'm offering. "I'm clean," I add.

"Me too. I've never gone bare with anyone. *Ever.*" His chest is rising and falling, heavy, needy.

Knowing he's never had anyone else like this? I want it even more. Fumbling to unbuckle his pants, I make just enough room for his heavy, solid cock to bob free. I suck in a breath as I look down.

Holy shit. He's big. And thick. And so fucking solid. Precum leaks from his tip as his hand chokes around his shaft and he's . . . pierced? I feel dizzy with need, imagining him inside me, trying to work out where the perfectly placed metal barbell on the underside of his crown will meet me when he fucks into me. *Oh God.* Nervous anticipation eats at me as I trace the piercing with my thumb.

"What will it feel like?" I whisper.

"Like I'm fucking everywhere, Livi," he growls, and I moan at the thought, loudly.

"Shhh, greedy girl. Do you hear them?"

I freeze. I had been so lost in Asher that I hadn't heard the sound of voices around us. Not everyone has arrived yet, but there are definitely people here.

Asher tugs my thong to the side even farther, though he doesn't bother to take it off as he slides the head of his cock through my soaking slit. My eyes roll back with the feel of the metal against me.

"Can you be a good girl? Stay quiet while I fill this tight little pussy?"

"*Oh . . . fuck . . .*" No one has ever talked to me like this before. "I don't know . . ."

Hell, even him just sliding through me feels incredible.

Time slows as Asher pushes in the first inch. My back arches with the feeling and I'm already seeing stars behind my eyelids.

I pant as I realize how full I'm going to be. He grips my hips and we both look down, watching the way he moves, sinking slowly, disappearing inside me. It's fucking hypnotizing.

"*Fuck . . . Olivia.*" He groans my name as he loses himself a little more and the voices grow louder. There should be laws against the dark and sinful way this man says fuck. It's so damn sexy.

"S-should we stop?" I ask, praying he says no because I've never felt anything like him.

Asher's eyes turn almost carnal as he pulls the white handkerchief from his suit pocket and shoves it into my mouth. My eyes water as he clamps his heavy hand over the top.

"I promise you, no one in this fucking building is safe if they get in the way of me burying my cock inside you right now, Olivia. Which means you *will* be quiet for me. You'll be my perfect, silent little slut. Got it?"

He groans deeply as he pulls out almost all the way, then pushes fully into me in one deep, heavenly thrust. I'm so full, I *do* feel him everywhere. The fullness reaches my stomach as I moan loudly into the cloth, but it softens the sound to a whimper.

"Aye, that's better. Now you can scream for me, Liv." His eyes darken.

I bite down hard to stop myself from crying out as he sets his pace.

"*So fucking tight,*" he huffs out as I begin to accommodate him. "Christ, baby . . . it's like you've never even been fucked . . ."

Him calling me baby is almost my undoing as he watches himself, holding me up like I weigh nothing.

"That's it." His eyes bore into mine. "You don't want gentle.

Do you?"

I shake my head as a tear slides down my cheek.

"Aye, you want me to fuck you so hard you'll remember me between your thighs tomorrow."

I nod a yes.

"Good girl," he growls as he slams into me, and I cry out, gripping him tighter. "When you wake, and it hurts, remember how you begged me for more . . ."

His piercing is pressing against the spot I try desperately to reach on my own with my vibrator. But Asher is effortless and every time he roots himself deep, I think I might die from the pleasure.

"Look at you. So damn pretty . . . swallowing my cock so well."

I don't know how much time passes as Asher fucks into me without relent, stretching me, filling me as he whispers my name, only slowing when he knows I am on the verge of coming. Asher fucks me like he wants to teach me exactly what it means to be owned by a man. And I'm completely at his mercy.

I'm inching my way up the wall of the bathroom stall with every deep thrust he offers. My hair is splayed out, my dress has fallen around my waist, and drool runs down my chin from being gagged as tears stream down my cheeks. Clamping his hand down over my mouth, he cuts off my breath even more. And suddenly I'm clenching him even tighter, somehow even more turned on by his sense of control.

"Show me who *you* are, Liv. I want every fucking ounce of your darkness." Dots line my vision as he squeezes my air supply. "This tight little pussy just gets wetter with every breath I steal from you. Come all over my dick now, Liv and I'll give you what you want. I'll fill you right the fuck up."

My legs tremble and I'm a whimpering mess as I do as he says, crying his name into the cloth against his heavy hand.

"Atta girl." He watches me intently while I fall apart, but I don't even care. All I feel is utter euphoria. I almost black out before he lets up a little and I suck a breath through my nose.

He slows his pace and, as I watch him, I realize I've never known a man so open with his own sexual needs. It sends a fire burning through me, knowing it's *me* who is making him this unhinged. My eyes roll back and the tight coil of heat centers again. His hand slides to grasp the back of my neck while he buries his face between my neck and my shoulder. He groans into me, his face buried against my skin.

"You're fucking ruining me, Liv," he admits, and the honesty slices through me.

The sounds of him fucking me fill the air, and just as I feel Asher grow inside me and inch closer to the edge again, the door to the bathroom opens and we hear someone walk in. My breath hitches as the water starts to run and my eyes snap open, focusing on him. But he doesn't even threaten to stop; he just keeps rocking into me. My pussy tightens even further, then he smirks before he whispers under the rush of the water.

"You like the idea of being caught?" he whispers low against my ear.

I nod.

"You want my cum dripping from you the rest of the night?"

I nod again.

"Then give me one more, pretty girl, milk every fucking drop," he orders as the water continues to run, and I'm helpless, my orgasm crashing into me without warning. My shoe hits the floor just as he stiffens inside me.

"*Fuck*," he groans against my bare shoulder, and we tumble over the edge together. His movements grow languid, but he's gripping my hips so tight I'm sure I'll be bruised. The cloth is pulled from my mouth, but I'm in a daze as his lips come down on mine and he spills into me, biting my bottom lip hard.

The water shuts off and I'm panting, sucking in my first full breath in minutes. It feels like I might pass out. Mortification washes over me as my shoe is slid back under the door by whoever was using the sink. I wait, breathless. Asher is still rock-hard and jerking inside me when the door to the bathroom opens. The voices get louder then subside as it closes and we're alone again.

"Holy hell . . ." I whimper, trying to catch my breath.

"Yeah," he breathes out, still holding me.

"I've never . . ." I mutter, trailing off as he pushes deep one last time and I feel him twitch. I moan involuntarily and he chuckles. Asher kisses my lips gently and my eyes find his.

"Still friends?" I ask.

"*Christ*," he murmurs, his laugh deeper this time. "If that's what you want to call it."

Asher moves to pull out of me but I stop him, gripping his waist with my legs a little tighter. In turn he squeezes my thigh like he doesn't want to leave me either. A rush of emotion washes through me and I bury myself against his chest. He tenses, then surrenders before hugging me back.

I expected today to be hard. I braced myself for watching another friend get married and start their future while I don't even have any prospects on the horizon, but this feeling of being wanted for even this small amount of time made things feel a whole lot easier. And so, for that reason, I cling to this dark mystery of a man just a little longer.

CHAPTER 15
Asher

LATE JUNE

P
> You have to call me, son.

I look away from my phone to glance up at Nash as he lines up his horseshoe shot. This is the third time my uncle Pete has messaged me in the last two weeks. Twenty-six months I made it with no contact from New York or my family, but my past life always seems to creep out of the woodwork when I least expect it.

ME
> There is nothing I'm interested in discussing, Pete.

P
> Your father is sick.

This isn't news. My father's been sick for twenty years. Side effects from too much daily whiskey and whatever his drug of choice is.

>ME
>Not my problem.

I set my phone down on the picnic table I'm sitting at, pushing Pete from my mind. He was told *never* to contact me, but a condition of helping me get out of my father's world was giving him a point of contact.

Nash tosses his horseshoe after all the buildup of planning his shot and lands it perfectly as he lets out a little "fuck yeah."

He's in his element: shorts, flip-flops, his cap facing backward. His brow is furrowed, deep in concentration, playing against Haden at Benny's Backyard BBQ. "Mama Tried" by Merle Haggard plays over the sound system and the air is both festive and casual. We've been here a few times; it's a cool place by the lake, on the beach, with a food truck–style take-out restaurant that serves ribs, wings, and burgers in white paper boxes with their logo stamped on top. It's no-frills, but out behind the truck there's a large grassy area with string lights hung up between wooden posts. Multiple picnic tables form a U around a gaming area with cornhole and horseshoe toss. Where the grass ends the sand begins, and there are nets set up right on the beach beyond for volleyball. It's the perfect place to ride my Harley to and hang out for an afternoon with a beer and some good grub.

"You overstepped the line!" Haden barks out as Nash lands yet another perfect shot.

"Nah, take the loss." Nash chuckles, flexing his arm. Haden takes a sip of his beer and shakes his head.

"I'll only let you get away with it because you're a married man now." Haden points his beer at Nash and grins. "That tossing hand's getting a little more of a workout these days, I'm guessing."

"Whatever gets you through the day, bud," Nash responds. "But for the record, pregnant women are wild."

"*Fuuuck*, just no," Wade bites out, taking a sip of his beer.

"Sorry." Nash shrugs. "At some point you gotta get over it."

"Nope," Cole warns from beside me.

My phone buzzes on the table and I expect to see another message from my uncle. I'm wrong.

> **LIVI GIRL**
> Shane says my demo is almost done! Thank you for recommending him.

Having her contact as "Oblivia" didn't seem right anymore after the night we had. The night that absolutely fucked with my head.

> **ME**
> Heard that. Great news, Liv.

I don't mean to be cold with her. It's been almost four weeks since we left the bathroom stall at the wedding after the hottest sex I've had in . . . fuck, as long as I can remember. Maybe ever. We both stayed and celebrated through the night with our friends, and every time I thought about how I was dripping down her thighs, it turned me into a man crazed.

She left with Jo, taking a ride home to the ranch like nothing had happened, and we've barely spoken since. It was exactly what we agreed to: one night, no strings. But I can't get her off my mind. There's just something about the goodness in her. That light with a desire for the dark that brings out this raw need in me—to protect her, to be with her, to *own* her the way she's owned my every thought for weeks.

"You know, I've known you for two years—" Nash says now, taking a seat across from me.

"Double or nothin'," Haden interjects, sitting down beside him and picking up a wing from his plate. "But first I gotta eat."

Nash nods to him. "Let me know when you're ready for another beating."

"Bite me," Haden mumbles jokingly around his wing.

"Where was I?" Nash looks at me. "Right, two years I've known you." He picks up a wing and points at my phone with it. "And never have I seen you look worried or stressed for more than one second. What gives?"

I shrug as I set down my phone and continue eating my rack of ribs. "No idea what you mean."

"Working all that OT got you worn out?"

"Being married has made Nash more in touch with his feelings," Wade pipes up as he dips a fry in ketchup.

I chuckle and swallow my bite.

"Well, when I'm looking for advice, I'll be sure to call the four of you first." I look to Nash. "But yeah, man. I'm feeling pretty burnt out."

"Sure it has nothing to do with the way you were looking at a certain redhead at my wedding?" Cole grins as he sips his beer.

I shake my head.

"Cassie said she thought someone was going at it in the bathroom and, funny enough, you and Liv were the only ones there before us." Haden grins. Fuckin' smug prick.

I say nothing.

"I had a friend like that once." Cole shakes his head and smiles wider. "Friends like that? They fucking sneak up on ya."

"Good to know," I grit out. I'm not about to explain anything to these nosey fuckers.

"As long as whoever was in that bathroom wasn't anyone's sister, I'm good. I don't know if I can take any more of that drama," Wade adds before he stands and pats his brother on the shoulder. "Let's go. Cornhole time."

"As much as I'd love to keep yapping about Asher's friend he doesn't seem to want to talk about"—Cole stands and interlocks his hands, stretching them out in front of him—"time to start tossing bags and taking names."

"That comment made me uncomfortable." Haden chuckles.

"I thought it was a-*maiz*-ing," Nash says with a smirk.

"Fucking morons," Wade huffs as he heads to the center of the grass with his beer. "No wonder you're looking for new friends."

"You off on the Fourth?" Nash asks as he sips his beer once we're the only ones left at the table.

"Off but on call."

"You should come over. We're doing a big barbeque at the ranch. Bring the Black brothers too, we'll play some footy."

I should say no. I know Olivia will be there, and the best thing for both of us is if I just stay away from her. But I'm a fucking sucker for punishment so instead I nod in agreement, understanding that, when it comes to this woman, I always seem to act *before* I think.

CHAPTER 16
Olivia

JULY

"I'm gonna head over to your house tomorrow. I bought a steamer online that will give the walls a really good wash."

I look up at my dad over our weekly pancakes at the Sage and Salt. It's a running joke that he has an online shopping addiction. Little gadgets show up at my parents' house every day—things for the yard, tools, T-shirts. More often than not, he'll start a conversation with "Look what I got online . . ."

"Red Rock cleaned already." I narrow my eyes at him. I'm on to him.

He shrugs. His skin is tanned from being outside so much, and he's in summer mode in his blue golf shirt, shorts, and flip-flops.

"Can't hurt to make sure it's perfect before they start rebuilding. How long did they say before it's done?"

"Another few months at least." Pushing that thought from my head and trying to forget I can't be in my own home, I stuff a bite of strawberry and whipped cream into my mouth. Every time I get down about being displaced, I try instead to picture how I'll redecorate. I have an entire Pinterest page saved and catalogued with rustic and modern country designs from the last six weeks, and that helps lift my spirits. "So what does Mom want you to do for her at the house?"

He grins and shakes his head. "Clean and reorganize the kitchen. Cut the hedge."

"It's the Fourth of July weekend. She won't give you a break?" I smile as I place my fork down and take a sip of orange juice. The moment it hits my lips, a sour feeling twinges in my jaw and I gag. I cover my mouth, my eyes wide as my dad looks up at me.

"Y'okay?"

I nod, my hand still clamped over my mouth.

"I think maybe the OJ is bad." I crumple my face and push it away.

My dad reaches over to try it. "Tastes fine to me."

"Must just be me then. My stomach has been off this week. I ate something that didn't agree with me a few days ago."

"That happened to me last winter. Took me a whole week to get back to normal. I'm sure it will pass," he says offhandedly. "Don't be drinking too much at the Ashbys' tomorrow night though."

"You know me." I grin as I pop the last strawberry into my mouth. At least that still tastes good.

"I know the Not Angels." He smirks as he shoves his last bite of pancake into his mouth.

"Except two out of three of us are married." I smile softly. "Plus, one has a stepdaughter and the other is *very* pregnant. It will be a mild night at best."

"Well, if you get through work and feel like popping in, I'll be at your place for a few hours with some Johnny playing and some pizza, cleaning up."

"Thanks, Dad." I smile back at him. "You know you can't hide from her to-do list forever, right?"

My dad chuckles as he leans back in his chair. "Maybe for another few days, at least."

He winks, but the truth is I love having my dad's help and I'm grateful every day that the universe gave me him.

GINGER
How gorgeous are we?

A photo comes in of all of us at the wedding outside the chapel.

CECE
Gah!! You got the photos back?

GINGER
Yes! We can look at them tomorrow at the barbeque!

I zoom in on the scene of all of us standing in a row; the white chapel creates a stunning backdrop and the sun is shining. Asher stands beside me, wearing the closest thing his face can offer to a smile, his inked hand just visible around my waist. It's been well over a month since the wedding, and I still find myself constantly thinking about him—the way he looked at me, the way it felt when he stuffed that handkerchief into my mouth and took my breath away, how hard I came all over him . . .

"Thank you so much! Enjoy the sun," Lucy says to the woman we both just spent thirty minutes helping pick out a new bathing suit. It's the thing I love most about my shop, the joy of making women feel beautiful in my clothes. I wave to her too. "Bye, Lori! Happy Fourth!"

"Holy, what a morning," Lucy says from beside me, pulling out her trademark snack, chocolate-covered almonds, and popping a handful into her mouth. We've been swamped the last few weeks, though I'm used to spending twelve hours a day here during the summer season. I'm sure that's part of the reason I haven't had time to search for a decent relationship too. I'm always working. Even when I'm at home, I'm contemplating social media posts, new inventory, staffing schedules, and how to keep everyone as organized as possible.

Aside from the fact it's good for business, being busy has also helped draw attention away from the slow-moving renovation of my home. With the Heritage Committee involved, Shane says the restoration could take us into fall. Which means spending so much time in the shop has been a blessing. Tomorrow is the Fourth of July, meaning Laurel Creek and the surrounding areas will be packed full of tourists. And it looks like the weather is going to be perfect—great for local business, terrible for townsfolk trying to get a seat on a patio or just navigate through town.

> CECE
>
> Liv, can you bring a cheesecake from Spicer's tomorrow?

> CECE
>
> I was gonna make one but with this heat my feet are the size of balloons.

I'm just about to type back that I'll bake cupcakes but another unexpected wave of nausea creeps up my throat so fast I gag, covering my mouth with my hand.

"Are you okay?" Lucy asks.

I swallow, trying to stabilize myself.

"Yeah. I've just been feeling off lately. I'm a couple weeks late for my shot." She knows I have a gynecologist appointment this afternoon. "I think maybe my hormones are just outta whack because of it. I'm gonna ask Dr. Allen today," I tell her, taking a shaky breath.

I retuck my white tank blouse into my sage linen shorts with paper bag waist. They're stylish but also comfortable against my tender stomach as I reach under the cabinet of the cash desk and grab two Sour Patch Kids from their package. I pop them in my mouth, quickly sucking the sour sugar off them as if my life depends on it. The birth control shot I've been on for two years has always made me slightly queasy and it typically makes my periods a little wonky.

"Almond?" Lucy offers her bag to me and that nausea almost brims up again. I suck harder on the sweets until it subsides.

"No, thanks. I'm gonna grab something to eat on my way to the clinic anyway." I grab my purse and a couple more Sour Patch Kids for the road. "You good if I head out now?"

"Yup. Rachel will be in at noon. I think I can manage to hold down the fort for an hour."

"Thanks, Luce. Have an amazing Fourth!" We're closed tomorrow for the holiday, so I look around my space. The shop is looking better than ever, even if my home isn't. "I'll be here by seven on Saturday."

Lucy nods, knowing as well as I do that it will probably be the busiest day of the year.

"I'll bring the coffee and pastries," she says with a smile, but the thought of coffee brings the sick feeling back. I add another candy to my mouth, shaking my head as I make my way to the door.

"If the shot isn't working for you, we can talk about the pill. It might be easier on your stomach."

An hour later, I'm wearing a white dressing gown and sitting on the bed in my gynecologist's office. The room is intimate, the walls a calming sage green.

"It's only been bad the last two weeks. I googled it and read that it could be from my hormones starting to balance again," I tell Dr. Allen. "I know I'm late for the next round, but I think I wanna give my body a break for a few months. Though I will definitely consider the pill."

"It can be your system rebalancing. When was your last period?"

I pause for a beat as I pull out my phone to study my period app. "It's been weird the last few months, but my last full period was May third."

"When you say full—how many days?"

"Two, maybe three? It's usually light."

Dr. Allen's brows knot as she writes in my chart. "And since?"

"I had a little spotting that started on May twenty-ninth, but that only lasted about a day. Though I did have cramps for a few days either side."

"Okay. Our nurse practitioner is checking the urine sample you gave us when you came in. We can make sure you don't have any sort of UTI that would cause cramps, and then you can decide if you want to give your body a break. It's not a bad idea if you aren't sexually active."

I laugh. "Nope, not active . . . at all."

The words haven't even left my lips before a flash of my back hitting the bathroom wall and the feel of Asher's lips crashing down on mine fills my mind.

"Okay, Liv." Dr. Allen smiles at me. "Just sit tight as I check on your sample. I'll be right back."

She isn't gone more than thirty seconds before my phone

on the small table beside me lights up and I see a text from Asher.

> **A**
> I was talking to Shane today. Seems they're going to have the electricians in next week. Have you been back? How's it looking?

> **ME**
> He mentioned about that the other day. It looks good. Empty but good.

> **ME**
> Thanks for the update and thanks for your help.

I wince as I hit send on that last message. I am grateful that Asher is still trying to help me with the house, but it's hard to pretend a spark doesn't shoot through me when I see his name on my screen. Which means that, no matter how hard I try, I feel like anything I say comes across as awkward and painfully formal. I facepalm and breathe out a sigh as the doctor comes back into the room.

"Well, interesting turn of events." Dr. Allen sets down my chart as I look up at her quizzically. "You must be a *little* active, Olivia. You're pregnant."

CHAPTER 17
Olivia

"E-excuse me?" The room spins as I grip the sides of the bed for stability. "No... I had... I was spotting. I was on the shot."

She shrugs with a small smile. "It's quite common to spot during implantation. Do you remember the date this could've happened?"

I feel dizzy as I try to catch my breath. That's one thing I don't have to think about as I give her Cole and Ginger's wedding date.

"That's the only time?"

I nod, tears welling in my eyes.

"And you said you had cramping on the thirty-first?"

"Yes," I answer, closing my eyes and willing my heart rate to calm down. Pregnant? *PREGNANT?* With *Asher Reed's* baby?

"I had my period... I think at the end of May," I offer. "Is this... normal? The light spotting?" I ask her, forcing myself to keep talking so I don't throw up.

"Implantation bleeding happens occasionally. And there are

times when the shot isn't perfectly effective, just like the pill. A number of things can alter its strength. Based on the dates, especially if it was only once, it sounds like your period on the twenty-ninth was implantation. I think your period at the beginning of May was your last true period, based on your HCG levels, which means you're right around eight to nine weeks along. That would explain your nausea, mild cramps, and fatigue too."

"Oh my God," I breathe out. "*Oh my God.*"

"I can see this is a shock." Dr. Allen has been my gyno since I was a teenager, and her face is now full of genuine motherly concern. "The father? Is this a relationship?"

"No, I . . ." I scoff out. I have no words. "I mean, we're acquaintances but. . . ." I'm struggling to breathe properly as my heart nearly hammers out of my chest.

I don't hate love. I just don't believe in it. Asher's words echo in my mind. Would he even want this child?

"You have lots of time." She takes my hand. "I want to make sure you know that, Olivia. All your options are on the table at this point."

"Options?"

I'm struggling to focus on her words as tears spill over onto my cheeks and panic washes over me. *I'm pregnant?*

"Yes. You can still choose to terminate this pregnancy, though you'd have to go out of state to do so. I can recommend a clinic in Ohio. If termination isn't something you feel you can go through with, but you aren't ready to be a parent, you can also look into putting the child up for adoption. I'm here to help you and support you with whatever you need."

I gulp back a sob as I nod. I always wanted a child, but *not* like this. Not with a man who doesn't want to settle down or have a family.

"I'd like to do an ultrasound," she continues now. "But we don't have to do that today. We can book that in for next week, after the holiday. Whatever you decide to do, I'd like to do one to confirm timing."

My thoughts are racing: I'm twenty-nine, own my own business, have good health insurance and a healthy savings account. I have an incredible support system and there is still a chance Asher will want to be involved, though I can't count on that. If I decide to keep this baby, I know I'd ultimately have the love and support of my parents, but I have to plan to do it largely on my own. I slide my hand over the flat of my belly. It would be me and this baby against the world.

Wiping my tears with the back of my hand, I think of my own childhood. How my mom, Nana, and I would bake together for every holiday, even when I was tiny. Of all the household projects I've worked on with my dad, and how he'd sit with me for hours helping with my science homework. I think of dancing in the living room with my mom when she got her dream job as principal of the local elementary school, and the three of us cozying up together watching a new TV series or film. I picture my parents as grandparents, and my birth parents, the grandparents they never got to be, and I realize just how much I want the legacy they weren't afforded.

Dr. Allen's words resurface as a thought as clear as day slices through the fog of the moment. *I can do this. I want to do this. I want this baby.*

Sure, I don't know how it's going to work. I don't know what Asher will say or do, or what my parents will think. But the thought of anything other than keeping this child is already out of my mind. Within the last two minutes, everything within my being has shifted.

"I'll give you a moment," Dr. Allen says, standing and passing me a box of tissues before she leaves the room.

I run my hand back and forth across my stomach as I let the tears fall. *I promise, no matter what happens, it's me and you.*

"Babe." CeCe sits across from me on the big house living room sofa, as shellshocked as I was earlier. I rang to tell her the news from Dr. Allen's office and she told me to drive straight to the ranch. I told Jo when I got here too, because Mama Jo knows all, and her advice is crucial right now. Of course, the first thing she did was get us a snack to soften the blow of the bomb I just dropped.

"I told you if anything happened, you'd be the first to know," I respond, laughing through the tears that threaten to spill over again. CeCe puts her hand over mine.

"You've always wanted to be a mom." My best friend starts to well up too.

"Yeah, but I never pictured *this*. I don't even know how this happened. It was *one* time. And I'm always careful."

Jo looks like a true farmhouse mama in her jean shorts and one of CeCe's old T-shirts. Her hair is in a ponytail as she sets a plate of freshly baked cookies in the middle of the kitchen table.

"Did you just have these on hand?" I ask.

"I know everything, remember?" She winks. "Something told me to bake when I woke up this morning, and cookies might not solve all your problems, but they sure make them taste better." She takes a seat beside CeCe and pops one into her mouth. "And FYI, in my experience, all it takes is one time, darlin'."

"He looks like a dark sort of superhero half the time," CeCe laughs, picking up a cookie. I follow suit because they look too good to pass up right now. I take a bite, and it soothes my tender stomach instantly. "Maybe he has super sperm."

"We didn't use a condom, I was on the shot . . ." I admit.

CeCe's mouth falls open. "So this was definitely a hot and

heavy moment..."

"I get it. Rookie mistake. But can we focus on the issue at hand?" I say as she straightens up and clears her throat.

"Yes, sorry. Kinda in shock here. When are you gonna tell him?"

"Half past never?" I retort. "I have no idea how he's gonna react. And I need to have a plan. I need to tell him and see how involved he wants to be, if at all. I just don't know when the right time is."

"Nash said he'll be here tomorrow," CeCe offers.

My stomach drops at the idea of seeing him.

"You can take as long as you need, but you have to ask yourself how long you think you can keep something like this to yourself, honey," Jo notes, picking up another cookie. I smile at them both. I'm so damn grateful to have them in my life and so grateful my baby will grow up knowing such amazing women.

My baby... "Not long," I mutter honestly. "But I need today at least."

Jo reaches across the table and places her soft, comforting hand over mine. I love this woman like my own mother, and I know she has nothing but the best intentions for me at heart.

"Taking today to wrap your head around this is something you *deserve*. Let's have some snacks, maybe a movie marathon?"

"Sounds...perfect." I breathe out.

"Our babies are going to be only a few months apart!" CeCe squeals, her eyes full of excitement as she reaches over to squeeze my arm. "I'm so happy we'll be going through this together."

My heart sinks at her words. There's such a stark difference between us. She has a committed husband, a ride-or-die through this.

I have a man I'm going to make this work with and co-parent with. The only way it *will* work, I realize, is if I let Mr. "I Don't Believe in Love" off the hook completely. Tell him I'm not in this equation. *I* expect nothing of him. Even if he wants to be involved with the baby, he doesn't owe *me* anything. I would take the pressure right off and just let him get used to being a dad.

"One more piece of advice?" Jo's calm, motherly voice cuts into my racing thoughts.

"Always." I smile softly at her.

"You're talking a lot about plans. You can plan all you want, but just remember, life doesn't give a shit about those plans. In fact, the more you plan, the more the universe will throw you twists and turns."

"I don't do well with twists and turns," I admit as CeCe starts to laugh.

Jo leans back, getting comfortable on the sofa. "Yeah, but sometimes those twists and turns bring you the greatest of gifts."

A tear spills over my cheek. I've cried so much today already. But this time it hits harder because I know she's right. This is a huge blessing, and though it may seem impossible, I already love this baby so much.

"No one plans their fate. But you can make the best of it and, trust me, sometimes people surprise you. You never know how he'll feel," Jo adds.

"He told me he never wants to settle down," I tell them. "His exact words were 'Romantic love just sets you up for grief one way or another.'"

"Okay, that is rather convincing," CeCe gives, and I can't help but laugh. This whole situation would be comical if it wasn't my life. "But, for your information, Nash wasn't up for that at first either. Sometimes, with the right person, it doesn't feel like settling."

"Look at you," I tell her. "A mama already."

She grins at me. "So are you."

Nausea starts to creep up my throat again, but this time it's from nerves. I can't keep this to myself. I have to tell Asher tomorrow.

I groan. "What do I even say to him?"

CeCe and Jo look at each other then back to me. CeCe shrugs. "How about 'Happy Fourth of July, Asher. You're going to be a dad'?"

CHAPTER 18
Asher

WALKER
This thing tonight at the Ashbys'. You only got one single one left in this group, right? She coming tonight?

ME
I dunno.

ME
But they're all off-limits. Got it?

It's a lie. I know she's single, and I know she's coming. But over my dead fuckin' body is Walker hitting on Liv.

WALKER
Just curious, Jesus.

I glance to my left out the window and notice Walker's truck is back in the parking lot after his last call.

ME
Are you texting me from down the hall?

WALKER
Yep.

ME
Why?

WALKER
I was gonna come in but you were wearing your don't-fuck-with-me face.

ME
I was working out.

WALKER
Still scary AF.

WALKER
If it was anyone but you, I'd think you got in a fight with a woman last night.

ME
Putting my phone down now. If you want to talk to me, grow some nuts and come down here.

WALKER
I'll wait till tonight when there are other people around.

Shaking my head, I set my phone down on the weight bench in the gym of the firehall, sweat dripping from my brow. It's been a fucking morning. We had a shit call where a man wrapped himself around a tree. Already drinking and driving at ten-thirty in the goddamn morning. It was all on the back end of yesterday's double shift. I love this job, but I don't love being short-staffed, overworked, and exhausted most of the time. Our new firehall on the outskirts of town was finished just last year. It's shinier than we needed in this county, but the board pushed it through. They've also pushed us more money to bring in two new permanent hires, but getting staffed properly takes time. We're stretched thin. It's not always the job people think it is, but it's worth it and rewarding if you can save someone, their pets, or their home. Even better if it's all three. There's a deep satisfaction I find in this career, one I've only just discovered since freeing myself from the evil clutches of my father's world and forgiving myself for my mother's death. The death I *couldn't* save her from. Protecting people who need it has been my main goal ever since, and I've come to the conclusion that this could be part of why I'm so drawn to Olivia. I just can't stand the idea of her being in need and not being there.

"You look wrecked," Walker comments as he enters the gym, ready to start his own set.

"I'm fine." I sip my water. "Here till three, then on call till midnight."

"I'm off till morning." Walker chuckles as he takes a seat on the rowing machine.

"The fuck are ya doing here then?"

"My house has two toddlers in it, so I wouldn't get an ounce of sleep there. Easier to catch some z's on the couch here."

I nod, knowing he's talking about his little nieces, and finish up to give him space. I've been at this workout for almost two hours already. Long, grueling workouts have been part of my day since my year in prison. Every morning and every night. The same routine mostly, and fuck have I needed them just to relieve the built-up tension in my blood. I'm wound up extra tight tonight because I know I'm gonna see Liv and I'm *still* fucking craving her.

The way I'm shamelessly keeping tabs on her is almost out of control. I can't even lie and say it's to make sure she's safe. It's because I *want* to know what she's doing, to see her. I know she's going mostly between her shop, Nash and CeCe's, Ginger's, and Silver Pines because I happen to drive by all those places more than I should. But I won't apologize to myself for checking in on her. Now that I've *had* her? The masochist in me just keeps watching.

Even if I know it can't continue, which it can't, Olivia should have the future she told me she's dreamed about since she was nine. And I'm almost certain that the man she envisioned isn't one with a dangerous, chaotic past. A man who might not even be capable of what she deserves. As if that truth needs to be driven home, I've got my uncle rearing his ugly head again for some godforsaken reason.

But even though I know all of that, Olivia's eyes as I fucked deep into her needy cunt never leave me. The way she cried my name around her gag. The way she *wanted* her gag. I see those eyes everywhere, whether I'm awake or asleep.

She wanted all the dark things I imagined doing to her, and I didn't expect that. Olivia might think she wants a steady suburban man, one who works a nine-to-five, has perfectly combed hair, and wears slacks and loafers. One who only fucks her on Saturday nights, holding back when he touches her, offering only half his attention. But I know what she really wants, what she *needs*, is a man who sees her every need before she even has it. One who appreciates the way she blushes when she trips over something, then cracks a joke about it. One who fists her hair with strong, steady hands while he kisses the fuck out of her. One who will offer her softness when she needs it *and* some pain with her pleasure. The kind her eyes beg for even when her words don't.

She needs a man like *me*. And that's the one thing I just can't give her.

"I still fucking got it." Haden leans forward in his chair and points at Nash with his beer.

"Sure do, Cowboy," Cassie agrees, squeezing his thigh then kissing his neck.

"Hey, your mama is right here." Glenda, Ivy and Cassie's mom, turns her head to her daughter.

"Don't pretend that you don't do the same thing with Geoff," Cassie scoffs, mentioning Glenda's boyfriend.

"I don't know what you mean."

Glenda blushes as Cassie nudges her playfully. The relationship between them reminds me of the connection I had with my own mother. An odd pang of grief I haven't felt in a long time hits my gut.

"I'm just sayin', it's been a while since you played football properly." Nash grins before nodding toward me. "We'll see if the boys want to get into it when they get here. I already told Asher."

I'm just about to agree to a game when Ginger and Cole come through the sliding door onto the patio that runs the length of the back of the Ashby big house with Mabel; Ginger's grandmother; and their dogs, Jake and Amy, in tow. Behind them is Walker and his younger brother Hunter Black.

"The great Hunter Black. Roper extraordinaire," Dean pipes up. "You best be giving me your autograph before the day is over, son."

Hunter salutes Dean. "You got it, sir."

Walker's younger brother is a sort of local celebrity, having just placed second on the southern tie-roping circuit. He's a playboy to a fucking T and very much enjoys the fruits of his rodeo celebrity. But he's a good guy and a hard worker in his craft. He still works with their older brother Beau on their family's ranch when he's needed. Hell, all the Black brothers end up back at that ranch even when they try to do something different. Their mother, Maeve, says that the land is in their souls.

"Football later!" Nash calls over to them now. "We're gonna kick Haden's ass."

"Hell yeah, I'm in." Hunter nods as he runs a hand over the scruff of his jaw.

One of the dogs, Amy, yanks on Cole and he almost drops the six-pack of beer he's carrying.

"Son of a bit—"

"Burgers," Ginger says over Cole's cuss with a smile.

"It counts anyway," Mabel says, not even stopping to look up. Cole digs into his pocket.

"Give it to Ginger, Dad. She'll eTransfer everything to me at the end of the week." Mabel grins.

"When did *that* start happening?" Cole asks Ginger, shaking his head and setting down his sixer as the dogs chase Mabel and the Ashby dog Harley into the yard.

"Who carries cash?" Ginger shrugs. "Besides you, Grampa." She pats his chest.

"She's got a point." Dean grins.

"I carry cash too," Ginger's grandmother, they all call her Granny Dan, pipes up. I remember her first name is Marilyn.

"I see you two brought my Fourth of July date." Dean smiles up at Marilyn as he pops his shades onto his face and leans back in his chair.

"They promised you'd make me one of your famous Tom Collins, Dean," she says, wagging a wrinkled finger at Dean and taking a seat beside him.

"Already on it." He grins. "Jo, can you bring me a fresh Tom Collins and one for my date?"

"In a minute," Jo calls out of the kitchen window.

"Coming right up," Dean tells Marilyn, folding his hands behind his head.

Marilyn laughs. "Isn't it nice how they serve us now?"

"Sure as shit is."

Dean is such a cool old man, the kind I would've loved to have as a father. Rather than the monster I was given.

"How many burgers is everyone gonna want?" Wade hollers, popping his head out the patio door. He's wearing a BBQ apron that says, *If you're reading this, bring me a cold beer* and his T-shirt has red-white-and-blue rocket Popsicles on it. I have no idea what he was thinking with that one until I see Ivy duck under his arm carrying Billi, their eleven-month-old daughter, who's wearing the exact same T-shirt.

I hold up two fingers to signal how many burgers I'll eat to Wade, and he nods.

"Nice shirt." I smirk. "Why do I have the feeling you picked that out yourself?"

"He did." Ivy grins. "I tell him that it's usually the mama who wants to match with her daughter, but he never gives me a chance."

Wade shrugs. "She's my best friend. I don't know what you want from me."

I chuckle quietly to myself, though a weird pang of envy strikes me out of nowhere.

I've never wanted a child before—fuck, I've never even thought of having one, not with my messed-up bloodline. But something about the way Wade is so in love with that baby hits me square in the chest.

Today, the Ashby yard is a hive of bustling activity. This is only the third time I've been here for a party, but ever since I started helping Wade on the wedding cabins in the spring, I've spent a lot more time here. I don't usually like spending too much time with people, but being on the ranch is easy; the Ashbys are always together and celebrating something. Plus, I've taken a liking to riding the breathtaking trails. That is, when I don't bump into runaways in need of rescue.

Today, Jo has the whole back yard decked out. A red-white-and-blue banner hangs from the pergola and on the big table are matching napkins and plates; red, white, and blue cake pops; and a cheesecake covered in strawberries and blueberries to look like an American flag.

I survey the happy scene around me as Wade finishes taking everyone's order and Ginger gets pulled into a game of ladder golf with Mabel. People are talking over the music, joking and laughing with one another. There isn't one member of this extended family who isn't open, loving, and honest. Until I met the Ashbys, I thought families like this only existed in the movies.

"I need a teammate." Ginger looks around the table.

"Don't even think about it." CeCe laughs.

Ginger focuses on Ivy. She shrugs then stands and, before I can protest, a giggling, chubby Billi is set into my lap. "Time to be christened into the role of baby watching."

Ivy smiles at me as she slides a bag full of toys over. "People line up for this, you know. She isn't walking yet, so if you spread this blanket and get some of these toys out, you should be good for a game."

"Wait." I'm not usually one to panic, but I've also never been so close to a person this vulnerable before. "What if she needs something?"

Billi reaches up and pats my beard, laughing as it tickles her hand, but Ivy's already walking into the yard.

"I just changed and fed her. All she needs is someone to play with her for twenty." Ivy's laugh echoes as she picks up her ladder golf balls. "I can still see you and hear you. It'll be fine."

I look down at Billi, who stares up at me with big blue eyes just like her mama's, and a strange, happy feeling takes over my chest. "You're actually really fucking cute, aren't you?"

"Oi." Cole cuffs me in the shoulder. "First rule of holding a kid. Don't say 'fuck' in front of them." He says it quiet enough that his daughter doesn't hear and charge him.

"Shit, sorry."

"Missing the point, bro." Cole chuckles. "Maybe don't have kids."

"Wasn't planning on it," I sigh as I try to figure out what I'm gonna do to entertain her.

"Shoot, me neither," Hunter says from behind me. "I wouldn't have a clue what to do with one."

"Y'all are missing out," Wade says as he flips burgers. "Best job I ever had."

It might scare the shit out of me, but as I look at Billi, happy and content in my arms and smiling up at me, I decide this isn't *terrible*. And, aside from my shitty language, Billi seems completely oblivious to my lack of baby knowledge. I can't help but smile back at her little face.

"All right, Billi bug. Looks like it's you and me then, yeah?" I toss the rainbow-covered bag over my shoulder and head to the grass at the side of the patio, holding on to this sweet-smelling little nugget for dear life. The last thing I need to do is drop her. I doubt I'd be welcomed back if I did.

"Ma ma ma," she babbles just as we reach our destination, which gives us a good view of the girls playing their game.

I chuckle as I pull the blanket out of the bag with one arm and hoist her up on my hip.

"I'd want your mama too if I were you," I mutter.

"You're a natural!" Ivy calls from the yard as I pull something called a Montessori Wooden Farm out of the bag.

"Who knows, maybe you're next?" Haden chuckles over the Kenny Rogers album that just started playing from Jo's Bluetooth speaker. He's pulling the cling wrap off a prepped salad Cassie brought.

"Fu . . ." I clear my throat and look at Billi as I set her down in front of me. "I mean, heck no."

I sprawl out on my stomach in front of Billie to move her little cow and pig across the blanket, making animal noises, which she seems to find pretty funny.

"Ya ya ya," she babbles, which I tell myself means *do it again*. She starts to giggle as I pretend the pig runs into the cow, falling over, and allow myself to laugh with her. So much so that I don't hear the patio door moving until it closes. I look up at the sound to see Olivia holding a big plate of cupcakes covered with red, white, and blue icing, staring down at me and the baby. She looks from me to Billi, then back to me. My fucking pulse is hammering in my throat. This is the first time I've been this close to her since the wedding, and I didn't expect to be affected in this way.

Olivia's eyes are bright, and her smile looks almost genuine as Jo takes the plate of cupcakes from her. She wears a checkered baby-blue sundress that falls just off the shoulder, clings to her small waist, and falls to her mid-thigh. The look is completed with a red bandanna tied like a scarf in her copper waves that blow in the summer breeze. Olivia's skin is glowing and her wispy bangs frame her heart-shaped face; she's close enough that I can smell her sweet, sugary scent and see that soft dusting of freckles on the bridge of her nose. The urge to run my hands up under her dress just to feel those curvy, silky thighs is overwhelming. Fuck, she takes my breath away and she has no goddamn idea.

"Christ," Hunter mutters under his breath with a chuckle

and a look that makes me want to backhand him as Olivia takes her time saying hi to everyone and I continue to entertain Billi.

"We think he's next," Haden tells Liv, hiking a thumb at me when Billi starts laughing hysterically at my best piggy impression.

Olivia chokes on air, as if the idea is preposterous.

I look down at Billi staring up at me adoringly. She seems happy enough. I lean in and tickle her cheek as she giggles again.

"The fuck do they know, Billi bug?"

CHAPTER 19
Olivia

Anytime I've ever had to do something I dread in my life, it's gone one of two ways. One: The opportunity to talk to said person or deal with said situation just *won't* present itself, and I find myself scrambling to make it happen. Or two: The opportunity *over* presents itself and I simply chicken out.

I realize I'm in the middle of option two when Asher walks into the Ashbys' kitchen after dinner. I wait for someone, *anyone* else to follow him in, but they don't. In fact, we're completely and utterly alone—the air around us filled with tension—as I pour my sparkling water into a red Solo cup. Nausea washes over me briefly at the situation, and I beg myself not to gag. Pregnancy sickness mixed with nerves really is the fucking pits.

I had a whole plan before now—come straight out with it, rip the Band-Aid off. But when I walked onto the big house patio to see Asher lying in the grass—looking drop-dead gorgeous in navy cargo shorts, a gray Carhartt T-shirt that clings to him in all the right places, his worn-in New York Giants hat turned backward, and playing with Billi—the sight threw me off my game completely. The smile he was wearing was so genuine and so unlike the broody, mysterious man I've gotten used to. The sight hit me in ways I can't explain.

Taking a deep breath, I turn to face him. His tan is deeper after a few weeks of summer heat and if my body wasn't already a total slut for this man before, it is now.

"You doin' your best to avoid me, Liv?" he asks as he cracks the top on a tall, skinny can of Corona Sunbrew and takes a sip.

"No . . ." I lie. My eyes drift over him as his throat works to swallow and I wonder if it's possible that being pregnant with a man's child makes him even more attractive. Because right now, I can barely find the strength to pull my eyes away and meet his all-consuming gray gaze. I hope our baby gets those eyes.

Holy shit. *Our* baby. I instantly start to sweat with the secret I'm harboring and blurt out the most generic question I can think of.

"Are you on call today?" I ask, noting the non-alcoholic beer choice as I take a sip of my bubbly water, trying to act cool when I'm in fact sweating like a pig.

He nods, but he doesn't break our eye contact.

"Are there usually a lot of fires to fight on the Fourth?" *Apparently, I'm interviewing him for the local news.*

"Always at least one daredevil lighting something on fire with a homemade bottle rocket," he offers.

"Sounds like a pain."

"Just part of the job." Asher takes another sip and his eyes study me as I look out to the yard.

He sighs as he sets his beer down, casually resting one big, inked hand against the counter. He points between us, giving me an upward nod. "What is this, Liv?"

"What do you mean?" I ask, my voice cracking at the end of the sentence. *Perfect.*

He watches me for a beat before slowly moving closer. There goes my damn heart rate again. I don't know if I've ever been so nervous around a man in my life. But then again, every single thing in my life, especially when it comes to him, feels completely and utterly out of my control.

"We're not gonna let what happened between us make things awkward." His deep rasp settles the blood pounding through my veins to a slower pace. "Understand?"

"Y-yeah," I say, looking up at him as his hand darts out to grab my cup, setting it down on the table, before he brings both to rest on my shoulders.

"We said we were friends, and that's what we are." His thumb grazes my bare arm just enough for my skin to begin to sizzle under it. "I'm not having any of this nervous Liv every time you're around me."

I watch his plush lips as he speaks, remembering what it feels like when they're pressed to mine. How his beard felt as it tickled my face.

"You good?" he asks, cutting into the memory.

My eyes flit back to his. "Right. Yes."

God, I am a total flake right now.

Asher's broad palms slide the rest of the way down my arms, and he takes my hands in his.

"I don't regret it," he offers honestly.

"Me neither," I say, a heavy feeling settling in my womb, as if my body is screaming at me to tell him the truth.

"From now on, when we see each other, it'll be just like it was before the wedding. Nothing's changed."

Everything has changed.

I can tell he senses my nervousness, and maybe he'd understand if I could just get the balls to blurt out why, but instead . . .

"I like to have a plan, always . . . and I didn't plan that night," I mutter.

"Aye, but sometimes life forces you to just live in the moment."

I scoff. "I don't live in the moment well."

"But you are capable of it, Liv."

"How do you know?" I ask, searching for any reassurance.

He leans in slightly and his delicious smell, how close he is to me, it all makes me temporarily dumb.

"Because I've seen you come, and there was no plan there." His eyes search mine. "I've never seen you look so fucking pretty."

I instantly blush with the idea of him watching me so intently that night.

"*Friends* are honest." His lips curve up as he fixes his still backward hat on his head. His arms flex as he backs up, and it's so damn sexy.

I'm pregnant!

It's on the tip of my tongue to say the words out loud, but they never come. Because apparently, I don't live in the moment. And I am a chicken shit.

"Hey, we're four on four," Haden says to Asher, breaking the moment between us as he pops his head in the patio door and taps the frame.

"Coming to watch, Liv?" Haden asks.

I nod with a nervous smile.

I'm pregnant! is still on the tip of my tongue as Asher tosses me a final glance before following Haden out.

Beelining to the bathroom, I splash a little cold water on my face. I stare at myself, knowing I have to tell him, I just have no idea how I'm ever going to muster the nerve.

I use a bouncing Billi on my lap to distract myself from all the incredibly gorgeous men in the middle of the Ashby yard ready to play an impromptu game of touch football.

Mabel has been picked up by her school friend to go swimming before coming back here to watch the fireworks Cole has planned. Ginger says he's been talking about this for weeks. I sit with Cassie at the big table while CeCe, Dean, Granny Dan, and Jo fill out the outdoor sectional on the patio. The two teams line up for their game of shirts and skins or, as they're calling it, Stars and Stripes. The large silver pines that frame the open space are the game's backdrop as the orange sun sinks low behind Sugarland Mountain.

Asher, Haden, and Walker are on one team. Wade, Cole, Nash, and Hunter are on the other.

"Can't wait to destroy you all," Hunter chuckles as he turns his worn-in hat backward and starts to stretch. He's a big guy just like his brother, fit from the rodeo circuit and training, I assume. His dark blond hair just touches his forehead, and I can see why he's earned his playboy reputation. Every girl who loves the rodeo loves to watch Hunter Black, and rumor is he uses it to his advantage.

"There's only three of us, but I promise you'll be begging for mercy, boy." Haden winks from the other side of the yard.

I turn and look at Cassie. "Men," we both say at the same time.

"Seriously though"—she laughs—"they have no idea what they're in for. I've seen Haden's old game tapes. He's gonna decimate the Ashby brothers."

Cole pulls a quarter out of his pocket.

"See, baby! That cash came in handy after all!" Ginger hollers, cupping her mouth so her husband can hear her. Cole flips her the bird, then shakes his head as he tosses it in the air.

I hear Asher call heads when the coin hits the air.

"It's heads," Cole announces.

Asher looks at Haden and grins that smile I wish he wore

more often. Haden nods for the three teammates to regroup for a chat.

"The art of intimidation, fellas," Haden says as they pull off their hats, then their T-shirts, before tossing them to the side of the yard.

Cassie whistles as my mouth turns to sand at Asher, Haden, and Walker putting on a little show, flexing at the other team in just their shorts.

"Christ almighty." Dean chuckles, flexing his frail biceps. "You three almost look as good as I do under a T-shirt."

Asher replaces his hat on his head backward. His eyes find mine across the yard, and my heart drops to the pit of my stomach as the chatter around me fades to an echo. My gaze is focused solely on him, as if I am in some sort of trance. God, he's even better under his clothes than I could have ever imagined. And I've imagined it. My eyes move to his wide, muscled shoulders and smooth chest covered in ink. Hawk wings and italic script illustrate his pecs, and his biceps and forearms are lined with thick veins that extend to big, tattooed hands. A light dusting of hair leads to a deep V that disappears into his shorts and holy shit . . . *abs.*

Haden throws him the ball and he licks his lips as he catches it.

CeCe leans into my side. "Blink, bestie."

I elbow her and pull my eyes from him as Cole calls the first play.

The next hour passes in a blur of hot, sweaty men talking shit to one another. Ivy takes Billi from me to put her to bed as I watch the boys toss plays and celebrate like they just won the damn Super Bowl whenever one of them gets a touchdown. It doesn't take long at all, just like Cassie said, for the Stars to beat the pants off the Stripes, finishing with a pass from Walker to Asher, then to Haden, on a double reverse as we cheer from the sidelines. After each time Haden scores, Asher and Haden do some sort of bro-code handshake that ends with a fist bump.

Watching Asher approach me at the end of the game has everything hitting me all at once. This man is the father of my child. I've got to put my big girl pants on and tell him.

"Good game . . . looks like your strategy paid off," I say, glancing once to his glistening chest, dripping with sweat, then forcing myself to move my eyes to his face as he chugs down some water.

"Glad I could keep you entertained, Livi girl." He wipes his forehead with the back of his forearm as I push his beautiful body from my mind and take a deep breath.

"Um, Asher, I'm pretty tired. Do you think you could walk me home?"

Time to rip off that Band-Aid.

CHAPTER 20
Asher

Something is definitely off with Olivia. I can sense it. I could feel it in the kitchen after dinner. An uneasy emotion runs through me as I say goodnight and thank-you to the Ashbys for having me.

"Hey, Olivia," Hunter calls now. "If you're looking for a fun night, hit me up. I'll get you and some friends good seats at the Buckshaw."

He's talking about the rodeo outside Lexington coming up, and the idea of her sitting in the stands, cheering for him with a cowboy hat on, sends an unexpected rage through me that I'm having a hard time swallowing down. *Get it together.*

"Thank you," she answers politely, giving him a friendly hug goodbye. "Summer is so busy for me and my shop, but maybe another time."

"Sure you guys can't stay?" Cole asks, excited to put on his fireworks display. "Mabes should be back any second, and I've got the whole show set up."

Fucking guy is wearing a red, white, and blue hat that says, *Fireworks director, I duck, you duck.*

"I'm tired, and I have some . . . kitchen stuff to go over with Asher," Olivia offers. I look down at her.

Huh?

"And I've got an early start tomorrow," I say. "I'll just walk Liv home then head out."

I shake Cole's hand and wave to everyone else, a feeling of dread settling deep in my stomach. As we leave the big house, I follow close behind Olivia down the steps and along the Silver Pines gravel walkway that leads past the main barns to the cabins. The night is quiet, and the sky is a deep, velvet navy, lit up with a thousand stars. My mind drifts as we walk. There's really no place like this ranch. It's the farthest cry from the place I grew up. Not just because of the breathtaking scenery but because of the peace it affords. I watch Olivia pull the scarf from her hair. As she prattles on nervously—about the food Jo put on, the Black brothers, the next day at her shop and how busy she's expecting it to be—I realize a world like the one I came from is one she could never even imagine.

The whole walk, she never stops talking. And by the time we reach the cabins, I've had enough. I stop dead in the middle of the road and she follows suit, turning to face me.

"What's wrong, Liv?"

"How do you know something is wrong?"

"You have a tell." My eyes lock to her baby blues. "You *talk*."

"Nothing's wrong. I mean something is going on, but I just don't know whether you'll think it's a bad thing or a good thing—"

"*Olivia*," I say firmly in an attempt to stop her spinning in circles.

Her eyes flutter closed as she sucks in a breath. What the fuck is going—

"I'm pregnant," she says so quickly the words are barely audible. "I haven't, I mean, there's been no one else since you, or long before you . . ."

Olivia is rambling but her words fade as the first firework ignites in the sky with a loud crackle and two or three more follow close behind. Though I don't properly register them as my heart stutters out. Hell, it feels like it stops dead with a heavy iron thud in my chest. I try to focus on Liv and what she's saying, but my mind is working to process the situation. It was supposed to be one night. No strings. No chance of exposing her to any part of my past life that could fuck with her future.

The screams that haunt me, the screams of my mother as she died at the hands of my father, fill my head. They normally only creep in when it's silent, but they invade my brain as I consider what this all means. Those screams get louder when men in my family get close to a woman.

"You're . . . *pregnant?*" I repeat her words, making sure I'm not fucking losing it.

She nods, clutching her hands in front of her as worry fills her eyes. I'm *always* careful and I'm sure she is too, but we weren't with each other. Suddenly, everything I've done up until this moment in my life feels pointless. I let the word replay in my head over and over. *Pregnant.*

Another firework goes off, and Olivia gestures to her door as pink and blue sparkles light up the sky.

"Maybe, um . . . we should go inside to talk?" She turns to walk up the steps, barely getting the words out before the next set of fireworks explode.

I snap out of my momentary lapse of shock and force myself to move, following close behind her into her cabin. She sets her purse down on the bench in the doorway and heads to the kitchen to fill a glass with water, but my feet are cemented to the floor.

"There is no pressure here," she continues. "I just thought you should know. I hope you believe me when I say I had no idea this would happen. I was on the birth control shot and I was faithful with it."

"Olivia . . ." I finally manage to get out, though it's like she doesn't hear me.

"I'm totally capable of having this baby on my own, and I'm not telling you this to force you to be involved, but I'm thinking—" She tucks a piece of her wavy hair behind her ear then brings her eyes back to mine. Christ, she's so beautiful.

"I want to keep the baby, Asher," she finally says, her brows pinched in determination.

My spine tingles and my heart thunders in my chest. I never saw myself with a child. My father was a fucking terrible parent, and my childhood was a total shit show. I have no idea how to be an example for another human, but somehow, in this moment, I know that I want Olivia to have my baby.

A few seconds pass, but it feels like hours as Olivia rambles on. "I hope you can understand, I'm the only home this baby has. I'm being pulled . . . toward the all-consuming light."

"The light?" My eyes snap to hers.

"Of being a mom."

She smiles softly with a shrug as a thousand images run through my head. Olivia's face in the early hours of the morning as she rocks in the soft overstuffed chair that sits in the corner of my bedroom, her belly swelling with our baby. Her soft copper hair tied back in a long braid, flying out behind her as she chases our child through the grass. They make me feel as though the air is being stolen from my lungs.

"Anyhow." She straightens up now, setting her glass down on the coffee table. "I know this is a lot to take in, and I only found out yesterday. There are still a million things I have to do."

She places a hand on her curvy hip and all I can think about is how soft they felt under my fingers.

"I have to go back to the doctor next week, and I need to tell my parents. But I've got lots of support, and you don't need to worry. I don't want anything from you . . . for *me.*"

"Olivia—"

"I want to keep this totally uncomplicated. Make the baby our priority."

It's as though she doesn't even register that I am here. The few feet of space between us feels too vast, and I fight the urge to close it. All I want to do is take her into my arms for one minute, to give in and breathe in the sugary scent of her hair. And fuck it, she's carrying my baby. So I do. And this action *finally* has her falling quiet as I press my lips to the top of her head and find my center and allow myself to listen to the steady staccato of our heartbeats.

"You're not doing *anything* alone," I reassure her, holding her tighter. "Understand?"

A whole host of emotions, ones that I try my hardest to always keep at bay, run through me and I can't get close to getting a handle on them. Shock. Because this is the last fucking thing I expected her to tell me tonight. Fear. Because, holy fuck, I have no idea how I'm going to keep her and our child safe from the darkness of my family's shadow. And strength. Because no matter what it takes, I *will* keep them safe. I *have to.*

Fuck, if I'm this much of a mess, I can't imagine how she feels.

I kiss her head through her hair again, lingering this time as I hear a tiny sob escape her throat. Animal instinct to take all that fear away kicks in.

"It's gonna be okay, Liv. This is . . ." I push her hair from her face.

"Unexpected?" She laughs, staring up at me.

"Fuck yeah, it is," I admit. "But we've got this. You and me."

Her fists tighten against my T-shirt and then she's pushing back, swiping at her tears. I give her some space.

"I don't want us to be a burden to you," she says with sad, pleading eyes.

Burden? The fuck?

"And I'm not asking for any kind of commitment to *me*," she continues. "But if you want to be involved with the baby, I need a dad who will show up every damn time."

It hits me square in the chest that Olivia thinks I could actually leave her high and dry.

I lift her chin to meet her gaze pointedly.

"So that we're clear, you could never be a burden. And if this is what you want, I'm in. *All* in," I tell her honestly. "From the get-go. The doctor, your parents. All of it. I have no idea how to be a . . . father—" I stop. The word feels foreign in my mouth.

"I have no idea how to be a mother," Olivia offers as tears spill over onto her cheeks. I can't help but reach out and wipe them away for her.

"Aye, that's why we're given months to prepare, to learn."

I take her hand. I can't help myself. This woman is carrying my child, so fuck it. I bring her wrist up to my lips to kiss it.

"What do we do now?" she asks helplessly.

I let my thumb trace her cheek, and stare deep into her pretty blue eyes.

"I don't have a fucking clue," I say bluntly, and she laughs. "But I promise, I won't let you down, Livi girl."

She drinks me in, and the way I want to kiss her right now is almost crushing. That heavy line between us, the one I keep between me and everyone, has faded just a little, overshadowed by the tether between us. It's clouding my judgment and logic, but although it's unnatural, there's a peace in letting someone in, even if it's only temporary.

"I'm *here*. In any way you need me." I sound a lot more confident than I feel, but I'm running on adrenaline right now and Olivia needs me to be the strong one.

She smiles up at me and the look softens the knot in my chest. "Well, um, I should probably tell you the next appointment is an ultrasound. They'll measure the baby and confirm my due date, which is currently February seventh."

We look at each other for a beat, letting this . . . twist of fate settle between us.

Olivia's eyes are glass, and I think of what she's been through over the last few days, having to deal with this alone. I can't help myself; I say nothing as I pull her to my chest again and she hums a little sigh. It's been too long since I last held her in my arms, but those weeks evaporate between us now.

"How are you feeling . . . physically?" I ask, realizing maybe I should've asked that first.

Olivia shrugs as she tilts her head to me. "Nauseous, a little lightheaded. Been living on Sour Patch Kids to curb the nausea."

"Lightheaded? Christ . . ." It hits me how much *more* clumsy pregnancy could make her. "We're gonna have to get you some bubble wrap to wear. For the baby's safety."

The baby. My heart thuds against my rib cage and I'm instantly hot.

Olivia swats at me, backing up. "Screw you . . ." She thinks for a beat, then smiles "Maybe you're right."

We both laugh. And then our eyes lock.

"So maybe we should, um . . . spend some time together? Get to know each other?" she asks hesitantly. It's fucking adorable how timid she gets when she's nervous.

"Yes. We should," I agree because I'm fucking hopeless when it comes to saying no to her. If that's part of the deal, I want it.

Fuck do I want it.

I watch as she heads over to take a seat on the sofa. I sit beside her, leaning back and running a hand through my hair. This is all so overwhelming, and I need a second before I go off half-cocked and ask her to move in with me. Which actually doesn't sound like such a bad idea . . .

"I have no misconceptions about what this is, just so you know," she says, extending a hand out for shaking. "No casual sex in bathroom stalls. Just friends."

The formality of her offer is almost funny given she came all over my cock mere weeks ago and is now growing my child.

Yet, I take her small hand in mine and nod. I need to be her partner, and she needs to feel in control when this situation feels so out of control. I don't want to do anything to fuck this up. But that doesn't mean I can forget the way we feel together. Her blue eyes start to heat as they trace my face.

I set her hand down in her lap. *Friends*.

I do my best to drill that word into my head, though I can still feel the heat from her skin burning into mine. The sound of both my radio and my cell vibrating in my pocket makes us both flinch.

"There's that firework catastrophe," she says with a shy smile. "Hopefully it's not Cole."

I pull my phone out of my pocket and read the message there. "Not Cole, but fuck, I have to go."

Everything begs me to stay as she nods, though I don't make to move.

"I'm fine," she tells me. I pull her close again before glancing down to her stomach, where my son or daughter lives inside of her. My hand hovers over the area but she nods, so I press it against her, almost covering her lower belly with my palm, and I swear to Christ I *feel* the life in her. My eyes meet hers and the corners of her mouth tug up. *Fucking beautiful*.

"Um . . . so, I'll text you tomorrow?" She tucks her hair behind her ear and it takes everything in me to turn and head for the door, the pull between my job and her is unimaginable in this moment.

"Yup. Night then, you two." I test the waters. Her mouth falls slack before pulling up into a small smile as she puts her hands in her dress pockets.

"Night, Asher. Thanks for being so great about this."

I nod in response as I force myself to walk through that door.

Making it to my truck at the main house, I climb inside, start up the engine, then lean my forehead against the wheel to take a breath as the guys at the station radio to say they're already almost at the scene. *Good men.*

When I pulled up here tonight I was a single man with no family, a past I try my hardest to forget, and the only person I had to keep safe was myself. Everything in my life was tightly controlled and I at least had a fighting chance of keeping my distance from the woman I can't and never have been able to stop thinking about. My heart gallops in my chest as I start to drive to the scene of the fire. Now we're tied and bonded forever, and I have no fucking clue how to navigate that because I am not the man she wanted for the father of her child. And the biggest, most glaring question is how the fuck am I supposed to stop myself from wanting to keep her now?

CHAPTER 21
Olivia

My phone is buzzing at six the next morning, and I know there's only two people on earth who text this early.

CECE
How'd he take it?

ME
As well as someone who got the bomb dropped on them that they're going to be a parent can. *shrug emoji*

ME
But he says he's all in.

CECE
I'm not surprised. It's obvious the way that man looks at you that he'd do anything for you.

I don't know how to feel about that as I open up the next message. It's from my father. He'll be up and ready for his morning walk.

DAD
> Morning, Sunshine.

ME
> If you can call it that.

DAD
> What is the most popular sport on the 4th of July?

I smile.

ME
> What?

DAD
> *Flag* football.

ME
> Haha. You're a day late.

DAD
> Gotta keep you on your toes. Have a good day. Breakfast this week?

ME
> You know it.

CeCe's text pops up when I close my father's out, and I wonder how he is going to react when I tell him he's going to be a grandfather.

> **CECE**
> Do you think having a baby with him will help us all solve the mystery of who Asher Reed really is?

> **ME**
> I don't know but he's been nothing but great, and he wants to come to my ultrasound appointment with me. *Crying emoji*

> **CECE**
> A word of advice for the woman who panics when there's no set path?

> **ME**
> Always.

> **CECE**
> If a good man wants to be there for you? Be there for his baby at every turn? Just go with it and let him. Planned or unplanned.

> **ME**
> Thanks, mama, but this is my current plan:

I send a meme of a dumpster fire followed by a thumbs-up emoji.

> **CECE**
> LOL

CECE

Last thing. When are you going to tell Ginger?

ME

I'll tell her at girls' night tomorrow. Then I'll go to the doctor, then tell my parents. And then I guess everyone else we know.

ME

So you'll have to keep it a secret just a little bit longer.

CECE

Rule number one of motherhood? Nothing ever goes according to plan. Try not to fret!

I look up at the cabin ceiling, exhausted already. I have to be at the shop in an hour, and then I'm meeting Shane at the house after lunch to go over some counter and trim samples. It's not like I'm going home properly. But it does feel like I'm getting a piece of stability back just being there.

That house will be where my baby and I start our future. I place my hand on my stomach, relishing a moment of peace before a wave of nausea hits and I'm running for the toilet.

By the time I settle my stomach and get ready for work, the sick feeling creeps back in as I think about my day. Pulling on a short but comfortable light blue short-sleeved sundress, I fluff my hair around my shoulders before applying my trademark ruby-red lipstick. I finish the look with a pair of leather espadrilles, my favorite red leather saddlebag purse, simple gold hoops, and a small stack of gold bangle bracelets.

My eyes drift as I stand in front of my mirror, running a

hand over my belly and thinking of Asher's hand in the same spot last night. The way it feels *every* time he touches me. Butterflies surface as another vision enters my mind, of Asher's head tipped back and the sound of his groan as he pushed his thick cock into me. I shiver as I remember the way it felt when the metal of that barbell slid through my pussy. The thought dampens my thin cotton panties and my nipples harden under the soft fabric of my dress as the ache grows between my thighs. *That's it, baby . . . open up for me. It's like you've never even been fucked.*

I let my eyes flutter closed, remembering how it felt to be like Asher, to have no inhibitions and to just take what I needed. I'm just sliding my hand down under my dress as my phone dings, pulling me from my daydream. It's the security system at the store telling me Lucy is in already. I settle my breath and meet my own gaze in the mirror.

"Damn hormones," I mutter as I push through my want. As I open the front door, I notice something sitting on my porch: a little brown bag.

I look around searching for whoever delivered it before carefully reaching inside to pull out a sachet of Pink Stork nausea tea and a little package of sour candies. Instead of being full of sugar like the ones I've been wolfing down, they're natural and organic. A little note sits atop the bag.

Better than that Sour Patch shit, A.

I bite my lip and smile to myself. *He's looking out for the baby. This isn't about me.*

Still, I can't resist texting him. I send a picture of the candies.

ME

How did you get this so quickly?

He answers right away.

> **A**
> Amazon.

He sends a meme of The Rock putting on sunglasses

I laugh, popping one of the candies into my mouth. Goddamn, it instantly settles my stomach. What kind of crazy science is this?

> **A**
> I'm helping Wade at the cabins this morning, but I should be able to pop over when you meet Shane at 1.

I breathe out a sigh of relief, glad he'll be there to ask the questions I probably won't think of as Shane discusses next steps. I definitely want to be involved in the design, but baby brain is a real thing and an extra pair of ears, particularly ones that understand all this stuff, can only be a good thing.

> **ME**
> You don't have to if you're busy.

I hate sounding insecure, but this man makes me feel like I'm floating half the damn time.

> **A**
> Liv, I think we're past this.

> **A**
> You're the mother of my child now. This is a way I can help you. Let me.

The butterflies resurface at the way he calls me the mother of his child, and my filthy mind goes wild as I think of a few moments earlier when I could've used his help. I wonder if that counts?

> A
>
> See you at 1.
>
> A
>
> Blue is your color, by the way.

He can see me? I turn in the direction of the new wedding cabins in the distance. My eyes fall on the closest one and I immediately spot Asher; he's on the roof, tool belt around his waist, wearing jeans that fit just right. Although I can't see his expression from here, he gives me the two-finger salute and tips his hard hat in my direction. I wave back, my chest heating as I head down the driveway to my car.

He's taking care of the baby, I repeat to myself. As I start the engine, I realize what I have to do, and that's build up my tolerance for the next seven months, because *this* is new territory for me.

I've handled quiet Asher, pissed-off Asher, I've even handled animalistic lust-filled Asher. But *this*? The doting dad? This is next level and I'm not really sure what to do with *this* Asher besides maybe invest in some extra batteries. Because something tells me my vibrator is gonna be working overtime.

CHAPTER 22
Asher

I tuck my pencil behind my ear and climb down the ladder off the roof just as Olivia backs out of her driveway. There's a part of me, a big part, that wants to follow her to work just to make sure she gets there safely. Not because I think she's weak—she's resilient as fuck—but I have an innate need to be near her right now and it's fucking crushing. Every second I laid awake in bed last night thinking about her and my baby was a fight as I wrestled with my thoughts. Men like me don't get to be regular dads, playing catch with their kids in the front yard. Men like me have been raised to train their sons to be ruthless. They marry their daughters off to the heads of other families to secure business dealings. Men like me cheat, steal, and lie their way through life. They don't love; they don't *feel*. Because of that, all these foreign emotions are running through me. I have to give Liv and our baby everything they deserve, but the idea of letting someone in makes me feel completely out of fucking control. If I bring them closer, I might lose them.

"How's it looking up there?" Wade asks when I come

through the front door of one of the wedding cabins he's working on. The smell of pine hits me as I enter; the cleaners are doing their best to get the place dust-free and we're pretty much complete after months of work. Soon we'll be starting on the outside, working on decking, landscaping, and driveways. Wade, Walker, and I laid the hand-planed four-inch maple boards as flooring—with cabinets to match—and did the same in pine for the ceiling. The kitchen is simple with quartz counters and stainless-steel appliances, and the front and bedroom windows have been designed to allow the natural light to stream in as bridal parties get ready and take wedding photos on their big day.

"It's looking pretty close to a finished cabin," I say, picking up my water. "The roofers did a great job where that flashing meets the trough."

"Thanks for having a look for me," Wade says, surveying the space and placing his hammer on top of the tool bag. "Fuck, I can't believe we're getting there. Just wish my dad were here to see it. He always wanted to work on a hospitality side to the ranch."

"You should be proud." I look out the front window to the open space and bubbling creek beyond. "This will be a pretty sought-after spot once it's done."

"You all good?" Wade asks, his dark brow furrowed as he examines me. I don't know if it's the fact that I've gotten to know him a little better over these last months, or because he has a small child of his own, but the need to talk to *someone* hits me like a ton of bricks.

"Fuck, not really," I say, taking a seat on an empty pallet in the center of the room.

Wade's eyebrows shoot up. "I didn't expect you to answer honestly."

"Yup. Trying something new."

"Any particular reason?"

I breathe out a deep sigh. "Olivia is pregnant. And the baby is mine."

Wade's mouth falls open in shock and we both sit with the statement between us for a beat.

"Holy fuck." He flips a pallet over just across from me and takes a seat. "Holy . . . fuck."

"Right?"

"Is this serious?"

"What's good, boys?" Nash pushes the door open just as I'm about to answer Wade's question. He's carrying a box of outlet covers. "Had to drive to Fallon Ridge for these. They don't stock black ones at the local hardware store."

Nash looks between Wade and me and his expression clouds over. "What's wrong?"

"We were just having a little talk," I offer. Wade stays quiet, knowing this is my story to share.

"Talk?" Nash's eyebrows shoot up in surprise.

"Yeah . . ." I begin. "Hell, I'm going to need all the help I can get for this one."

Nash folds his arms over his chest, unsure what to expect.

"Olivia is pregnant."

It takes Nash all of five seconds to make the connection between this statement and why it's significant to me.

"Holy *fuck*." He bites out the same response as Wade. "When did you two . . . ? Wait . . . is this *serious*?"

I shake my head, scrubbing my beard with my hand and looking down at the scuff of my work boots. "I don't know what it is. My head is fucked."

Talking to other people about my personal shit doesn't come easily. But, for this, I *need* some advice.

"I take it, seeing as you're telling us now, that she's decided to keep the baby?" Wade asks now as Nash leans back onto the kitchen counter.

I nod. "And I'm all in. But, fuck, I'm so out of my element

here. I want to do the right thing by her. I just don't have a clue what that is."

Nash pulls some covers out of the bag and moves around the room, placing them at each outlet. "I'm eight months in and I still don't know if I've done enough," he admits.

"And I've been a dad for a year almost and I don't know either," Wade adds.

"*Christ*," I mutter under my breath. "I'm fucking doomed then."

"Do you have feelings for her? It always kind of seemed like you had a thing for her." Nash side-eyes me.

I revel in a moment of silence before answering.

"There was a connection when I first met her. A draw. Like she's the goddamn sun and I can't help but want to be near her." I struggle to get my thoughts out. "I've always felt, I dunno, protective of her. And maybe that's not normal. But the way she fucking injures herself isn't normal either."

Nash chuckles. "I followed CeCe to Seattle once because I was worried about her safety. So no judgment here."

He raises his hands in surrender and I quirk an eyebrow, though he offers nothing more as I stand. So does Wade.

"After the fire, we went our separate ways. But not because I didn't want to know her better. I'm just not the man she's looking for. She's the town sweetheart, and I am . . . well, not that. Plus, I've never seen myself as the type to settle down."

"Neither did I," Nash says, "not until CeCe. With her it was different."

His words resonate with me. Because in a way, that's how I've always felt around Olivia.

"You must have some feelings for her?" Nash assesses.

I start cleaning up because I can't sit still.

"How can you tell?" I grunt out as I load my drills into their cases.

"You wouldn't be talking to us if you didn't," Wade pipes

up.

I stop cleaning for a moment. "I have this nagging need to take care of her, to make sure she's settled and happy. And, fuck, when I see her . . ."

Nash chuckles, moving closer to pat me on the shoulder. "That, my friend, is feelings."

"Feelings or not, it's best for *her* if we just stay friends."

Nash doesn't question my motives, just eyes me slowly. "A man's past doesn't define him, Asher."

I nod curtly. "And I won't let it hurt her either."

"When is she due?" Wade cuts in. It's the thing I like most about these guys. They never pry about my past.

"February."

Quick calculations line his face. "Well, that tells me you've got about seven months, give or take, to figure all this out."

I carry my drills and tool pouch to the door.

"In the meantime, just let yourself get to know her," Nash offers with a shrug. "In case you haven't noticed this about yourself, you aren't exactly the easiest guy to get close to."

I don't answer. *And for good reason.*

"We know you keep to yourself," he continues. "And you keep your past buried under that prickly exterior. But this situation? It's something entirely different, so maybe *you* need to do something different."

I turn to face him.

"Let your guard down a little. It's not easy, but take it from me: Demons from the past will haunt you if you let them." Nash grabs a water from the fridge. "They'll stop you from forming relationships, from living. And then the demons win." He cracks the lid on his bottle as his words sink in. Something tells me he is speaking from experience.

"Let my guard down . . ." I repeat, registering his advice.

"Yeah. Just take as much off her plate as you can and the rest will work itself out," Wade adds. "We're all here for you both."

I nod; no one has ever "been there" for me, and the offer of help feels foreign.

"Thanks." I look between them. "Before I moved to Laurel Creek, I never had any friends who didn't want something from me."

"Aww shucks, bring it in," Nash says exaggeratedly with a deep laugh. He pulls me in for a hug, clapping me on the back, and the contact causes me to stiffen. I rarely have people try to hug me.

"Congrats, man! You're gonna be a father!"

Hearing him say it out loud makes it *that* much more fucking real. *Holy fuck*.

CHAPTER 23
Olivia

"Well, I guess a little bit at a time. Right?" I ask as I look around my house, my voice wavering. I didn't expect that seeing my house still so barren would hit me so hard. I look around what used to be my kitchen. It's stripped down to the studs and wiring, and half the kitchen floor is ripped out.

"It's really not as bad as it looks," Shane attempts to convince me. We've been here for about thirty minutes, and I've managed to both panic and talk myself down at lease twice about the state everything is in.

"It's great that the old wiring and plumbing were redone before you bought it. If it hadn't been done already, when we opened up those walls, you would've had to replace it to code."

"That's good, I suppose," I offer with a small smile, trying my best to stay positive. Asher hasn't shown yet, which tells me he may be hung up on a fire call.

We wander the space some more and Shane shows me how they'll build out the drywall to make it meet the existing plaster. Sheila, the Heritage Committee member, has been more lenient than I expected and is allowing me to use drywall because it's safer and more eco-friendly than plaster. I just have to make sure the finer details—floors, cabinets, and anything that can be made period appropriate, is.

"Sorry I'm late." Asher comes through my front door with a light knock. I turn to face him as all the air inside feels like it's been sucked through the door he came in. He's not in his gear, but he's still covered in soot and sweat. The bravery of being a firefighter command hits me, and I feel a heady mix of both desire and fear. Asher is gorgeous, of course, but the bubbling fear I feel . . . I shudder at the thought that anything could happen to him, at any moment, and there would be nothing I could do about it. A wave of nausea rises as I imagine my baby being left without a dad, just like I was once.

"Barn fire on Highway 12," he says quickly.

"Everything okay?" I ask gently.

"Yeah, the owners are fine, but they lost part of the barn and two pigs. They're at the beginning of their journey, just like you were." He gives my shoulder a light squeeze and looks around. "But look at this place now." He seems pleased with the re-studded walls, the exposed electrical wiring and pipes.

"Yeah, a real beaut." I snicker as I follow his gaze.

"Nah, this is nothing. Go on, tell her," Asher says to Shane.

"I already did." Shane grins. "More than once."

"It's just because I don't understand how to fix it," I offer. "But I trust both your judgment. I just can't wait for it to be done. Thank you so much for all the work you are doing."

"No problem. Can't wait to see what you do with the cabinets. We've found some flooring to match the wood you're using." Shane turns to me and pushes his blond locks off his forehead. "Wait till he finishes with your cabinets. Then you'll see what a genius this guy is with wood."

I bite my lip to keep from grinning. *Definitely already witnessed that.*

Asher clears his throat. "All right, I gotta head back to the hall but, tonight, let's have dinner when you're done with work?"

My mouth falls slack for a moment.

"You know, get to know each other better," he adds, awkwardly hooking his thumbs into his suspenders.

"Okay, sure," I answer. *This open and compromising Asher is . . . new.*

Neither of us say anything for too long, both waiting for the other to speak. Shane's phone rings and he heads to the other room, which makes me feel the need to break the silence between Asher and me. I give in to the smile twitching at my lips.

"So . . . I hear you're a real genius with wood?"

Asher shakes his head as he turns and heads to the front porch. I go with him.

"Aye." He wags a finger at me. "Don't you dare fucking flirt with me, Liv. I'm having a baby. My emotions are all over the goddamn place."

I laugh as he pushes his sunglasses down to cover his eyes. He smiles at me even wider and then he laughs. A real laugh, not a chuckle. I realize it's the first time I've ever really heard it. It's a deep, clear sound that warms me from my toes up. It's intoxicating. And, suddenly, all I want to do is make him laugh again.

CHAPTER 24
Olivia

My store is so busy all afternoon with the nicer weather that I don't even have a chance to be nervous about dinner with Asher before the front door dings precisely at five o'clock and my gaze lifts to meet a six-foot-five firefighter still in his khaki-colored workpants and a fresh LCFD T-shirt. Heavy work boots cover Asher's feet, and his black hair haphazardly touches his forehead. It looks damp, like he showered at the firehall before he came here. *Stop staring, Liv.*

"Ready to eat?" he asks, reaching the counter, turning the full force of his gaze on me. "Mama's choice."

Close your mouth, Liv.

"You could bribe me to do crazy things with a good cheeseburger and fries right now," I blurt out, because apparently Asher Reed cancels out the normal filter between my brain and my mouth.

"Noted." He chuckles deeply, and the sound is like wrapping myself in a soft, warm blanket. "Well, my main goal for the next seven months is keeping you fed. So I'll start a list."

I try to push down my dirty, hormone-enhanced thoughts

as Asher waits patiently while I lock up. Once I'm done, he leads me out of the store.

"Where should we go?" I ask.

"Sounds like . . . the Burger Barn?" He eyes me cautiously. "Then we're going to my house."

Laurel Creek is bustling at the dinner hour. Flowerpots hang from every lamppost down Main, brimming with petunias and vibrant green foliage. The patios are full of people chattering while they sip wine and eat their dinner, and the ice cream shop already boasts a lineup that slinks all around the block as we cruise through town. By the time we hit the sprawling fields that dot the Kentucky countryside in Asher's pickup truck, I'm still talking myself out of any sort of attraction to him. He has zero interest in what I want, which means I have to keep my head straight. We have a long road ahead of us.

The Burger Barn is an old-style diner that offers takeout just at the edge of town, no drive-thru, so we head inside to order, but I'm surprised when Asher doesn't even ask me what I want and goes to order a bacon burger with cheese, lettuce, tomato, extra pickle, and mustard, sweet potato fries on the side with Cajun mayo.

"Am I that predictable?" I ask as he orders the same thing for himself, but doubles the meat and subs the fries for regular potato.

He glances down at me, always as if he's assessing me. I say nothing as I let his wheels turn.

"And a strawberry shake. Extra thick," he adds to the server behind the counter.

I busy myself while he pays, though I can't help my mind straying to check out how well his uniform pants mold to his perfect ass. *Holy hell. I'm a mess.*

"Nope," he says as he turns back to me. "Just a perk of serving you for two years at the Horse and Barrell. I know exactly what you like."

"I am always ordering strawberry margs and burgers," I agree. *But the fact that he remembered?*

The smell of food makes my stomach growl as I listen to Asher tell me how his guys ran a betting ring today on who could empty their truck fastest after a call to an eighty-year-old's house for an electrical fire. Sadly, she lost her dog, but they managed to save her.

"You don't find it hard to make light after such a sad afternoon?" I ask.

"No, we do," he admits as he stares out at the road. "It's taken a few years with the same team for me to feel comfortable enough with them to do more than simple small talk, but we have a good group, and if we don't take moments like that to unwind, to remember that we're a team, that's when you get buried under the day-to-day stuff that threatens to pull you under." I listen intently because it's rare for him to talk this much. "There's a lot of injury and sadness and loss in this work. But the one good day, where you save everyone . . ." He shakes his head. "That makes every second of the bad worth it."

I don't notice we're slowing down until we're almost at a complete stop just below the base of Sugarland Mountain. Asher turns off the main road and onto a paved, narrow track that disappears under a canopy of trees. The entire property is flat and expansive—fenced in by thick black iron—and we cruise down the driveway for at least half a mile until the house comes into view.

The main building is a two-story white farmhouse, atop of which sits a black metal roof. There is a main porch at the front that continues all the way around, and I can see what looks like a newish wooden deck in the back. Beyond the house is a barn that appears almost bigger than the house itself. It's red and rustic—but looks restored—and I can see the double barn doors slightly ajar, with Asher's Harley parked out front. Asher cuts the engine and hops out before coming around to my side and opening the door. As my feet land on the concrete driveway, I look around and the smell hits me before I see it.

Lavender. So much lavender that it takes up an expansive portion of the yard at the side of the house. My breath catches in my throat as I take in the beauty of the violet field swaying in the gentle evening breeze. It's so peaceful, the only sounds the spring peepers and crickets.

"Y'okay?" Asher asks.

I look back at him with a nervous smile.

"Yeah. It's just . . . lavender is my favorite. You have so much of it."

"Aye. I figured. Lavender Grove." He says the name of my store. "This was a farm before I bought it. A woman from town buys bushels of it from me to make soaps now."

"What a beautiful place to live," I observe, still taking in the surroundings.

"Mmm," he gives.

"At the base of a mountain." I smile, remembering what he told me his mother said.

"As soon as I saw it, I knew it was right."

"I can see why." I'm happy that he felt he could share his home with me. I startle when a big, black, burly head pokes out from the barn, until I realize it's a dog, a dog that seems very uninterested we just woke him from his slumber as he yawns and saunters toward us. Asher crouches down to rub the fur behind his ears.

"Were you a good lad today?" he asks as the dog jumps up, his front paws settling on Asher's thighs. He's both massive and intimidating, but it's obvious he's Asher's baby.

"Hold down the fort?" he continues as the dog nuzzles in.

"Yeah, you did. And now you're looking for your dinner, aren't ya?"

The dog paws at him, tail wagging like crazy, and I almost melt into a puddle with this softer side of him I'm sure no one ever really sees.

"Who's this?" I ask, moving toward them and holding my hand out.

"This is Duke," Asher says as his bear-like best friend hears my voice and strolls over to investigate me. He's calm as he sniffs me, so I go to pet his head as he cozies up to me.

"A gentle giant," I say.

"He doesn't meet a lot of new people," Asher admits. "But he seems to like you."

A flash of orange catches my eye before I can answer, and I spot a tabby cat milling around one of the doors to the barn. *He has a cat too?*

The cat rubs his back against the edge of the door as he looks at me, curious and utterly adorable. My heart swells in my chest as I think about my little Biscuit. This cat looks very similar, only he's still very young, hardly more than a kitten.

"Quite the animal lover," I note as I narrow my eyes at Asher. I can't figure this man out.

Asher's face morphs into a scowl. "*He's* not mine."

"He's in your barn."

"Yeah. But he's not mine. Although he thinks he owns the place, and Duke likes him."

"Well, at least Duke has some common sense," I say to Duke, who gruffs in what I'd like to think is agreement as I let go of his head and make my way over to the cat. I stop about a foot away and kneel down. He seems a little skittish, unsure of me at first. But after a moment, he comes right to me, purring as I scratch behind his ears.

"I'm pretty sure he's a runaway from the farm about a mile down the road." Asher shrugs. "He just hangs out here."

"What's his name?"

"I call him Dick."

I turn and frown at him. "That's not very nice, is it? Is he a big meany?" I ask, turning back to Dick. "Maybe he just isn't a pussy guy after all, huh?"

"Christ, woman," I hear Asher grit out as I pick up the cat. He's heavy and warm and purrs into the crook of my arm.

"He just wants some love. How long has he been showing up?"

"A few months."

"What do you eat, big guy?" I ask Dick as he lets out a little meow.

"He eats the mice around here, and whatever I bring out for Duke from my kitchen."

I nuzzle into his fur. "Tell the big bad meany you'd like some pumpkin too." I turn and face Asher. "Pumpkin was my cat's favorite treat."

"Pumpkin?" Asher queries as he picks up a stick from his grass and tosses it for Duke to retrieve.

"Cats usually have temperamental stomachs. It's good for them."

Asher lets out a grunt as Duke finds the stick and redelivers it. "I'm not about to spoil the damn barn cat."

I watch as he pulls our take-out bag off his front seat. "Okay, pussy whisperer. Let's eat."

My stomach growls at the thought of food as I follow Asher and Duke across the green expanse of his yard and into his house, fighting how comfortable I feel just being here with him.

"And this was from when I broke my arm when I was nine." I

hold my arm out so Asher can see the thin line at the bend of my inner elbow.

He cocks his head to the side. "I don't get it."

"Well, I was still growing, which meant they didn't want to put plates in or screws or any of that. They just wrapped the cast really, really tight. So tight"—I take a sip of shake—"my fingers swelled up and started turning blue."

"Horseshit." Asher stuffs a fry into his mouth.

"Seriously." I laugh now. It seems unbelievable, but it's true. "They had to cut the cast up the center to relieve the pressure then rewrap it."

"Christ. How does that happen? Your parents should've sued."

"That's what I'm saying!" I laugh, scooting closer. "And this—" I hold my hair back at my forehead and show him the tiny scar at my hairline. "This was from playing baseball in my neighborhood with friends. Same summer. I wasn't even doing anything dangerous, just waiting my turn to hit, and the girl in front of me threw the bat after her line drive. Hit me right in the head."

"Fuck sakes." Asher starts to laugh, but I'm still not used to the sound or how it makes me feel. It's a reward. "You really are a fucking walking accident."

I nod as I take a sip of my drink.

"Between that second toe and all these catastrophes, how are you even still alive?" He leans back in his chair, relaxing his thick thighs.

"I have no idea," I say, glancing around Asher's little kitchen. As you would expect from a man who likes to dabble in woodworking, everything that can be crafted from wood, is. The cabinets, the floors, the counters, the beams. It's stylish but also warm, homey, and clean. It also smells amazing, just like him. Citrus and leather with a hint of pine. I look away first when our laughter putters out, and Asher stands to pick up our take-out garbage, stuffing it all back into the brown paper bag and setting it on the spotless kitchen counter.

"These cabinets would fit a heritage mold suitable for your house," he says, walking toward his own. "They're maple, but I got the wood from the same place I told Shane to look for the wood for your floors. When I'm done sanding and refinishing yours, they'll look something like this."

I stand and make my way over to his cabinets to run a hand along them. "They look really similar to what I had before we painted my old ones white."

Asher scoffs in disgust. "Terrible fucking choice."

"What?!"

"Painting natural wood should be a goddamn crime." He mutters the last part.

"Could I see the wood?" I ask.

He rinses off his hands and dries them on a tea towel, then nods toward the barn. "Aye."

He whistles and Duke stands up.

"Let's go." I can't tell if he's talking to me or Duke, but we both follow him regardless.

As we cross the yard and head back into the barn, I wonder how he ever finds the will to leave this place. The sun is just sinking into a dusty blue-and-pink sky and there are so many tree frogs and cicadas buzzing, it's hard to hear anything else. Out here, we're so close to Sugarland Mountain, it feels like I could reach out and touch it. I still have no idea what made him decide to open up and bring me here. But I'll take it if it means getting to know him a little better.

When Asher flicks the lights on in the barn, I gasp. It isn't a barn at all. Rather, it's a full-scale, high-end woodshop. His shop doesn't take up the whole barn, but it's most certainly been redone to fit even the most avid carpenter. Floor-to-ceiling shelves hug the whole west wall, filled with wood of various cuts and sizes, so much that I wonder what on earth he's planning to do with it all. The east wall boats a variety of hanging tools: wrenches, clamps, a sea of yellow DeWalt power tools, backed by black cabinets lined with novelty stickers.

And, in the center, a big American flag is pinned taut to the wall between the cabinets with a laser-cut sign underneath that says, *People come and go, but Johnny and June are forever.* I smile at that one because my dad is a Johnny Cash and June Carter fan and it makes me think of him.

In the middle of the room is a table of full-scale equipment. I have no idea what any of it does, but I believe Asher could make anything from a rough piece of wood in this shop. I stare at the space as Duke lies down in the corner with a grumble in a really comfortable-looking dog bed and Dick comes moseying in behind us, curling up beside him.

"Is it air-conditioned in here?" I ask as I feel the chill of cool air on my skin.

"Yeah, and heated. My laser is temperamental." He nods to one of those big machines. It looks like a big plexiglass box with a motor under it.

"Hmm. Kind of like its owner." I fold my arms over my chest. Asher just grunts, turning and heading over to his wood shelf while I give myself the tour. Like his home, everything in here is clean and precise, each item in its own place.

Dick gets up and comes to nuzzle my leg again as I'm admiring Asher's stickers on his tool cabinets.

I turn wood into things. What's your superpower? My eyebrows shoot up when I eye the next one.

Measure twice, cut once, then force it to fit.

Images flood my mind, mostly ones of his face while he watched himself fuck into me, *slowly,* forcing himself to fit.

Suddenly, even with the air-conditioning, it feels hot in here. I hear Asher clear his throat from behind me and I flinch.

"You ready to see this wood, G.I. Toe?" He smirks.

Prick.

CHAPTER 25
Asher

When Wade and Nash told me to let my guard down, to do something different, I figured bringing Olivia to my home would help us both get to know each other a little better. The man I am *now*, the man I want to be for our child, the man I was destined to be. But I wasn't thinking about how I'd get to know her in return. And how easy it would be to *like* her.

"You just push it through here?" she asks now, her voice soft and clear in my barn. I've always watched Olivia, wondering who she was and why. And I realize that having a baby with her is dangerous in more ways than one. It gives me a *reason* to get to know her. It's the logic that *almost* pushes past the worry in my gut that something bad will happen to her if I let her get too close to me. Especially when she's in my home, my space, and she's enticing as hell.

Running her hand carefully over the white oak sitting on my planing table, she examines the wood I chose for her cabinets. I might die a little inside if she decides to paint it. It's from a one hundred-and-fifty-year-old tree from Johnson

County; the grain is fucking incredible and once I lacquer the finished product, it'll really pop. I pat the machine she stands in front of and nod.

"You just push it through."

"And this is safe for me? To be out here," she asks.

"In my shop, yes. It's entirely dust-free." I point to the hose and system that sucks the dust from the space and the HEPA filter in the corner.

That satisfies her as she crouches down to check out the gadgets attached to my industrial planer. Her pert, round ass is on full display, as if she doesn't realize how perfect she is, or how desperately I want to take a fucking bite out of her.

"We'll run the wood through maybe four times," I say in an attempt to steer my mind away from the enticing curves of her body. "It's a process."

"I'm sorta invested now," Olivia says. "Could you maybe show me how it works?"

She eyes the blades enclosed in the center box of the massive machine, like my wood shop is the most interesting thing she's seen in a while. I can't imagine it is. But if it keeps her here a little longer, I'm all in.

"This thing looks like it could flatten a car."

"Pretty close," I admit.

It's a Fray 800 and, at over twelve feet long, it's a beast of a planer. When this thing fires up, it vibrates the damn floor around it. I pull a pair of clear glasses down for her.

"Safety first," I say, placing them on her face. She flashes me a grin in response. *Goddamn that's cute.* "This is a powerful machine. It would be really difficult to hurt yourself on it. Still, it's *you*, so we're going to take every precaution."

Olivia sticks her tongue out at me, and my cock involuntarily twinges with the sight. One taste of being close to this woman after weeks of starvation and I'm a fucking teenage boy.

"I'm gonna push this piece through here." I grip the piece of rough wood and refocus, pointing to the center where the cutter head is partially housed, protecting us from the blades.

"These tables don't do anything? Nothing sharp?" She pats the large expanse of stainless-steel table in front of us.

I shake my head. "Nope, they're just a resting place. They allow me to plane very big pieces of wood. This side holds it as the machine sucks it in, the other side spits it back out when it's done. Do you understand?"

She nods like a good little pupil. *Everyone* I've ever known looks ridiculous in safety glasses. But somehow, when Olivia puts them on, I want to hoist her up onto the table and fuck her into next week.

"Let the machine do the work. Slow hands are better than fast ones. Got it?"

"I think so," she replies, studying my movements.

I gesture in front of me and back up. "Okay, you're gonna do it now."

"I am?"

"You are," I assure her. "Lean up against the machine and guide the wood through. Once it's free, I'll bring it back and you can push it through again."

"Sounds easy." She shrugs, leaning against the wide table.

I reach over her and turn on the safety then hit the start button to fire up the machine. Olivia startles as the table comes to life and vibrates gently. It's a smooth, deep, and steady hum, and I fucking love the sound.

"I'll help you get started." I lift up the two-foot-wide by six-foot-long board, deciding which side to smooth out, then lay it flat in front of her. She places her hands on the board, and I rest mine behind hers, as we begin to push it through the machine.

Olivia presses further into the table, holding the board in front of her.

"Don't be afraid of it," I say, low in her ear. "You're the boss."

She nods and continues to work the wood. Once it's halfway through the machine, I make my way down to the other end of the table, ready to grab the finished product. I bring it back to Olivia.

"See how much better this looks already?" I ask, flipping it over to show her how the new wood compares to the rough side. She nods before moving back into position. Standing just behind, I steady the wood as my arms reach around her.

Everything about this turns me on. Our proximity, her eagerness to learn, the combined scent of her and the wood. *Everything.*

As we begin to push the wood through again, a tiny whimper escapes her lips and at first I worry she's hurt. But when I look down to see her bottom lip between her teeth, I realize she's fine. *More than fine.* Apparently, I might not be the only one turned on by woodworking.

But it takes me a second to understand *why* she's worked up. The height of this table is perfectly lined up with her body. Right against her needy little pussy. But Olivia doesn't back away. Instead, she leans into it more.

"That's it, nice and slow."

I breathe in her sweet-smelling skin. Her soft neck is just below my lips and the brush of her hair against my jawline begs me to lose my fingers in it. The steady purr of the planer is like background music as the heat from her body radiates to mine.

"Like this?" she asks, almost breathless, as we push the piece of wood through the planer.

"Perfect," I tell her as the last of it disappears through to the other side. I'm rock-fucking-solid right now and I'm planing wood.

Olivia's practically panting as she presses up against the vibration until her hips rock back and her ass grazes my hardened cock. At the movement, her lips part and a soft moan escapes her, barely audible under the hum of the planer. I could withstand it if I thought it was accidental, but when she grips the sides of the table and her head falls back, my control snaps and I'm spinning her around, lifting her body up so she's sitting on the table as I turn the machine off. Olivia tosses her safety glasses to the floor—just as eager as I am—and I press my body against hers. She moans as I slide my hands up to cage her face with them, hovering my lips just above hers.

"I just . . . This damn table is *torture*," she pants out.

I stop dead in my tracks with *that* word and the question I see in her eyes. *Torture.*

It's like a sucker punch to the gut. A trigger. *What the fuck am I doing?*

Images of torture—real torture at the hands of my father—flash through my mind. I squeeze my eyes shut to dispel them. But they don't disappear, and I'm listening to my mom's screams once again. They're the last straw as I fight this with *everything* in me.

"Fuck. I'm sorry . . ." I grit out as I let her pretty face go.

"No, *I'm* sorry . . . I don't know what happened." She blushes furiously. "It's just the table and these . . . damn pregnancy hormones. Who knew wood was such a turn-on—but we agreed, no complications. Right?"

"Right," I agree so quickly there's no chance of me changing my mind. "It's best if we just stick to the plan."

Fuck, I sound like such an asshole. Her gaze drops to the floor, and I have no idea how to keep my head but also let her in. I wish I could tell her that I *want* to pick her up and carry her inside my house. That I want to bury myself in her until the sun comes up, until she's completely wrung out and begging for mercy. But instead, I find the will to back up and help her down off the table. Without saying anything more, I move to take her home. Where she's safe.

CHAPTER 26
Olivia

What the hell just happened?

One minute I'm helping him plane my oak boards, the next I'm almost kissing him on that damn table, and that is *not* the way to keep the lines between us clear and let him be just a father to our child. How can I keep things uncomplicated if I'm the one rocking my ass against him and practically begging him to touch me? He may not believe in love or relationships, but he is still a man. And there's clearly a physical pull between us.

As we got ready to leave, Asher was a perfect gentleman, gathering my things for me and asking me if I wanted to stop anywhere on the way back. What I *wanted* was him. What I *wanted* was to feel his hands running through my hair as he groaned into my lips.

"I think we shouldn't be too hard on ourselves," I say when we pull up to the cabin and he cuts the engine. "So we almost had a slip-up. This is a lot to be going through together, and we're gonna be spending a lot of time in each other's company. But I want you to know I don't, um . . . expect *that* from you."

Asher's silence is stifling in the darkness of the truck.

"It's not about what you can expect," he says finally. "It's about what you deserve. I can't be the shining knight you have in your head, Liv." His hand covers mine. "That Prince Charming you want. I'm not *him*. I'll never be him."

He takes a deep breath as I sit quietly, unsure how to respond. I already knew this about him, but the words still sting.

"It's not just that I didn't come from a good place." His admission takes me by surprise. "Where I came from is *unthinkable* for someone like you."

A shiver runs up my spine as he turns to face me. I can *see* it. I can see the demons he harbors deep inside.

"I swore I would never look back. I changed my last name to Reed, my mother's family name. But the curse of the man my father raised me to be still haunts me. Because I was almost him."

My mouth falls open as I register what he just told me.

"What was your last name . . . before?" I ask cautiously, still in shock at his openness. I get the feeling he doesn't do this ever, and I don't take it lightly.

"I was born a Donovan." He says the name as if it pains him to admit it. "I come from generations of men I'm not proud of. But I can promise you now, that cycle ends with me. I'll always be there for you and our child. I'll never hurt you. You both are my priority."

"I know," I admit. We sit quietly for a moment; it doesn't feel as though either of us wants to get out of his truck just yet.

"Can you tell me more about your father?" I say softly. Another beat of deafening silence passes.

"He is . . ." Asher pauses. "A ruthless businessman. No one crosses him and everyone is at his command. Even me for a time. The world was whatever I wanted under him: drugs, women, money. And then, I went to prison for thirteen months for him, Liv. And that's what finally changed something in me.

It's what made me realize I needed out, but still it took me years to do so."

I think I make a weird kind of squeaking noise as my mouth falls open again. Prison? The father of my child was in *prison*?

"Why were you in prison?" My voice is a shaky whisper.

"Assault. It wasn't my crime, but I claimed it was to protect my father. It's what we did. My world was hard as fuck to survive in. I was young and I took one for the team to save *him*. The men who caused the assault got away; I didn't. I wasn't fast enough. I wasn't strong enough. I told the police that I was responsible for hurting a man very badly in one of my father's warehouses."

Shame lines his face, and my heart hurts for him.

"It was my choice to take the blame."

"What *kind* of world is this?" I ask.

"The kind where the lines are very, very blurred between my father's ruthless business empire and the criminal world." His throat bobs as he swallows, and my stomach drops. My hand instinctively moves to my low belly to cover it. His eyes follow, then return to mine.

"So he what? Took bribes? Worked with criminals in exchange for the growth of his business?"

Asher grips the hand that rests against my belly, and I feel the scars that line them in a new way.

"Yes. Among other things."

"How could your father let that happen to you?" My brain can't wrap around this. My father would die before he'd let anything happen to me. Yet his father let him take the fall for something he didn't even do?

"I don't let myself think about that," he replies. "Going to jail was the best thing that ever happened to me. It pushed me to listen to my mom and finally escape my dad. When I was in jail, my 'family' was nowhere to be found. After, I knew I needed a career, one that could help me leave his world behind."

He runs a hand through his hair.

"I know this is scary to hear. But it's not who I am now. It's not the man I'll be for you and the baby." His thumb strokes against mine. "But I need you to understand why talking, expressing, feeling . . . it doesn't come easy for me."

"It *is* scary," I admit. "But we have no choice about who we're born to or the path their lives take, Asher. I know that better than anyone. Is your father still alive?"

"Barely," he says. "He's been sick for years."

His brow knots and I can tell there's more he isn't telling me, but I don't push him.

Maybe I should be more afraid. I don't know the details of his horrors, but I do *believe* him when he says he wants to be different. He's here, a fire chief in a small Kentucky town, and he's been disconnected from that dangerous world for over two years. The thought of him being some dark prince? What he *could* be but chooses not to? His honesty matches his strength of action, and it makes me respect him *more*.

"Does anyone else know this?" I venture now.

"No."

I look down at my hands in my lap. "Why me?"

"Because I need you to understand why I am . . . how I am."

I say nothing. Asher is right; just because I'm having his baby doesn't mean he can simply change his mind on relationships. And why would he? After a life like that? How could he ever trust another person when his own parents let him down so badly?

"We can do this." I move the conversation on. "Maybe we make a pact?"

I need to set boundaries because, when there aren't any, I'm tempted to cross them. Especially now, when he's been so open and honest with me.

"A pact?" he repeats, a hint of curiosity in those charcoal

eyes.

"Yeah," I answer. "We strictly stay friends. Co-parents. And we always put the baby first. We still get to know each other, but for the pact's sake, maybe we stay out of your woodshop?"

His jaw tenses but he nods slightly in agreeance.

"And . . . a safe word? Something to signal if we notice that we're, you know, looking at each other like we might want more . . ." I offer.

Asher's eyebrows shoot up in question. "A safe word?"

God. He must think I'm some sort of horny, sex-crazed lunatic. He pulls his hand back into his own lap, and I hate that I feel the loss of his warmth so much.

"I don't need a safe word, Liv. I don't want to fuck this up."

Glad he's got lots of willpower because I'm fresh out.

"So it's a pact." He states evenly. I still have so many questions, but I don't want to push Asher tonight. He already seems a little lighter, more relaxed, than I've ever seen him. I want to tell him that I want to know *him*, the real him, that he isn't a shadow of his father. That all that trauma is what makes him who he is. But I can already tell that will take time for him to see.

So instead I just give him a small smile, letting him know I'm grateful for his honesty.

"A pact," I repeat as I pray to the pregnancy gods to help me resist those eyes, those hands, and that *body* that I'm almost positive will make me wish more and more every day that the line we just drew didn't exist.

CHAPTER 27
Olivia

"You're *what?*" Ginger's slaps both her hands down to the table, her eyes as big as saucers as we sit in the big house backyard the next evening. It's an at-home girls' night because there's no way we were getting CeCe to the Horse and Barrel when she's so pregnant. Plus, after what almost happened in Asher's woodshop last night, I needed a night in.

The only sounds to be heard under the Ashbys' big pergola as the sun starts to set are the trees swaying in the breeze at the edge of their manicured property. It's the kind of summer night where the temperature's just right—not too cool, but not too hot either. There are times this place feels like heaven and, tonight, it's the perfect escape from the absolute ass I made of myself when I rubbed up against the father of my child, practically begging him to fuck me.

But the way he opened up to me about his past is a staunch reminder that, even though there is an obvious attraction between us, it's not enough for Asher to change his mind about relationships, but I respect that and that he wants to put our baby first.

"When did this happen, and *how* did *I* not know about it?" Ginger continues, sipping on her ice-cold lemonade.

"At your wedding." I cringe as Ginger lets out a high-pitched squeal. *There it is.*

"You've been together for *that* long and I didn't know?"

"Well, no, technically it was only once. Well, and some light groping on his planer table last night in his workshop."

That gets CeCe's attention, and Cassie almost spits out her drink all over the table.

She starts choking before it turns to laughter. "Do tell?"

I blush a hot pink and meet the eyes of the women I trust more than anyone in the world.

"It was a little heated moment. Nothing came of it." *Because he stopped it.* "He was showing me how to smooth the rough wood for my cabinets."

"Oooh! Even that sounds hot." Cassie giggles. Ginger and CeCe follow suit.

"It wasn't my fault, but I lost control. He had me pressed up against the table and, well, it vibrated right in the . . . perfect spot."

"Oh shit!" Ivy starts to howl. This is her first kid-free night in a while as Wade holds down the fort, so she's already on her second sangria. "You dirty little slut you."

"Okay, I'm a happily committed woman now." Cassie's blue eyes dance. She's so relaxed and at home at Silver Pines. She slotted straight into our friendship group and has really settled into Kentucky life as she focuses on writing music now. It's as if she's a whole new woman since she stopped performing. "I mean, there's no man I love more than my own, but we gotta know. That man just *knows* what he's doing, doesn't he?"

"I'd put money on it," Ivy chimes in. "He's got that same BDE I loved about Wade."

"Gross." CeCe covers her ears.

"Sorry." Ivy winks at her, looking not the least bit sorry

with a tipsy glow taking over her pretty face.

"Oh, he knows," I admit. "Too much. Even when I'm crampy and nauseous and moody, I still want him. And, God, there are moments I think he wants me too. But last night, in the woodshop, it was like a wall went up when we got too close."

"He's definitely a bit of a mystery," CeCe chimes in. "And it's not the same thing, but Nash has trauma in his past. It took some time for him to trust that he deserved me."

I nod, knowing now that these two men don't share the same kind of trauma, though Asher's story isn't mine to tell them.

"Maybe you just need to give him a little more time," CeCe continues. "Maybe letting someone in isn't easy for him."

"Asher is a lone wolf. He's got his property, his job, his dog, and now here I am, barging in, baby in tow. I can't ask him for more." I smile. "Although he seems genuinely excited about the baby."

"And it's hard not to want him when he looks like that." Ginger snorts as she picks up a chip from the bowl in front of her.

"That's the problem. It's like I can't control myself. I almost always want him, *physically*," I tell them. "Is that normal?"

"Oh hell, wait until you hit your second trimester," CeCe says knowingly. Ivy nods but keeps her mouth shut at the other end of the table.

My eyes grow bigger with a little bit of fear. "I'm gonna want him *more*?"

CeCe leans in. "Well, everyone is different, but let's just say that there were times when I could've been with Nash and my vibrator in the same hour and I still wouldn't have been satisfied."

Ginger starts to laugh beside me. "Thanks for that picture."

"My pleasure," CeCe fires back.

"He's coming with me to the doctor tomorrow. But we

made a pact: We're just friends and the baby is the priority. Asher and I are gonna keep things as uncomplicated as possible."

"A pact?" Cassie's eyes twinkle. "That's cute."

I side-eye her. "It's a big move, him stepping up like this. Especially when he has no desire to be married or even in a serious relationship. I'm not forcing him into any corner. I just want him to be a good dad."

"He seems like the kind of man who will just take care of business. I think he'll be a great dad," Cassie observes.

"He left me pregnancy candies the other day and this tea that stops morning sickness," I tell them. "It was sweet."

"Ooooh, we love an acts-of-service man. *Hot*," Ginger says. "That's maybe his thing. It's easier to show you how he feels. You know? Take care of you."

"So he is sweet and protective, but I want to climb him like a tree? Should be the *easiest* seven months ever," I joke, throwing my hands up as the girls laugh with me. God, I love them.

"What's his own dad like? Do you know?" Cassie asks curiously, shoving some popcorn into her mouth as the timed twinkle lights above us kick on, illuminating the darkened sky.

"Apparently his family life was bad," I give, not willing to offer any more on the subject right now.

CeCe stands up and starts turning on the flameless lanterns around the patio.

"Nash always said that Asher didn't speak to his family. Something about them being bad news back in New York."

My stomach drops at her words. An image of him in prison flashes through my head and still freaks me out a little, though mostly I feel empathy that he had to endure that.

"I'm hoping as time passes he'll open up a little more," I add, sidestepping her comment as I sip my own lemonade.

"Well, I say focus on the here and now. In the words of Ted Lasso, be a goldfish," Ginger says, raising her glass to me.

"The man he *was* doesn't matter. What counts is the man he is now. For you and your baby. To the new mama," she adds. "May this pregnancy always make her glow."

"May her nausea slow as her baby bump grows . . ." Ivy pipes up with a tipsy rhyme.

"When it comes to food cravings, may she not have to wait," CeCe adds, holding up her own glass of iced tea.

"And may her baby daddy's woodshop tables always vibrate!" Cassie snorts.

I can't help it, I start to laugh. These girls are my rocks in a lake of uncertainty, and I couldn't survive without them.

My phone buzzes on the table as they continue their chatter.

A

This is the size of our baby?

I pick up my phone and see a link to a pregnancy website telling me the baby is the size of a grape.

ME

Maybe, but with arms and legs.

A

A grape with arms and legs.

He sends me through a photo of himself. He's at the firehall, in his uniform, but he's making a "What the fuck?" face.

I laugh out loud as all eyes at the table land on me. I'm glad because, even after last night, it seems like things won't be awkward between Asher and me.

ME

Well I for one think he or she will be a cute little grape baby.

> **A**
> Can't wait to find out tomorrow, mama.

My heart clunks in my chest at the same time I hear Cassie whisper "I don't smile like that at my *friends*" to one of the other girls.

> **ME**
> Me neither. The app I have says to eat lots the day before so the baby will be active. I'm definitely doing that.

I send a photo through of myself eating a slice of Jo's lemon loaf.

> **A**
> Good girl.

Praise kink activated. I bite my bottom lip as his next message comes through.

> **A**
> Night, you two.

"You know you're totally screwed here, right?" Cassie asks when I look up. I take a sip of my drink in response. At this point I can't even argue.

CHAPTER 28
Olivia

"This may feel a little cold, Olivia," Dr. Allen says as the chilly gel hits my abdomen. "We'll try the ultrasound like this. Sometimes, at this stage, we need to do them transvaginal. But let's see."

I've already been here for almost an hour and have had a full physical while Asher's waited in the other room. They've drawn blood and asked me a million questions about my preferences and whether I'd like to take advantage of the midwifery program this clinic has. It offers a more natural approach during labor and delivery. Asher knocks as he enters the room with a nurse just as Dr. Allen is spreading the gel.

"You must be the dad?" she says to him with a friendly smile.

I watch Asher's throat work into a hard swallow. He nods as I try to place the look he's wearing. If I had to guess, I would say it's a mix of protectiveness and pride.

"Well, come on over then. You're just in time for the show."

I wince as Dr. Allen presses the wand with more pressure into my abdomen.

"Ugh . . . that doesn't help me forget how much I have to pee." I squeeze my eyes shut and Dr. Allen laughs as I feel Asher slide his hand over mine. It's big and warm and instantly settles my nerves.

"Oh, here we are," Dr. Allen says as I squint at the screen. Smack in the center of what looks like a big black hole is a little peanut-shaped being.

"Is . . . that him?" Emotion creeps up my throat faster than I could have ever prepared for.

"Possibly." She chuckles as she continues the slide of the wand. "Or her."

Asher squeezes my hand as he side-eyes me and everything hits all at once. My throat feels thick, like I just ate something really sweet, and I'm having a hard time swallowing as tears flood my eyes.

"And there, that little fluttering right in the center?" She points to the screen. "That's your baby's heartbeat. Looks strong too, measuring . . ." She takes a second. "About one hundred and sixty-four beats per minute."

I watch in sheer fascination as four little nubs move when the peanut does.

"*Fuuuck*," Asher breathes out, his eyes glued to the image.

I start to laugh, turning to face him. "You took the words right outta my mouth."

I've never seen him look like this. He's beaming as he leans down to brush a tear from my cheek.

"Look what we made, Livi girl," he rasps. "Look what we made." His words are almost a whisper as he kisses my forehead.

"You're measuring nine weeks and one day, which means your due date will stay the same at February seventh. If you're a little late, maybe a Valentine's baby." Dr. Allen grins as she clicks away on her computer.

"Is that normal? To go past your due date?" I ask.

"Very. Especially with your first baby." She's still moving

the wand over my abdomen, but I don't feel the immense way I need to pee, or the fear that should be creeping up my throat at the thought of growing a whole person inside me. Because I'm utterly high in a fog of baby bliss.

"Everything looks great. Let me get you a picture and we'll schedule you another appointment once you've had some time to consider if you'd like to utilize our midwifery services."

I turn my eyes back to the screen for one more look before Dr. Allen swipes the wand off my belly and hands me a paper towel to soak up the gel.

"I can give you some of their pamphlets, and if you do want to use them, I'll work hand in hand with the service. Ours is a unique clinic here, so you're in good hands."

It's a lot of information to take in at once, so I just nod and hope Asher is listening. My mind is on the human inside me, and maybe I'm also a little lost to the man tucking his photo into his shirt pocket like it's his most prized possession, still firmly holding my hand and looking down at me like the proudest dad ever.

The rest of the day passes in a blur. Asher brings me back to my cabin before he heads down to the police station to discuss an accident he was present at this morning. Once inside, I pin my ultrasound to the fridge; Dr. Allen printed one for each of us, and as I make myself a grilled cheese sandwich and heat up some of Glenda's homemade minestrone soup, I get lost in the little black-and-white peanut stuck to the stainless steel, in the hundreds of visions of our future, allowing myself to imagine who he or she will be. I'm still in my bliss when a text comes through from my mother, reminding me of our planned dinner. The one where I'm supposed to tell them I'm pregnant.

I think about Asher's words, that he wanted to come with me. I know he's off tomorrow, and the idea of him being there makes me feel a little stronger.

> **ME**
> Did you mean what you said? About coming with me to tell my parents?

> **A**
> Of course.

> **ME**
> What if I told you that they want us to go out for dinner tomorrow and that they will ask you a hundred questions, probably stare at you and make you entirely uncomfortable, and it's highly likely my dad will ask if you're planning to marry me.

> **A**
> Stop spiraling, Liv. I can almost feel your nervous energy through the phone.

> **ME**
> They want to go to Dolcetto's.

> **A**
> I love Italian.

He's not even slightly nervous, but I am here sweating with the thought of telling them.

> **ME**
> They won't be expecting you is all.

> **A**
> A man?

> **ME**
> No *you*. The mysterious and rather intimidating town fire chief.

> **A**
> It will be fine, Liv.

> **A**
> Just tell me what time and I'll be there.

I close out his chat and pull up my mom's, chewing my bottom lip as I type. Once I send this text, there is no going back.

> **ME**
> Dolcetto's it is.

> **ME**
> Also don't freak out or make a big deal. But I'm bringing someone.

"*Fuckity, fuck fuck!*" I bite out after I send the message and stare at the ultrasound photo.

There's no going back now. It's time to tell my parents they're about to level up to grandparents.

CHAPTER 29
Asher

Growing up, I had no idea what I'd be exposed to at any given time. Like the Christmas morning my father came home from a brawl, coked up, and passed out on the living room floor, but not before taking the whole tree down with him. Or the time I was playing hide-and-seek with my cousins at my uncle's deli only to realize someone was tied up in the back room, beaten so badly that their face was unrecognizable. Or the time I found a severed finger under the workbench in our garage when I went out there to work on my brand-new bike at the ripe age of twelve.

Looking back, I'm pretty sure I learned to harden from as soon as I could register those memories. I always had to be on high alert, to remain in fight or flight. And when I wasn't, everything felt off. I started to *need* the chaos to feel normal.

Which is why I'm feeling on guard tonight as I get ready to take Olivia to dinner with her parents. It could also be partly because the other night I spontaneously decided to tell her more about my past than I had ever intended to.

I just couldn't stop myself when I could see her thinking I

didn't want to kiss her, didn't want to touch her, when the truth is I've thought of nothing else. But I needed her to know I was only denying anything between us because I would never want to hurt her. My darkness haunts me and I won't let it haunt her too.

Even though I was able to open up to her, I couldn't tell her everything. The full truth was on the tip of my tongue, but when I saw the horror in Liv's eyes when I told her about prison, I froze and decided to tell her only what I thought she could handle. And I'm not sure she could handle me being the heir to the largest organized crime ring between Boston and New York. Not yet at least.

Though I'll admit, even telling her the little I did feels like a weight off of my chest.

I turn up "1800 Miles" by Colter Wall on my Bluetooth speaker as I change my shirt for the third damn time, and I spend a little time making sure my hair sits just right. I don't remember the last time I gave a fuck about my appearance, but I want this to go well. Olivia cares a lot about what her parents think, so that makes *me* care what her parents think.

Shutting my speaker off and making my way down the steps of my house, I head to the workshop carrying two containers of food. I feed Duke a whole food diet, no store-bought bullshit, and tonight it's ground beef, green beans, and sweet potato. He's already waiting as I open the door, his tail wagging nonstop when he sees me.

Dick peers out from behind my workbench. He usually avoids me, but when I have food it's a different story. And while I don't like cats, I'm not gonna see him starve. Plus, I guess he gives Duke a friend.

Pulling out the second container, I add a scoop of raw pumpkin to a smaller dish and set it down.

"Don't get used to it, fucker." I grimace, sliding the dish over to Dick. He gets his back up at the sound of my voice before hissing at me. "Baby steps then, I guess, ya horse's arse?"

We still aren't friends, and Dick knows it, but he sniffs around the pumpkin and starts to eat it anyway.

I turn to make my way out of the barn, heading for my truck, as I think about Olivia, imagining the happy smile she'd offer if she knew I fed the damn cat. I may tell her, just to give her something else to focus on other than her parents, me, and the baby. I'm learning quickly that, when she can't plan something or control something, she panic talks. Nonstop. About anything and everything. The fear of telling her more details about my old life hits me even harder when I realize *everything* about my family, my past is chaos.

I push that thought away as I drive. In my mind, I'm already halfway through all the things I can say to her to help her relax. I tell myself that's the normal, supportive thing to do, and I've almost got myself convinced my thoughts are strictly chivalrous. That is, until I pull up to her cabin.

Olivia's already waiting, standing on her porch in a short, off-the-shoulder pink dress. It's pretty from the front, of course, but when she turns to make sure the door is pulled tightly closed and I see the low back tied at the top in a big exaggerated bow, it hits me that she looks like a wrapped present. One I'm almost desperate to claim for myself. Her hair blows in the summer breeze as she holds a platter of freshly baked cupcakes. *Goddamn*, no matter how many times I tell myself she deserves the kind of man she says she wants, or that I shouldn't try to keep her, I already know I'm quickly becoming fucking *obsessed* with the mother of my child.

CHAPTER 30
Olivia

I shift the container of red velvet cupcakes in my lap as we drive through Laurel Creek to my childhood home. I didn't really have time to bake today, but my mom loves red velvet and when I get nervous I bake.

We're having dinner in town but, since I never bring men home, my parents want us to meet them at their house so we can all leave together for the restaurant.

As their neighborhood comes into view, nostalgia settles within me and happy memories of me learning to ride my bike—during summer nights just like this—make my heart squeeze. When we turn onto my parents' street, Asher whistles. "This is beautiful."

He takes in the canopy of trees that meet in the middle over the long street. Large, stately homes sit back on their properties; many of them boast winding driveways, beautiful lawns, and manicured gardens. It's not the wealthiest part of town—that's where Ginger grew up—but it's close. Safe and quiet.

"My parents have owned this house since the street was new in the early nineties. Back then this was an average-priced home for two working-class people."

Asher nods as he watches a mom push a baby stroller along the road. She walks behind another child trundling along on his tricycle. He can't be more than three.

"No going back now," I mutter under my breath as Asher pulls into my parents' driveway and cuts the engine. He turns to face me, and the way he's looking at me now is the same way he looked at me when he pulled up to my cabin twenty minutes ago. Heated, and I'm having a hard time fitting it into this "friends only" pact we've made.

It doesn't help that he looks absolutely incredible. He's usually in jeans and black T-shirts, or sometimes in his uniform, so when I see the effort he made to share this news with my parents, it takes my damn breath away. His white fitted button-down hugs his body in all the right places, and he's paired it with navy chinos, a brown belt, and brown boots.

I nervously suck in a breath because the flash of the curtain in the front window tells me my parents already know we're here. I move to unbuckle my seatbelt, but Asher stops me, taking my hand in his own, his presence as ominous and commanding as ever.

"You and me here. Yeah?" He squeezes lightly.

I nod and swallow down my anxiety. "Yeah."

God, I fucking hope so.

"What a nice surprise," my mother says with a happy, yet clearly confused, tone as she opens the door to me with Asher.

"Nice to see you again, Chief Reed," my father says, extending his hand for shaking.

Asher takes it and pumps it firmly. "Please call me Asher. It's good to see you too, sir. This time in better circumstances."

"Now, that is true." My father chuckles. His white hair is shorter than when I last saw him and I know my mother made him get a haircut, which means she also had no idea what to expect when I said I was bringing someone.

"These are for you, Mrs. Sutton." Asher's voice is low and full of gravel as he hands my mom a beautiful bunch of lavender and wildflowers from the fields at his house.

"Lynn and Ken, please," she insists. "And thank you. These are gorgeous."

"I'm glad you think so," Asher tells her. "They're from the fields that surround my home."

His affluent, albeit horrendous, upbringing is front and center of my mind as he speaks. It's obvious that he knows how to turn on the charm—despite his usual brooding manner—and I find myself wanting to unravel the mystery that is Asher Reed even more.

"Oh, even more lovely," my mom says, disappearing into the house for a moment to put the flowers in water.

An awkward moment of silence hangs between us when my mom returns, and my parents look at me. They have no idea why Laurel Creek's fire chief is in their foyer.

"Okay, well, now that we're all on a first-name basis," I say nervously, turning to set the cupcakes on the entry table. In my haste, my heel catches on the rug and I almost fall. Panic hits my chest as Asher's strong arms steady me and I manage to keep my cupcakes upright. No one says anything as I blow my hair out of my face and look up to the ceiling.

"You have no idea how often I have to do that," Asher jokes, and my parents laugh.

"I had stocks in Band-Aid Corporation while Olivia was growing up," my mom adds, taking the container of treats from me. Everyone chuckles as I blush pink.

"Glad my clumsiness could help break the ice." I shrug. Maybe Asher's right and I do need that bubble wrap after all?

"Well, on that note, let me just pop these here." She sets the cupcakes down on the table that I had been aiming for. "We can have them for dessert. Shall we go?"

My mom tucks her arm into mine, leaving Asher with my father as we head down the driveway. I glance back over my shoulder at him and he winks in reassurance. I hope he's ready for Lynn and Ken.

Dolcetto's Ristorante is bustling—just as one would expect for a balmy summer night—as we're seated on the patio shaded from the last of the day's sun. On the way here, Asher spoke to my father about the custom cherry banister and staircase in our family home. The woodworking in my parents' house is my dad's pride and joy, so it doesn't surprise me that they're already off to a good conversational start by the time we take our seats. My dad suggests that he and Asher head up to the massive bar area in the restaurant to view the craft beer on offer.

I look around in a bid to settle my nerves; I already felt the nosey eyes of at least two people I went to high school with when I entered the building with Chief Asher Reed.

"He's hunky," my mom says with a little shimmy when we're alone.

"*Mother*." I laugh.

"Well, he is. I never had a thing for tattoos, but I must say—"

"The food smells so good in here, doesn't it?" I interject to keep my mother from reminding me how hot the man is. I definitely don't need *that* reminder. She laughs as I survey the space again. It's a really pretty setting; most of the walls boast rustic exposed brick, and twinkling string lights decorate the charming patio we're sitting on. Dolcetto's is Laurel Creek's number one first-date spot.

"I wish you would've told me this was the official 'meet the parents' dinner." My mother winks at me before she picks up the menu. "I would've been more prepared."

My father's deep guffaw from the bar makes us both pause, and with it a low chuckle from Asher. I watch him for a moment. The smile he wears as he chats to my dad like they're old friends is something I wouldn't have been able to dream up a few months ago. I have to remind myself this is Asher. The man I've felt drawn to, but have also been slightly afraid of, for over two years.

Turning back to my mom, I want to correct her and say this isn't a "meet the parents" dinner. But for fear of getting into a "what the hell is he doing here then" conversation before I'm ready, I decide not to say anything as my father heads back over to us, leaving Asher at the bar. I take the opportunity to sneak a glance at him. He's looking down at his phone, silencing it with a grimace, and I wonder briefly who could make him look even more irritated than normal.

"I'll just grab our drinks at the bar, Lynnie," my dad says now, leaning down to kiss my mom's cheek. "We can get the next ones with dinner."

My parents' love is enviable after over thirty years.

"Asher likes the good stuff." My dad hikes a thumb over his shoulder. "We're gonna get a Brown Bourbon Ale. What do you two want?"

My mother looks up at me with a smile.

"California red?" she asks. This is something we always order when we're together, but the thought of it now turns my stomach.

When I shrug and say "I'm gonna just stick to sparkling water tonight," my parents both look at me suspiciously.

"Are you feeling okay?" my mother asks, worried. The people at the table next to us glance over at the tone of her voice.

"Yes, Mom, I'm fine. I just don't want any wine tonight," I reply as quietly as I can.

"Not even a tiny bit? For tradition's sake?"

"I'm not having any . . ." I stammer. "I *can't* . . ."

"*Can't?*" she asks way too loudly. All her attention is on me, and I can all but see her spidey senses tingling. "Why can't you—?"

Her eyes drop to my stomach, then back up to my face. *Fuck*.

"Oh my gosh!" Her hands fly to her mouth as she gasps. "Olivia Renee Sutton!" She whisper-yells, though not quietly enough. The people next to us glance at us again, as well as one of those girls I went to school with.

This is my nightmare.

My father says nothing, and he doesn't look as happy as my mom.

"You're pregnant?" His voice has an edge to it, as he looks toward the bar where Asher is still standing. The silence between us while they wait for my answer is deafening.

"How long have you even known each other? Are you in love?" he asks hopefully.

"I mean . . . this wasn't planned," I mutter as Sandy from the Sage and Salt pats my dad on the shoulder on her way to take a seat two tables over.

My mother starts to giggle, and it's a weird, excited sound that makes even more people look at us.

But my eyes don't leave my dad's as my heart squeezes in my chest for him. Something I wasn't prepared for in all my planning for tonight was seeing all the dreams he's talked about with me die in his eyes at the thought of this pregnancy being some sort of frivolous mistake. A result from a one-night hookup. My dad is seventy years old and very traditional, especially where I'm concerned. He's talked about walking me down the aisle so many times, and daydreamed about the day I tell him he's going to be a grandpa.

I freeze, panicking as I sit here by myself, with no sound, reasonable mind to stop me.

I look my mother then my father straight in the eyes and smile. "Yes, of course we're in love."

I see my father instantly relax, and his eyes fill with something new. Happiness.

"I'm going to be a grandpa?" he asks.

I nod, a tight smile on my face.

"Well, then I guess we've got some things to celebrate, don't we?!" he says.

"We didn't mean to. I mean we weren't expecting . . ." I start.

"Oh, honey, we're not prudes. We know what it's like to be young." My mom stands and comes around to my side of the table. She clings to me, so I don't even have time to take it back and tell them the truth, nor do I have the guts to. "The main thing is that you have someone to share it with and you're in love. Oh, this is wonderful! We have to congratulate the father-to-be."

Oh God.

My mother doesn't let go as my father makes his way over to Asher, and I realize after he hands my dad his beer that my dad has just congratulated him. His eyes meet mine and I really, really hope he'll go along with my lie, at least until I can figure out another answer that won't break my father's heart.

CHAPTER 31
Olivia

My dad returns with Asher just as my mom releases me and makes a beeline straight for him.

I cradle my head in my hands; I already know this gossip will be all over town tomorrow. The others in here may not have heard that we're having a baby, but they will know we were out for dinner to celebrate something with my parents. What else is gossiped about will depend on what the lady sitting next to me heard. I cast another glance at her and realize she's come into my store in the past. Fuck. It's true: Everyone knows someone in Laurel Creek.

"I didn't know when I went to get us this beer that I'd be toasting my first grandchild!" my father says to us now with a genuine, easy smile.

Asher's eyes flit to mine in question as he sits. I plead with him silently, hoping he'll understand the look on my face.

"Come on, Lynnie, a toast!" my dad continues. My mom is wearing the world's biggest smile; her cheeks are flushed as she clutches the glass of red my father brought her and nudges my lemon water to me.

"A mocktail," she whispers. Asher's eyes never leave mine, and he's clearly wondering what the fuck just happened.

"To expanding our family and welcoming this new baby," my father says, raising his glass. Okay *that* was loud.

Asher raises his beer cautiously and smiles at them. I am settled slightly as he graciously takes a sip.

"And to the two of you falling in love," my dad adds just as Asher is mid-drink, causing him to nearly choke on it, though he recovers quickly.

"Let's order so we can eat. It smells delicious." He rubs his hands together.

"And then we can go home and talk more about all the specifics over dessert!" my mother adds animatedly before turning to Asher. "And we'll have to get to know your parents, of course!"

"Unfortunately, my parents are no longer with us," Asher answers. "But I can say, without a doubt, that my mother would've loved to be a grandmother."

There's a truth in his eyes when he speaks of his mother that makes my chest tighten. I don't understand his loss really—because I don't remember my birth mother—but I can imagine how it would feel to lose the mom sitting next to me, and the thought is gut-wrenching.

"So sorry to hear that, honey. But let me be the first to say, welcome to our family." My mother reaches her hand out to pat his. Oh shit. This is *not* what he signed up for.

CHAPTER 32
Asher

Well, well, well.

Miss "I Have a Plan for Everything" is totally fucking winging it, and when she made that conscious choice to lie to her parents, it was like a switch flipped for me. I should be given an Academy Award for holding it together when her father said we're in love, because now Olivia's gone and done it. The battle that wages in me constantly settled out completely when I realized Olivia had made the decision to put us in this false relationship, and now there's no going back.

She watches me cautiously—she has no idea I'm on board with this plan—but her expression feels like I'm her anchor in this storm. Which is exactly what breaks through my carefully crafted armor.

Sitting across from her parents, I brace myself for the twenty questions Olivia warned me would follow as we eat. I can't say for sure, but I'm guessing she couldn't bring herself to tell her mom and dad, the epitome of old-fashioned tradition, the truth about our situation. Not to mention every local in the place has their eyes on us right now.

"So, Asher, Olivia's place is in shambles right now. Is your home in town?" Ken asks me in friendly conversation. I look at Olivia; her eyes are pleading, her cheeks rosy. She's told her parents we're in love. And wouldn't that mean that the best place for the woman I *love* and our child to stay is in my home, with me?

The answer isn't even a fight.

"We can make a nice home at my place." I pop a bite of this damn good lasagna into my mouth as I feel nails dig into my thigh. "I have a good chunk of land just on the outskirts of town, plenty of room inside and out." I grunt under my breath to stop myself from wincing as Olivia squeezes harder.

"We didn't decide on that a hundred percent yet, remember?" Olivia hisses. I turn to face her as I swallow.

"I remember, *kitten.*" Now I'm just fucking with her. But I don't miss the way her mouth falls open when I call her the nickname that suits her to a fucking T. "My house really is the safest place for you and the baby."

"Did you hear that, Ken? *Kitten?*" Lynne gushes. "Oh . . . our baby's in love."

Olivia and I keep our eyes locked on each other, and I smirk. The lady on the other side of Liv appears to be leaning in, listening for gossip. So I double down.

"All that land to roam, fresh air, Duke to protect you when I'm at work. You were just saying how peaceful it is."

"Well, that sounds lovely," Ken pipes up. "Who's Duke?"

"He's my cane corso, my best friend, and he's tough as hell." I pull my phone out and show Ken a photo.

"Ah, nice-looking dog. You can tell a lot about a man by his choice of pet."

"You have Dick too," Olivia blurts out. Her mother's mouth falls open and the lady next to them drops her fork. I try to swallow my smirk.

"Excuse me?" Ken says, looking between us as Olivia turns a bright shade of pink.

"His *cat* . . . Dick," she tells them.

"The barn cat," I correct.

"Yes, *darling*. But remember you said he can come inside the house more since it's so hot out lately?" She cocks her head and gives me a "fuck you" with her eyes. Now *she's* playing hardball, but Christ if I don't want to kiss the fuck out of her right now.

"Hmm, I don't remember that." I take another bite and address her parents. "Olivia has taken a liking to him. He just showed up on my property a few months ago. But, for the record, he *is* a dick."

"Cats aren't my animal either." Ken chuckles as I side-eye Olivia. "But what Olivia wants . . . she usually gets. And your place sounds like the perfect space to start a family."

"I couldn't agree more." I turn to Olivia with a wide grin, feeling way too amused by all of this. I *like* the idea of her moving in way too much for our friendly pact, but I'm not backing down now.

"Right?" I coax.

"I suppose it is," Olivia grits out through clenched teeth as I feel her hand slide a little higher up my thigh and squeeze the muscle. Hard.

Definitely don't hate that. I reach my hand under the table and pat hers.

I push the warning voice in my head aside—because I'm quickly losing my will to fight—and Olivia just keeps on stumbling into my corner even when I try to keep her at arm's length.

We spend the rest of the dinner answering all their questions: when the baby's due, what each of us think the sex is. We talk about Olivia's reno and my job, and by the time we're done Olivia seems more relaxed, especially when she sees how happy and supportive her parents are about our "we're a couple" ruse.

I'm sure it's a huge load off her shoulders that I'm in her parents' good books already. They're a little tipsy by the end of the night, telling us stories about when Olivia was young, and I watch her blush as her parents talk about her childhood. The slow, steady creep of pink that moves up her throat reminds me of other scenarios, which has me gripping the table to stop myself from reaching out and grabbing her.

I haven't even finished my first beer, but I'm almost drunk on Olivia as she talks. Her closeness with her parents makes it clear why she cares so much about what they think, and for the first time in my life, a flash of *want* courses through me. I want to sit at a table with my son or daughter in thirty years and talk about their childhood. But the voice in my head stops that dream in its tracks: Men in my family don't get that lucky.

The stories continue as we drive them home, and when we sit down to eat Olivia's red velvet cupcakes, which are bakery-worthy delicious. Her parents tell me about how Olivia always had a wild imagination and could be found out in the yard with the boys from the neighborhood, leaving the girls behind as she chased butterflies, or climbed trees, in only her bare feet. Then they tell me about her teenage years, when she fell in love with sewing and making clothing from old sheets or, once, from a set of curtains.

By the end of the night, we've even settled on a four-way wager about the sex of the baby. Ken is with me and thinks we're having a girl—he says he's always imagined he'd have a granddaughter—and Lynn is with Olivia in thinking the baby is a boy. Everything is easy, happy, and full, and as we ready to say our goodbyes, I'm in an odd state of acceptance.

I have no right to want Olivia. And she wants to keep things platonic and uncomplicated for the child she's growing. But, despite knowing all of that, as I sit here breathing, I know my home is *exactly* where Olivia and our baby belong.

CHAPTER 33
Olivia

"Well, you certainly won them over, didn't you?" I ask, not looking at Asher as we drive through the dark countryside. In this light the massive rolling hills along the highway are intrusive but beautiful, and the moon is high in the sky. I'm full, and relieved that this is out in the open, but also feeling so guilty for lying to my parents.

But I'm also surprised. I didn't expect Asher to fit in so easily with my parents, or to go along with my lie. I didn't think he'd have me move in with him, but I don't hate the idea either. And if I didn't know any better, I'd say he really seems to think us living together as friends will actually work. Right now, I need Asher Reed. I need to feel settled in at least one space in my life because everything feels as though it's spinning out of control.

"You didn't really give me a choice," his low voice taunts with obvious amusement.

"Look, I don't like lying to them. But I just couldn't break my dad's heart. I couldn't bear to tell him his first grandchild is the result of a one-night stand."

Asher remains silent, so I keep rambling. "We're going to have to tell our friends we're moving in together and make it clear this is a co-parent thing only. CeCe and Ginger know my parents, so they'll understand why, but I'll have to tell them tomorrow."

The truth of it is, after that dinner, I'm sure half the town will know I'm pregnant by the end of the week. I have no idea how we're getting out of that after the baby comes, or at least until my own house is complete.

"We can't control town gossip," Asher says, matter-of-fact. *How is he so calm?*

"I just—" I pause for a moment, searching for the right words, feeling the need to explain my harebrained behavior. "I'm sorry I put you on the spot. But I want to give our baby the family I lost, and the gift that is the family I was lucky enough to be raised by. I know we can't continue this charade forever, but maybe just until we can figure out the next step. I mean, how is it *actually* gonna work for us to live together? What happens when you meet someone one day? Or I do? I'm still getting matches on my dating app, for God's sake."

"Christ, woman." Asher cuts the engine when he pulls up to my cabin at Silver Pines. He turns to face me. "I don't like people in general. Maybe three or four, and my dog. That's it."

His eyes meet mine and he slides closer across the bench seat of his truck, his gorgeous face now just inches away.

"And I definitely don't connect with anyone easily. But *we're* connected now."

Even though it's hard for him to tell me this, I can see how important it is to him that I understand. This man has likely never experienced the support that he's so freely offering to me.

The continual stroke of his thumb creeps up to my wrist, sending goosebumps over my flesh, and I can't look away. I feel like his gaze is home to a deeper longing too. Though that's probably just the hopeless romantic in me begging to see what's not there.

"And about either of us meeting someone else . . ." He looks down to my wrist, probably feeling my heart stutter out. "The *only* thing I'm focused on right now is you and the baby. And I can pretend to be in a relationship with you for your parents' sake too. Though I have some conditions."

"Conditions?" I ask meekly.

"Yes. A change to the pact." Asher's eyes flick back to hold mine. "Due to the change in . . . circumstance."

I swallow down the lump in my throat and nod. "Okay . . . like what?"

"If you need something, Olivia, from here on out, you come to me." His jaw is so tense it looks like he's about to pop a tendon. His dark eyes are bottomless as they drink me in. "There will be no other man for you while you live in my house. *Or* while you carry my baby."

The pad of his thumb continues to trace lazily along the inside of my wrist. "If you're hungry, I'll cook. Thirsty? I'll bring you water."

Asher's pupils are blown wide as he inches even closer, and his big hand slides up to hold my face before his fingers settle through my hair.

"If you need a man to touch you"—his eyes drop to my lips—"you understand, that man is *me*."

I nod, unable to speak.

"And it's time to delete that fucking app, is that clear?"

I swear my heart is about to beat out of my chest. The way he's looking at me is all-consuming and, as he removes his hand, my body begs for its return.

"Yes," I manage.

"Good girl." His voice is gravel as he leans in and kisses my cheek so unexpectedly it takes my breath away. I almost melt at the touch, and I swear I hear him groan against my skin before he pulls away.

"Now get some sleep. Tomorrow I'm moving you both in with me."

Asher moves back across his seat to exit the truck, but I don't move. I'm a puddle for this man who I'm getting to know more and more with each day. Asher is fucking enticing, sweet, and hot as *hell*. Even the danger he knew in his old life, the unknown that lingers in the background, turns me on. Hell, I think that little bit of danger might just be what I've been searching for this whole time.

When I'm safely inside my cabin, I watch through the window as Asher backs out of the driveway. It's only when his headlights have disappeared that I finally feel as though I can breathe again.

Padding through the house, I fold some laundry and start to pack a bag of essentials to take to his home tomorrow before hopping in the shower. I take my time as I lather soap over my body and wash my hair; thoughts of his lips on my cheek flood my brain as I will myself not to fall for this man, to remember what we are to each other.

I could lose Asher to his old life, to his job, or to another woman when the novelty of this situation wears off and the reality of being a parent hits. But I don't have a choice: I have to trust him.

I'm still thinking about this situation we've gotten ourselves into when I step out and dry myself off. So much so, my brain almost doesn't register when I look down to my bathmat and notice something I know I'm not supposed to see for at least another seven months.

Blood.

CHAPTER 34
Asher

> P
> He doesn't have long now.

> P
> I didn't say goodbye to my father, and I've always regretted it. I don't want that same fate for you. And there's a lot to go over. Everything will change once he's gone.

Pete's father, my grandfather, was a man I don't remember much—he died when I was young—but from everything I know about him, he was more like Pete. Which means there's a big fucking difference between his father and mine.

> ME
> My father is not like yours was.

> **ME**
> And I can assure you, I have nothing to say. That won't change.

> **P**
> I think you'll regret that, son. But regardless, we need to talk.

> **P**
> In person.

It may seem cold or callous, but I have no desire to see or speak to my father, and I know that's not what is important to Pete anyway. This is how my family works. Pete needs me for business, especially if my dad is on death's door, and having me come home will just create a crack he can slink through. But I'm not fucking having it.

Duke is snoozing in his usual seat when I grab a towel and head for the shower. But as I do, my phone starts buzzing on the table beside me. It's a New York area code. *Pete.* Fuck it, I'm done fucking around with him.

"You need to stop calling me," I half growl into the phone.

I know he won't say too much over the phone; his line is probably bugged by at least one government agency.

"Long time no chat, son." The old country accent is much thicker in his voice than mine. He came from Ireland two years after we did.

"Aye, for good reason."

"It's time to let bygones be bygones, and there are some issues we need to discuss."

I'm done speaking in tongues. "My father has had his funeral planned since I was a child. I won't be coming back. I have nothing to say to him."

"You know what happens when there's much to be said and

one party doesn't cooperate?" my uncle asks me.

"Yeah, I fuckin' do."

I can picture exactly what happens a hundred times over thanks to the man rotting in New York.

"You have a good night, son."

Pete hangs up after muttering those words, but they're all I need to hear. He's telling me he'll come looking for me. Normally I wouldn't give a fuck. I've hidden from them this entire time. Shit, even my home is owned by a numbered company rather than me. But if he comes looking now, he might find Olivia and the baby too. Over my dead body will the dark shadow of my father come anywhere near the only good sliver of light in my life.

I haven't hurt a man in a long time. But I fear if my uncle takes this any further, if he ever finds me, I won't just hurt him, I'll put him in the fucking ground.

My rage has barely subsided when my phone rings again, but when I see Olivia's name, my chest tightens with the thought of talking to her again before tomorrow. I couldn't stay in the cab of my truck one second longer or I would've kissed her senseless, and I really don't know if I would've had the strength to stop.

"Yes, you can bring the cow slippers," I say gruffly into the phone.

"Asher?"

I sit up straighter on my sofa, immediately on high alert at the tone of her voice.

"Can you, um . . . I'm sorry, I know you haven't been home long . . . I just—"

"Olivia, what is it?"

"I'm bleeding and I don't know why."

It feels like all the blood drains from my face, but I'm already grabbing my keys and blasting through the front door before she can say another word.

"I'm on my way."

The hour-long wait in the ER while Olivia is taken back with the triage doctor is the longest of my life. I can't sit, so I pace and read pamphlets on the bulletin boards, though all I can think about is Olivia and the baby.

I never expected this twist in life, but the sorrow in my gut at the thought of anything happening to the baby now is unbearable. I'm just about to reread the same hearing aid brochure when I see her emerge. She's in a pair of black yoga tights and an oversized WKU hoodie. Her hair is loose and wild. I know she let it air-dry so it's full of waves and curls and there isn't a stitch of makeup on her face. She looks so beautiful. It's fucking killing me.

"Sorry to make a whole big thing about this."

"What did they say?" I ask cautiously, my heart beating erratically.

"The doctor said it was just minor spotting, probably from my physical the other day. Everything is good, but he said, um, that it might be best not to have sex until I'm through my first trimester . . . although orgasms are fine if I . . . feel the need, on my own that is." She looks down at her clutched hands in front of her, blushing furiously for panic rambling. As usual.

"Not that you needed to know that or anything—" Her cheeks turn a deeper shade of red. "Sorry, *shit* . . ."

"*Olivia*," I stop her.

"Oh." Her eyes widen as the lightbulb goes off. "The baby is perfectly healthy and the heartbeat is really strong—"

"*Fuck*." My chest tightens and I don't even let her finish her sentence before I pull her into my arms. I can't control my body's reaction as I kiss the top of her head, then her cheek, sliding my hands up to cradle her face. "Thank Christ."

Olivia's eyes glisten and I don't care where we are, or who's watching, as my lips press to hers. Softly and slowly once, twice, and then again when she doesn't pull away. Everything that grounds me floats upward in this moment as I breathe her in. It's like I have no control over my own actions, and I swear my fucking soul leaves my body when I'm this close to her. Just the feel of her lips on mine threatens to ruin me, and it has me lingering for just a second longer than I should before I pull her into my chest again. She whimpers and it almost breaks me as I slide my hand down to her belly and over the life we made together.

"Our baby is a little bear then, after all. A little fighter," I speak firmly into her hair.

"Seems like it," Olivia whispers back. "I have to be careful for the next couple of days. Stay hydrated. And no physical exertion, though the doctor said it was probably just an isolated issue. She also said stress doesn't help and that's something I've seen my fair share of over the last few months."

"Not anymore," I tell her as I take her hand, and we make our way down the long hallway and through the hospital doors. The walk to my truck is quick since we're parked right at the emergency entrance.

"All that stress . . ." I tell her as I open her door and help her up, placing my hand on her thigh. "You're gonna give it all to me. Understand?"

I reach for the seatbelt and she takes it from me with a pretty smile playing on her full lips. "I can buckle my own seatbelt, Asher," she laughs, grabbing my arm gently. "We're okay. I promise."

I watch her face in the moonlight as I stare down at her, my mind already made up. "I want you to come home with me now—"

"Okay," she says gently.

"Fuck, I expected you to argue." I reach down and squeeze her hand in her lap. "I had reasons ready to go."

Olivia tucks her hair behind her ear. "I don't need them. If it was ever gonna get worse, I'd rather be with you."

As she looks up at me with those pretty blue eyes, all I can see is the man *she* sees in me. The man she feels safe relying on. It sends both a thud to my heart and a deep pang of fear coursing through my blood. Not because I don't think she'll be safe with me, because I'll do everything in my power to make damned sure she is. The devil himself wouldn't get past me if he came for Olivia or our child.

When she looks at me like this I *want* to be the man she thinks I am, but caring about anything or anyone that much when I know how fast life can take it away terrifies the living shit out of me—and I don't get scared.

"My house it is," I say as I close her door, making my way to the driver's side of the truck.

She turns to me as I settle into the seat beside her. "But I really do want to let the cat into the house."

I let out a small laugh as I start the engine.

"Gotta shoot my shot." She grins. I reach into the center and cover her hand with mine, feeling those last threads of control I'm clinging to slipping through my fingers faster than I can even think of grasping them.

CHAPTER 35
Asher

My property is dark, aside from the lightning bugs that decorate my garden, when we pull up, and Duke is at our side the moment we come into the house. I'm sure he could tell I was stressed the fuck out when I left in a hurry earlier.

I crouch down to greet him and give him some love but the fucked-up thing is he doesn't even seem to care about me. Instead, Duke goes straight to Olivia, sniffing her and brushing up against her leg with a whimper. She gets down to her knees and rubs him behind the ears.

"Uh huh. I get it," I tell him as I toss my keys into the basket on my table. "Y'only met her once, but the pretty girl comes home and I'm chopped liver."

I pull open the fridge to grab two waters. "I just feed you . . . take care of you . . ."

"I think if you *were* chopped liver, he'd be paying more attention to you than me." Olivia flashes me a grin as she nuzzles him.

Duke is extremely smart, as most cane corsos are, and it

hits me as I watch them together that he probably senses she's pregnant. It could even be part of the reason why he instantly took a liking to her when she came here the first time. I pass Liv a water and she stands to take it from me.

"Come on, you must be wrecked," I say. "I'll show you my room."

"Oh . . . I can just sleep here." She gestures to the overstuffed leather sofa in my living room. "It looks really cozy."

"Fuck no." My voice is almost a rumble. "Non-negotiable."

She must know I mean it because she nods before giving Duke a final pat and turning to follow me through the house. My dog doesn't want to let her go and follows close to her heel. I push my bedroom door open and give her the tour; as if I would ever let her sleep on my sofa while I slept in my California king like a total fucking asshole. It makes me wonder exactly how men she's been with in the past have treated her.

She looks around and smiles, shaking her head.

"What?" I ask her, setting her bag down on my bed.

"Nothing, I just . . . you have a Himalayan salt lamp . . . which is not what I expected when I met you is all."

I look around my room, viewing it through her eyes. The entire wall behind my bed is black-stained wood and, above it, is a laser-cut, multifaceted deer head made out of rare bird's-eye maple. My bed takes up a lot of the center space and is covered in thick, white bedding. I don't sleep well, so I sourced the most comfortable material I could find to get the most out of what little sleep I do get. Floating shelves keep the space clean on either side of the bed, and a nine-foot patio door looks out onto my deck and the woods beyond.

"This will do then?" I ask her, patting my bed. She could never know she's the first woman to ever see this space.

Olivia kicks her sandals off, stuffing her hands in the pocket of her big hoodie and wiggling her toes in the thick shag area rug.

"Mmmm..." she moans, her eyes fluttering closed, and the sound forces my cock to jump to attention, especially when she adds a throaty little "Yes, so good."

I don't know how I'm going to survive this pact with her in my space. Every single thing this woman does seems to turn me on.

In a bid to distract myself, I show Liv the attached bathroom—including where the soaps and shampoos live—and open an empty drawer for her to house her own things. When we're done, we move back to my room and I hand her the remote control, showing her how to work the TV.

"I have streaming services but no cable," I tell her.

"Perfect, I pretty much live off Netflix." She takes another look around then brings her eyes back to mine. "If I'm going to be staying here, you'll probably be watching a lot of Netflix too."

I look at her questioningly.

"Rom-com-athons mostly," she continues, as if I have the slightest clue what that is.

"The fuck is a rom-com-athon?"

She smiles at me like she knows something I don't, though I'm sure as fuck I will find out soon enough. I expect a witty little retort but, instead, her blue eyes turn soft as she studies me.

"Thank you, Asher."

I let myself stare at her. She's so beautiful right now, not a stitch of makeup on her pretty face. I understand exactly what she's saying; she didn't want to be alone, she was scared tonight, and just knowing I could offer her a safe space to land makes me remember Nash's words: *Just do everything you can to take as much off her plate as possible.*

I brush a little copper curl from her forehead, letting the pads of my first two fingers trail down her cheek.

"It's what I'm here for, Livi girl."

She leans in, her eyes turning playful, that sugary scent stunning me.

"Don't you mean *kitten*?" she practically purrs.

It's meant to be a joke—throwing the nickname I gave her on a whim back at me—but instead, with how close she's standing and the soft rasp of her voice, the air between us turns electric when my gaze drops to her mouth. I can't fucking help but look at her juicy goddamn lips. I swallow as they curve upward, then she starts laughing. "How did you even come up with that?" She pushes my shoulder playfully, oblivious to the fact that my cock is stiffening by the second.

"Easy." I muss her hair just to get some much-needed distance. "I've decided you *were* a fuckin' cat in another life."

"Is that so?" Her eyebrow shoots up. Even that is fucking sexy as hell.

"You keep to yourself. You're always snacking and knocking things over. Yet, for some goddamn reason, you always manage to land on your feet." I lean in closer. "Plus, I don't know about most cats, but Dick has really long toes. Seemed like the easiest correlation."

"All right, that's it, Reed." Olivia pushes her red hair off her shoulder and puts one hand on her hip. With the other, she makes a come-hither motion. "Let's see your feet."

"I don't want to make your feet feel bad. Because mine are perfect, in every possible way."

She scoffs. "No man has nice-looking feet."

"I do," I counter.

"Are you gonna make me throw down some cash for the privilege of seeing them?" Olivia glances down, and I'm happy that she's distracted from what happened tonight. "Come on, off with the socks."

Rising to the challenge, I pull off each of my socks—slowly, like a little striptease—before tossing them into the hamper in the corner of my room.

She takes her bottom lip between her teeth as she looks down at my perfectly shaped, model-worthy size thirteens and mutters the cutest little "fuck sakes" under her breath before she looks away.

"You were saying?" I gloat, folding my arms over my chest, feeling light and I think even happy for the first time I can remember.

Olivia narrows those baby blues at me. "You get pedicures."

"*Fuck* no." I scoff into a laugh, then shrug. "Just naturally perfect. It's my superpower."

She pushes past me in a huff of defeat. I can't help it as I tip my head back and laugh without any hesitation. Goddamn it feels good. *Too* good.

"Jealousy isn't your strong suit," I offer as she heads to her bag of belongings on my bed. I reach out to grasp her arm, pulling her close to my chest. I'm flying through the gates of hell straight on now by keeping her here, which means there's not a chance on earth she's living in my home and I'm not touching her. I kiss her forehead, pushing the limits of our own boundaries, but she doesn't protest.

"Your feet are beautiful, Liv, just like the rest of you. I'll love our little bear even if he or she gets your toes."

Our.

That twisting feeling in my chest is back suddenly, but so is her fist pounding against me playfully.

"Jackass," she mutters. But I saw it, if only for a moment. The same heat in her eyes as I harbor in mine. The air stills and the crickets outside grow louder as our laughter putters out. The pull to her is so strong I could really use that safe word I told her I didn't need right about now.

"All right, well, I'll leave you to it." I back up. "I'm gonna hop in the shower, but I'll check on you when I'm through."

Because I want to see you again before I sleep.

"Okay," she says. "I'm just gonna put on a girly movie and

try to get some sleep."

I bow out, grabbing my toiletries and heading to the guest bathroom upstairs, where I stand and soak in the hot water for a good, long time.

I let myself think of those perfect curves just a floor below, of every single time she's touched me. The jolt of electricity that shot up my leg when she gripped my thigh under the table at dinner. The way my body begged for more as her nails dug in, and how I imagined them raking down my back as I fucked into her, slowly, taking all fucking night to worship every single part of her. Claiming her the way I need to but know I shouldn't. I think of the tiniest whimper that escaped her lips without her even realizing when I kissed her gently in the hospital.

All three times.

I think of her eyes when she saw the barbell under the crown of my dick, and how they went from needy to desperate in one second flat. At that image, I lose all control and the shameless side of me takes over as I spit into my palm, then grasp my solid cock. It's not the first time I've made myself come with her face in my head, but the fact that I'm doing this with her in my home means I've reached a whole new level of depraved. A sort of desperate haze takes over with her so close, as I picture her tight, pink cunt stretching so well to accommodate me, coating me in her arousal with every deep, intentional thrust.

I imagine nothing but handfuls of that shining copper hair spilling through my fingers as she looks up at me from her knees, choking on my cock. In this second, she's right here in this shower with me, her hair wet and heavy, her eyes lust-filled as she gags and drool drips down her chin.

I imagine her in *my* bedroom, in *my* bed, wearing nothing but those flimsy cotton panties I can't forget. How wet she was, soaked, all for me, as she dripped through them.

How she *tasted*.

Christ, if I ever get the chance, I'll feast on her sweet cunt for so long she'll be begging for me to give her even a moment to breathe between the desperate cries of my name while she falls apart, again and again. She'll cry into my pillows as I spread her ass wide, watching my fat cock fuck into her tight, hot pussy. As I stiffen further in my hand, my mind wanders to how she'll look in a few weeks, a few months even, when her body has changed with my child. How she'll glow, how her tits will grow even fuller.

"Asher . . . please . . . I need you."

I hear her screams in my mind as water hits my back and I press my free palm into the shower wall. My eyes screw shut as a sort of static lines my vision and fire licks up my spine and hips.

Giving myself a final tug, I picture those blue eyes on me.

"Fuck, Liv," I grunt out as I come, hard. Spilling into the shower, I bite my lip to contain my groan, then try to catch my breath as my cock jerks in my hand.

I've reached a new level of fucked, jacking myself off just because she's sleeping in my home. All my fucking control—the rules I've had my entire life—officially broken.

As I push my hair off my face, my heart rate slowly starts to come down. I have no idea how long I'll make it like this with her here. Taking care of her while also wanting to strip every bit of clothing from her and get her between my sheets, is a balance I worry I won't be able to find.

I towel off, tossing on my boxers, then my sweats, before making my way downstairs to check on her. I search for Duke as I pass through the kitchen. But he isn't in his bed in front of my fireplace. I continue my search for my suck of a dog until I find him curled up in my bed with Olivia, as if that has always been his home.

My patio door is open and a light breeze blows through the

room. The sounds of summer cicadas and tree frogs outside fill the air as I lean on my bedroom doorframe for a moment, allowing myself to watch her. The glow of the TV—which I assume is playing one of her rom-coms—is the only light in the room, illuminating Olivia's sleeping form. Her copper hair is splayed around her, the red tones a stark contrast to my white bedding, and her full, pink lips are slightly parted as she breathes softly with one arm up over her head. My duvet is untucked and messy—surrounding her in soft tufts—and her cow slippers peek out from just beneath the heavy throw. Even those stupid things are growing on me. *What is this woman doing to me?*

I couldn't tell you how long I stand here, just watching her, noticing the tiniest details I normally force myself to look away from. I could easily forgo sleep to just look at her like this until the sun eventually rises. I've watched her for years, but this is different. She stirs with a soft moan, and it brings me out of my trance. Tapping the side of my leg lightly, I signal for Duke to follow me. He lifts his head up but makes no sign of movement, simply grunting and lowering his head back down beside her feet. It seems he has zero interest in coming with me.

"Don't blame you," I mutter to him as I flick the TV off and cast one more glance at Olivia sleeping peacefully in my bed. And that's when I hear it, another tiny moan that sends all the blood in my body rushing back to my cock.

"Asher . . ."

Yep. Fuck it. I'm keeping her.

CHAPTER 36
Olivia

"*Mmmm . . . that's it, kitten.*" *I look down into those dark mercury eyes to the beast of a man nestled between my thighs, gripping them tight to hold me close. He uses his free hand to spread me apart before running his tongue firmly through my soaking core. The ache is too strong. I want him too badly. I need him. He doesn't hide the way he wants me either as he groans against my clit, his eyes closing as he tastes me. My legs begin to shake as I cry out his name. "Asher!"*

I'm panting so hard I feel dizzy as my body quakes for him and desire rolls through me at the sight of him on his knees for me. I moan as he sucks my clit firmly into his mouth and those eyes spark open, now vibrant and light as he burrows his face deeper, watching me.

"Show me how well you ride my tongue, Liv. . . ." Asher feasts on me in a way no one before him has. I do what he says and rock my hips. I can't breathe. I can't think. I exist only for the pleasure his tongue and his perfect mouth offer me. I can't keep up as he trades between licking, sucking, and nipping at me. My legs shake and, in mere seconds, I feel the orgasm taking its firm hold, centering every

cell in my body. My eyes meet his, and he lets out a rumbling growl as his tongue laps against my clit.

"Your cunt is always so needy, always fucking dripping for me, isn't it?" He smirks against me. "Only for me. Because you're mine, Olivia."

I bolt up in bed, sweating, my heart beating erratically fast. The ache between my thighs is real, even though I was dreaming.

My attention is brought back to the present when I feel something move at my feet. Duke gruffs and lays his furry, warm head on top of my blanket-covered feet. I slump back down into the pillows.

"You stayed with me all night, boy?" I say. He isn't interested in waking up yet and, instead, slumps against my feet as his pillow.

I glance out to the woods behind Asher's house. The lightening gray sky is a stark contrast to the mountain, and the patio door is still open. The morning breeze enters the space, bringing the sound of birds with it. Asher's bed was so comfortable to sleep in, and as I look around the room now, rested but still very turned on, I breathe in the delicious scent of him that lingers in the plush pillows. I flip my phone over on the bedside table to see that it's just after six A.M.

I listen for movement anywhere else in the house but find nothing. I do, however smell coffee . . . which tells me Asher is already awake? Mortification washes over me as I wonder if he just heard me, if I was *actually* moaning his name in my sleep.

All I have to do is sit up for the nausea to creep in. I reach for my bag beside the bed and grab two salted crackers from the stash I brought last night when we stopped at my place on the way home from the hospital. Popping them into my mouth, I close my eyes as I chew, willing my stomach to settle and

CHASING THE FIRE

reminding myself it's good that I feel this. The ER doc said morning sickness is a sign of a healthy pregnancy.

After a few minutes my stomach feels calmer, so I slide my feet out from the blankets and stand, stretching as I grab my hoodie and toss it on over my tank, my pajama shorts still on from when I crawled in last night. I toss my mass of tangled hair back into a bun, then pad out to the kitchen. I'm surprised when I don't see Asher anywhere, though there is a pot of coffee brewed and an empty mug in the sink. *What time does this man get up?*

I spy a Post-it note on the counter. *Went for a run. This is half decaf, there's cream in the fridge.*

I putter around the kitchen, pulling out a mug from the mug cabinet—all black, all in a neat row. I pour myself a cup of coffee, breathing in the delicious smell and taking a big sip. Then I look for the ingredients I might need and, surprisingly, Asher has everything. I wonder if it's overstepping but then decide it's the least I can do to thank him for being so supportive.

It takes me no time at all to whip up a quick batch of pumpkin spice muffins from the puréed pumpkin in his refrigerator. As I wait for them to bake, I scroll through my pregnancy app to understand the changes I can expect this week. This week, the baby has officially leveled up to fetus, and it says he or she is already an inch and a half long. I'm watching a 3D rendering of a little alien when the oven beeps. The smell of pumpkin and spice fills the air when I pull the muffins out to cool.

I yawn and top up my mug as my phone buzzes on the counter,

MOM

Make sure you let us know if you need anything today.

DAD

> We can bring you over some lunch if you want, but just get some rest.

ME

> I will. I promise.

I tell them both I love them. I know they're probably worried after waking up to me telling them about my scare. Setting my phone down, I notice the sun is fully up now and beating through Asher's French doors, so I decide to take my coffee out to the house's wide covered deck. From the kitchen window, I spy a rather comfortable-looking sectional sofa that faces Sugarland Mountain. Duke trots alongside me as I head for the door. I know Asher lets him have free rein of the property so I pull the door back and let him out first, expecting him to take off into the yard. But he doesn't. Instead, he just turns to look at me with a cocked head that seems to say, *Let's go, lady, I don't have all day.*

I make it outside, balancing my coffee, a warm muffin, and my phone as Duke heads out into the flat of the yard to do his thing. I'm so intent on not spilling my coffee that I don't notice the massive aluminum tub on the other side of the deck, or the almost naked beast of a man sitting inside it. My stomach drops and my mouth almost waters after the dream I just had as my gaze lands on the sculpted, inked arms—dripping and glistening—outstretched over the sides. My eyes trail up to Asher's dark, wet hair that is brushed back off his forehead. His own are closed, as if my arrival into what I assume is an early morning ritual does not faze him in the slightest.

"Is that *ice*?" I ask, shivering just looking at him as I take a seat on the sturdy outdoor sofa.

He smirks, eyes still shut. "Good morning to you too. And yes."

"*Why?*" I ask, my voice sounding appropriately horrified, which makes Asher chuckle.

"Because, after I work out, I bathe in ice. It's good for circulation and blood flow."

"You enjoy self-torture?" I query, taking a sip of my coffee.

This makes him open his steely eyes, and a shiver runs through me as he turns to face me. *Fuck me.* The sheer beauty of this man stuns me as I watch him raise a muscled arm and run a hand through his wet hair.

"A little pain is never a bad thing, Livi," he says in that deep timbre, and I'm damned if that sentence doesn't turn me right back on. "Helps remind us we're alive."

I decide to steer our conversation toward something that doesn't remind me how close to naked he is ten feet away from me.

"Would you be able to give me a ride back to Silver Pines to get my car this morning, please? I have to be at the shop at eight."

"Your car is here. I had Haden pick me up this morning and take me to the ranch. I drove it back. Keys are in the basket on the island."

"This morning? As in what? Four A.M.?"

"Four-thirty." He says it like it's nothing, and I have to force myself to pull my eyes from him as I will my brain out of the deepest depths of the gutter that is his glorious fucking self.

"Pumpkin . . . muffins," I blurt out of nowhere.

"Pardon?" he asks, genuine concern lining his face. I take a breath and hold my muffin up.

"I baked. Pumpkin spice, you had everything."

He leans back and closes his eyes again. "You used the pumpkin in the fridge?"

"I hope that's okay. I just wanted to bake you something for being . . . so great."

His lips tug up. "Dick's gonna be pissed you used his pumpkin."

He fed his "not my cat" pumpkin? Before I have a chance to tell him how sweet that is, Asher's phone starts to beep with a timer and he rises like Poseidon from the sea, and my brain descends right back into that gutter as water slinks slowly down the crevices of his chest and abs like tiny rivers running downhill to meet the band of his black swim trunks. Swim trunks that are stuck to him and outline his cock perfectly. My mouth turns as dry as the desert as I watch him.

"You're staring," Asher says with a grin, his accent thick as he wraps a towel around his narrow hips. Slowly, my brain cells start to rebuild, and I'm able to look away.

"Sorry, I . . . just . . . *Damn dream.*" I whisper the last part under my breath so he doesn't hear.

"What dream now?" he asks, not missing a beat. *Fucking hell.*

"Do you have supersonic hearing?" Fuck it. I decide to just be real with him. "You *must* know how you look right now."

Asher moves closer and leans down over me as icy drops of water fall from his skin onto mine. I shiver as he kisses me on the forehead, just as he did last night.

"I'm gonna grab a coffee, one of those incredible muffins, and put on a shirt to help you control yourself. But if you think I'm letting you off the hook about that dream, you're wrong."

Another shiver runs through me.

"It wasn't about you," I lie as he straightens and begins to head in.

"You're a shite liar, Liv," he says with a chuckle.

I close my eyes when he's gone, take a deep breath, and secretly commit the image of him dripping wet and half naked to the official Asher Reed dream bank.

CHAPTER 37
Olivia

LATE JULY

Ten little fingers, ten little toes, eleven weeks along, little bear grows.

CECE

My mom heard at the senior center that Asher proposed at Dolcetto's last week. *Laughing face*

GINGER

I'm gonna be best friend offended if this is true.

ME

How on earth would anyone get that from what they saw?

I picture my mom clapping and laughing.

CECE

I'm sure if my mom heard it at the center, the whole town is gossiping.

ME

Well, the only way they could prove otherwise is if they snuck into Asher's and saw us sleeping in separate rooms every night.

GINGER

Eye roll emoji

CECE

How long do you think you can keep this charade up before, you know . . . ?

GINGER

The levee breaks. And by levee I mean *Eggplant emoji* *peach emoji*

GINGER

There are definite feelings between you and Chief Reed, aka your hot baby daddy, who gives you his bed and I'm sure has a huge *eggplant emoji*

GINGER

Remind me again why you two aren't trying to make a go of this?

ME

Because I'm not about to trap him into something he doesn't believe in. I'm fine just being co-parents and friends. And after my little scare, I'm happy to be at his house.

> **ME**
> I don't want to complicate things any more than they are. We'll figure the rest out later.

As I read my message back, it's obvious I'm trying to convince myself at this point.

> **GINGER**
> Sex is the least complicated thing there is, darling.

> **ME**
> You're impossible.

> **CECE**
> She's got a point.

> **ME**
> You can't both be devils on my shoulder. I need at least one angel to tell me to keep my head straight.

> **GINGER**
> Need I remind you? We're NOT Angels. You'll have to look elsewhere.

Lucy hands a customer her bag with two bikinis and a cover-up as I set my phone under the counter, ignoring my devilish best friends. The shop has been swamped all morning. It's an absolutely perfect day weatherwise, a sunny seventy-five, and we've sold enough designer swimsuits today alone to operate the store for the next week, but my feet are sore, my breasts are aching, and I'm absolutely exhausted. On the upside, it's been two weeks since Asher took me to the hospital and I haven't had any spotting since. I've been living in my newest line of strapless floral A-line dresses, since they're nice and loose around my waist, and every day that goes by, I'm breathing a little easier, learning to accept what the ER doc said about it just being a one-off from my exam.

My needy hormones have calmed down a little too, which I think can be attributed to the fact I've barely seen Asher since he's been working doubles.

"So will you take a few months off? Or what will you do?" Lucy asks, cutting through my thoughts. I told her my news the other day.

"I haven't really gotten that far yet." I shrug, realizing I'm not ready to think about leaving my first baby, my shop, for any length of time just yet. "I'm not sure yet."

"I've got you here, Liv. The shop basically runs itself now, and you could just do all your buying from home. I'm so excited for you." She smiles wide. "You're going to have a little fashionista!"

I smile in return. "I'm thinking the baby is a boy."

"Excuse me, but there are many men who are incredibly fashion-conscious, like . . . *holy hell* . . . him." Lucy's eyes drift to the door as she holds up the universal sign for chef's kiss. I turn, expecting to greet a customer, but instead I get Asher looking like a fucking snack. He's in dark jeans, a black T-shirt, and his trademark sunglasses. But what confuses me is the big, deep brown, tattered cowboy boots on his feet and the cowboy hat perched on his head.

Another image for my dream bank.

"Livi," he greets, kissing my cheek right in front of Lucy. I hear her suck in a breath when she realizes who he is. "You must be Lucy. It's nice to meet you in person."

"Y-you too," she answers quickly. Asher extends a hand over my head and I turn in confusion to see Lucy handing him my purse and phone over the cash counter.

She's smiling like a schoolgirl now, and I turn to look at him through her eyes. He's so gorgeous it almost physically hurts, especially in that damn hat.

"What is this?" I ask, looking between the two of them.

Asher reaches up and strokes my cheek with his thumb.

"I took the day off, and I thought you could use one too. One you can't say no to because I prearranged it with your shop manager. Told her you had a date."

"Congratulations," Lucy says to Asher, and he nods in response.

"Ready?" he asks, as if I'd ever say no.

I nod and hold up a finger. "Gimme one sec?"

"'Course," he says, saluting Lucy goodbye, who is smiling at Asher adoringly as he heads for the door.

"Holy shit," she whispers. "He called the shop this morning before you got here and asked what you had on the go. I did *not* expect him to look like he just walked off the pages of fucking *GQ*!"

Asher clears his throat. "Aye, the store's not that big."

Lucy blushes beat red as she looks from me to him. "You better go with him before I do."

"Can still hear ya," Asher quips as second-hand embarrassment washes over me for Lucy. But she doesn't seem fazed as Asher just shakes his head and I turn to follow him.

"Have fun!" Lucy calls to us.

Asher slides his hand over mine to lead me out of the store, and I'm not sure if I'll ever get tired of how it feels when he holds my hand. I'd know his anywhere with the scars that line his palms. The feeling is wholly and uniquely him.

"What are we doing?"

"Well, we're gonna see if we can help you with that stress the doctor talked about avoiding."

His presence is warm and safe and makes me want to crawl

into his arms and breathe him in until the pact we put in place is completely nonexistent.

"Oh, and I got us lunch from the Sage and Salt." He gives my hand a little squeeze. "I knew you'd be hungry, little mama."

Fuck. What pact?

Twenty minutes later I'm finishing the sandwich he brought me, still trying to guess what we're doing as we pull down the driveway of his property.

"This is just a stop. So you can change."

I sip my lemonade as the sun streams through the trees, marking the gravel drive with dappled light. We slow down as the smell of lavender hits me, and I turn to watch the bees buzzing in the swaying purple field.

"Spa?" I continue my guessing.

"Nope."

"Hmm." I tap my chin as I look out the window. "We can't go trail riding." I gesture to my low belly. "And my days of riding on the back of your motorcycle are over."

"For now," he says with a promise that rushes through me.

"We aren't day drinking."

He chuckles. "Pregnancy really is just a long list of fucking passes, isn't it?"

"Yup. I can't do shit anymore." I laugh with him. "You can still do it all, though. I could live vicariously through you."

"I'll be riding bareback just trashed through Silver Pines holdin' my half-empty bottle of JD while you watch on the sidelines in your bubble wrap, Livi."

Asher is really laughing now—it's such a beautiful sound—and he leans over to pinch my thigh.

"You wouldn't dare," I say as that familiar sizzle runs up the top of my leg.

"No, I wouldn't," he gives. "Sadly, it wouldn't be any fun without you."

We grow silent as I let those words sink in, because lately that's exactly how I've felt, and knowing he could be feeling the same is both scary and exhilarating.

When Asher parks the truck I look around, still none the wiser as to what his full plan is as he comes around to open my door.

"Right. Come on then," Asher grunts out. I laugh, because even when he's being sweet, he still has this edge to him.

Nothing seems out of place when I enter the house, until I see a little flash of orange in my periphery.

I have to look twice because it looks like Dick but . . . cleaner and more . . . fluffy. I look to Asher in search of answers.

"Still don't like the fucker. But I know you do, and I want you here. So we made an arrangement, he and I."

"An arrangement?" I raise an eyebrow.

"I took him to the vet and then the groomer this morning. He got a clean bill of health, so if you want to keep him inside more often, or all the time, he's yours."

My mouth falls open as Dick rubs against my legs. He's so soft after being treated, such a handsome boy that looks so much like Biscuit the sight makes my heart squeeze in my chest.

I nuzzle into his freshly groomed fur before setting him down, and he wanders off, exploring his new home with cat-like curiosity.

I face Asher, tears brimming in my eyes, trying to understand how this man even wrangled Dick to get him to the vet.

"Animals really help with stress." He says the words like it's no big deal, but I see how much thought he put into making me happy. Something in me snaps. *This fucking man.* "But I draw the line at him sleeping in my—"

I jump into his arms, his words trailing off as I hug him tight. Asher hesitates not a moment before his strong arms come around me. I stay right here like I've been dying to all this time, allowing myself to breathe in and let his warmth surround me. Feeling how good *he* feels. Right now, our situation isn't complicated because, in his arms, like this, I just want him. Even if I can't have Asher forever, I want him now. I *need* him now.

Pulling back, I finally look up and prepare to thank him again but, when I do, it's as if time freezes. Because when Asher's eyes meet mine they're dark, and his hold tightens on my lower back, pulling me closer like he doesn't want to let me go either. We drink each other in as the afternoon sunlight streams through the windows.

"Fuck, Liv . . ." His voice ripples through me as he tips his forehead to mine. We breathe the same air as I find bravery, moving my palm to his bearded jaw, my hand small against the wide angle of it.

I'm practically panting as I stand on my tiptoes, close my eyes, and kiss his cheek, my chest pressing to his as I linger there way longer than I probably should if I want to keep my heart intact through all of this.

A sound I can only compare to a low growl rumbles in his chest.

"I'm so fucking tired of trying to fight this . . ." he warns, but it's not the tone of a man fighting. It's the tone of a man *begging*, and that alone makes me throw caution to the wind.

"Kiss me, Ash," I whisper into his lips as I grip his face and pull it down to mine. The smell of spiced pine washes over me, igniting my entire body as he growls.

"*Fuck*." Asher crushes himself to me and seals his mouth over mine. I go limp as his hands press hungrily into my lower back, squeezing me like he can't get enough, and it's clear, pact or no pact, neither of us has a shred of restraint anymore.

This kiss isn't soft or gentle. This kiss is full of want. This kiss makes me feel completely breathless as his tongue meets mine, licking and tasting, toying with me like he's been thinking about this as much as I have. Like he wants me the way I want him. Everything around us fades, and all I hear is our beating hearts.

The possessive greed Asher kisses me with is all-consuming. I'm lost in him, overwhelmed with the way he knows what I need without asking and the way his hard length is pressing against my abdomen.

"H-hear me out," I start with a pant when we finally part, trying to gather a proposal because his thumb grazing under my shirt across the skin of my waist has me reeling. Either pregnancy or temporary insanity makes me bold and unashamed because I slide my hand down and press my palm to his solid cock through his jeans. He sucks in a breath and I moan when I remember his size.

"We're pretending anyway, right? Half the town thinks you proposed to me . . . and the other half knows I'm carrying your baby." I stroke him softly as my eyes find his, feeling him stiffen further under my touch. Lust makes his eyes dark and stormy in that way I've envisaged for weeks. "Being pregnant makes me *a lot* more needy than usual and, the way I see it, this is all your fault." I stroke him again, and this time he bites back a groan. "You kinda owe me, Reed."

"Christ, woman." His hands fly to either side of my face and he presses his lips to mine, kissing me deeply until I'm dizzy with my palm still stroking his cock. I pull in a breath when his lips move to my neck, then my shoulder.

"Maybe, just when absolutely necessary, we can be friends with benefits. You know, do each other a solid." I smirk at my choice of words because he's *so* solid right now. "Unless of course you'd like me to reopen my eMatch profile instead?"

I'm bluffing as I back up and let go of his cock, trying *any-*

thing to make him give in.

Asher's fast, tight grip over my forearm stops me, then he's tugging me back tight against him. My breath catches as his heavy chest presses against me and his deep gray eyes search mine, hungry and alive with need.

"I'm a man of my word," he growls, his voice pure gravel. "If your needy little cunt is desperate to be touched, the man who touches you is *me*."

Shit.

I look up at him through my lashes, the sun illuminating his broad silhouette as his chest heaves. "So touch me, Asher, I *need* you."

CHAPTER 38
Asher

"*I need you . . .*"

Those words will break me every damn time, because I want her to need me. I want her to need *only* me.

I crush my lips to hers in a knee-buckling kiss. A moan escapes her as my hand slides under the thin cotton of her shirt and her lips part, letting me taste and savor her until she's kissing me back, eagerly, like she's been waiting forever for me to give in. She's fucking stunning like this. No care about where she is, no worry about right or wrong, just taking what she wants without thought, which I know for Olivia is rare as hell.

And fuck, do I ever give in.

This kiss isn't like the ones before it. This kiss is full of something I've never felt before: fucking emotion and a growing connection that I'm having a really hard time understanding. This connection is deep, split equally between us, only becoming one when we're connected like this with my lips, hands, and my body on hers.

I cradle the back of her head as I hold her so close there

isn't enough space to breathe between us. Olivia slides her hands up and twists her fingers in the hair at the nape of my neck, trying to pull me even closer. We both moan as she moves her hand over my cock between us. We slow, nowhere near done kissing each other as she meets my tongue with her own in a perfect, teasing pulse.

I'm ready to come in my fucking pants as she takes my bottom lip between her teeth and bites down.

"I've never stopped thinking about *that* night," she says in a breathy whisper. The words make me give in entirely as I slide my hands under her skirt and grip the soft skin of her ass tight. She's so fucking silky and warm as the tips of my fingers graze her cotton thong. Knowing I can't have her, that I still have to wait until her next trimester, is a special kind of torture all on its own.

"I never stopped thinking about how it felt when you were deep inside me, Ash . . ."

Goddamn.

She strokes my dick again, squeezing a little harder this time, letting her free hand reach up to rest on my shoulder and I suck in a breath. "About how good it felt for you to stretch me, fill me."

"*Fuck, woman.* What are you doing to me?" Flames lick up my spine as she lets out another throaty moan, rocking into me further, adding more pressure.

"Do you think about it too?" she asks, so needy. *Fuck.*

"Every. Waking. Fucking. Moment," I growl, gripping her ass so tight her breath hitches. Another throaty moan and my dick is leaking for her. I'm so fucking hard.

"Me too," she breathes. I press my heavy palm against her clit through her panties, knowing she's fucking soaked for me. I remember the way she clenched around my dick and it sends another thrill through me.

She's fucking perfect.

"I can't wait for you to fuck me again," she admits in a dirty whisper, trading between gently stroking her fingers over my cock then gripping it tight. My eyes nearly roll back; the contrast is driving me mad.

"Fuck, if you keep that up, I'm going to blow in my fucking pants, Olivia."

Her plush pink lips pop open as she whimpers. "Maybe that's exactly what I want."

She's a little brat. Sexy as hell and she doesn't even realize it.

"I *want* to make you come . . ." she trails off in a moan. I force myself to back up from her before pulling my T-shirt off with one hand and tossing it to the floor. Next, I lose my jeans, and then my boxers, until I'm standing stark naked in the room in front of her, calling her bluff. There's no stopping this now. She hasn't moved; she's frozen and her eyes are moving quickly over my rigid body. I see the tiniest hint of fear in those eyes and *that* spurs me on even more. It's as if she knows she's awakened something in me that can't be pushed down any longer.

"You and me, yeah?" I affirm.

"Yeah," she wisps as her hands slide over her hips like she can't wait to touch her needy little pussy. My eyes trail over her soft curves, desperate to see those thighs slick with the mess I know is all for me.

"That means we come *together*." I nod to her. "Now take off your clothes. *Slowly*, I want to see all of you."

Olivia

Asher looks every bit the dark prince standing before me, waiting for me to do as I'm told.

The slight tic of his jaw, the intensity in his eyes. It's all for me.

I've never been so desperate for any man as I pull my T-shirt off over my head and a low rumble leaves his chest as he watches me. His hand moves to his thick cock as he begins to stroke. The cooler air has my nipples aching and hardened under the soft cotton of my bra. Slowly, as I hold his eyes with mine, I unbutton my skirt and let it slide down my legs, stepping out of it slowly just like he asked. His chest rises and falls steadily, though his pupils are blown out, giving him an almost crazed look.

"So eager to please me, Olivia. You want to be my good girl, don't you?"

His tone alone makes my pussy throb with want as I give him more. Nodding, I pull my hair to one side over my shoulder as I reach behind and unclasp my bra, which falls forward and drops to the floor. Then, I slowly slide my thumbs under the fabric of my light gray cotton thong at my hips and start to pull them down too.

"No. Leave them," he orders, and I freeze with his command, waiting for the next, wanting nothing more than to please him. The ache between my thighs is overwhelming as I watch him continue to stroke his huge cock in his hand. I'm so desperate to touch myself; he's so hard, so rigid, rippled with veins and covered in ink. So ready for me as he closes the space between us. He dips his head down, spitting into his hand before returning it to his thick shaft; I whimper.

"You like that?" he asks, something wicked in his eyes. I'm a total goner for him at this point and manage nothing more than a nod.

"Sit down." He tips his head to the sofa. I move the short distance and do what he says, taking a seat as I watch for his next order. The power in his eyes as I submit to him is a drug. One I know I'll *never* be able to give up.

"Lean back, spread those thighs, and show me how wet you

are. I bet you've soaked right through those fucking panties for me."

I say nothing but keep my eyes on him as I lift my heels onto the sofa. His pace increases on his cock as the deep V of his abs flexes. I'm completely exposed like this, and I'm sure he can see the wet spot I can feel in the center of my thong.

"Aye . . . Just as I thought. Fucking *dripping* for me. Pull them tight. Show me that swollen little pussy."

Oh fuck.

I obey his dirty instruction, understanding more every time I experience a moment like this with him that it's what I've always missed. Tugging on the top of my thong so the outline of my pussy is apparent for him, I lick my lips and wait. Even the friction of my panties is better than nothing.

"Mmmm . . . fuck, so wet, so needy for me."

I stay still, desperate to touch myself, but I don't dare until he tells me I can.

"Throbbing too . . ." he assesses calmly, studying my expression.

"Yes." I practically whine the answer and I don't care how desperate I sound. Just watching him jerk his cock standing over me is everything I've ever wanted.

"Take them off now. Touch yourself for me, kitten."

Holy hell. Normally he uses that nickname jokingly, but like this? It feels different. Special. Like it's only for me. Sliding my panties off, I lean back again, exposing myself fully to him.

"Thank you," I breathe out without thinking, and I hear him groan as my eyes flutter closed and my fingers move to rub my aching clit. My free hand moves to my tits and I let my first finger ghost a nipple as he strokes, moving close enough that he's standing right over me.

"Fuck . . . Asher!" I take a breath, slowing my movement to stop myself from coming so quickly.

"I didn't say stop," he grits out as he reaches down and

pinches my nipple. Hard. I cry out as he soothes over the pain with a gentle touch. "Play with those beautiful tits for me, Liv."

He pinches again then rolls it between his finger and thumb. *Fuck, that feels good.* His hand moves to stroke my face tenderly as I pinch my nipple gently. My other hand still makes sweeps against my clit as electricity sizzles through to my core. Asher watches intently when I let out a long, drawn-out moan, allowing my eyes to flutter closed.

"Atta girl." His pace continues. "There's nothing more beautiful than you . . . just like this." Asher drops to his knees, pulling me up against him and licking a trail along my bottom lip.

"Gimme a taste of that sweet fucking cunt now."

I mewl into him with his gruff commands but slide my first two fingers through my pussy. They're covered in my arousal as I raise them up and trace his lip.

"Don't tease me, Olivia. Fucking *feed* me."

"Fuck . . ." I whimper as he sucks them right into his mouth with a deep groan. I'm rocking my pussy against his cock now because I'll take anything, any part of him. Being this close, yet unable to have him, sends pure anarchy through my bloodstream. My eyes nearly roll back as he backs up slightly on his knees, gathering my arousal with two fingers, sweeping them up over my clit, and gently pinching it as I begin to breathe heavier. I'm clinging to him as he teases me, continuing to work his fingers at a pace that has me spiraling. Just before I'm about to come all over him, he stops.

"Greedy fucking girl. *Together*," he reiterates. "I wanna see how you make yourself come, Liv. Show me what you do to yourself when you think of me."

His own hand has returned to his cock, and he doesn't need to tell me twice. I lay back against the sofa and replace my fingers. The faster he strokes himself, the faster I work. Both of us getting off on each other's actions. Asher isn't even touching me, and this is the hottest fucking thing I've ever done. The sounds of my soaking pussy fill the air as he strokes himself over me.

"Listen to that sobbing cunt." He growls. "It gets you off knowing how hard it makes me. Just fucking looking at you..." Asher groans as his head tips back, and the muscles of his arm flex. "How fucking sexy are you spread out for me like this?"

"I love it," I admit as I reach up with my free hand to pinch a nipple.

"Fuck yeah, keep those eyes here, baby." He points to his own then settles his free hand across my inner thigh. "And these legs spread wide. I'm gonna paint this pretty pink cunt with my cum."

"Please..." I whimper, wanting him to make a mess of me. Wanting him to mark me.

Asher's expression is one of satisfaction at my begging and, finally, my orgasm takes a foothold. There's a deep-seated hunger in his eyes as he fists himself, and I feel the wave begin to crash over me.

I start to come apart at the shameless way he strokes his cock, how confident he is in his own sexuality, how he knows exactly what he wants, and he has no fear of showing it. His eyes are dark and wild, his bottom lip steady between his teeth.

"I'm gonna... come," I pant. "Please come with me, Ash... please."

"*Fuuuck*, Olivia..." He growls my name as hot ropes of cum coat my fingers and my pussy. I come with him, my body rocking as I shudder, trying to catch my breath. Asher pulls me up to him, but I'm in a daze as he kisses my lips, weaving his hands through my hair as our naked flesh presses together and his cock slides through my pussy, covered in both of us, and the feel of his barbell against me when I'm still so sensitive has me desperate for more already.

"Christ, you're beautiful," he murmurs as he pulls back to

look at me. "So goddamn beautiful."

"You're pretty beautiful yourself," I say honestly, my heart beating fast.

He smirks. "Aye. You always get naked on the first date?"

"No," I admit. "Do you?"

Asher pinches my ass and I squirm. "No." His eyes grow more serious. "In fact, you're the first woman I've been with since I came to this town."

I stare at him for a moment, letting that information wash over me.

"So, um, what does this mean? Best co-parents ever?" I kiss him again and shrug. "Moment of weakness?"

"Aye." He smirks at me like he can't help himself, and this side of him, the side that only *I* get to see when he wants me, is like a spark before the flames. I realize as his lips return to mine that I felt it the very first night we were together, and I know now I've been chasing the fire he offers me ever since.

"Fuck . . ." he mutters, looking to the clock over my head as my breathing slows.

"What?" I ask with concern.

"We're gonna be late."

"Where are we going?" I hum into his lips. "I'm already feeling completely relaxed."

Asher chuckles, tipping his head back, and it cracks my chest wide open to see how happy and light he is.

"Uh-uh. Come on, little mama, let's get you cleaned up. I'm taking you to the rodeo."

CHAPTER 39
Olivia

I've lived in Kentucky most of my life and I've never been to the rodeo. It was just never of any interest to me, but sitting here now at Buckshaw Farm's annual rodeo in Fallow Ridge, Kentucky, just outside of Laurel Creek, with Asher, Hunter Black's brother Beau, his twin daughters, and his mama Maeve, I can't stop smiling.

"All right, rodeo fans, here we go. Contestant number six of twelve all the way from Lexington, Kentucky, is Andy Yarrows. Ten and four is the time to beat, y'all, ten and four."

I listen intently to the rodeo announcers who have been keeping us entertained throughout this tie-down roping competition as I take in the sights and sounds around me. The large dirt arena we're sitting in is one of four, surrounded by metal fencing. Just beyond the fence are bleachers filled with spectators, most of them wearing cowboy hats. Even the kids are decked out with the best boots and hats, talking happily as they munch on popcorn and candy. "Thank God I'm a Country Boy" plays over the loudspeaker, rivaling the announcers' voices as Andy takes off out of the gate just after the calf he's set on roping.

"He looks young," I comment to Asher beside me. "Surely he can't be more than twenty."

The father of my child is all cleaned up now, as am I, from our moment of weakness. The deep brown and tattered cowboy hat he was wearing earlier sits on his head, hanging low over his intense eyes. His black T-shirt is partially tucked into another pair of perfectly fitted Wranglers and his thick thigh rests close to mine under the table. Thanks to Hunter, we're in the VIP section right near the gate and our view of the arena is impeccable.

"He's only eighteen," Beau Black says, bouncing one of his three-year-old twins on his lap. He's a big, burly man just like Hunter and Walker, but he's older, and it's obvious he doesn't live life like the fun-loving, free-spirited Hunter. He's reserved and stoic, with dark hair, a thick beard and mustache, and haunting green eyes that tell a story I can't imagine is filled with joy since the twins' mother died when they were one.

I smile down at the toddler, safe in his big hands, as she returns a gummy grin. I'm not sure if she's Sadie or Piper—since they're virtually identical with bouncing dark curls and big blue eyes, chubby little rosy cheeks and hands, and the most infectious smiles you ever did see. Seeing them makes me so excited and intrigued about who our baby will look like.

"He worked on the ranch the last few summers, but he's heading to college this fall," Beau continues in his deep timbre. "Any other sport—football, baseball, basketball—you can't play at the professional level when you play for the school. But tie-down roping has no restrictions, so he can rope all he wants."

"Helps his mama pay for that schooling," his mom, Maeve Black, pipes up.

She's a breathtaking woman who looks to be in her sixties, with long, flowing blond hair that has an almost silver tinge to it and deep green eyes you could get lost in. Her style is completely boho country, and I envisage her to be the type of woman who forges for berries in her bare feet on the Grosvenor Ranch.

"Rumor has it he's gonna be a doctor," she adds.

"This town seems a little like ours," I comment as I watch Andy wrestle his calf and wrap his rope securely around its legs as the crowd cheers. The opening strings to "Sweet Home Alabama" start to play as the announcers let us know he had a bit of trouble on his dismount; his time will easily be beat at thirteen and six.

"Everyone knows everyone's business?" Maeve guesses with a grin.

"Precisely." I smile back as the breeze blows my hair and the scent of hot gravel and barbeque wafts over to our stand. Asher squeezes my thigh gently under the table and it sends those sparks I'm doing my best to understand through me. After this afternoon's session, my body has fully gone off the rails. My mind tells me we need to keep things uncomplicated—for the baby—but it's a losing battle when he looks at me with those charcoal eyes.

"Hungry, mama?" he asks low, as if he's reading my mind. The way he dips his head down to whisper in my ear, closing the gap between us, warms my chest, and I realize I am hungry.

"Whatever the barbeque is smells delicious," I tell him.

He gives my thigh a little squeeze. "On it."

"Anyone else want anything from the stand?" he asks Beau and Maeve as the next roper is sent from the gate.

"Want Daddy to get you some french fries, Sadie-baby?" Beau asks the twin in his lap, his voice gruff but gentle. He kisses her chubby cheek.

Sadie nods and little Piper pulls on his shirt from Maeve's lap. "Me too!" she says happily.

"I'll come with you." He looks to Asher as Piper reaches her hands up to him. "Up," she tells him as he easily switches one twin for the other before planting a kiss on his mother's head. "Anything for you, Mama?"

"No thank you, darlin'." She shakes her head as she swipes Sadie's curls off her cheek.

"He has his hands full, doesn't he?" I say once the boys are out of earshot. I finish playing a little game of peekaboo with Sadie, who giggles as Maeve strokes her soft hair.

"He does," she confesses. "But he handles it with grace."

I don't ask what happened, figuring if she wanted to tell me, she would.

"I've met Asher a handful of times," Maeve continues, picking up a little toy and placing it in Sadie's hand. "But he's different this time. How far along are you?"

My mouth falls open slightly before I manage to close it and flash her a rueful smile. No point in lying. "Eleven weeks."

"Mmm." She muses.

"How did you—"

"I just know things, darlin'." She smiles sweetly at me. "I *feel* things. Some people say I'm a witch. And I do come from a long line of them. Generations of them."

"That's incredible that you know your history that far back," I say as a pang of jealousy cuts through me, knowing I'll never know my history like that.

"When we can't discover everything about our own past, it's important to create a future. Pass it on to your child, then they'll pass it on to theirs. Make your own history."

I study the woman next to me; her deep green eyes twinkle with wisdom and her silvery blond hair swirls on her slim shoulders. She nods toward the concession booth where Asher and Beau stand.

"There's deep trauma there." She's looking at Asher. "But his spirit seems lighter now. And it's because of you."

I smile softly. "I think maybe it's because of the baby."

As if he senses we're talking about him, Asher turns over his shoulder. I admire the way his T-shirt clings to the wide expanse of his upper back, and how his jeans hug tight to that perfect ass. He winks at me, tipping his cowboy hat to shield his face from the sun, as longing hits me in the chest.

"He'll be a good father," Maeve says firmly. "But trust me on this, the way that boy is looking at you? That has everything to do with *you.*"

CHAPTER 40
Asher

This was the best idea I've ever had; I'm not sure I've *ever* seen Olivia look as happy and relaxed as she is right now.

I've been to the rodeo to watch Hunter a handful of times and I've been on the Grosvenor Ranch with them just as many. Immersing myself into this Southern culture came easily to me when I arrived from New York. I had been craving a simpler life, and the people here have an easy way about them, like they've got it all figured out. Hard work is something you enjoy, not dread, and your family is your life. Being with the Black family now, Olivia sitting beside me, smiling ear to ear as she plays with Beau's twins and chats easily with Maeve, settles something within me.

"Want the rest?" Olivia turns her pretty face up to me. Her hair is tied at the nape in a blue scarf, which is a stark contrast to her shining copper waves, and she's wearing a tattered straw cowboy hat. Her shorts are denim cutoffs and she wears a billowy white eyelet tank top in the summer heat. The kicker is the pair of light blue cowboy boots that show off her tan and the curves of her legs. The whole package has had me half hard the entire afternoon. With Olivia, there's no trying. Everything is just fucking effortless. As simple and perfect as a warm summer's day—breeze on my skin, sun on my face without a place to be kinda perfect.

I take a wing from her plate, and can't help but grin as I swipe barbeque sauce off her cheek with my thumb and she blushes a hot pink. Fuck, she's cute.

"Like a little gremlin." I chuckle as she shrugs.

"Mama's gotta eat." It's a simple sentence, but my cock pulses at her words nonetheless.

"All right, folks, we've got a treat for you here now. We all know you're here to see the Wild Boot! Hunterrrrr Black!"

Hunter's always a crowd favorite, so the cheering explodes as two buckle bunnies clap for him and jump up and down at the fences. Hunter flashes his playboy smile at the crowd, rope between his teeth and looped in his hand as he waves. Maeve cheers with little Sadie on her lap and Beau shakes his head with a grin.

"Fuckin' rock star."

"Let's go, boy!" I call out, cupping my mouth as the excitement builds and the gates fly open to let Hunter do his thing. He's roped that calf with lightning speed and is off his horse in no time to flip the calf like it weighs nothing, looping his rope with precision through its front legs then its back, throwing his hands in the air when he's done. I look at Olivia, whose jaw is almost touching the floor.

The crowd explodes as "Kick the Dust Up" by Luke Bryan starts playing.

"Christ almighty, that's a record." Beau chuckles as Maeve cheers, "Yeah, baby!"

Hunter's mom is clapping her hands as little Sadie mirrors her.

"It's the mustache," the announcer roars into the mic. "Makes that boy faster, I'm sure of it. Which means all I gotta do is work on my 'stache. That there is your favorite and mine, the Wild Boot coming in at ten even!"

Our table goes crazy as Hunter gives the crowd a wave before turning to wink at the buckle bunnies. I already know he'll probably be taking them both with him at the end of the day. He lives the celebrity life, but he'd give you the shirt off his back if you needed it.

Beau stands as Hunter rides back behind the gates and dismounts, giving some love to his horse.

"Good man." Beau claps Hunter on the shoulder when he comes to stand by our table. "That's a time to beat."

"Yeah, we had some luck." His brother grins back at him as he pulls Maeve in for a hug.

Once Hunter is done embracing his family, I hold my hand out to him. "Thanks for having us."

"Thanks for coming, man." He turns to Olivia and leans down. "And congratulations, darlin'."

Olivia beams in response, a hint of surprise on her face. "Thank you, good job out there!"

"Anytime you two wanna come to something, you just holler."

"Hunter . . ."

He turns over his shoulder at his name to eye up the blonde striving for his attention at the gate.

"Duty calls." He kisses Sadie on the head and ruffles Piper's hair.

"Be good," Maeve pipes up.

"'Course, Mama."

"You told him I was pregnant?" Olivia whispers to me as Maeve and Beau attempt to wrangle the girls from straying too far in the busy area.

I reach down and squeeze her hand. "Fucking right I did."

"Why?" she queries.

"Because I really like the guy." I shrug. "And I didn't wanna have to break his fingers if he decided he might be worthy of touching you."

Olivia scoffs. "I think pregnancy might be making you crazy, Reed."

She's smiling, but that semi-needy look in her eyes, the one that tells me she secretly likes my possessive side, is ever-present. It makes me question if I have time to make her come again before I even get her home.

Goddamn. She's right. I am fucking crazy. For *her*.

CHAPTER 41
Asher

"I have my phone with me at all times, Chief. I won't miss the call," I say into the phone as I look out onto my yard. Even after two years, the natural beauty of Kentucky and the peace it offers me still catches me off guard sometimes. There are some beautiful places in New York, but everything there was tainted by my father.

"Good. There are currently twelve burning now. The boys almost put them out, but damn wind picked up again and now they're dangerously close to Franklinville. If one hits the town head-on, the team just don't have the resources to fight this on their own. They're already flying in hotshot teams from Washington to California. But they aren't experienced with the structural side, and we may need all hands on deck. Can you talk to your team?" The head of Kentucky Emergency Management, Dale Brenner, is a straight shooter, and he wouldn't be calling me if the wildfires in the eastern part of our state weren't a worry. A *big* fuckin' worry.

"Yes, sir," I tell him, knowing we have enough men to look after the town. "I can leave most of my volunteer deputies in charge here. I can bring Walker, and probably also three or four fairly experienced hose jockeys too."

> **ME**
> Just got the call from the head of K.E.M. Stay on alert. With what's going on in Franklinville, they may need us if it gets any worse.

> **WALKER**
> You got me any way you need me, Chief.

> **ME**
> Thanks. I'll be in touch.

"Everything okay?" Olivia asks with a hint of worry as I emerge from my bedroom.

"Everything is fine. Just lining up the possibility of helping with the wildfires in Franklinville. If the wind stays on course, and they can't get it under control, it could hit the town head-on."

"Is that normal to call in firefighters from other towns?"

I nod as she checks her sour cream cake in the oven.

"Yep, if there is a threat of damage to the town. Wildland firefighters aren't any more trained on the structural side than we are on the forest fire side. In an emergency, it's best to have experts from every field. All hands on deck."

"Hopefully they'll be able to control it." Olivia bends down to pick up the new love of her life as he purrs into her. *Dick*. "That seems scary."

"We ready to get this show on the road?" I try to steer the conversation away from work as she sets her fluffy pet down. The wide-necked Mötley Crüe T-shirt she's wearing distracts me every single time she bends over because it gives me the perfect view of her full tits, and I'm already itching to touch her after watching her wander through the vendors at the rodeo this evening, hair blowing in the breeze, her heart-shaped ass on full display.

"Yep." She smiles as she washes her hands. "Icing making one oh one."

I move to the other side of the island—whiskey in hand—and watch her. If anyone would've told me three months ago that I'd be letting the mother of my child baby talk a fuckin' cat as she taught me how to make icing with a movie called *13 Going on 30* on the TV in my living room, I would've told them they were fucking high. But watching Olivia like this lets me get a glimpse of the nurturing woman she is, the kind of woman who will love my child more than anything in this world. And that might be the sexiest fucking thing I've ever witnessed.

Duke moves closer as she works, sniffing around to assess what the fuck is happening. My boy is already used to having Dick around, so the new addition of him in the house doesn't seem to faze him.

"I'm supposed to be cooking for you, not the other way around," I say to Olivia as I watch her check the consistency of the butter in one of the bowls.

"I like to bake. It calms me. And I have the best memories because of it."

"You and your nana, right?"

She blinks up at me with a surprised expression.

"That's right. *The Joy of Cooking* was her bible." She looks away for a moment, the reminder that it no longer exists hitting her all over again.

Olivia tucks a lock of red hair behind her ear. "Can't be sad while I bake. It's illegal. So get over here, cream this butter."

She holds out the bowl to me, which I take and dump into the stand mixer.

"This is gonna be a glaze. We use it in two steps. One, when the cake comes out and we flip it on the plate. We'll add just a drizzle. Then we'll use it again after the sponge has cooled."

"Yes, ma'am," I say, turning the mixer on low.

"Now add this icing sugar, slowly," she says, and the way the soft light of the early Kentucky evening hits her face right now is fucking unreal. "Half a cup at a time. Don't go getting all impatient and dump it in there. It won't cream right. It will be too wet."

Christ. How is baking with her doing it for me?

I let my eyes trail over her, lost for a moment in the way she shifts her hips as she checks how level her sugar is in the measuring cup.

Olivia lets out a laugh and pokes me in the chest when she catches me staring. "Stay focused. Remember, moment of weakness? Best co-parents? Keeping things uncomplicated here, Reed?"

I look down at her as I tweak her chin. "Right."

Wrong. I want to complicate the fuck out of things. Averting my eyes from hers, I get back to the task at hand.

"Tell me. What part of Ireland is your family from?" Liv asks tentatively as we watch the mixer do its thing. The leaky faucet to tell her the whole truth about my family and my father drips constantly in the back of my head.

I'm silent as she continues with a devilish grin. "It will help me feel *relaxed* to know more about your family history."

"Such a brat," I mutter as she giggles, pouring a little vanilla into a teaspoon and adding it to the mixer bowl.

"Plus, since I didn't know my birth parents," Olivia offers, "it might help me to know more about yours."

I hate talking about my past, but I know she deserves to know as much as I can offer. The memory of my mother's screams creep in but I push them away, forcing myself to give a little to Olivia. At the very least, sharing this with her will keep my mind off wanting to fuck her right here in my kitchen.

"I'll tell you what." I study her pretty face. "I'll tell you about my family if you tell me about yours."

"Deal," she answers almost immediately, her smile widening. As if I could deny her anyway.

"Belfast," I say slowly. "My family is from Belfast."

"You still have a bit of an accent."

"We came here when I was six. I don't really remember life in Ireland." I can feel my body tensing as I speak, and I try so fucking hard not to let my history control me.

"How old were you when your mother passed away?" Olivia asks as if she's interviewing me for a documentary.

I shake my head. "Uh-uh. My turn. Tell me about your birth parents."

"I don't remember a lot, though I do remember snippets from my fourth birthday. They come to me in dreams. I swear sometimes I remember the way my mother smelled. The smell was like sugar cookies or vanilla, and when I smell it, mostly when I'm baking anything sweet, it's comforting."

Olivia blows out a raspberry as she continues talking.

"I have quirks that remind me of my adoptive parents, probably just from being raised by them." She uses a spatula to push down the icing as it mixes. "But I have no idea who I'm like at my core. In a sense my entire personality, who I am, is a mystery."

She takes a lick, and some of the mixture sticks to her lip.

I move closer. She doesn't back up, but her breath increases as I swipe the sugar off her lip with my thumb then suck it into my mouth. I love the way she has to force her gaze from my mouth back to my eyes and, when she does, her pupils are blown wide as the pink I crave climbs her cheeks. The air between us is so charged you could power a damn city block.

"I was seventeen when my mother died," I answer her earlier question, pointing to the bowl. "You gotta add something else to this?"

She looks down in question at the icing. It's perfectly whipped.

"Shit, yes. Just a little milk."

She grabs the carefully measured-out amount and pours it in.

"What do you miss most about her?" Olivia asks as she assesses the icing, slowing the mixer down a little.

I haven't spoken about my mother with anyone ever. But, with Olivia, I want to. I have the strong sense that my mother would fucking love her.

"I miss the way she looked at me, with an unconditional sort of love. She knew all our family's demons. I wasn't the best . . . version of myself when I was a teenager, but she loved me exactly how I was." I think for a breath. "And she always made sure I knew it."

"What happened to her?" Olivia's eyes search mine as I fight the walls I've so carefully put in place all these years. I reach out and tuck a copper lock behind her ear, thinking maybe the best way to protect her is to arm her with a little of my truth . . .

CHAPTER 42
Asher

AGE SEVENTEEN

My heart is thumping faster the closer I get. I'm almost done; the battery is the last piece before I add all the fluids to the motorcycle I've been working on for months. My phone says it's one o'clock in the morning. I shake my head. I shouldn't be surprised. My dad said he'd be home by now, but I know he's with Denise, or one of his other side pieces. He doesn't bring them here to Scarsdale, our upper class neighborhood outside New York. He stays in the city with his mistresses. It used to piss me off that he cheated on my mom, but now I know that's just the way it is when you're the king of the Saints. You get all the pussy you want.

At seventeen, I'm not the king yet, but I'm James Donovan's son and the fly half on our school's varsity rugby team, so I already get all the pussy I want too.

Moment of truth. I stand back and look at my bike. A 1973 vintage Harley. A gift from my uncle Pete. I've restored the whole thing with the money my father gave me for my seventeenth birthday when he told me I have only a year left to play. After that, I belong to the family. I'm old enough now to know what that means: One day, I'll control this empire.

I turn the key and my bike fires right up, filling the open garage with a beautiful deep rumble.

"Fuck yeah," I grit out, turning up my iPod in celebration. Eminem fills the space and adrenaline rushes through my blood because, tomorrow, I'll be riding. I'm so consumed by the sound of the bike, my music, and the thought of what I have to do next that I don't hear the group of men as they make their way across our vast property to the house. I don't hear the windows break as lit Molotov cocktails are thrown through them.

It isn't until I smell the heady scent of smoke coming from somewhere close by that I pause and turn down my blaring music. And that's when I make my way to the door of the garage and see the flames a hundred feet away. I hear screaming and then, I'm running, knowing, once again, that my father pissed off someone he shouldn't have.

I pull my gun from my hip, ready to shoot any motherfucker on our property the way my father and my uncle trained me to. My stomach lurches as I round the corner of the yard to see the east side of our house burning.

It's *been* burning. Flames shoot through the living room window as I hear the sound of glass breaking. I don't see anyone on the premises, but I hear another scream, and I feel like I might throw up because I know it belongs to my mother.

"James! Asher!" she cries as the heat hits me like a fucking tsunami the closer I get to the house. I search for an open space to get inside. The front door is impossible; the flames are out of control behind it. I have no idea what the fuck I'm doing as I run to the back door off the kitchen and kick it in without thought.

Another wave of heat blasts over me and I can hear my mom's sobs. I cry out for her as my lungs fill with smoke. I know I'm too late because, holy fuck, our entire living room is on fire.

Panic rises; I can't even *see* down the hall where the screams are coming from. My mother's bedroom is on the other side. The horrific sounds continue over the deep crackle of fire and the crash of items falling and smashing on the ground. I hold my shirt to my face and keep trying to find a way through the burning rubble because I can't leave her. I have to save her. *My mama.*

Images of her flood my head as I call out, telling her I'm coming, while I choke back sobs; in our yard, on the swings, chalking in the driveway when I was young. The way she kisses the top of my head before ruffling my hair. The way she watches from the stands when I win my rugby matches. Birthdays, breakfasts, masses, family gatherings—it's all flooding me now as I narrowly miss being smothered by one of the ornate beams from our living room as it falls and hits the floor. The sounds of sirens fill the air, drowning out the screams of my mother that are already dimming. My lungs grow heavy and dots line my vision as I try to lift the searing beam. It's too big, too heavy, and the wood is charring my flesh, but still, I try. I still have to try. I can't let her die.

Olivia's eyes are filled with tears when I look up at her, finishing my story.

"It was too big to stop by myself. I was living a life of insolence: drugs, arrogance, entitlement. I wasn't a man. I was a boy who thought he was a man." I swallow the boulder in my throat. "And I wasn't strong enough then. The smoke was too thick, and I guess I passed out. Firefighters pulled me from the room and said I was moments from death myself."

She swipes a tear from her cheek. "The scars on your

hands?"

I lift them, studying, remembering. "I didn't feel anything. All I could focus on was her screaming: my father's name, my name, crying out to God to save her. And then it was over. Everything was quiet."

The silence is what haunts me the most.

"I'm so sorry." Olivia's face is full of genuine sorrow and understanding. "That's why you fight fires now."

I nod. "After she died, you'd think I'd stop partying. Stop living that life. But I ran toward it to do my best to bury everything. I was angry at everyone and everything, so I used people, women mostly. I drank too much, took every drug I could get my hands on. I let that anger fuel me to work for my father. I told myself it didn't matter, but I always heard her voice in my head telling me there was another way, that I should get out. But after I went to jail, I never touched a drug again. Never took advantage of another woman drawn to the power of my father's world. Prison changed me. It made me a better man, but it also put up solid walls around me. I vowed to never again let in anyone that could hurt me. About a year after I got out, my uncle told me Staten Island was looking for recruits at the one-thirteen station."

"Is that when you left?"

"Not quite. You don't just leave my family. I had to train first and find a way to ease out. But I remember thinking, maybe I could save someone else's mother."

It's been a long time since I've thought of that, fuck.

"When I was about twenty-three, I began distancing myself, because I felt like a better man when I wasn't in that world, but there were too many ghosts. The pull was too strong. I was still heavily involved, and family was always trying to suck me back in."

"Your father included?"

"My father *especially*. My guess is he *still* wants me to come home." Now would be the perfect time to tell her exactly who my father is, but as I look across the table at her beautiful face, I can't do it. I'm too selfish to give her up.

"I saw the ad online for battalion chief in Laurel Creek almost three years ago. I had just enough experience to apply, and I knew that a small town in Kentucky was the last place my family would come looking for me."

"You've overcome a lot . . ." Olivia focuses on stirring the icing, her lip between her teeth as she tries not to let the tears in her eyes spill over.

"Seems you've just got a lot more information than you bargained for," I say. "I've never told anyone that before. Feels good. Fucking cathartic even."

She smiles softly as she sets the spatula down.

"Your story is safe with me." Olivia reaches across the island and puts her hand over mine, stroking the scars there. "And, for what it's worth, I think your mother would be really proud of you."

I clear my throat and pull my hand away, the momentary fear of losing her crippling me. I carry the dirty dishes and measuring cups to the sink, needing a second and internally scolding myself for pulling my hand away.

I'm still lost in my memories, washing the last few bowls, when Olivia moves beside me. I turn to face her and her hands slide around my waist as she angles her face to mine. I can't help but stiffen as her arms hug me tight and she leans her head on my chest.

"I'm sorry," she whispers, pulling back to look me in the eyes, and my chest twitches even more. "A loss like that. It's unthinkable."

I let the moment wash over me as I watch the way her blue eyes focus on mine.

"You're a good man, Asher," she whispers, just as Dick jumps up onto the counter beside us like a fuckin' dumbass, thinking the handle of the spatula is a good perching point. It goes flying through the air—eventually landing on the floor, but not before icing flings everywhere, flicking onto my face and hers. I look down at her at the same time she looks up at me in shock. Dick takes off down the hall; it obviously scared the shit out of him too.

Olivia's mouth tugs up and I'm left wondering if this was the universe's way of lightening the mood after all the heaviness. Because, fuck, she looks damn edible covered in icing.

"All right then, guess we're having a proper taste..." I lean in and run my tongue along her chin, letting the sugary icing melt on my tastebuds. It doesn't taste as good as she does.

Olivia half whimpers and half laughs before she turns, a coy look on her face as she reaches into the bowl and smears icing across my lips with her finger.

"Fucking beautiful asshole," I faux-snarl at her, sucking her finger into my mouth and licking the sugar from it. The feel of my tongue on her finger has those sapphire eyes heating instantly.

"I hate to break it to you, buddy, but you aren't so scary with icing all over your face," she challenges, and before I can stop myself, I'm swiping my own finger into the bowl, then smearing it across her lips, then dragging it farther down her neck. Her breath quickens and I know I'm done for. Because, before she can take another inhale, I'm hoisting her onto the counter and crushing my lips to hers.

Hands down, the best fucking treat I've ever had.

CHAPTER 43
Asher

Olivia sucks in a breath when my counter meets her short-clad thighs as I press my already solid cock against her pussy. I'm only wearing sweatpants over my boxers and I can feel everything as her legs tighten around me.

The sugary vanilla flavor mixes with the taste of her and I groan into her mouth as I devour it. Taking my time, I grip either side of her face and kiss the fuck out of her as her lips and tongue match mine effortlessly. Her legs tighten further as I pull her shirt off over her head; she's not wearing a bra, and I don't waste a second before wrapping my arms around her, my skin on hers.

I lift another scoop of icing out of the bowl and drop it to her pebbled nipple. She whimpers as I bend down to suck it into my mouth, my tongue flicking over her as she rocks, begging for me. I fucking love it.

Every single cell in my body is buzzing with the feel of her as I lift her and pull down her panties, leaving her naked and glistening in the middle of my kitchen.

"You have no idea what you do to me, Liv."

How you make me feel so fucking out of control.

I trail more icing between her tits and she pants as my mouth chases the sweet line to heaven. I drop to my knees, spreading more over her belly, licking that off too, leaving small bite marks in the wake against her skin.

Then I move to her inner thighs. I haven't even reached the apex where she wants me most yet, but Olivia cries out and pushes her hips against me, begging for friction. I rub her thighs softly, taking my time to torture her. I already know it's what she needs, but my girl doesn't want me to give it to her easily.

I take another slick of icing, and using my thumbs to spread her pussy wide, I paint either side of her lips with it before licking a trail over her with the flat of my tongue. I groan as she goes fucking animalistic, gripping my hair so tightly it hurts.

"Ash . . . I need . . ." Olivia moans and the sound courses through me as I lap up the icing and move on to her soaking cunt. *Fucking unreal.*

Her soft, warm thighs hug my face, and I can't hold on to her anymore.

"We both *need* things, Olivia." I flick my tongue over her clit. "You need my tongue, and I need my fucking dessert."

I groan as I devour her, curving my arm around her hips and pulling her down closer to my face, holding her in place as I let myself feast on her pussy. Her hands grip the counter and her legs begin to shake, so I push my tongue deeper. Olivia cries out, not a care in the world, as she grinds down on my tongue.

"Christ, you're fucking beautiful riding my face, Liv. Now, come for me, baby . . ."

"Fuck, Asher!" she cries out as she falls apart, every part of her trembling. But I don't let up as I lap up every drop of sweetness she offers me until she's no longer rocking but boneless in my arms, running her fingers through my hair.

I kiss my way up her skin until I'm standing, her hot naked body pressed against my bare chest as I stroke her back through her waves.

"Didn't know . . . you were so hungry," Olivia says breathlessly, her lips curving up into a coy little smile.

"When it comes to you Liv? Motherfucking starving."

I seal my mouth to hers, my tongue dipping between her lips as she lets out a soft whimper. Fuck, I could devour these lips all day, every day. Because Olivia's lips are pure and good and I want to kiss them like the sinner I am, begging for her to save me even when it's the last thing I deserve.

"You're way too good at that, by the way," she whispers. "It's something a woman could get used to quickly."

"I told you. Whatever you need from me, mama, I'm here."

"So chivalrous, *Daddy*." She grins in a way that has my cock aching for her. "Maybe I should get on my knees for you now?"

Well, fuck, I have no idea why the hell it affects me so much when she calls me Daddy. It's fucking raw and dirty and instantly makes my cock stand to attention as she drops onto the soft mat in front of my island, looking up at me, icing stuck to her thick red waves, lips swollen from kissing me.

Olivia gives me the same sort of rush of adrenaline that fighting fires does. The feeling that I'm freefalling, risking everything with no net. She runs a hand over my cock, a question in her eyes that I'll never be ready to stop answering.

"Take my cock out, Liv," I command.

She doesn't hesitate, and the dirty side of her I crave takes over as she shimmies my sweats and boxers down while I sit back and watch. My solid cock bobs free, slapping against my stomach. Her eyes heat as she takes me into her soft hand and runs a finger down my shaft. I slide my thumb down to her bottom lip, holding it open. Her tongue moves on instinct and her big blue eyes widen through her lashes. The sight pushes me over the edge.

"Open," I say as I tap the head of my cock against her mouth. She slips her tongue out to lick the barbell under the crown of my dick. My eyes threaten to roll back but I hold my gaze steady as I let her toy with me for a beat, trying to control myself when all I want to do is fuck the back of her throat.

I pull the clip from her hair and it tumbles down around her shoulders. Her tongue continues its swirl over my piercing.

"You're so pretty on your knees for me. Now *suck*."

Olivia doesn't wait—so eager to please—hollowing out her cheeks and sucking me in deep. I look down at her, noticing the way she squeezes her thighs together, and grin. So fucking ready. Gripping her hair, I take over. I don't take it easy and thrust deeply into her mouth; the back of her throat feels like my own personal heaven. Sliding my thumb down her jaw, I pull it open as wide as I can and she accommodates like the good girl she is.

"Look at you, taking me so well, your mouth was made for this cock."

I have no idea how long I fuck her throat. I'm lost as I continue to pull myself out slowly then push back in, just to relive the feeling as if it's the first time. I fight to last even one more second as she moans around me. Every dirty thought I've had of her since the first moment I lost myself to her rises to the surface as I take in the mix of fear and want in her eyes. I know how I must look right now above her, unrelenting, half mad with lust. I pull back, stroking my cock over her face.

"Squeeze those tits together for me, kitten, so I can cover them in my cum."

Olivia smiles up at me so sweetly, so innocently, as she pushes her aching breasts together. *Goddamn this view.*

Just when I think I can't take anything more, she smirks as I give another tug. "Ready for you, *Daddy*."

"Jesus, woman . . ." I roar as I erupt, painting her tits and her slender, bitable neck with my cum. I've never seen anything this enticing in my fucking life as my cock jerks in my hand. Not being able to fuck Olivia is gonna be the goddamn death of me. I lift her up and place her back on the counter, pressing into her as my lips gently come down on hers.

"I don't think I'm ever going to look at baking the same again."

"Funny" I answer. "I was just thinking how much I like baking."

She's laughing as I grab a warm cloth to clean her up. Music plays on the TV as the credits to her movie roll, and the sky outside is an inky black. I have no idea where the animals are. Everything is a mess—so at odds with my normal sense of order—but my house feels *lived* in. Leaning in to kiss her plush lips once more, my phone starts buzzing on the counter. I groan as I pull away, because I know if my phone's ringing at ten-thirty at night, there's a reason.

My thoughts are confirmed when I answer the call. Franklinville is burning, and they need me.

CHAPTER 44
Olivia

AUGUST

THIRTEEN WEEKS, FIVE DAYS
Mama's hungry morning, noon, and night,
baby is growing, and a new phase has
bloomed. Second trimester, here we come.

Fifteen days.

For fifteen days I've watched along with the rest of Kentucky while Franklinville and the forests surrounding it burn. I've gotten up every day to watch the local news, praying for rain, hoping for the wind to change. And, finally, it seems as if the crews that have been brought in to help control the blaze are making progress. Asher has been added to a team of structural firefighters—made up of men and women from surrounding states—working tirelessly and staying in temporary camps like the wildland firefighters to prevent and put out fires in the wealthy neighborhoods of Franklinville on the west side. Most of the homes affected are in the wooded mountains, and a lot of them have been lost. I've barely talked to him, only briefly over text because he's been going nonstop, and there are times when he just doesn't have service. His longest shift was eighteen hours as all the crews battled to save one of Franklinville's most historic streets.

The only thing keeping me centered is visiting my house every day and seeing the progress there. All the walls are drywalled, and they'll be mudding and taping this week before putting down flooring. My Pinterest page is full of shelving ideas, décor, and furniture, like new stools for the island and an updated kitchen table and chair set.

I officially entered my second trimester a week ago. Apparently, little bear is the size of a peach, and every time I check my app I wonder why the hell they compare the baby to the most random of foods.

A few breakfasts with my dad, shopping with my mom, and a lunch with Ginger and CeCe have helped pass the time over the last two weeks too. I've even run into Nash and Haden a couple times—Haden just outside my shop, and Nash at the gas station down the street from my house. With everyone around me, it's hard to feel lonely, though there's still a void with Asher gone.

At almost fourteen weeks pregnant, I'm no longer feeling sick. I'm feeling incredible, and at my last ultrasound I was measuring a few days ahead. Asher was so upset to miss it so I recorded the ultrasound and texted it to him along with a new photo.

I've been walking with Duke every day down the path through Asher's wooded property to the basin of his creek. It's a great little hike to clear my head, and the reward comes halfway through when the channel opens up into a small center pool of crystal-clear water. Wild lilies grew around it in July—though they're now dying off now.

Although it's been only two weeks, it feels like so long since I've seen him. I can tell Duke is missing him too.

"Thinking about him, aren't you?" Cassie asks me now from the other side of the clothing rack as we shop in the cutest little baby boutique in town.

"That easy to tell?" I ask.

"Well, yes, seeing as I just asked you what you thought of this, and I didn't get a response because you were off in la-la land." Cassie holds up a little dress.

"Too fussy. CeCe's baby will be sporty," I say, matter-of-fact. "Nash will have her in skates before she's two."

"True." Cassie laughs as she places the dress back on the rack. "So . . . penny for your hot firefighter thoughts?"

I breathe out a sigh as I sift through the clothes.

"We had this pact. No strings. Keep everything uncomplicated for the baby," I explain as Cassie nods in understanding. "But we just felt so in sync before he left. Every time I looked at him, every time our fingers brushed, it was like my skin was set on fire."

"Been there," Cassie admits.

"Now with him gone, I miss him and, I don't know, it reminds me that . . ." I lean in so no other shoppers can hear me. "We aren't permanent, and this is the life he lives."

"His job worries you?" Cassie queries, and I'm instantly glad to have someone to talk to.

"Yes. It's such an unpredictable life; things can change in an instant."

"On the flip side," she notes with a smirk, "it's hot as hell."

I laugh as I pick up a little sleeper decorated with tiny bears and a matching hat. This *has* to come home with me.

"Most see what he does as brave and heroic," Cassie continues.

"And I do too. Of course I do. But I also see the giant, glaring risk."

"How are you ladies doing? Anything I can help you with?" Maria, the owner of the boutique, asks.

"Great, thank you." I smile at her. "We're just browsing."

She reaches out to pat my shoulder. "I heard about your

little bundle. My mama ran into Sandy from the Sage and Salt, who said you're engaged to our hot local fire chief?"

I shake my head as I'm about to protest.

"Ain't it funny how rumors spread around here?" Cassie interjects, trying to save me from having to explain Asher's and my situation. "Thanks for offering to help! We'll let you know if we need anything."

She smiles warmly at Maria, who looks slightly confused but nods before heading over to help another customer.

I turn to Cassie. "Thanks for that. I can't wait to hear what everyone thinks when it's time for me to move back into my house."

"You're worrying about tomorrow's problems." She studies me for a moment. "I mean this with no offense, and in the best possible way, but I think maybe your adoption has put up a big roadblock for you. It's made you *too* afraid of anything unplanned or unforeseen."

"Maybe," I agree. I've definitely always had this fear of not being there for my child when I became a mother. Now that I'm actually pregnant, that anxiety has grown stronger by the week.

"I think my therapist would say . . . it's like if you feel like you can plan everything out, you can control it." Cassie looks at me over the rack of baby clothes. "But you can't control everything, Liv." She offers me a reassuring grin. "Your baby is the perfect example of that. Thomas Rhett said it best: You can make all your plans but life just changes. They're words to live by."

I laugh. Deep down, I know she's right.

"My advice? Just go with it. We could all be dead tomorrow."

"What a beautiful sentiment," I say sarcastically.

"I mean, the whole town thinks you're together anyway." She stops to spin on her heel. "Look at it like baking!"

I crumple my face up at her. "Mmmmkay...?"

"You have the flour. That's Asher. You have the... sugar. That's you. And the baby, naturally the egg. All this other stuff..." She leans in close. "The yearning, the chemistry; it's like the baking soda and the vanilla, the butter. Alone, they don't do anything. But together... pure magic."

"I have no idea if that made any sense." I let out a snort. "But I'll take it."

"So... are you gonna tell him you're catching *real* feelings for him? Not just the orgasmic kind?"

"We'll see. He has to come home first." *Home.* Just the thought gives me butterflies.

"Haden said they've got the fires over fifty percent controlled. He could be back any day now."

We continue to shop, and I also start putting together a list of the baby items I still need to buy for my own little one. Twenty minutes later, when we're in line to pay, my phone buzzes in my pocket.

> **CECE**
> A little birdie told us you might need some girl talk.

> **CECE**
> Come for dinner tonight?

> **GINGER**
> I second. I need my girls tonight.

> **CECE**
> Your house, Liv? Yes, I'm inviting us over but we'll bring pizza. *Smile emoji*

> **GINGER**
> Maybe if we get it extra spicy it will evict this little princess from you.

> **CECE**
> One could only hope. She's overstayed.

I look up at Cassie. She shrugs with a sheepish smile on her face, and I know she messaged them while we finished shopping.

"Thought you could use a girls' night?" she offers.

> **ME**
> Sure, as long as one of the pizzas you bring has extra pepperoni on it.

CHAPTER 45
Asher

I lift my hard hat and wipe the sweat, grit, and soot from my hot, filthy forehead. The last two weeks have been nothing I've ever seen before. The Franklinville fires were just like a blowtorch on a mission to ignite and destroy the thing next to it. What wasn't on fire was soon to be on fire. One hundred and eighty volunteers are here from all across the country, and the sheer devastation is shocking; the number of homes burned, the way the fire came down the mountainside and impacted these communities and their life stories is fucking gut-wrenching. We've been working seven days a week with one day off before the next shift, which we spent in a spike camp in the next town over. We had one day to shower, eat, and try to sleep before we were bused back into town to start the whole process all over again. Three fires are still burning, although they're contained enough that our work is mostly done. The fire department in the county, along with wildland firefighters in the forest and the mountain, will continue to fight this for another week or so, I'm sure. Rain is expected today, which will be instrumental in putting an end to what I can only call a fucking nightmare.

I offered to stay because I'm naturally a fixer and that is my only mindset out here. My life, my health, my mental health—all of it is an afterthought when I'm on the line. In this job, you have to give a lot to save a lot. So even when you have a fire that officials call unstoppable, even when you have officials screaming to be properly funded so you can help the communities around the blaze? All you want to do is prove the experts wrong and save everything you can.

But after fifteen days on the scene, my emotions have never been more torn. This is the first time I've fought fire and *wanted* to leave. Probably because I've never had anything to go home to before. It's been the hardest fight of my life to stay away from Olivia and the baby. I've thought of nothing but them since I got here; so I've kept my head down, ignoring the pleading messages that still stream in from my uncle, knowing my boys at home have Olivia watched and safe. I've barely had the chance to talk to her but, when I do, Olivia doesn't push me about how bad it is here. She knows not to ask me questions I can't answer.

Instead, she sends what I *need*. Photos of herself, clothing she's bought for the baby, bunnies in my yard, her food. Anything that could bring a touch of light in these dark days.

A pang of longing floods my veins. I fucking miss her so goddamn much, I feel as if my heart has ripped in two. It's all such a new experience for me, but Olivia, and fifteen days in hell, will do that to a man.

My helmet comes off as I climb into the truck with my ride-or-die for the last two weeks: Walker Black. He's on the phone—just as exhausted as me—but hangs up as I shut the truck door.

"Everything okay on the home front?" I ask, taking a chug of electrolytes as sweat pours out of me. I'm wearing almost seventy pounds of equipment and it's ninety-six degrees already out here.

"Kinda. Beau is going a little crazy," he says honestly. "Dad's going through a rough patch again *and* the girls don't sit still." The smoke is still thick outside his window as he gazes out of it. "They're so fucking cute but they can also be little buggers, and they've got him wrapped around their finger. Fucking miss the hell out of them all though."

He shows me a photo on his phone of the two dark-haired cuties smiling at the camera with ice cream–covered faces. "That was yesterday."

I think about my own baby on the way. "I can't believe he's raising them both on his own now."

"It's tough, man." Walker shrugs. "But they've got all of us. My mama's got them outside barefoot in the grass every day; best up brining there is."

He takes off his helmet to reveal dark hair matted to his forehead with sweat and grime. "I'm gonna jump from one inferno to the next when I get home. Fall calving coming up. We'll be going nonstop."

I chuckle. "At least you'll be able to shower and eat something other than camp food."

"True fuckin' story." Knocking my bottle of Bio Steel with his own, Walker grins. "I'll fucking drink to that."

"Thanks for stepping in, brother," I say honestly. "We needed you out here."

"Any time." He smiles wide as my phone lights up. "I live for this shit."

NASH

> All the girls are at the big house tonight.
> Just thought you may want to know.

HADEN

> Yeah, I saw Liv when I dropped Cassie off.
> She looks good, relaxed.

> **ME**
> Thanks, boys. I appreciate you checking in on her for me.

These guys are the closest thing I've ever had to friends. Because they know me well enough to know I don't ask for help with anything or even open up. But the funny thing is, I didn't have to. They've all just been keeping watch on Olivia, as if they knew I'd want to know she was all right while I was gone, and I'm damn grateful. I would've gone insane out here otherwise.

> **NASH**
> Seriously though, it's been fun running around town like PIs.

> **NASH**
> But it'll be good to have you home.

> **ME**
> Can't fucking wait to get back.

I open my photos and look at the one Liv sent me earlier this afternoon. It's her and Duke on their daily walk to the creek. She's in a pair of shorts and a tank, but as I zoom in, I swear I can almost see the hint of a swell in her lower belly. Her hair is back off her perfect, makeup-free, smiling face. *Oh hell yes.*

I think of how we got here. And of how goddamn tired I am of fighting the way I feel for her. These last couple months have been a blur—a blur of red hair and blue eyes, an addictive laugh, and plump, pouty lips that turn up into that pretty smile. My blood starts to race as I start the truck, roll down the windows, and turn up Waylon Jennings as we hit the road. It doesn't feel real, but in less than ten hours I'll be home.

CHAPTER 46
Olivia

"Please, they're huge." CeCe holds up her foot. Her ankles are so swollen at four days overdue and she looks so damn uncomfortable. "At least with my swollen feet I won't have to cook for the next few days." CeCe gives me a wink. If it wasn't also possibly my fate, I would be laughing with her. To give her the best possible start, I spent the better part of my afternoon before shopping with Cassie making her a tray of freezer lasagna and shepherd's pie that she can just heat and serve after the baby finally makes her appearance.

"It'll all be worth it when you hold that little love muffin," Mama Jo says.

CeCe, Ginger, Cassie, and Mama Jo are sat outside on Asher's back deck and Ivy is at home with Billi, who is teething and miserable. We're eating snacks and talking shit, and Cassie was right, it's exactly what I needed. For the first time in two weeks there is life here, and I welcome it.

"You're next." CeCe points at me when I laugh.

"Right now I feel pretty good." I shrug. "No more morning sickness."

"That's because this is the honeymoon part of your pregnancy." She smiles at me. She's so round and adorable right now. "You're in the 'my boobs are a little bigger, my ass still looks great, and all I want to do is eat and fuck' phase."

"Darlin'." Jo scrunches up her face.

"Sorry, Mama, but it's true."

"How long does that last?" I ask as I pet Duke's big head. He hasn't left my side since the girls arrived. "I've almost resorted to sleeping with my vibrator," I admit and they all laugh, but it's true. Lately, I can't get myself off *enough*.

All I can think about is Asher—the way he looks at me with that burning desire, and how desperate it makes me to have him. I keep picturing the way he digs his hands into my thighs and hips, and how his dark brows furrowed as he fucked into me, over and over.

"She's thinking about it right now." CeCe hikes her thumb over her shoulder at me and pops a chip in her mouth, snapping me from my vision. Ginger, Mama Jo, and Cassie all laugh.

"For me it was until about seven months," CeCe continues. "After that, I was just tired and growing bigger by the day. Now I feel like a beached whale."

"Well, you're the prettiest beached whale I've ever seen." Ginger grins.

"When's it your turn?" Cassie turns to ask Ginger, who looks around at all of us.

"Um . . . well . . . actually," she starts sheepishly. All our heads snap to her. "We just found out."

Screaming ensues around the table as we stand and hug Ginger one by one.

Tears stream down my cheeks. "We're all pregnant at the same time?"

"Cole wants our kids to be as close in age to Mabel as possible. She's almost ten already, so . . ."

"Kids?" Jo asks. "How many are you two planning?"

Ginger shrugs. "I don't know . . . a baseball team full?"

CeCe sits up, lifting her feet to rest in Ginger's lap. "Our babies are gonna be such good friends. Not Angels next gen."

"I'm due in the spring, so I'll be right behind you." Ginger pops some Skittles into her mouth with a smile as a vision of our kids growing up together washes over me. Hell, I must be getting sappy in my hormonal state because I can't stop the tears from gathering in my eyes again.

We spend the next hour in easy conversation, talking baby stuff, what music Cassie is writing, how Mama Jo is going to cope with three grandbabies in tow. I show them photos of my house now that it's nearing completion.

"Shane thinks it will be only another three weeks or so before it's done."

"And then what?" Ginger asks, piling her unruly curls into a big messy bun. "You seem pretty cozy here."

I sigh. "I don't know."

I take a sip of my homemade mocktail, a strawberry daiquiri made from a Pinterest recipe. The girls seem to like it.

"You'll know when he gets home," Jo chimes in. She's been helping us solve boy, and then man, problems since we were fifteen. "Those first few seconds with him will solve everything. I'd bet my last dollar on it."

As if on cue, my phone buzzes in my lap.

A

> Looks like you and little bear are gonna have to get used to having a roommate again.

I smile down at my phone as a thousand butterflies take flight with just the sight of his name on my lock screen.

> **ME**
> You're coming home?

> **A**
> Filling out the paperwork as we speak.

My heart hammers in my chest with anticipation.

> **ME**
> Are you okay?

> **A**
> I'm wrecked.

> **A**
> But I can't fucking wait to see you, Liv.

My stomach drops with his honesty. *God. I really miss him.*

"If he looks at you anywhere close to the way you're looking at your phone, I'd say it's written in the stars," Jo says as she fills her bowl back up with potato chips.

I look around at my best friends, so damn grateful for them.

"Total gaga." CeCe laughs and the rest of the girls follow. But I let them, because the excitement rushing through my blood and the smile I'm wearing isn't going anywhere anytime soon.

Daddy's coming home, little bear.

CHAPTER 47
Asher

It's just after four in the morning when I come in through my front door as quietly as I can. Olivia will absolutely be sleeping, and I don't want to wake her, but Duke is already wise to my arrival and is at the door waiting for me when I open it. I drop to my knees as he whimpers into me.

"Such a good boy, ain't ya? Watching the fort for me?"

He gruffs against my leg; it's the longest I've ever been away from him, so I know he's been wondering where the hell I've been. I'm so fucking glad Liv was able to be here. I would've hated to board him.

He doesn't let up, mewling into my chest, giving me the best dog hug he can.

"Where's Mama?" I ask him in a whisper as I set my gear down at the door. I'll fuckin' deal with it tomorrow. All I want to do now is have a hot steaming shower and crawl into bed. My arms ache to hold Olivia and, as I look around, I'm shocked at how much she's managed to ingrain herself into my fucking soul. Lavender from the side garden sits on the counter in a big vase and freshly baked cupcakes are covered just beside them.

Olivia and our baby have taken these four walls and a roof and made this house a *home.*

I round the corner, walk down the hall, and peer into my bedroom. My heart hammers in my throat at the sight of her sleeping so peacefully. One panty-clad hip peeks out of the blankets parked on a pillow she's cradling, and my eyes quickly roam over her as I take in all the tiny details I've missed over the last two weeks.

The way her soft copper hair curls around her, how her full lips pop open as she breathes softly. My gaze tracks the fleshy curve of her hip, her perfect ass on display, and goddamn if I'm not almost salivating for her. The sight has me dreaming of waking her up with my face between her soft thighs and envisaging how pretty she'd look riding my cock until she came all over it. I adjust myself in my pants, rock-fucking-solid as I head for the shower, realizing it's the only thing keeping me from crawling in beside her and doing just that.

As I take off all my clothes and step into the steaming space, I wonder what she's dreaming about. Because I hope it's me. *I hope it's always me.*

It takes me a good twenty minutes and a few passes with the shampoo and soap before the bottom of the tub is clean again and my skin has returned to its normal tone. The adrenaline races through my veins as I imagine my hands roaming Olivia's every curve, taking her fast and hard at first, and then slower so I can worship her the way she deserves.

"Fuck." I grip my cock, ready to shut off the water and go make all these visions reality, when I hear the door open and turn to find Olivia standing in the middle of the bathroom in her underwear. Her hair is wild as her chest rises and falls; her eyes are glassy from sleep but focused solely on me. Her nipples are hardened to points under her white tank top, begging for my lips, my teeth. The bottom of her shirt sits just at her belly button, and the sight of the slightest bump below it almost takes me out at the fucking knees.

My baby.

She doesn't even take off her clothes when I open the glass shower door. She just closes the space between us until she's in my arms and my mouth slams down on hers, kissing her like she's the breath I need to fill my lungs. And fuck, in this moment, she *is*.

Olivia

The absence of Duke on top of the comforter at my feet when I roll over wakes me from a deep dream, one where Asher's hands were on me. Touching as his lips tasted me, driving his solid cock in and out of me as my back arched and I moaned his name. As happens almost every night, I wake up positively soaked between my thighs, about to explode from the ache. I'm just about to reach for my vibrator when I hear it.

Water running. I freeze, listening to make sure I'm not imagining the sound.

And it's now that I realize I smell smoke. Not smoke like the house is on fire, but a deep campfire-like scent, and I know instantly he's home.

I don't even think or question myself as I race up the stairs as fast as my legs will carry me, pushing the bathroom door open to find Asher in the shower, his hand on his cock, his hard body even harder, even more defined, than when I last saw him. The veins in his arms and hands are more prominent after three weeks of grueling labor, though he's no longer dirty from the road. He's clean, and all that is left is this incredibly stunning man, scars, ink, and all.

There's no darkness in front of me. It might as well have washed down the shower drain with all the dirt and soot that I'm certain was covering him when he got home. Asher is fucking incredible—my brave hero, my broody man of few words with everyone else but *me*.

His gray eyes land on me and his mouth morphs into a smile.

I don't wait one more second. The moment I see his hand on the door to the shower, I'm moving, not even bothering to take off my clothes before I'm in the rushing water with him, the heat and warmth washing over both of us as Asher wraps his strong, powerful arms around my waist and kisses me with so much passion I can barely breathe.

It's beyond demanding. It's his lips, tongue, teeth, hurried yet slow, hungry yet calculated. Asher is wild and frenzied as his hands sink into my wet hair and tilt my head for better access. I meet him just as eagerly, just as desperate, and kiss him until I'm breathless.

He drops to his knees and wraps his arms around my waist, lifting my sopping tank top to pepper soft kisses on my belly.

"How's my little bear?" His deep rasp sounds so damn good as I run my fingers through his hair. "Fuck, you've grown since I've been gone . . ."

He's having a private conversation with our child, and it melts me from my head to my toes. But not as much as when he gives my belly one final kiss and then stares up at me with those molten gray eyes, his pupils blown wide.

"Hey, little mama."

"Hey," I whisper back, a sob catching in my throat. And then he's up and kissing me again. I moan into his mouth as he pulls my wet top from my body before tearing at my panties and tossing them to the shower seat.

"*Fuuuck*," he groans as his eyes move over my naked flesh. His lips roam my throat, my collarbone, while I press my body into his. He moves his mouth down to my breasts as he cups them in his big palms and toys with one nipple between his finger and thumb, sucking the other between his lips and swirling his tongue over it.

My head falls back in release because my nipples have been so sensitive. And, somehow, Asher knew that.

"Ash . . . fuck," I whine as he continues, taking his time. "You're going to make me come just from *that*."

He growls as he moves to the other bud and takes it in his mouth, playing with me, offering me sweet torture as my pussy positively throbs.

"I'm going to take my time with you, Livi girl. I'm going to fucking worship this stunning body." He rises and tips his head to mine. "But I don't fucking have it in me right now. I want you too fucking badly to be gentle with you."

"Yes. Gentle. Later," I manage as he continues the roll of my nipple between his thumb and forefinger. "Please, just fuck me."

I barely have two brain cells to rub together as Asher's teeth graze the space under my chin, biting gently and throwing little sparks into that fire I chase. I'm groaning, and the sound echoes off the glass as his lips trail across my jaw. He slides his hand up to my throat, turning my face to hold his gaze. His dark, stormy eyes are on mine as that free hand trails between my legs and runs through my soaking pussy.

"Goddamn, kitten. All this fucking mess for me?"

Asher smirks as he backs up slightly, his lip between his teeth as my fingers move to my clit, unable to stop myself. He watches as I take over, the sounds of my fingers sliding through my soaked and aching pussy filling the shower.

"That's it, fuck." He watches me, stroking his own leaking cock. "Such a good girl getting yourself good and ready. That tight little pussy is just begging for my thick cock, isn't it?"

"Oh God, please . . ." I breathe out as he moves to lift me up, pulling me down into his lap as he sits on the bench seat in his shower. Water rains down on my back as he holds me here, looking up into my eyes.

"I've thought of nothing else but you for fifteen days," I tell him as one finger slips between us, inside me, and my head falls back. My breath is ragged, and my body begs at the sight of him when I open my eyes. His gray eyes are hooded and dark as his huge cock strains to claim me.

I run my hand through his wavy hair, gripping tight as he slowly finger-fucks my pussy, getting me good and ready to take him. I don't want him to stop, but he removes his finger—leaving me feeling hollow—and I whimper against his lips with the loss.

"Tell me how many times you've used that vibrator I know you stuff under my bed on this hot little pussy while I've been gone."

Asher strokes my G-spot perfectly as I rock with him. I'm gonna last about zero seconds with him doing this.

"Every day," I admit. "Every damn day, Ash."

He removes his finger gently and smacks my clit in a tight little slap with a tsking sound.

"So impatient, my greedy girl."

He smacks my clit again and I whimper as he smooths over the pain as a thrill runs through me.

"And what have you thought about, hmm? Making yourself come in my bed, my dirty little slut . . ."

His words are so brazen. But I want them. I want *more*. Every part of me is hypersensitive after dreaming of him for days on end.

"You . . ." I grit out. "Fucking me, filling me . . . God, I want you to fill me."

Asher looks down, positioning himself against me. His cock slides through my soaked pussy, and the feel of the metal barbell against me makes goosebumps erupt all over my skin. He grows even harder beneath me—his dick leaking precum—before he lifts me mercifully, beginning to push that first few inches in so slowly I think I might die.

"Hands on the glass, Liv," he orders. "I want to watch these perfect tits bounce."

I do as he says, reaching out for the glass behind him. We both groan when he pushes a little deeper, and I watch as he takes his lip between his teeth, squeezing my hips so damn tight my pussy clenches around him. Everything is heightened as I continue to sink onto him and fiery tingles race up my spine. Asher makes it only about halfway before he all but roars into my lips, and the sound is like a shot straight to my core.

"*Fuuuck*, I missed you, baby . . ."

I don't know what this is, or how to control it, but for once I don't try to. I don't think at all. I just let go of my fears and worries and speak from my heart.

"I've missed you so much," I whisper as he holds me tight and I see my hands leave prints on the glass. "Let me move, Asher . . . please."

That last word leaves my lips like a plea and soon he's giving in, thrusting slow and deep inside of me. Our breathing accelerates and we both sigh in satisfaction as he pulls out halfway, then pushes back in, all the while squeezing my flesh to hold me steady as his abs and arms flex and he watches where we connect.

"Fuck . . ." He breathes out as he pushes deeper. "You take me so well . . . *this perfect body begging*, sucking me in so deep. So beautiful Livi girl."

Water streams over us, and the tiled bench bites into my knees as I lean forward for a scorching kiss. He pushes deeply into me again and my thighs grip his as my pussy clenches around his size. After three months, everything feels brand-new. We both huff out a breath as he fills me to the hilt, and it's in this moment that I realize I'm exactly where I'm supposed to be.

I mewl into him as another thread of control snaps while we still, both of us just existing from this moment to the next.

"Now . . ." He grazes his scarred thumbs over my hips, then reaches up to pinch my nipple just enough to make me whimper. "Fuck me like you own me, Liv. Fuck me like I'm yours."

"Yes, sir . . ." I whisper into his lips as I rest my forearms on his shoulders, sliding up then back down, moving faster, taking him deeper, my submission fueling him as he groans.

His eyes are unhinged as he moves with me, fighting his own need for control. We set a deep, delicious pace, and I fucking love this side of him, the side that only *I* get to see. I want to push him like this forever. To watch him become wild, out of control, and utterly lost in his desire.

"That's it, baby. I want to feel your pretty pussy fight to take all of me."

Asher thrusts his hips, taking me as deep as he can. I whimper as he forces himself to fit, and the pain is bliss.

"You're gonna use *me* now, kitten." His voice is a warning. "Do you understand?"

"Yes . . ." I say as heat coils in my core as he reaches up and grazes my cheek with his thumb.

"I'm gonna give you everything, I see *you* pretty girl . . ."

My eyes flutter open to study his; they're maniacal and lust-crazed but it's like he's seeing my soul the way no one has before.

"You want *rough*." He pinches my clit between us, hard, and I almost come all over him on the spot. "You want me to claim this tight little pussy, don't you?"

"Yes . . . please!"

He times his thrusting hips perfectly with mine, watching the way he fucks into me.

"Mmmm, yes . . . look at how pretty you are, taking my thick cock . . ." *Thrust.*

". . . how you become the woman you were meant to be when you're treated right." *Thrust.*

"To remind you, I'll still be dripping down these thighs

when you wake up baby . . ." His hands tighten their grip at the top of my legs.

"Fuck yes . . . please!" I cry. "That's what I want!"

"Aye, that's just what my dirty little slut *would* want."

With his next thrust he hits the spot inside me that makes me almost shatter.

"Christ . . ." he groans as I clench around him. And then he takes over for me because I'm too far gone. He works his hips with an expert pace, and I can't keep up; each time he bottoms out, I lose a little more of myself to him. His hand slides from my hip to my hair as he angles my face to meet his eyes. He's so big and overwhelming, I lose the ability to function as my orgasm begins to roll through me like a thunderous wave about to crash.

"Asher, I'm gonna come . . ." I moan out as I bury my face into the crook of his neck.

"Then come," he orders with a deep growl. "Show me that I'm the only man who can fuck you into this desperate, whimpering mess."

His depraved words are everything I've always needed as my legs tighten around him. And then I'm falling apart, coming so hard it's like fireworks have ignited through my blood. I'm floating as my pussy tightens around him, and I'm crying out his name.

"*Ah fuck* . . . Atta girl, Liv. You're so fucking good to me, now I want to hear my name when I fill this pretty pussy, got that kitten?"

"Yes! Asher . . ." his movements grow slower and deeper as his hands grip my ass so damn hard. I'm helpless to fight it, helpless to anything but his words, existing in the perfect way he fucks me. Everything comes crashing down, but then the heat coils again as if I have no control over my own body and I cry his name out again.

"Olivia . . ." He groans my name like a prayer as he spills

into me, wrenching another orgasm from me in the process. This feeling between us reaches out and grips me in an iron chokehold as we fall apart, together until all I feel is his warmth all around me, and inside me.

I wind my fingers through his dark hair, clinging to him as his movements slow and his breathing softens. This feeling isn't temporary and it has nothing to do with my hormones. This feeling is terrifying. I'm falling in love with the father of my child, and I have no idea if he can ever truly be mine.

CHAPTER 48
Asher

"That's the thing with all this girly shit. The plot's so fucking obvious."

"Yes, but we love it. And I think you love it." Olivia kisses my lips. She's right. I do. And I never want it to end.

"And it's not *that* predictable," she adds.

"It'll be a happily ever after, you wait and see," I tell Olivia as we watch the movie she chose: *The Ugly Truth*. So far, Gerard Butler's character in this movie has been a dud. But by the last third, I find myself oddly rooting for him to get his shit together and win over the girl. I reach over and take a bite of Olivia's ice cream straight out of the carton. She tugs it away. "You just said you didn't like chocolate cherry."

"It's growing on me." I take another scoop and pop it in my mouth, along with a final bite of a chocolate cupcake from the batch Olivia made the other day, then lean back against my pillows resting against the headboard. We're naked in my bed after the shower where she let me wash all that beautiful hair; it's so thick and soft, so vibrant and such a stark contrast to my scarred, inked hands. *Christ, even this woman's hair makes me hard.*

"Just keep this stocked for the next few months and you'll remain firmly in my good books, Reed."

Olivia holds up her bite of ice cream before sticking it in her mouth. The twinge in my chest is back as I watch her.

"I'm not already in your good books?" I pinch her pretty pink nipple and she squeals like a little mouse.

"You're growing on me."

She pops in another bite; she's happy, and safe, eating ice cream and cupcakes for breakfast in my bed at eleven in the morning. Fuck, if heaven is real, then this is it. This is all I'd want. Olivia's silky, naked perfection beneath my blankets.

"It probably doesn't help that everything I'm craving is sweet," she says happily. "Even though I'm pregnant, I'd really like to not gain a hundred pounds eating ice cream and peanut butter and jelly sandwiches."

I look at her and tuck my arm behind my head. "Peanut butter and jelly?"

"Specifically, Uncrustables with the raspberry jelly. The market near my shop stocks them and I've been living off them the last week." She mentions the premade sandwiches you can buy from the store.

"Fuck, those are full of chemicals."

"I know, but they're *so* good." She laughs as she sets down her empty carton.

I flip over so I'm propped up on one arm, trailing my finger over her collarbone, and her nipples pebble the moment I touch her. I fucking love it.

"You'll be beautiful even if you gain a hundred and fifty pounds," I say to her. "Hot as fuck, and I'll take my time getting to know every single new curve."

"You say that now . . ." she says as my finger dips lower. When I reach her abdomen, I gently press my palm to the small swell there. The connection to the life growing inside her almost cripples me. My own son or daughter, my own blood, and *my* chance to be the kind of father he or she deserves. At first I had no idea if I could really be the man Olivia and our baby deserve, but now, every day I have Liv by my side, I'm starting to believe I'm exactly the man she needs and that I can be the father mine never was too.

I inch down the bed.

"What are you doing?" She giggles as I kiss my way down her center until I reach the little bump, kissing her there too.

I look up at her from my place at her low belly. "I read that the baby can hear me."

"Not yet, I don't think." She shoots me a grin.

"Hey," I say, pointing at her, trying to keep my face serious. "Don't bring that negative vibe here. This is between me and the baby."

"Oh, is it now?" Her smile is ear to ear now. Goddamn, I'll never tire of how gorgeous she is.

"Hey, little bear, it's . . . your dad." I swallow down those words that seem so powerful and *right*, while swallowing the fear that always threatens to take over when I think of keeping our baby safe and happy.

"Tell your mama, please, that no matter what happens while you grow inside her she'll be a fucking knockout because she's doing something amazing." I look at Liv. "She's growing you."

"Even when I have stretch marks and my feet are double the size?" she challenges.

I rest my head on her stomach as I continue. "I'll kiss every single inch of you, Olivia, and stretch marks? Those are fucking badges of honor for how miraculous this body is." I slide my hand up and down her thigh. "They'll be the proof of the badass woman you are, what you're capable of."

Her hand continues to stroke my hair as she watches me with glassy eyes.

"You and me, yeah?" I breathe out.

She nods as I turn my face back to talk to little bear. "But please, if you get anything from me, little one . . ." I cup my mouth as if to whisper. "I hope you get my feet."

Olivia laughs and swats at me as I pounce upward to hover above her.

"Fuck you, discriminating against my toes!"

She writhes under me as I move downward before springing up to my knees and lifting her heel, bringing her pretty pink toes to my lips and kissing the pads of them while I stroke the underside of her foot with my thumb. Her breathing starts to quicken as she pulls a finger to her lips and takes it between her teeth.

"I only joke . . ." I kiss the next one, then the one after that. "But the truth is, I find every single part of you fucking flawless."

I kiss the last one then move to run my lips against her ankle, and then the inside of her calf as I stroke the underside of her knee.

I push her thighs apart and settle my hips between them, pressing my already aching cock against her core as I look down at her panting, the needy look in her eyes back already.

"I'd lube up and fuck the arches of your feet if you asked me to."

She laughs as I kiss one cheek, and then the other. "You're insane."

"Maybe . . . because I'd do anything to see that perfect little O your pretty lips form into when you take my cock deep." I tip my forehead to hers. "The only thing I won't do is stop burying myself deep in your sweet, perfect pussy. I'd fucking beg to live and die here."

I push into her with one languid thrust, and the crushing worry I live with constantly leaves my mind as I kiss her. My selfish want, the need I have that I can no longer push down, takes over as her lips part and I fill her.

"Aye," I say, watching her moan. "Just like that, baby."

Olivia's thighs wrap around me and I lose myself to her body, mind, and soul, which is when I know that every single thread of fight in me is gone. This tether I have to her is something I can physically feel, it weaves between us and my need for her pushes right through our crafted boundaries. It sends me into no-man's-land. No-man's-land being the fact that there's nothing pretend or short term about the way I feel for Olivia. I don't know how to tell her, so I have to show her, and the only way I can do that is to worship her until all my fears are gone, faded with the sun as it sinks behind the mountain and the intoxicating sound of my name on her lips.

CHAPTER 49
Asher

I'm scared. He only gets really mad like this when she disobeys him, and when this happens I have to go to my hiding place.

I'm crouched down behind the toy box in my bedroom. I'm in my closet but I can still hear him.

"You think you're gonna threaten me, Sierra? I'll fucking destroy you."

I flinch. I've heard him speak to her like this for the ten years I've been alive but I still hate it. I silently pray to Saint Michael to protect me and Mom, whispering the prayer she taught me for when Dad gets mean.

"She was my friend! You promised!" my mother cries. "You promised you wouldn't—"

"My business is my business. She's just a hole, I don't give a fuck whose friend she is!"

I squeeze my eyes shut as I summon all my courage to run into the room. My mom is on the floor, cowering from him and covering her face.

"Why can't you just behave?" I ask her as tears stream down my face. He wouldn't get angry at her if she did.

"Aye, son, you tell the stupid little skank how to behave. He's fucking ten years old and he knows you're out of line."

I ball my fists at my sides. I hate when he calls her names. He turns to go—anger radiating from him—and when I hear the front door slam shut, I follow in his footsteps to make sure he's gone. When I can see his car lights through the window, my shoulders relax just a little. He's gone.

My friend at school just has a mom. I wish I just had a mom. I take a deep breath and run as fast as I can back into the living room.

"Asher..." I hear her call me, though I can't get to her fast enough. "My little hawk..."

"I'm sorry, Mommy," I tell her as I round the corner. "I didn't know he would hurt you again. I was trying..."

"It's okay, baby," she whispers, holding my hand. "Get my ice and a cloth, okay?"

I nod and she flashes me a crooked smile. "Promise me, Asher. Don't be a Donovan. Everything a Donovan man touches dies."

She places her hand on my face as she mumbles in the weird way she does when she drinks too much wine.

"I'll get you some ice," I tell her, trying to hold in my tears the way Dad told me I should.

"Asher..." she calls as I run through our house to get her what she asked for. The house is very big, and it takes time for me to get to the kitchen. "Asher!"

"Asher."

I sit up in a cold sweat to the incessant sound of buzzing and a warm hand on my arm.

I turn quickly to try to focus on the space around me.

"You're shaking." I realize the voice belongs to Olivia and the buzzing is my phone. I flip it over and see my uncle's name on the screen. It's as if he has some sort of direct connection to my brain; my past haunts me, whether I'm awake or asleep.

Olivia wraps her arms around me and I take a deep breath, steadying myself.

"You were dreaming. You were saying, 'I'm not him.'" She kisses my head. "Are you okay?"

I grip her tight, burying my face in her hair, reliving my dream. The trauma of my early childhood and my father's abuse is buried in the deepest parts of my brain.

Olivia moves to unwrap her arms, but I hold her tighter.

"Stay," I tell her. "Please, just stay."

Everything a Donavan man touches dies. I squeeze my eyes shut to push my mother's words away. I don't want to let her go.

"I'm not going anywhere, Ash. I'm right here."

"Olivia," I whisper, trying to catch my breath. I'll never be the source of any pain for her. "I'll never hurt you, I promise. I'll break the cycle. I'm not him."

There's a burning need inside me to tell her everything, even if it means losing her. I look to her in the dark.

"My father, he's not just a cutthroat businessman with a shady empire. It all runs deeper than that. Much deeper. The things I had to do, things for my fucking dad to keep him happy, things I need to tell you—"

Olivia places her finger to my lips, silencing me.

"I don't want to know, Asher."

I stare at her, stunned by her words. She doesn't *want* to know?

"Is the man you were then the man you are now?" she whispers as she holds me. Her voice is soft and calm and soothes me as she traces the outline of my jaw with her fingers.

"What?"

"Is the man you were then who you'll be in the future for me, or our baby?" Her eyes search for answers. "Are you still that man, Ash?"

"No," I answer gruffly. "I'm not . . ." *But I still don't deserve to keep you.*

"I don't need you to confess all of your—or your father's—sins for me to trust you. I only care about who you are now, who you'll be tomorrow, for me and for little bear. If you want to talk about it I'm here, always, but I don't *need* it. Understand?"

Olivia places my hand over the life growing inside her. She's radiating strength and resolve, and this mercy is greater than any other. She accepts me, sins and all, and the sheer relief of that is damn near overwhelming.

"I want to be . . . the best man that I can be for you and our child," I tell her before dropping my lips to hers and kissing her with a passion I've never felt in my life.

"Your father has nothing on you now," she says as she strokes my hair. "He can't touch this life you've built."

Suddenly, something in me breaks for this woman. Olivia could push me, could ask me to talk more about how I feel, but she doesn't. Instead, she simply holds me in the dark and smiles, the smile I already know I don't want to go a day without seeing.

"You're fucking incredible," I tell her, not knowing what else to say because this feeling is fucking overwhelming me. *I can't live without you. I love you.*

This isn't a matter of allowing myself to speak these words. It's a matter of being *unable* to. It's years of mistrust and trauma and abuse, but I know I'll get there. For now, all I can do is show her every goddamn day how much I love her.

"You know what always makes me feel better when I'm thinking of my parents? How I lost them? How I can't change where I came from?"

"Hmm?" I ask as I tighten my hold on her, drinking her in.

"Rom-com-athon." She smiles.

I look at the clock. "It's four A.M."

This woman is a lunatic, but she's *my* lunatic. And oddly

enough, the idea sounds good. Because anything sounds good with Olivia Sutton.

"Perfect time for a little . . . hmm . . . let's see." She picks up the remote. "Ohhh, I know, *The Proposal*."

She starts prattling on about the plot as she selects the film and presses play. Less than an hour later, I smell my coffeemaker brewing its daily fresh pot. The sun is just starting to rise, casting a warm glow through my balcony doors, and I've forgotten all about my dream and my uncle calling me. I'm completely satisfied and whole with Olivia in my arms as we watch Sandra Bullock realize Ryan Reynolds is the richest guy in Alaska. *Okay, maybe these rom-com movies aren't so bad after all.*

We both doze off toward the end, and it isn't until after seven, when we wake up and Olivia hops in the shower, that I read my uncle's message.

> P
>
> Your father has passed on, son.
>
> P
>
> We still need to talk.

I stare at the message for a long moment, letting it register how unaffected I am to hear that the man who made me, the one I lived under since the day I was born, has died.

I don't have one cherished memory of him. Not one pang of grief for him. All this means is that maybe I'm *finally* free of the shadow that has haunted me for years. I can't bring back my mother, but maybe now I can just live my life as my own man and finally make Olivia mine for good. Maybe the deep, dark sins of my past can be buried with my father.

Rising out of bed, I leave Duke snoozing at the foot of it as I toss on my sweats and move quickly through the dewy morning grass into my workshop, placing my phone on the top of the butcher block work desk.

> P
>
> I'm meeting with Cale McAllister this morning. You really should call me and we can discuss arrangements for your father's service.

> P
>
> Come home, Asher.

Pete was my safe space when I was young, but I can feel his fingers trying to pull me back in, and I want nothing to do with it. Letting him go is how I protect Olivia and the baby. So no trace of my former life can touch either one of them.

As I pick up a hammer from the hooks above the bench and bring it down harshly, striking the screen of my phone, I feel fucking free. I'll have to get a new one, with a new number, later. But for now, I can say goodbye. My father is gone.

I strike again as memories run through my head—of every time he screamed at my mother, struck me, or made me watch him beat somebody without remorse. Of when he paraded his mistresses around like my mother wasn't watching, like she was *nothing*. Of the nights I slept on that cold, hard cot in prison, realizing my family caring about me meant making sure I had enough in commissary but never coming to visit me as I rotted for them.

I remember them all as the phone turns into dust, my chest heaving as I stare down at the remnants. Tossing the hammer down, I swipe the broken glass and components into the trash before steadying my breath, feeling better than I have since I arrived in Laurel Creek. Because I'm no longer running from my past. I'm saying goodbye to it.

James Ari Donovan, good fucking riddance.

CHAPTER 50
Olivia

SEPTEMBER

EIGHTEEN WEEKS
Fall is coming. A quickening in the air like a baby's first movements. Little flutters as gentle as the leaves falling from the trees. Seasons change and so do we, inevitably and beautifully.

My thumb traces the soft, warm face of my angel niece Ruby Rae Carter, who was finally born in the middle of the night, fast and furious, three weeks ago. No matter how many times I've seen her since she was born, I can't get enough. Her mouth moves—like she never stops being hungry—while I rock her gently back and forth.

"I might never give her back," I tell CeCe. She's sitting on her sofa in her and Nash's home, happy but utterly exhausted. Her blond hair is piled high on her head and she's wearing a soft pair of nursing-friendly pajamas. Nash is home with her and the baby for another week, and I love watching the adorable way he fawns and fusses all over Ruby.

"It's amazing how someone so tiny can turn your life completely upside down," CeCe says with a tired smile as she sips the matcha we brought over while munching on her favorite from Spicer's Sweets, a jumbo blueberry muffin. "It's taking moments like this when you can just rest and let someone else hold her for a minute that feel so good. Make sure you do that," she orders me, already such a mom.

I look out to Asher sitting on the back deck with Nash, drinking coffee and watching the bubbling creek behind Nash and CeCe's house.

"Are you two going to find out what the sex of the baby is?" she asks around her bite.

I shake my head. "No. We sort of made a wager with my parents, and it might be fun to find out at the time. Ash says there are very few real surprises in life, ya know?"

"Ash?" CeCe's eyebrows shoot up, ready for the tea. "You two are getting close?"

I shrug. "Hard not to when you live with someone."

"Mm-hmm," she muses as she takes another bite. "But that could end soon, right? When do you get your keys back?"

Ruby yawns in her sleep and my heart melts just from watching her perfect little face.

"In a couple weeks. Asher spent last weekend sanding and lacquering my new cabinets, but he won't let me see them yet. He says the lacquer is bad for me to breathe in. He's been in his woodshop every free moment he isn't at work."

"Or in bed with *you*?" She laughs, knowing all about our situation because, of course, I told her and Ginger.

"I suppose."

"Okay, Liv, time to get honest." CeCe pops the last of her muffin in her mouth and sets her plate down on the table.

"Yes, Mom," I say, not lifting my eyes from the perfect little bundle in my arms.

When I side-eye CeCe, she gives me her best stern face, though it's full of the love she's always given me since we were fourteen.

"I've never seen you this . . . settled. You've always been in a rush. To move on to your next step, your next part of the plan. But now, with him . . ." She gestures over her shoulder to where the guys sit outside. "And this baby. You don't seem like you're in any kind of rush at all."

I look down at little Ruby happily napping in my arms. "There are moments when I feel like we're perfect for each other."

"But?" CeCe asks.

"But we have an understanding about the physical stuff, and I'm not sure that, if I wasn't pregnant, he'd be in this deep with me. I never want the baby to be the reason he decides to settle down. I'd want it to be because he wanted *me*."

"I don't know if you see it the way the outside world does . . . He looks at you like you're his whole universe. In his own possessive and intimidating way."

She laughs and I know she's right. Even now, when I glance at him through the glass, Asher's dark brow is furrowed and he's positioned himself so that he can still see me, and the whole yard, as if an attacker may rise from Nash's creek at any point. I'm sure it's a side effect from always having to be on guard as a child.

I shrug. "I know how he feels now. But will he feel this way after the baby? I'm too afraid to ask him. All I know is that, right now, it's perfect."

I shift Ruby in my arms as I continue. "He's not the type of man I thought I'd fall for. Everything about him is a risk: his past, his job, how much *I'm* starting to care."

"Life is a risk," CeCe says pointedly.

"I'm starting to see that. I can't control my future even when I think I can, and if I'm being honest"—I look out at him on the porch with Nash—"from the first moment I met him, there was something about him. I always know exactly where he is, like I can feel him, like there's this invisible tether between us."

I glance back at CeCe as I bounce on my toes, rocking Ruby back and forth.

"He doesn't let anyone in, but I think he's letting *me* in. He's choosing to open up to me, and that gives me peace. It's like, when he's around, I can breathe a little easier because Asher makes me feel steady and secure. I don't know if that sounds silly or if it even makes sense..."

CeCe smiles at me while she adjusts her pillows under her. She's still a little sore.

"That makes total and perfect sense."

"It does?"

Ruby stirs in my arms and opens her pretty little eyes to look up at me, probably hoping to see her mom.

"Yep," she confirms. "Sounds like maybe you aren't really interested in moving back into your house at all. And if I didn't know any better, Liv, I'd say you were in love with that man."

As Ruby starts to cry, I hand her off to CeCe. My arms feel empty when she's gone, and I run a hand over my own growing baby bump. I'm barely fitting into my shorts these days, so I've resorted to wearing mostly dresses. Being pregnant has shown me how limited cute fashionable maternity clothes are and has inspired me to dig into a deep search and order some sweet designs I've found for the store, and for me. Over the last couple weeks, I also swear I've felt the baby move. They're tiny little flutters, like real butterflies.

"Asher's home feels like our home and, you're right, I love my house, but I'm dreading leaving his." I shake my head. "I never expected to be here."

CeCe starts to nurse Ruby—the sweetest smile on her lips—and it's such a beautiful sight. We've all grown up together and, now, we're all going through this journey of motherhood together. It makes me teary just watching her.

"Maybe how you got here doesn't matter. Maybe all that matters is how you move forward together."

Ruby suckles effortlessly and I realize just how truly miraculous our bodies are. I watch as CeCe picks up a glass of ice water and drinks half of it.

"I swear, the second my milk lets down I'm so parched." She grins. "Pro tip if you nurse: Always have ice water."

"Noted."

It's going to be a serious blessing having CeCe a few months ahead of me, and then me a few months ahead of Ginger.

"I really love you, you know," I whisper to her as Ruby makes adorable little grunting noises at her breast.

She holds eye contact as she sips her water. "I love you too. And you guys are gonna be a great team. Maybe the prince you always dreamed of is just a little different than you planned."

I look out the window.

"It's scary to give your heart to someone who may not be able to give you his in return," I reply softly.

As if he can sense we're talking about him, Asher looks through the window at me and smirks with a little nod. I know now that it's his way of making sure I'm good. I smile back at him and nod quickly too. Letting him know I am.

CeCe grins as she watches us. "That doesn't look hard at all, babe. It looks as natural as breathing."

CHAPTER 51
Asher

"I kind of figured you'd be taking a step back now," Nash answers after I tell him I'll be leaving the bar permanently. With getting Olivia's cabinets done, and her living with me, I just have no desire to spend my nights in the bar when I could be home with her. I knew he'd understand, and it seemed like the perfect time to tell him as we sit on his deck, drinking some good coffee and watching the fish jump in the creek behind his house. It's already obvious that the cooler weather isn't too far off; the afternoon sun streaming through his pergola isn't as warm on our skin as it would've been a few weeks ago.

"We had Matt doing your job when you were away in Franklinville anyway and most nights since. He needs the hours, so I'm sure he'll take on the extra responsibility."

I nod. "Thanks."

"No problem. I get it." He looks over his shoulder then leans in a little. "You still working on her cabinets?"

I nod. "Yeah, almost done now. And I'm thinking about what I can make for the baby, for the nursery."

"Have you managed to talk about where that nursery will be?" he asks as he leans back in his chair.

I shake my head. I'm still getting used to opening up to people like this, but Olivia has made me want to try. "Not yet. We're long overdue for a talk like that, but we both have a problem with making waves when everything is great as it is."

"Been there." Nash drums his fingers against the arm of his chair. "But trust me when I say it will help to talk it out."

I take a deep breath. I know I can trust Nash; with Ruby being so new, he knows exactly what I have to lose.

"There are some things about my life before I met her that I feel she deserves to know. When this all started, it just seemed easier not to explain the connection I still have to my family." I look out at the water as I take a deep breath. "A few weeks ago my father died. And I was gonna tell her everything."

"I'm sorry, man."

I shake my head. "Don't be sorry. He isn't worth it."

Nash just nods. It's what I like most about him—he's a good listener. "She told me she didn't want to know and that it was easier to leave it all in the past. I know I need to let go of that part of my life. But I'm just living in this state of fear that they'll get me one day."

"You're constantly on edge," Nash says like he knows the feeling well.

"Exactly. And I'm really struggling to allow myself to accept the good right in front of me."

"Like you're not worthy of it."

My eyes snap to his. "Aye."

"Things have changed between you two now. It's pretty obvious," Nash comments as he looks out at the lush green land in front of us.

"They have. Drastically. I think . . . fuck, no, I don't think, I *know*, I'm in love with her, man. But I have this incessant need to protect her. And I will not put her in harm's way because of where I came from."

Nash looks down at his coffee, then back to me. "Your past isn't my business. I only know what you've told me, but it's all I need. I only care about the man you are now, and I know you're a good man. A friend. The way you look at her, it's obvious how you feel about her. And the way she looks at you? That makes it obvious she feels the same."

I glance at Olivia; she's perched on the sofa just across from CeCe, holding the most adorable *and* terrifying little person I've ever met. But Olivia's not scared at all. She's a natural, smiling down at Ruby with so much goddamn love in her eyes it makes me desperate for it to be our turn, for us to get our happy ending.

"It just scares the shit out of me thinking that I could lose her, especially when, hell, I think this is what it feels like to be happy."

Nash smirks. "Olivia is like a sister to me. She's one of the kindest people I've ever met, and one of the most understanding. Take it from me. Not facing your demons? Letting them cripple you? They'll catch up to you at some point, regardless of whether you try to keep them at bay. In my opinion, and speaking from experience, it's better to get ahead of them then deal with the aftermath. You have to learn to trust that she'll love you anyway, accept every part of who you are, even the ugly parts. All love really is, is finding someone who brings you so much happiness, so much fuckin' joy, that the devils you're haunted by don't stand a damn chance."

I raise my mug at him with a grin. "When did you get so fucking smart?"

"Since they became my life." He nods inside. "And I'll let you in on a little secret. You may not have told her yet, but Olivia and your baby, they've already become your life. It's written all over you."

I look out at the lake. I've never been good at talking, so the fact that we're even having this conversation astonishes me. I don't think I could put into words how I feel about Olivia, but I know I have to try. As I bring my mug up to my lips, my eyes land on a stack of wood out near Nash's shed at the water.

"That olive wood?" I ask, pointing toward it.

"Yeah." He nods. "Shame. I had to cut the whole damn tree down in the summer. It was getting too close to my power lines. It's pretty rare for them to get that big, from what I'm told."

"It is," I confirm. "What are you doing with it?" I'm curious now; I must be hanging around Olivia too much because I'm starting to hatch a plan.

"Right now, you're looking at it." He chuckles. "Maybe firewood."

"Fuck no," I grumble. "Mind if I take it off your hands?"

"It's yours," he agrees right away. "You'll be doin' me a favor, to be honest."

"Thanks, and uh, thanks for the talk too." I tip my chin to him. "I mean it."

"That's what friends are for." Nash lifts his coffee in a cheers and, as we finish our chat, I'm already designing in my head. I may have a hard time expressing to Liv exactly how I feel, but I know for damn sure I can *show* her.

CHAPTER 52
Olivia

MID-SEPTEMBER

TWENTY-TWO WEEKS
Together, we created a life. Half you, half me, and entirely ours. Now we're over half-way there.

"What is all this?" I ask as I slide open the patio door after the longest Thursday I can remember. My mouth hangs open as I take in Asher's deck. It has been totally transformed, and I'm having a hard time looking at everything all at once. I should've known by all the questions he was asking me over text this afternoon—when I'd be home, how much I still had to do at the store—that he was planning something. He knows I've been working a lot lately, and that I have lists upon lists of things I need to get taken care of and planned for before the baby comes. Duke is already outside with Asher, but Dick follows close by my heel, giving my ankles a quick, loving rub (and nearly tripping me in the process) before disappearing into the yard.

"Thought you could use a night to relax, little mama, get you through the last day of the week tomorrow." He smirks that beautiful grin at me, and my heart skips a little beat with how incredible he is. "Rom-com-athon."

Dear universe. Please let me keep him?

Asher has moved all of the outside furniture, which now sits against the railing facing the back of the house on the fully covered part of the deck. The sofa is covered in blankets and cozy pillows and the side tables are decorated in flameless candles, their glow lighting up the darkening sky as twinkle lights hang overhead from the beams. The coffee table boasts a pizza, salad, and garlic bread, as well as a charcuterie of dark chocolate, fruit, and movie candies.

"You're too good to me." I set my purse down on the sofa and toe off my comfortable Birkenstock sandals.

Asher approaches and kisses me lightly on the lips, then places his big hand over the swell of my belly, which he does every day now, saying hi to little bear too.

It's amazing how much I've grown. At twenty-two weeks we can see an actual baby, a real human with arms and legs flailing around, very active inside me. I've felt tiny kicks and flutters recently, and I'm so excited to really feel him or her moving around so that Asher can experience them too.

The last few weeks have been a blur with Asher working doubles because Walker has had to be at the ranch a lot of nights. Which means we're only meeting in passing. Well, specifically, in bed, devouring each other until the early hours of the morning before we both pass out and start another day. Which means this night means everything to me. Finally, a night just for us.

I still haven't worked up enough nerve to tell Asher I want me and the baby to stay with him permanently. He's installing my cabinets soon, the last piece of finishing my house aside from paint touch-ups, which means that conversation needs to happen soon. Because I'm almost out of time. Though, right now, all I want to do is enjoy this moment, this evening.

"Come on then, we've got a good selection tonight. I think you'll be proud of me. I worked fucking hard on picking the movie lineup."

It's only now that I notice a small outdoor projector set up on the table, pointed at the brick of the back wall on his house.

"Oh yeah?" I laugh, sitting down and picking up a slice of pizza. It's topped with everything I've been craving. Mainly all the meat. "What've you got, Reed?"

Asher takes a seat beside me, sliding his hand up my thigh and over my leggings. Those familiar sparks crackle at my skin with just the simplest touch. On my top half, I'm wearing a cute, oversized, wine cable-knit sweater. Today was just one of those days I needed to be comfy.

"Hey, you joke, but I took this shit seriously," he scolds, wagging a finger at me. "Even looked online for the best rom-coms. These are ranked. *Cosmo* says so."

I laugh a little more as I watch him, utterly in awe of his thoughtfulness.

"We've got some classics tonight. First up, it's *Never Been Kissed*. And then, for the later o'clock showing, with dessert"—he leans in to kiss me—"maybe after a nice hot shower—" Goosebumps break out over my skin. "Maybe a massage . . . We'll be playing everyone's favorite, *Pretty Woman*."

This night sounds like pure heaven. I settle in beside him, satisfied but also unsure of how to put my current feelings into words. No one has ever taken care of me like this, and with everything I've planned for all my life, since that little journal I started when I was nine, I never planned for *him*, the perfect blend of sin and grace. And the way he treats me? It almost makes me feel like maybe none of this was by chance, and maybe there's a world where Asher Reed was *meant* to be mine.

"Awww, remember this one?" my mom says the next evening, passing me a photo of my fifteenth birthday. Asher and I have stopped by for dinner to bring my parents their own copy of our twenty-two-week scan.

I look down at the next photo my mom hands me; it's of me, Ginger, and Cece at the local roller-skating rink. We're so young and carefree, with our arms wrapped around one another. Ginger's hair is pin-straight—back then she hated her curls—and all of us are wearing Twilight T-shirts. CeCe and I have Edward Cullen on ours and Ginger is wearing a Chief Swan T-shirt that says *Team Charlie*. Funny now since she's married to the town sheriff.

I pass it to Asher. "My mom was never not taking photos."

"It's the most important thing you can do!" she defends, continuing to rummage through the box of pictures. I squeeze her hand; it's the best thing she could've ever done. Being able to look back on the life my parents gave me is the biggest blessing.

"I had a slight obsession with Twilight that year, and the party was an all-nighter," I admit as Asher examines the photo.

My dad chuckles. "I remember the manager's face when I told him I wanted to rent the rink for the whole night."

"Twilight?" Asher asks, brows raised in question.

"The book series?" I blink up at him. "The movies? The billion-dollar franchise?"

He stares back at me, utterly clueless. "Edward and Jacob?" I add.

Asher shakes his head.

"Basically, it's four movies about a regular girl who has to choose whether she loves a wolf or a vampire more," my dad chimes in.

"Five actually," I remind him.

"Right." My dad lets out a loud laugh, mock shock on his face. "How could I forget *Breaking Dawn Part Two*?"

"I hope she chose the wolf," Asher comments.

I look at my mom then back at him. "Nope."

He shakes his head. "Stupid move."

"Why?"

"Because a wolf can protect her. Plus, he won't eat her. So there's that."

"Edward—the vampire—doesn't *eat* her, he only *wants* to. Until she becomes a vampire anyway. Then the wolf falls out of love with her and he imprints on her baby."

Asher's jaw falls slack and he rubs his forehead and chuckles. "Imprints? All due respect, but what the *fuck* kind of movie is this?"

My mom and dad laugh at his assessment. When you say it out loud, I guess it does sound weird.

"You had to be there." I swat at him, unable to hold myself back from laughing too.

My mom looks to both of us, a warm smile on her face. She hands me an empty photo album.

"I thought you could choose photos to put in this album. That way"—she steadies her voice—"the baby can look through it when he or she gets older. Get to know their mom a little better."

"Thank you, Mom," I say. "This is amazing."

She shrugs. "You used to love spending hours looking through Nana's photos. And now your baby can do the same."

My eyes glisten as she pats my hand and we both bask in the memories.

"Well, since we're giving photo gifts," Asher says, standing and looking to my dad. "Should we do this?"

My dad grins as he makes to get up. "It's your show."

I look at my mom, confused, as they both duck out of the

room.

"What is this about?" my mom asks.

"I have no idea." It's an honest answer because I am just as confused as she is.

"I wasn't going to give this to you until the baby shower, but it feels more appropriate to do it now," Asher says as he reenters the room carrying two identically wrapped rectangular gifts.

My dad takes a seat next to my mom, all smug and happy like a Cheshire cat.

As if . . . "Do you know what it—"

"Here we go." Asher sets one of the gifts in my lap and one in my mom's. It's heavy and perfectly wrapped in silver paper.

I run my hand over it and look at him as he sits down across from us. Asher's dark jeans hug his thick thighs and his standard black T-shirt, one of twenty that live in his closet, clings to his still-tanned, muscular arms. His beard hasn't seen a razor in weeks but, somehow, even the overgrown scruff on his jaw is perfect too. Especially when it's tickling my arms, or neck, or inner thighs.

"Well, go on then!" Asher coaxes us now, his accent coming through a little stronger than usual with his subtle excitement. As excited as Asher *can* get.

I look at my mom, who's smiling giddily as she starts tearing the paper. I do the same and pull out three frames, each filled with . . . I gasp as my eyes move quickly over the contents. In front of me is a collage of little photos of me and my nana at various stages of life, and next to them . . . My stomach drops and my eyes instantly fill with tears when I register what I'm looking at.

"Her recipes?" I croak out, swallowing the giant lump in my throat. I look back down at the gifts, barely able to see them through the blur of my tears. Asher kept and removed the salvageable recipes from the burned-up old cookbook I

CHASING THE FIRE

thought was lost to the fire? He took my prized possession and turned it into . . . art?

"I hope you don't mind. I took the book and found a restoration company to help remove the soot from the ones that could still be read," he explains.

My fingers trace the glass as tears spill over my cheeks. I look at my mom, who grabs my hand in hers. She's crying too.

"Your dad told me which dishes you used to make with her the most," he continues. "And helped supply the photos, of course."

Each frame houses two or three different recipes, decorated with charred edges, but somehow the burnt design makes the paper prettier. My nana's scribbled notes are all still visible, thanks to the restoration.

In one of mine sits our favorite chocolate cake recipe next to a photo of my nana and a twelve-year-old me making it in her kitchen. I'm laughing in the picture; she'd just swiped batter onto my nose. The other two frames are much the same. One boasts how to make her famous pineapple upside-down cake and is set next to a photo of me, Nana, and my mom at Christmas one year. We're all grinning, wearing our festive aprons at the kitchen island.

I glance at my mom's frames; Asher has included a few photos of when she was little too, in which my nana's eyes twinkle with her own youth. I look over every recipe, every photo, and it's only when I'm done that I see the engravings on the bottoms of the wooden frames.

"Your dad helped me with that too," Asher says with a shrug as my fingers trace the writing on each frame.

"The gravy makes the meal," my mom reads.

"Life is short, eat dessert first," I counter, tears streaming down my cheeks.

"This icing is perfect," my mom says as we turn to look at each other. "Not too sweet," we say in unison.

All my nana's favorite sayings, written into the frames as a homage to her. My heart feels as though it could break inside my chest right now with love, with grief, with joy. *This gift. This man.*

I'm sobbing as I set them down and throw myself into Asher's arms. And then my mom is there in a blink, pulling both of us close.

"Thank you," I say to him. "This is the greatest gift I've ever received. I thought they were lost forever."

My mom moves over to hug my dad, and I follow suit.

"The two of you were in cahoots," she says, wiping her eyes with a laugh as she returns to her seat to study the frames in more detail.

My dad grins. "It was all Asher's idea. I was just there to assist."

I try to catch my breath. "Don't you know better than to do this to a pregnant woman?!"

"I know they were too important for you to lose," Asher says softly, leaning over to place his hand on mine. "You'd already lost enough. Now you can each hang these somewhere special and keep them forever."

And then he's turning to pull two more items out of the bag he carried the frames in, handing us each an unwrapped, new edition of *The Joy of Cooking*.

"And these are to write your notes in. Maybe you can use it to cook with little bear so she can make her own memories with her mom, and her nana."

More tears threaten to spill over, and by the time we've each looked at each other's frames, my mom and I are a blubbering mess, and my dad and Asher are toasting themselves on a mission well done.

And I finally admit to myself without a doubt, in true Olivia fashion, I've fallen for Asher Reed, hook, line, and sinker.

CHAPTER 53
Asher

"What's going on in that mind, Livi girl?"

I can feel her gaze on me as I cradle one of her feet in my hands, rubbing it out after we're home from her parents' house.

"That gift, Ash. No one has ever given me anything so special, and I guess..." She struggles with her words. "I just want you to know how much I appreciate it."

She's stretched out on the sofa, feet in my lap. The windows are open slightly and it's raining outside. The sound beats a slow rhythm on my metal roof as a fire blazes in the hearth. It's only mid-September, but it's been cooler than normal.

"But that's not what's on your mind," I say, knowing she's not being entirely honest.

Olivia is so goddamn beautiful like this by the firelight. It serves to illuminate the fullness of her hips and the swell of her pregnant belly in the soft red dress she's wearing. It has slinky straps and fits tight to her full breasts, cinching her just above her little bump before flowing outward to her mid-thigh. Tonight, her auburn hair cascades onto her shoulders and a red silk scarf pulls it back from her pretty face. The rings and layered bracelets she was wearing earlier in the day are discarded on the coffee table.

"I didn't expect you." She looks around the room, then back down to where I'm rubbing her feet. "I didn't expect any of this. What I mean is, I didn't expect to like you so much . . ."

I chuckle at her bluntness.

"That sounded bad. I just didn't plan . . . any of this. I really did think we could stick to the pact."

She's laughing, but I don't mind, because I know she rambles when she's nervous. Instead, I focus on smoothing out the arch of her soft foot to keep her relaxed. She moans as I work my fingers over her skin, and my cock twitches with the sound.

"I sure as fuck didn't expect you either," I say honestly. "But now I can't imagine my life without you, and as for the pact . . ." I pull her ankle up to my lips to kiss it. "I want a rewrite, kitten."

"A rewrite?" Olivia's coy little grin and raised eyebrow tell me I have her attention.

"Yeah, *no* pact. I say fuck the rules, fuck the boundaries. Let's make a pact to just be there for each other, in any way that feels right."

"Okay . . ." She takes her bottom lip between her teeth and I see her eyes glisten as she watches me. "Ughh. I'm just so sappy."

I press my thumbs into the sole of her foot, causing her head to tip back, and I feel her body physically melt into the sofa.

"My hormones are just all out of whack. I can't decide what I want."

I press again and she moans this time, a throaty little sound, as she flexes her pretty pink toes. And now I'm hard.

"One minute I'm terrified, the next I'm happy and full of joy. And then the next I'm desperate to fuck." She lifts her gaze, her blue eyes sparkling in the light. "I'm even *dreaming* of fucking, for God's sake. My body can't make up its mind," Olivia rambles.

"Tell me what you dream about," I order as my massage trails up her calf.

"You," she answers as I set her leg down. Her foot presses against my swelling dick and she smiles when she notices the effect she's having on me.

"The fuck do you expect?" I deadpan, picking up her other foot. "You make the same noises when you eat, when I massage you, when you fuck. It's always the same."

"So basically I always sound like I'm fucking?" she queries, cocking her head to the side.

"Exactly," I answer. "Which means I'm almost always hard. It's fucking torture."

Of the best kind.

"I think at this point I deserve to hear those dreams as consolation," I continue.

She shrugs her shoulder, flexing out her foot.

"Sometimes we're doing things I've never done before."

Olivia is shy now and doesn't meet my eye as she moves the pad of her foot again, grazing my dick in the process. Though this time I know it's on purpose. My eyes meet hers as she continues.

"Like maybe you're tying me up, keeping me in one place, making me come over and over. Other times I'm just dreaming of the way you speak to me."

I can already see the blush in her cheeks, even in the dimly lit space.

"Using me like I exist only for your pleasure. Though it . . . seems so wrong. I shouldn't want that, should I? It goes against everything I was taught about boundaries, taking control . . ." She trails off and her nipples pebble through the thin fabric of her dress as I grow harder just listening to her. My fingers graze the underside of her knee.

"But I can't help it," she breathes out, letting her legs fall open a little, taunting me. "It gets me off and I wake up *so* wet."

Fuck if I can help myself. At her words, I let go of Olivia's foot and climb up to settle between her thighs, holding my weight above her. I lean in to kiss her lips.

"Listen." I slide one strap of her dress off her soft shoulder. "I'm going to need you to understand that there's nothing I wouldn't do for you." I push down the other strap and it slinks to just above her breast as I duck my head and press my lips to her pulse point.

"Tell me what you want, Olivia." I move to kiss the other side of her neck. "If you're happy, I'll be happy with you."

The back of my knuckle ghosts her nipple through her dress.

"If you're desperate to fuck—" I slide her dress downward until it pools around her waist and her perfect tits bounce free. They're even fuller now with pregnancy and, fuck, they're *begging* to be pulled into my mouth. "I'll make every fucking fantasy you could dream of come true."

I pinch and taunt her right nipple as I continue to murmur against her pillowy skin.

"Whatever it is you need." I wrap my lips around her other nipple and her body arches into me as my tongue flicks over the pebbled little bud.

"But one thing you won't be is afraid to tell me what you want. Understand?" I kiss her lips and she nods. "Think of it as my job to do things with you you'd be fucking *ashamed* of in the morning with anyone else." I trail my thumb over her soft cheek. I already know I'm going to spend my life doing the dirtiest fucking things to her just to please her. "There's no room in this pact we have for judgment."

"O-okay," she agrees as if she's building the courage to admit what she wants. But she doesn't need to. Because I already know. I back off and help her up to sit beside me so she's facing me on the sofa. I can hardly stand how unreal she looks in the orange light.

"You like it when I tell you what to do?" I let my hand trail up her thigh, taking the skirt of her dress with it as her breath rises. "You like it when I tell you how pretty you are as you obey me?"

"Yes," she admits. "I want to be your good girl."

Christ.

I pinch her nipple again to reward her and she bites her lip.

"Mmm, fuck, Liv, you aren't my good girl. You're my only girl, yeah?" I kiss her painted red lips. I know that any praise makes the hunger in her eyes build further.

"It's you and me, Livi girl." I move my kiss to the shell of her ear. "Which means there's no being ashamed. The number of times I've come with my dick in my hand and your face in my mind . . ." I press my lips to her sweet-smelling throat. "It would fucking shock you, baby."

A long, breathy moan leaves her lips as I drag my teeth up her neck. "If you want to be my princess, let me bury my face between your thighs as you come while I tell you how fucking beautiful you are." I kiss her again, then use the pad of my thumb to press her pillow-soft lips, smearing her lipstick across her cheek. *Fuck, that's pretty.* It'll be even prettier wrapped around my cock.

"But if it's something darker you crave. If you want me to use you, make you my perfect little whore, just to feed your depraved, slutty side, then give me your words, Liv."

My girl doesn't even consider it.

"Yes . . . Please, *please* use me, Ash. Make me your good little whore."

Her hands move to my hair as a surge of need and exhilaration washes over me. All I want to do is drive my cock home, but I manage to exercise some semblance of control, which isn't easy when it comes to Olivia. But even more than I want to fuck her, I want to tease her. I want to wind her up so damn good that, by the time I finally do bury my cock inside her, she'll be coming instantly, screaming out my name in the process.

I find the will to stand over her and pull the silk scarf from her hair, tilting her chin up to me. She's so trusting, so curious.

"My greedy little toy... that's who you are tonight, hmm?"

Her eyes close as I let the silk brush her cheek. Even that makes her shudder.

"Yes..." she whispers as I take my time folding it carefully into a long makeshift blindfold, looking down on her as my cock aches behind the zipper of my jeans.

"You trust me to take care of you, kitten?" I ask her as I hold the blindfold over her eyes, then tie it gently behind her head. The rain thunders on the roof and her breath is heavy as I secure it, the ties hanging down into her long, thick waves. Her skin breaks out in goosebumps when her eyes are fully covered. I give myself a moment to stare down at her before reaching behind her and unclasping her bra and tossing it to the floor. *Fuck*.

"Yes..." She moans as I lose my shirt and unbuckle my jeans. She sits still in front of me, exhaling a slow, ragged breath in anticipation.

Fisting my solid, aching cock in my hand, I bend down and breathe her in, letting my lips skim hers. She flinches with the touch.

Sliding my free hand down to each of her thighs, I push them open wide, slowly, because I like the way she looks like this. It's a fucking sight to behold.

Her silky legs spread wide, blindfold on, with her hair spread around her shoulders and her mouth gently parted, sitting before me like my own eager little doll in just her panties.

I could give myself one or two good tugs and come all over

her just like this.

"Just let your body feel," I tell her. "What do you want to do?"

"Whatever pleases you," she answers so quickly I smirk in response and graze her cheek with my thumb.

"Do you want to touch yourself?" I ask, knowing the answer.

"Yes, please," she says and, fuck, I don't know how much more of this I can take.

"Do it."

Olivia reacts to my demand by sliding her hand into her panties. I watch her fingers work under the soft cotton fabric while she rolls her hips. Taking her jaw in my hand, I tap my leaking cock to her lips. Her tongue darts out to taste the precum that waits for her there.

"Good girl. Now open your mouth for me," I say in an even tone.

She does what I say as the barbell at the crown of my dick nudges her lips. Her tongue darts out to trace it and my head tips back. *Christ*, she feels good. I pull her bottom lip down.

"Lick," I grit out. Her tongue drags all the way from my base to my crown, and then I'm sliding into the wet heat of her mouth as her fingers continue to work against her clit. She responds instantly to my movement, taking me as deep as she can.

"Now suck, my little slut."

My eyes roll back as she hollows her cheeks with a moan. Her mouth feels like fucking heaven.

With every deep thrust of my hips, her mouth relaxes a little more, until she's moaning and drooling around my cock, her red lipstick coating me. I watch her suck me in deep as pleasure builds in my balls, tightening when she moans around me again, her fingers still working her dripping little cunt.

"Don't you dare come," I growl, gently removing her hand

from her pussy. She whimpers with the loss as I regretfully pull my cock from her mouth and lift her up, carrying her to my bedroom and depositing her on my bed when we arrive. I pull her soaked panties from her body. This woman, my submissive little beauty, might be the damn death of me. But I wouldn't want it any other way.

"Now lie back for me, spread your thighs, and feed me my messy little cunt."

Olivia's still blindfolded, butt-naked, when her legs fall open, and fuck that makes me even harder. The way she submits to me makes me feel like her fucking king. I'm crazed, almost animalistic, as I watch her wait so patiently for me to claim her.

Not yet. The masochist in me takes over as I slide a finger into her. She clenches around me as I pump it in and out, my tongue dancing over her clit until she's writhing, begging. I slow my pace, pulling back just as she nears the edge.

"Asher . . ." She's pleading with me now, but I'm in a haze. Sucking each nipple into my mouth, I finger-fuck her until the sounds of her wet cunt and the rain on the metal roof fill the room.

"I can't wait anymore . . . Ash . . . please let me. I need to come!" she cries out as I continue to stroke her G-spot.

"That's it, my good girl, you're gonna gush down my fingers. Let fucking go, kitten." A rumble builds in my chest as I grind my cock into the mattress, aching to fuck.

"Asher!" she cries out, soaking my bed as I dip down to suction my lips around her swollen clit while she rides her high.

"I never . . . I never . . . What happened?" she asks breathlessly, my hand and my sheets covered with her cum.

"You showed me how my good little toy can soak the bed." I kiss her. "Now you're gonna soak my cock."

"More . . ." Olivia orders. And she doesn't have to tell me twice. I lift her up and place her on her knees on the bed.

Climbing up behind her, I slide my aching cock between her swollen pussy lips. The sight of her heart-shaped ass framing my dick is . . .

"So fucking pretty . . ." I murmur as I help guide her hands. "Grab the headboard, Livi girl." I slide through her again, gripping her full hips. "And beg me."

I notch the head of my cock that first euphoric fucking inch. She's so fucking wet, so warm, and *I'm* the one who's close to begging. But I know she gets off on being told what to do. "Beg your fucking king, baby."

"Please," she whispers so softly it's almost an inaudible pant. She sucks in a breath. "Please, *sir*. I'll be such a good little slut, I promise. Just make me come again."

Fucking hell. The rush of adrenaline that courses through my blood with her dirty words sends me reeling. I grab her hips and sheath my cock into her with one deep thrust, and we both groan together with the feeling.

Olivia wastes no time, rocking back onto my dick, fucking herself, desperate again already. I give her just what she needs, holding myself steady while I wind my hand in her hair for leverage. Every time I fill her, every time I sink my cock deep, I fuck away any man who's ever laid their hands on her, any man who's ever wanted her, hurt her, or thought they could have her for themselves.

"Tell me who this pussy belongs to." I don't hold back, driving into her relentlessly as she fists the sheets. "Who this body belongs to."

"You. It's all yours . . ." she cries out as I steady myself, letting her rock back on my cock.

"That's right . . . now fuck me," I tell her as she grips the sheets with a long, strangled moan and I still completely.

"Show me how much you want to come for me, greedy girl." Her whole body shudders as she moves, taking what she wants. And Christ, it's so beautiful. Her ass ripples as it slaps against my balls, her back arching, her pussy tightly clenching. She moans my name, and as I slide my hand over her hip and pinch her clit, she *screams* it.

My body responds in the most visceral way at the sound. Flames fly through me, up my hips, and the raw and uncontrollable current between us pulses us as I pull her up. Her warm back rests against my chest and I whisper softly into her ear.

"Remember this . . . Every fucking fantasy you have, Liv, it's yours." I crush my mouth to hers until I'm coming so fucking hard I see stars. I let myself spill into her, feeling myself break with her as she falls apart all over me, dripping down me. I fall into a million little pieces as I hold her tight. The dread of losing her still courses through me, and I wonder if there will ever be a day it doesn't. But I know now, without any doubt, that every single broken piece of me belongs to her.

CHAPTER 54
Asher

OCTOBER

TWENTY-SIX WEEKS

> **LITTLE MAMA**
> My parents would like to come too.
>
> **LITTLE MAMA**
> Well, actually my mom insisted.
>
> **LITTLE MAMA**
> She's as excited as I am, I think. She's gonna pick me up from the store.

I pull my pencil out from between my teeth. I was just ready to mark the start of my screw line when my phone buzzed on the completed part of the deck. I push the sleeves up on my thick flannel shirt and the fall sun warms on my skin as I read Olivia's messages.

It's a beauty of a day today, the kind of day where the air is crisp but the sky is a vibrant blue, highlighted by the dogwoods and sumacs on the Silver Pines property, which have turned an unmissable red and purple. The maples around the creek have recently made the switch from lush green to a burnt orange, and the view is not too shabby as Wade and I finish fitting the decking on the last wedding cabin. We've got two boards left to screw down, which won't take us long at all. And then that will be a wrap.

> ME
> I'm almost done here. I'll stop at home to feed the troops and then I'll meet you there.

> LITTLE MAMA
> Sounds good, Daddy.

> ME
> Don't start with me, woman. It's gonna be hours before I get you alone.

Suppressing a smirk, I set my phone down. I started working on Wade's wedding barn and the cabins with him last fall. The time we've spent together has allowed me to really get to know him better. I just couldn't say no to helping Wade when I heard the crew he had lined up backed out last minute. I've always been a natural with woodworking, and I spent my summers in high school working for one of my uncle's construction companies, which taught me a lot too. And, I have to admit, I've loved every minute I've gotten to spend on the ranch.

"So, what are you gonna do with all your free time now?" Wade asks as he pulls his box of screws toward him and drills down a row.

"Well, Olivia has about a hundred things she wants to shop for now that she's almost into her third trimester."

"Shit's getting real . . ." Wade huffs out, not looking up

from his work.

"Fuck yeah it is," I retort. "Time is flying."

"I'm still trying to figure out where the last fourteen months have gone since Billi was born."

I measure again for my chalk line. "And you just knew, when she got here, what to do?"

I turn to face him. I'm on one side of the deck and Wade is on the other, both of us on our knees as we screw boards.

"Fuck no." Wade laughs. "But you figure it out. You *have* to. I can't explain it, but when that baby girl gripped my finger for the first time, I knew my life would never be the same. She had me hook, line, and fucking sinker. There are very few occasions in a person's life that can bring that much joy."

"Fuck, that's deep." I chuckle, yanking his chain, but the truth is, hearing that settles me a lot.

"You'll see what I mean, prick." Wade nods at me then gets back to work.

These last screws mark a new chapter for me. Having worked my last shift at the Horse and Barrel weeks ago, once these cabins are done, I'll be able to spend all my free time helping Olivia get ready for the baby's arrival. Every day flies by in a mix of work, food, fucking, and talking. Not always in that order but it's like a heaven I never want to give up. Today Olivia's house gets the final inspection, and I'm nervous as all hell. Not because I don't think she'll like the custom white oak cabinets I've made and installed for her, but because, with the restoration complete, when we walk in that door and her keys are handed over, it will be a glaring reminder that she can leave my house whenever she wants and return to her own.

It's been almost two months since my father's death, and although I've heard nothing from my uncle since trashing my old phone, I still never really feel settled. Like Nash said, I have this *need* to always feel on edge; it's what keeps me alive. But with Olivia around, it's easier to work through it.

"Billi! Slow down!" Ivy calls out to Wade's little daughter toddling at speed down the path to the cabin we're working on. She's carrying a bag in her tiny hand, and Ivy and Ginger trail right behind her.

Wade's smile is instantaneous as Billi looks up at him on the deck.

"What'd you bring for Daddy then, bean?" He scoops her up, and the idea that my own child will look up at me in the very near future the way Billi looks at her dad blows my mind.

"Coo-kie," she says.

"Cookies!" Wade exclaims, animated as he pulls one out of the bag and shoves almost the whole thing into his mouth. Billi starts to laugh.

"No wonder she eats as messy as she does," Ginger calls out to Wade. "Just look at her daddy!"

She's already looking more pregnant, only a couple months behind Olivia.

"Have you seen your husband eat?" Wade asks around a mouthful of cookie. "Your baby will be worse."

"Nope," Ginger says, matter-of-fact, running a hand over her small baby bump. "Just found out yesterday we're having a girl. She'll be a lady like me and Mabel."

"Since y'all aren't finding out what you're having," she continues, turning to me, "I get first dibs on Ivy's baby clothes. Though I promised Liv I'd share whatever she wants *when* she has her girl."

I raise my eyebrows. "So you're on my side?"

"No." She shakes her head. "You're not getting me into shit. I'm only saying you're having a girl because I think it's our destiny to produce another generation of Not Angels."

I lift my chalk line and let it snap, giving me a nice blue trail to follow with my screws. I shake my head.

"We brought you some hot cocoa too," Ivy says with a soft smile. "Since you're working so hard out here on this fine fall day."

Wade trades Billi to Ivy for a thermos.

"You want?" he asks me.

I pull my phone out to text Liv back—telling her I'll be on my way in the next couple of minutes—as I stand and carry the box of screws to the back of Wade's truck parked in the driveway. I pat him on the shoulder.

"I'll take mine to go," I say. "I'll be late otherwise. And, in case you don't remember, it's never a good thing to piss off a pregnant woman."

Wade grins as he extends a hand. "Well, I can't thank you enough."

I accept his firm grip and look around. "Some damn nice cabins, aren't they?"

They're newer replicas of the five already on the property, and they'll earn Silver Pines a pretty penny from spring through fall. Ivy already has bookings for next year.

"My dad would love this," he notes as I squeeze his shoulder goodbye. I wonder what it'd be like to have the kind of father that you'd want to make proud. Fuck, I can't wait to be that kind of dad for my baby.

"Oh, Asher," Wade calls as I take a thermos from Ivy, thanking her on my way over to my own truck. I turn to face him. "It doesn't end when she has the baby. The only thing riskier than pissing off a pregnant woman is pissing off a mama."

He chuckles as Ivy swats at him, and I check the time on my phone. It's perfect that Lynn is picking up Olivia. That leaves me just enough of a window to get home to pick up the surprise I made for her before I head back over to her house.

As I drive through town and into the surrounding Kentucky countryside, I think of my mother. I think of everything that has come before. Something settles deep inside me. It feels like the Donovan curse is finally broken. It feels like today is the perfect day to make Olivia Sutton mine.

CHAPTER 55
Olivia

"I feel like I'm on one of those shows on HGTV. You know, the ones where they do the big reveal?" my mom says excitedly as we wait for Shane and Asher to arrive.

The wind blows on the front porch as I watch Asher pull up, and I move to pull my thigh-length, cream sherpa coat a little tighter over my short-sleeved, wide-necked navy dress. It's a loose fit and flows to my midthigh, perfect for my growing baby belly.

My mother's smile is full of pride as my father makes his way down the driveway to shake hands with Asher and Shane. Just like every time I see the father of my child, my heart starts to beat a little faster in my chest. His beard is a little thicker than usual—he's just coming off a nine-day stretch at work—and I think I like him best like this, a little scruffy. He's wearing his trademark jeans and a long-sleeved charcoal-and-ivory flannel that complements his eyes and fits tight to his strong, chiseled chest. He's rolled the sleeves up to his elbows to show off those corded forearms. But the kicker? The LCFD ball cap on his head, backward, and his trademark sunglasses. He pulls them off as he approaches me.

"Stop looking at me like that with all these people around," Asher whispers low as he kisses my cheek. *Am I that obvious?*

"Ohhh, here comes our surprise!" Mom calls to us as I turn to the road and see a white SUV with RE/MAX decals driving toward my house.

"Mother . . ." I breathe out. "What is this?"

I look at my dad, who's shrugging at me as Lorraine Bridgman, my mother's high school friend and top Laurel Creek real estate agent, steps out of the vehicle. Her dark hair is pulled back in a high bun, her deep brown skin is flawless, and she wears ruby-red lipstick that matches her fingernails and a light gray power suit.

"Ahhhh, look at you, Olivia! You're beaming!" she exclaims, quickly making her way over to me.

She pulls me in for a hug, which I return, though I have no idea why she is here. I feel Asher squeeze my hand before I turn to my mother, hoping for an explanation, and fast.

She tucks a lock of her blond hair behind her ear. "I just thought with the baby coming and how busy you both are, it might help if I set up Lorraine to come and give you an appraisal. This way you'll know how much it's worth when you want to sell."

Oh my God. Lynne Sutton means well. But I haven't even had a chance to talk to Asher about staying with him permanently. And here she is, selling my house out from under me.

We manage to get through the walkthrough with Lorraine without my mom surprising us with a priest ready to marry us. Everything is perfect in the house. Better than perfect. The cabinets that Asher made are sanded and clear-coated to perfection. They're a shaker style with sleek black hardware and they perfectly match the cabinets Shane installed. The walls are painted a soft white and are accented with the same light wood as my cabinets. They've done a beautiful job.

I have tears in my eyes by the time we've seen everything. But I'm surprised that it doesn't feel like home anymore. I've been out of this house for months now and, for four of them, I've lived with Asher. Now I can't imagine being anywhere else.

I watch him as he chats easily with Shane and my father, then look back to Lorraine as she exits the main bedroom with my mom. I can tell by the look in her eyes that she's worried she overstepped. She has a tendency to do that; she wants a plan for everything.

She flashes me a smile from across the room and I feel my lips tug up in return. Maybe I'm a lot more like my mom than I realized.

"I think with these renos you could really ask top dollar right now," Lorraine says, examining the custom moldings Shane repaired. "This area in town is quickly becoming very sought after."

I look from her to Asher across the room. He's listening to our conversation but doesn't say anything, and I wonder what's going through his mind.

"And we'll offer you the full red-carpet service so neither of you have to worry." She looks to Asher. "With an upcoming wedding and a baby, you probably have your hands full—"

"Oh, they're not getting married just yet," my mom pipes up.

Asher turns back to his conversation with Shane, and I wish I had the superpower to freeze time and then rewind it so I can ask Lorraine very nicely to please shut the hell up.

"Oh, I could've sworn someone told me that . . ." she begins to my mom. I squeeze my eyes shut. This goddamn town.

CHAPTER 56
Olivia

"I'm sorry about that. I know we have to figure this out. The whole of Laurel Creek thinks we're together, my parents think we're together, but now, with my house done, I know we can't keep this up any longer and I have no idea how we're going to get out of this . . ."

I know I'm talking a mile a minute, but with my parents now questioning why I'd keep my house, I know we've come to the end of Asher and I *playing* house. I just don't know how I'm going to—

"Liv." Asher's calm tone settles me instantly. "I can see your mental gymnastics from here."

"It's just . . ." I take a deep breath. What I'm about to say is gonna make me feel either better or worse. But at least I'll feel like I'm speaking the truth. Fuck it.

"I haven't been very honest with you, Asher," I blurt out, staring out the window as the countryside passes us by in a sea of oranges and reds. Running a hand over my swollen belly, I hope with everything in me this doesn't make him feel trapped or like I broke our pact. Most of all, I hope it doesn't make him feel obligated to agree to something he doesn't want to. "I've been pretending that I'm okay with right now and temporary."

I turn to face him. "But, Asher, I'm not," I say softly, my heart thudding in my chest as if my entire future rests on this moment I definitely didn't plan.

"I know we were supposed to stay friends, co-parents. But—and I think this is entirely your fault because you've been so damn incredible—I think . . ." I look down at my lap. "I know, I'm falling in love with you."

My voice is a whisper, and the moment the words leave my lips I start to panic. Because Asher is silent, a tic in his jaw, as he turns down his driveway. The mere moments it takes us to park feel endless, until he cuts the engine, turns to face me, and reaches out to cover my hand with his.

"I think there's something you need to see, Liv."

He gets out of the truck and comes around to my side. *That's it? I confess my love and there's no "I've been pretending too" or "I feel the same way"?*

"*Stop* spiraling," he reiterates, kissing my forehead with a chuckle as he opens the door. His big hand swallows mine and I have to remind myself that he's always been a man of few words as he leads me up the steps to his house. The smell of freshly fallen leaves and wild winter pansies drifts through the crisp fall air as we walk, reminding me of all the nights he's made me hot apple cider with cinnamon, and the mornings we've explored the creek with Duke. All these small moments that have made this house feel like home.

I don't know how I'm ever going to say goodbye to it.

Once inside, I toe off my sandals as Asher does the same with his boots. My heart flutters in my chest as his knuckles come up to graze my cheek, and then his hands move through my hair to pull the orange scarf from my head before folding it into a blindfold.

"You know I'm not the best at expressing my emotions, Liv.

When I was young, I was told it was a sign of weakness. But, for you, I'm learning." He pauses for a beat before pressing on. "I'm much better at working with my hands when I'm inspired. And I've never been more inspired than I have been since you tripped into my life . . ."

Asher lets out a chuckle and I smile softly as he ties the blindfold securely over my eyes. When he's sure I can't see anything, he runs a hand down my arm, sending goosebumps over my body, before peppering a kiss on my cheek.

"Now, come with me, mama," he whispers, "and watch your step." I can almost hear the smirk as he leads me to the end of the long hallway where his office is.

I hear the door open. "If you think for one second, Olivia, that I've been doing any kind of pretending with you, then you're wrong."

Asher places his hand on my lower back as his lips move to under my ear. "All I've wanted to do is respect you. I never wanted to push you; I wanted you to want *me*. I just never in a million years thought I'd be lucky enough to get to keep you. I always thought there'd be a time when I'd have to give you back, let you go, because I've never had anything good . . ."

His words trail off as the scarf is untied and slips from my face. At the same time, he flicks on the light and my eyes fly open. I'm standing in the doorway, only his office isn't his office anymore, not really. I swear my heart stops beating at the sight before me.

Asher's desk has been moved against the wall beside me and, in the center of the room, amid some storage totes and a filing cabinet, sits the most beautiful crib I've ever seen. It's been crafted from natural wood and engraved with intricate sleigh details.

"It's olive wood. Rare."

I watch as he moves closer, running a hand along it. I follow suit. The wood is so smooth and the design is breathtakingly beautiful. I can tell how much time, care, and love he must have put into making it. "As rare as someone like you giving me a chance."

My heart stutters with the raw honesty and, when I lift my gaze, I notice two words laser-cut in cursive hanging above the crib.

little bear

My eyes grow wide. It's too much. All the emotions this man is making me feel; cared for, safe, wanted.

"A-are you asking me . . . to stay?" I stutter out.

He grips both sides of my face, stroking my cheek with his thumb and looking deep into my eyes. They're so intense—vibrant gray—and his pupils are blown wide.

"I'm not just *asking* you to stay, Liv. I'm trying to tell you that living with you, loving you, is the easiest thing I've ever done." He bends down and presses his lips to mine. "I'm fucking *begging* you to stay."

My entire body tenses. The words are so unexpected, so raw, that I feel them everywhere.

"Say it again," I whisper, tears spilling over my cheeks as I close my eyes.

He takes his time. Kissing one cheek.

"If it isn't painfully clear, I'm so madly, insanely in love with you." He moves to kiss the other. "I'd die before I let you go, Olivia. I made this crib for our baby, and I'd really, really fuckin' like it if it lived here in my home, instead of going back to yours."

I smile up at him, narrowing my eyes.

"I thought you didn't believe in love?" I query, my eyebrow raised, though I'm so damn happy I could burst.

"Aye." He chuckles. "You gonna make me work for this, are you?"

"You know it." I kiss him.

"Beautiful Olivia, never in all my thirty-two years did I ever think there was a woman for me. A match who would excite me." He kisses my nose. "I never believed in soulmates. I thought the men in my family were cursed for love, for true happiness." Asher lifts his hand so his thumb grazes my cheek. "But it's taken you less than seven months to prove to me that I am the man I always wanted to be, with you. My soulmate, in every possible way."

"I love you, Asher," I whisper. "Of course I'll stay."

Reaching down, I take his big hand in my smaller one and place it against my stomach.

"This is where we belong," I say, and my heart soars as I kiss him. Every bit of love I can muster up courses through me now, for him, and for our child, as he kisses me.

Asher is warm and inviting as his hands search and knead. Hunger takes over as the fall wind howls against the roof and Asher groans. I feel him stiffen with our kiss, and then he's moving me backward out of the baby's room and into the hall. We don't even make it past the foyer before he's spinning me around, sliding his hands through my hair, and lifting my head up so that I can look over my shoulder and into the mirror above the table near the front door.

The soft light from the kitchen casts shadows over both of us, and I watch intently as his gaze trails over my back. A look of tortured need lines his gorgeous face as he flips my dress up over my hips and squeezes my ass tight. I moan and his jaw tics at the sound.

His expression has me so turned on that a feeling I've never experienced before takes over. A desire to own him how he owns *me*. Driven by instinct, I reach back, cupping his cock through his jeans, and his heated eyes flick to mine as I start to stroke him. I smirk and then slink out of the way so he's left standing in front of the mirror.

"Take your shirt off," I tell him in my most sultry, commanding voice, power coursing through me when he listens. "And stay there."

His muscular chest rises and falls as I move behind him, reaching around his waist and unbuckling his jeans.

I peek at his reflection in the mirror, expecting him to lose his patience with me and take back the control he always clings to. But, to my surprise, he doesn't move an inch. He waits as I loosen his jeans around him just enough to pull his hard cock out.

"You want me to touch you?" I purr. His cock is so hard and leaking for me, telling me he likes me taking control just as much as I do.

"Yes," he answers.

"Yes, kitten?" I correct him. He doesn't hesitate.

"Yes, kitten."

Holy hell, I'm practically dripping down my own thighs. I spit into my palm intentionally while he watches me. His jaw locks again as I reach around and begin to pull on his cock, not moving my eyes from his in the mirror. His bottom lip is clasped between his teeth, and as I toy with him, running my first finger over his piercing, his eyes roll back in pleasure.

"Uh-uh," I tell him firmly. "Eyes here, Daddy."

"*Fuck*, woman," he bites out as I continue my stroke, watching us both in the mirror. The strain of his thick neck, the veins in his abs, sending all that blood to his aching, solid shaft. I've never felt more high than when he groans a long, deep growl. This beast of a man, this absolute alpha, handing all the control to me. Because he's *mine*.

I'm drunk on this power as I back away. Asher doesn't dare move as I drop my hand. He pulls in ragged breaths, like his lungs are working overtime, and his eyes are wild as he waits for my command.

"Now you spit," I order, not breaking eye contact. "Stroke

yourself for me, Ash. Show me how you make yourself come when I'm not around."

Asher smirks, the kind that tells me that when he gets his hands on me, I'm done for. But he listens as he spits into his palm and takes his huge dick into his hand, stroking for me.

"That cunt is crying for me, isn't it, *pretty girl?*" he asks as he continues his steady pulls.

"Yes," I answer honestly. "You want it?"

"Fuck yeah," he answers right away.

"Beg me," I breathe out, lifting my dress off over my head, moving out from behind him, just enough for him to see my lacy white bra and panties. "Tell me when you can't take it anymore." I hook my thumbs into my panties, letting them slink down my body and onto the floor.

"Don't you *dare* come," I say as I step out of my panties and cock a hip. His eyes go to the swell of my belly as a low growl erupts from between his lips. His teeth are clenched, his jaw taut.

"Too much yet, baby?" I ask as I ghost my middle finger over my clit.

His eyes are dark as he speaks in a low tone. "Please, my bossy, messy little brat, give me your hot, tight cunt so I can fucking ruin you."

I move to position myself in front of him, bending down to lean my forearms against the table as he spits onto his first two fingers, running them through my soaked core and pushing them into me. There is no gentleness, no moment to savor. Asher is on a mission and I'm so wet already, but the lewd act causes my pussy to throb even more and my head to fall back. Moments pass as he runs his cock through my arousal, my pussy lips hugging tight to him. I'm panting, I'm about to beg for him. He knows it.

"Since you asked so nicely, you can fuck me now." I lock eyes with him in the mirror and a tingle of fear runs up my spine for just a moment as I consider maybe I pushed him too far. *Fuck it.* I push him further. "Make me scream your name, Daddy."

CHAPTER 57
Asher

Fucking Christ, how is this woman mine?
Dominant Olivia turns me into a sort of fucking beast. Desperate to claim her with a bond that can't be broken. Her beautiful tits peek out from the lace of her bra, her perfect ass on display, but it's her eyes that send me wild, hooded and glazy, her cheeks flushed with want.

I want to do the dirtiest, darkest things I can to her. But right now, I'm unabashedly at her mercy. She holds all the power in this moment. Power I hand over gladly if it means she's mine forever.

"Do you know how fucking tempting you look like this?" I groan into Olivia's ear as I thrust my cock deeply into her. She moans and her head tips back. *Gorgeous.*

"The curves of this body." I pull out before driving deep back into her.

"Ash!" she moans, clenching around my dick.

"You're a fucking dream. And you're all mine."

I'll fill this pussy day in and day out, forever.

I grip her throat, angling her face, as I refuse to take my

eyes off her.

"Look at the way your pussy begs me." I slide down to play with her clit with one hand and a hardened nipple with the other, my finger and thumb rolling the bud between them. "Do you know why I love seeing you this way?"

I thrust deep, and her hands tighten around the wood of the table.

"A whimpering, greedy little slut for my cock?" My voice is husky as Liv's eyes flutter open and she takes in the view of us in the mirror.

"Why . . ." she whimpers, and the sight of her, pulling her lip between her teeth, her eyes glassy with want, almost does me in. I bite down on her neck in a frenzy as her sweet pussy strangles my cock in a vice-like grip.

"Besides you being the most beautiful goddamn thing I've ever seen," I groan as she angles herself into a new position that almost makes me unload in her on the spot.

"It's knowing that no one but me will ever see this." I slow my pace just to torture her, but I don't stop my sweep of her clit. I know she's about to go crazy.

"Harder."

"No, kitten. Not quite yet."

I look down to where we connect before reaching around and spreading her soaked pussy lips even wider, adding pressure over her clit with the pad of my middle finger as her legs start to shake.

Her eyes turn to a blazing fire in the mirror, watching me take her painfully deep and slow.

"It's knowing no other man will ever be where I am again." I thrust deeply and feel her body shudder. "You're mine, Olivia."

"Yes . . ." She breathes out.

Thrust—"Come for me. Now, baby," I tell her, replacing my fingers over her clit with her own. She takes over, rocking back, and fuck if it's not the prettiest sight I've ever seen.

I grip her curvy hips tight and fuck into her—harder and harder—while she plays with herself. I watch in the mirror as she fucks me, my balls churning as her eyes flutter closed. Her mouth pops open and her tits bounce as she trades between moving fast, then slow, her free hand gripping the table. My girl is not self-conscious in any way, and it's so fucking beautiful to see her bloom into this woman with me. A woman who knows exactly what she wants and how to take it.

"I'm coming, Ash!" she cries, and goddamn, so am I.

"Fucking Christ, Olivia . . . I love you . . . I love you so fucking much, baby . . ." I growl as I spill into her with a force that has a dull buzz clouding my brain.

I'm dropping kisses to her shoulders, tracing her skin as I whisper into her ear how much I love her again before sliding my hands over her full belly.

"*Mine*," I whisper, and the moment I do a firm little kick nudges my palm and my whole body stiffens. My eyes lock to hers in the mirror. Olivia has been feeling the baby moving for weeks, but I've never been given the chance. Until now.

"Fucking . . . Christ . . . was that?"

"Yes." She giggles as I drop to my knees and kiss her stomach. I'm jabbed with another little kick and I start to laugh, incredulous. "*Mine* . . ." I say gruffly again, looking up at her with so much goddamn love as her fingers run through my hair.

"Yes, Ash. We're yours, always."

CHAPTER 58
Olivia

DECEMBER

THIRTY-TWO WEEKS
Baby is the size of a coconut and weighs close to four pounds. He or she misses nothing; they hear all of your sounds. So here's to smiles, laughter, patience, and joy. A day to be showered and a healthy girl or boy.

"Just letting you know we're closing very soon," I tell the man who's been browsing around my store for the last twenty minutes. I'm leaving early to head to Silver Pines for the winter-themed baby shower my mom has been planning for weeks.

The shopper turns and smiles at me.

"So many lovely things in here." He has kind eyes. Yet, for some reason, I keep my distance. It's not often men come into the shop alone. This man is not threatening, but something about his gaze makes me feel on guard. Plus, I know he's not from around here.

"Maybe you can help me. I'm looking for something for my . . . girlfriend," he says as he picks up a five-hundred-dollar shoulder bag. "She loves bags like this, and I just can't decide which one would suit her. What do you like?"

The man has an accent not unlike Asher's, only much stronger. He looks to be in his late fifties with lots of salt in his black hair, and his face is clean-shaven. Deep, vibrant blue eyes peer up at me, and he wears an expensive-looking leather jacket and black jeans.

I suddenly feel very alone in my shop. It's already dark outside, and everything in me tells me to make this encounter short.

"Um, that one is classic. Pretty," I tell him. "We have it in basic black too . . ."

He follows me as I weave through the store. He doesn't say much, though I'm overly aware of his presence as he watches me.

"This is a quaint little town. Seems like the kind of place everyone knows everyone."

"Yes, it is," I say truthfully. "Been here my whole life."

"We'll go with the black," he says after a few more minutes. "Thank you. You have a lovely store."

"Thank you," I answer quickly, hoping to end this conversation as soon as I can.

"Your husband must be very proud."

I only nod with a tight smile as I assess him for a moment. He hasn't said anything out of line, yet he's unnerving me all the same.

"You're not from around here," I note as I scan the bag and bring up the total for him.

"No, love. Just passing through."

His lips tip up in a wide smile as he hands me cash with his ring-lined fingers. He has a friendly smile, which makes me relax a little. He takes the receipt from me and tips his head in a farewell before turning to leave the store. I tell myself I was just being paranoid because this man has been nothing but kind. Plus, he just gave me a really good sale.

"Take care of yourself now," he says over his shoulder.

"You too," I call back, waiting for him to leave. Everything about this encounter should feel fine, but, for some reason, the moment he's through the door and disappears down the sidewalk, I breathe a sigh of relief. I don't have to lock up yet, I still have to cash out, but that doesn't stop me from heading right over and locking the deadbolt tight behind him.

The subtle scent of sage and lavender fill the main hall of Wade's wedding barn, emanating from the centerpieces that sit on every table.

They're made from the lavender we harvested and dried at our property in October. I say *our* property because my old house just sold for over asking and, after moving my own belongings in, Asher's home feels like it's more my home than anywhere I've ever lived.

I'm sitting in a comfortable white wingback chair, wearing a long, soft sage dress with off-the-shoulder puff sleeves, gold layered necklaces, and a sash that says *Mama-to-be*, my feet covered in strips of wrapping paper. CeCe and Mama Jo scramble to pick it up and toss it in the recycling bag beside me. They're having a hard time keeping up because it feels like my mother invited the entire town to shower me with gifts. My worry over the encounter with the man in my shop earlier feels silly now that I sit here, happy and safe. My emotions are all over the place this far into my pregnancy.

"You got a spare room to keep all this in?" Jo asks with a wink.

"I think I'm gonna need it." I look to the table beside me, which is filled with clothes, toys, diapers, and every single gadget I could ever need to care for this baby.

"You look so happy, darlin'," Jo comments as she squeezes my shoulder. She's right. My cheeks hurt from smiling so much today, but I've never felt more grateful or blessed.

"I really am." I draw my palm over my thirty-two-week belly.

"See how good fate is at making plans for ya?" She winks as my mother picks up one more box.

"Last one, sweetheart," my mom says, handing me the gift. "Your dad told me I had to wait until they got here." She nods to the front of the hall, where my dad and the man who takes my damn breath away every time I look at him have just come through the doors. Everyone starts clapping for Asher as the dad-to-be.

My eyes meet his across the room and I know he's uncomfortable. Being the center of attention is not his thing, but I flash him a reassuring grin, which he returns, looking like a straight-up baby daddy snack. He's all scrumptious in his fitted jeans and uniform black T-shirt, but it's those bottomless eyes that cause the familiar drop in my stomach I fear will never go away. It also causes a strong kick from little bear. He or she knows Daddy is here.

Asher makes his way over to me and kisses the top of my head with my dad close behind. They've spent the day together putting the finishing touches on the baby's space so we could bring this payload of gifts home.

My dad gives me a little side hug before nodding to the gift in front of me.

"Go on. I've been waiting twenty-five years to give you this." His eyes crinkle as he beams down at me. How I got so lucky to perfectly join my past and future together I'll never know. Though I won't take one second of it for granted.

"You're gonna make the pregnant lady cry, aren't you?" I ask him as emotion bubbles up and threatens to spill over.

"Aye," Asher says, kissing me. His hand comes down over my belly, and he whispers into my ear so no one can hear what he says next. "If you're feeling like you need something after, there's a good bathroom down the hall."

He chuckles darkly with another kiss to my cheek. I grin up at him and someone takes our photo; it seems fitting that the shower is being hosted at the scene of the crime. I love that our baby was made here at Silver Pines.

Pulling the paper back carefully, I lift the lid on the large box. Inside are two laser-engraved boxes. They're identical in shape and size but one has the words *Olivia's Story* engraved on top with an ornate-looking border. The other has the same border but the name space is blank. To be decided.

I open up the first one and I'm met with . . . my life. An old baby book with two little teddy bears on the front I've seen many times before. I pull it open and note my birth mother's handwriting. I haven't looked at this in so long. I start to cry softly as I read her words; they tell me when I got my first teeth, my sleep schedule or lack thereof, my first foods, how old I was when I first rolled over, and when I took my first step. The story of my life continues all the way until my fourth birthday, when my now mom and dad take over. Photos of the first day they brought me home, my childhood bedroom, notes about how I adjusted to living with them, the first birthday I spent with them, and then my first day of school in Laurel Creek.

Photos of me as a little girl soon turn into so many photos of the three of us on road trips, at my graduations, dance recitals, soccer games. And then I'm looking at mementos I never even knew my parents kept. Movie stubs from seeing the Twilight series at the cinema, a ticket from my first concert, the Jonas Brothers. My dad took me and Ginger to it like a trooper. Cards I made them, report cards, pictures I drew, the memories feel never-ending.

I pause for a beat, realizing I've never been more grateful for two people in my life. The stars were aligned when I ended up with Ken and Lynn Sutton. No planning could have prevented what happened to my birth parents; their loss will always be profound for me, but there isn't one part of me that feels empty now. Asher helped me to realize that. I know now that I'm a perfect blend of all my parents, and the confident woman the people I love have helped me to become.

"She kept everything," my dad says, pointing to my mom. "We saved it all, and your mother thought now would be a good time to hand it over to you." Tears line his own eyes. "But Asher made the keepsake boxes."

I look up at this man of mine, so proud, so gorgeous and strong. "Of course he did."

"What do you call that, Lynnie?" my dad asks my mom. "Cahoots?" He chuckles.

My mom swipes her tears away. "Yup, cahoots."

Asher bends down and kisses my cheek. "Open the next one."

I do as he says, opening it slowly to see a much emptier box. Inside is just one baby book, "The Story of Little Bear" written across the front. I trace my fingers along it.

"Now"—my dad struggles to get his words out—"you two can start your own memory box."

When I lift the book out, I notice some small items already inside. Ultrasound photos, a piece of quartz we found on one of our walks to the river, dried lavender, a receipt from the Burger Barn the first night he brought me to his house. A cupcake pick from one of the cupcakes I brought to the Ashbys' Fourth of July party. A selfie of me and Asher he took while we were working on the baby's room last month.

One of me just a couple of weeks ago on the sofa in one of his T-shirts, shorts, and the last thing to still fit me: my cow slippers. Duke's head is nuzzled in my lap, and my hand is on my belly. Underneath the book is a little bag and when I look inside, I start to laugh. Asher has bought a tiny pair of slippers. They're cow-shaped, just like mine.

"We're gonna fill this box to the brim, Livi girl," Asher whispers, and my heart squeezes in my chest. "You and me, yeah?"

Everything around us disappears as his lips meet mine and his hand lowers to meet my belly. The baby obliges it with a kick, and I smile. For the first time in my life, I don't feel the need to plan everything out. I just want to live in this moment with him and hope everything will always be this perfect.

CHAPTER 59
Olivia

JANUARY

THIRTY-SIX WEEKS, FIVE DAYS

"The baby isn't going to kick just because your head is there," I giggle, naked in bed with Asher as he drops tiny little kisses to my almost thirty-seven-week belly. Every night feels like this, like we're in suspended time waiting for our baby and even though it feels perfect, and even though I know how much Asher loves me, I have an underlying feeling of worry. I've chalked it up to a fear of the unknown and for a planner like me it makes sense. I'm afraid to to become a mom, and afraid of not being enough for both the baby and Asher.

"Come on, little bear, say hi to Daddy."

"He's running out of room," I tell him. And it's true. I can't imagine another three weeks of growing because, at this point, I feel like an overstuffed turkey. I'm still measuring for the beginning of February, but the baby is big, which is not surprising because their daddy is a giant.

"Take a sip of the smoothie," Asher commands. "I read if you take a cold drink, it can get her to move."

I rake my fingers through his thick hair as I peer down at

him.

"Her? You're awfully convinced, aren't you?" I say. "And since when did you become a fountain of knowledge?"

"Gotta read the baby books, Livi girl."

I take a sip of the fresh juice and shift my hips just a little, right at the precise moment Asher slides his broad palm over my growing bump. Our eyes lock when we both feel it, the firm little boot for changing my position when our little nugget wasn't ready.

"Holy fuck, that was a good one." His mouth falls open and he grins so wide it melts my heart as another kick knocks right against his splayed palm.

Asher goes crazy at the movement, kissing my belly over and over.

"Daddy loves you so fucking much, little bear," he whispers against my belly.

Snow is falling outside the house. A lot of it for January in Kentucky. It's been piling up for hours, but I don't mind; I'm perfectly cozy here in bed with this beast of a man.

"I don't think you're supposed to say 'fuck' to the baby," I huff out, shifting slightly to ease the ache in my back that has been bothering me all damn day.

"Shit, right." He laughs, and then he's kissing my belly, kissing my lips, hovering over me with the biggest smile on his face.

"I love you, woman," he rasps against my lips, sending that familiar thrill through me. He kisses me for a few moments, stopping only when his radio and his phone start to alert. He's on call tonight, and this is not the first time work has interrupted my being ravished by him. I'm also sure it won't be the last.

"Fuck," he mutters, climbing off me and pulling the alert up. "Yeah, I gotta go. But stay right where you are," Asher orders, wrangling his clothes on around his hardened cock.

I laugh. "For hours?"

"I'll be as fast as I can," I hear him call out from down the hall. Then the front door closes and his truck starts. The ache between my thighs is still very much there when I hear him pull out of the driveway.

I realize I am going to have to keep myself busy or I'll be reaching for my vibrator before he gets home, so I stand and get dressed. The office has now been fully cleaned out to make way for the baby, and Asher and I have spent the last few weekends painting the walls a soft sage green and putting shelves and a closet organizing system in place.

All the baby clothes, bedding, and toys have now been washed, and I've been folding them and hanging them a little at a time while Asher works. Tonight's plan is no different as I have a nice long shower—letting the hot water pelt against my aching lower back—before blow-drying my hair carefully, all the while dreaming of the ways Asher is going to please me when he gets home.

Once I've finished my hair, I feed Duke and pop some popcorn to take into little bear's room while I organize. I'm just pouring it into a bowl when I realize Asher's woodshop light is on, though I can barely see it through the snow coming down in fluffy tufts. I don't remember him being out there today. I have no idea when he'll be home, so I decide to head out and shut it off for him.

"Come on, Duke," I say, patting my thigh and bundling up in my most sturdy boots and winter coat. Asher keeps the walkways and the driveway plowed well; it's necessary when he gets called out.

Duke rises up from his bed and pads alongside me as we trek out the back door and through the snowy yard. I'm so lost in my little daydream—thinking about the baby and seeing Asher later tonight—that I'm startled when Duke barks into the night. It's a menacing bark, and one I don't hear very often.

"Duke!" I start to say but freeze when I realize there is a man standing in the shop. Asher never locks the side door and it's wide open now, though I couldn't see it from the kitchen. The man turns to smile at me as a shiver runs through me. It's the same man who came into my store a few weeks ago, the day of my baby shower. Only now he's holding a briefcase. Duke continues to bark rapidly.

"I'm not going to hurt you, love," the man says.

Duke growls low and snowflakes hit my lips as I stay rooted to the spot, watching him through the door.

"Who are you?" I ask, understanding his visit wasn't by chance. This man wasn't just a tourist. Has he been here this whole time? Is this why I've felt uneasy? Dread rises as I realize I should've told Asher about him. I should've trusted my gut. I study his features from my spot outside and, the way the light illuminates his face, I realize this man is related to Asher. I can't believe I didn't see it before.

"I hadn't considered *you*," he says, tilting his head to the side.

I don't reply.

"Sorry, how rude of me not to introduce myself. I'm Peter Donovan, Asher's uncle."

I blink for a moment. His uncle who runs his father's business . . .

"Asher isn't here, is he, love?"

I hold Duke tight. If this man threatens me, Duke'll rip him limb from limb.

"No, he's not." My voice is shaky as I start to back up. "Why didn't you introduce yourself that day in my shop?"

"I didn't want to make my nephew suspicious; it's my job to observe first, dear. I had to wait for the right time. He hasn't exactly been interested in seeing me."

Peter smiles at me, though even that terrifies me. "I think I'll wait. This reunion is a long time coming. Maybe you invite me in?" He nods to the house and Duke growls again.

Hell no. Make an excuse.

"Why don't I call Asher?" I pull my phone out, showing him I have it. "See if he wants me to invite you in?"

"Don't," he warns, and for the first time since I found out I was pregnant with Asher's child, I realize how stupid I've been not to ask more questions. Because standing in front of me isn't just a man who runs a ruthless business. Everything about this man screams danger, and I feel the intense need to know exactly what kind of family I'm bringing my baby into.

Peter moves closer, and I take a step back in response.

"If you know what's good for you, lass, you will let me in."

I take another step but trip and stumble as I do, almost falling backward before I steady myself against the rain barrel outside the door.

Before I have a chance to dart for the house, I hear Asher's truck careening down the long drive and turn to see snow flying from his winter tires. He must see Peter in the shop, because when he gets in view of the barn he speeds up. Slamming to a halt in front of us, he's out of the truck in seconds as Peter sets down the briefcase he was holding and moves even closer to me. So close I can smell the heavy musk of his cologne as he stands beside me.

"Duke!" Asher orders in the tone that stops Duke dead in his tracks, though he remains at my side.

I watch Asher's fists flex open then close. He doesn't move, or come closer, or even blink as he watches Peter. The look in his eyes isn't something I've seen before. His expression is dark and terrifying. It's ruthless.

Deadly.

"Pete," Asher greets him through clenched teeth.

"She tripped on her own, clumsy little thing." Peter grins. "I'm not going to hurt her, don't worry."

"You're fucking right, you aren't." Asher's voice is pure

gravel.

Pete holds up one hand. "I'm only standing so close to her so you don't pull yer Glock out and shoot me before you listen to the reason I'm here."

Asher smirks, but it's not the smirk I love.

"I don't carry a weapon in this town." Asher's steaming as he moves closer, and I feel Pete tense, like he's prepping to stand his ground. "And I don't need a gun, Pete. I'll rip your throat out with my fucking teeth and my dog will eat your remains if you don't step away from the mother of my child. Right. Fucking. Now."

CHAPTER 60
Asher

I left the fucking gates open.

I got too comfortable, and I should've told Olivia everything. I shouldn't have kept any of the pieces of my past life from her, and *this* is why. Had I told her how dangerous my family is, she could've been prepared for something like this. It takes everything in my body not to snap my uncle's fucking neck for coming here, and the only reason I don't is because of the woman just inches away from him. I would never want to scare her, and I'd die before I'd do something that could take me away from her and the baby.

Pete moves a step away with my threat, and I move robotically, reaching down to cradle Olivia's hand in mine. She looks like a perfect little snow angel in her white winter coat, fur-lined hood pulled up over her copper hair.

"You're safe. Go inside. Take Duke with you. I'll be in in a moment," I tell her, kissing the top of her head. I can feel her shaking and I fucking hate myself for getting her involved in this life.

"He came to my shop the day of my shower," she whispers

so he can't hear.

Red. That's all I see as I look into the blue eyes I love. "It's okay. You're safe, baby. I promise. Go inside."

She nods but her eyes are full of questions as Duke leads her into the house. The moment she's safely behind the heavy wooden door, I'm gripping my uncle by his shirt collar and pinning him up against the shop wall. I pull back and knock his head against the exposed brick. He grunts in pain.

"The fuck you'll come here and scare the woman I love. Go to her store, when she's unprotected? I should fucking gut you where you stand. She's almost ready to give birth, you piece of shite." I seethe as I hold him so tight his collar almost chokes off his air supply. His face reddens and the version of myself I've fought for three years comes coursing back through me.

"You didn't answer me," he bites out, fighting to speak. "And then your number was cut off. I *don't* want a fight, son. Christ. I'm here because I *have* to be!"

My head reels and I grip him tighter. The need to fucking hurt him burns inside me, blending with my need to be the man Olivia loves.

"If I wanted to hurt her, I would've slit her throat the moment I walked through the door."

A rage I've never felt before races through me as I hit him in the jaw, hard, but it's not enough. So I rear back and go again.

"And it would've been the last fucking thing you ever did," I remind him.

"Let me fucking go, son," he bites out, spitting blood from my punch. "I've spent fucking weeks here dwelling on how to talk to you and months searching for you before that. You're a tough nut to crack."

The rage pulsing through me forces me to let go of his collar. I can't be both men; I *have* to choose who I am. I look my uncle up and down, then nod my head toward the table in my shop.

"Aye, then say what you need to and get the fuck out," I order.

"You aren't going to ask for my gun?"

I smirk at him as I sit, leaning back in one of the workshop's chairs. "You'd be dead before you drew your gun. Now tell me exactly why you're here and who else knows where I am."

Pete takes a deep breath and straightens out his collar before taking a seat opposite me.

He nods to the black handheld safe he set down. "I know you have trust issues, boy, but fuck, I loved your mother. I wouldn't come here to fucking hurt you."

"Try to hurt me," I correct. "You'd *try*."

"Potato, *potahto*." He smiles at me, then winces from his split lip. "I'm here because your father asked me to be, which is what I've been trying to tell you since the summer."

"Stop being fucking cryptic, old man, and tell me what the fuck you mean." I'm goddamn exhausted and I just want him out of here so I can explain all this to Olivia.

"Your father wanted to see you before he died. He wanted you back in the fold. It was all he talked about. I didn't come the day I arrived because I had to make sure I wasn't walking into a trap. You really are unprotected here."

"Which is exactly *why* I didn't answer you, I want nothing to do with this life." I affirm, folding my hands over the table.

"Your father knew it left . . . a dark spot in you. When you went to prison."

I cock my head. "A dark spot? No . . . that's where you've got it wrong. It made me see the truth. It took me years to get out."

"And you wouldn't have if you didn't have my support." Pete pulls a pack of now slightly squished cigarettes from his pocket and pulls one out with his teeth, lighting it with a silver Zippo lighter. I wait as he takes a deep inhale.

"As he became sicker, all he talked about was you leading the Saints into the future. He said you were born for it." He blows out the rest of his smoke. "And he left you everything, son."

The fuck? My stomach drops. When I told my father I wanted out, he told me I was *dead* to him. He said I wouldn't see a cent.

I scoff. "I don't fucking want it." I don't even need to *think* about it. I have everything I need here, and I wouldn't touch one penny of his filthy blood money.

Pete shakes his head on the exhale. "You might want to think about it. It's millions."

"I didn't fucking stutter," I bite out just as quickly.

"I'll admit I was going to do my best to try to convince you. I miss having you with me, the family misses you. I figured you'd be done hiding out here when you learned your father was no longer at the helm."

I refocus on my uncle's weathered blue eyes, understanding just how much I've changed in the last three years and, more importantly, how much I've changed since Olivia came into my life.

"I'm not fucking hiding here. I'm *living*."

Pete takes another draw of his cigarette. "Aye then." He exhales. "As much as it pains me, I have to respect that."

He can't force me, he knows that. I went to jail for the family, staying in is my choice after that, and he knows I'll take any secrets to my grave.

"This is paperwork." He nods to the briefcase. "You have to read through it, regardless of whether or not you want to. It's all drawn up by Cale." He mentions my father's longtime lawyer. "His number is there should you want to consult with him."

"I don't." There's no time to even consider this. My uncle

can have it all; I'd rather fucking die than go back.

"Your father was adamant you'd come back, but Cale insisted we put these conditions in during his last days, should you be stubborn." Pete leans back in his chair, a little more confident now that I'm not going to kill him. "Now I see why you won't cooperate."

"Why would he want me to run things?" I ask. "He told me I was dead to him."

"He changed a lot after he got sick. A man lives with a certain amount of regrets on his deathbed." He exhales a plume of smoke. "He would mumble for long nights about you, how he treated your mother, how she died, and it was his fault."

"It fucking was."

Pete grimaces. "I *promised* him I'd find you. It was his last wish and request. And I needed you to know you were welcome back anytime into this family. There's no ill will here. You and I, we could do great things together."

I shake my head, my eyes never straying from his.

"For what it's worth, he was sorry."

I run my hand through my hair. "I don't want to know this."

"I get it," Pete says, slowly assessing me. "It's easier to hate him. Hell, I hated him. I loved you and your mother and he was a cocksucker in those days." He points between us. "But I need you to know that if you sign these documents, everything will be in my control."

And?

"Which means if things ever went south between you and Red"—he nods to the house, and just his mention of Olivia has me ready to kill him again—"or if you simply decide you wanted the rush of the old life . . . once these documents are signed, I'm afraid you won't be able to do that. At least not as the boss? Is that clear?"

I chuckle. "Fucking crystal."

Pete looks toward the house, the soft orange glow from inside a stark contrast to the snow barreling down out here. Pete looks over at me, a puzzled look in his eyes.

"Never come back. Your mother wouldn't want it."

Our eyes lock for a second before I make to stand, moving to pick up the briefcase. It isn't heavy as I set it down on the table. I don't care what's inside. I'll sign it all if it means I'll never see him again. If it means the ghost of my father is truly dead.

"You never told me how you found me," I ask him as I grip the handle and open the briefcase. "And who else from the family knows you're here?"

Pete stands with me, lifting a boot to put his cigarette out on the bottom of it, tossing the dead butt into the snow out the open door of my shop.

"No one knows. Declan helped me try to ping your number." He mentions my younger cousin. "I needed him to help me find you. He's quite the whiz with computers now, but even *he* couldn't find you. Not really."

Thoughts of me and Declan playing together as kids flash through my head but I push them away.

"He doesn't know it was your number I was looking for, on my honor." He pats his heart, and I know it's true. His word is his bond.

"And no one even knows these documents exist but me and Cale." He looks down at the case. "The last known ping off your phone was a Lexington tower, but I knew you'd be more low-key than that. I started going through local fire halls, newspapers online. The only reason I found you was because you helped build the cottages on some ranch nearby. It was in the local newspaper, though it never said where you were from." He grins. "Asher isn't a common first name, and when I saw you were going by Reed now, I knew it was you. I'd been out here for a few weeks, moving from one small town to the next in the vicinity, asking people if they knew you. I just happened to stop at the bar in town and the server said he did. Young guy. Told me about your girlfriend's little shop."

Matt.

I can't even be upset with him. He'd never think twice about saying he knew me.

Pete hands me a pen and I flip through the papers, finding the sectioned tabs put in place by the lawyer. If I know one thing about my father, he was lawyered to death. This paperwork will be fair and complete, but I read through it anyway as Pete waits.

"You expect me to believe you came all the way here unprotected?"

"I knew you were. What's fair is fair." Pete moves closer, pulling back his jacket so I can see the gun at his hip. "Plus, I had faith you'd be understanding."

Signing the last space, I flip his pen over to hand it back to him.

"The Saints are my cross to bear now." He mentions the street name for my family. "If it's your true wish, you'll never see me after today."

I swallow and watch his expression. Pete may have done terrible things, but he isn't the soulless monster my father was.

"Your mother always wanted more for you." He looks toward the inside of my house. "You've found better now?"

I nod curtly but say nothing. The less I speak of Olivia the better.

"Good." He pats my arm. "Then live this life, son. And my best advice? Take care of it with everything you've fucking got."

Regret he can never outlive, regret for the family he never had, peace he's never known, lurks in his eyes as I turn to face my snow-covered yard with a sigh.

"This is my life now; my old life is dead and gone. Ashes to ashes," I mutter an old family saying. "And if *anyone* comes looking for me again, including you, they'll be in pieces at the bottom of my creek before they can even tell me why they're here."

"Then that is my bond," he agrees, leaning in to hug me. "I won't come looking for you, but you know where to find me if you need me. Just stay away from the Saints. They're mine now." He chuckles. "I'm proud. She would be too."

It's the first time any man in my life has said that to me. And it affects me a lot more than I'd expect. I cling to the last member of my family I'll ever know—just a moment longer—before backing up and giving him another nod. I pat his shoulder as he makes his way down the drive and into the black SUV parked on the road.

As he drives away, I take a moment to watch him go, knowing I need to face the music and tell Olivia who my family really is, whether she wants to know or not. I glance back toward the house, wondering if my father has actually managed to blow my world apart one final time, even from beyond the grave.

The look on her face as I come through the door says it all. My eyes sting with the threat of the first real tears I've felt since my mother's death. But they're not tears for my uncle or my father; they're tears for Olivia, our baby, and what I may lose by not being totally honest.

She normally rambles when she's nervous, which is what I expect from her now, though it's not what I get. Olivia's calm, sitting on my sofa with Duke perched beside her, her hand on his head.

I take a seat on the sofa beside her, angling my face to hers.

"Is he gone?" she asks.

"Yes. For good," I say, placing my hand over hers. She almost flinches at my touch. It feels as though she's already distancing herself from me.

"Your father wasn't just a ruthless businessman," she says, the words defeated.

"No," I answer honestly as I take a deep breath, pinning her with my gaze. "All I can offer you is the truth, Liv. I tried to keep it from you to *protect* you. I tried to tell myself it was all in the past, that my old world didn't exist in this new one. But I should've known they would find me eventually, that my father's hand would reach up from the grave to try to strangle me one last time. Especially when things are going fucking good for the first time in my life."

Dick brushes against my leg. It's as if both animals can sense the tension. I reach down and pet him. Fuck, I'm even scared to lose *him*.

"The truth," she says firmly.

I feel the tension in my jaw as I ponder my next words before allowing my eyes to return to hers.

"Once I tell you this, things will never be the same. You may not want to stay here, and I want you to know I wouldn't blame you. I'll suffer for my father's sins because I have no choice. But you don't have to, Liv."

"*Who* was your father?" she demands, choking back a sob. "I changed my mind, Asher. I need the whole truth now."

CHAPTER 61
Olivia

I should've let Asher tell me about his past the first night he woke up in a cold sweat from a nightmare.

No grown man has nightmares like that unless he's lived through something very, very bad. And instead of letting him, I brushed it off, my head in the clouds, believing his father was a businessman with some shady ties. I told him it *didn't matter*. But I know now unequivocally that I was wrong.

The look in his uncle's eyes told me I'm missing a lot of vital information about the father of my unborn child. Now I'm not backing down until he tells me everything.

"I wanted to tell you, that night . . ." he starts.

"But I stopped you." I breathe out a sigh as he sits, placing his head in his hands.

"I used to be like him." He sniffs in a breath, looking at me with so much sorrow in his steely eyes. "I told you I couldn't be the Prince Charming you wished for. And that's true, but not because I couldn't give you what you need. Because I *was* the villain," he adds, his voice hoarse. "I've hurt men, Olivia. I've watched my father *kill* men and stood by idly."

CHASING THE FIRE

My breath catches and I adjust my position. My damn back is killing me.

"I don't expect you to ever want to look at me again after I tell you this," he says, defeated, sucking in a deep breath. "My family name *is* Donovan, just like I told you. But . . . my father was James Ari Donovan. He was the head of our family before he died. In the world of organized crime, my family is known as the Northern Saints."

My mouth falls open, because there aren't many people who don't know who they are. The organization is as notorious as the Hounds of Hell or the Capones. I guess I just never knew their leader's name.

"Mafia," I whisper what I had already assumed.

"Yes," he answers firmly. "I've stolen, lied, cheated, beaten men within an inch of their life. All before the age of eighteen."

Oh my God.

"I watched as my father hurt my mother, tortured her with other women, with his words. He was evil, and he raised me to be just like him."

My spine tingles at what he's telling me. But when I look at Asher, I don't see the man he's speaking of.

It all makes sense now why he never got close to anyone, was so closed off to real emotion, and never wanted to settle into anything real. How does a man who was raised on pure hate ever believe in love?

"My uncle had been trying to get in contact with me for months. I kept it to myself when I should've told you," he says, his jaw almost popping in frustration. "I knew my father was sick, and even though my uncle tried to get me to see him, I had no desire to. And I told him so, repeatedly. I thought he would go away, I thought all of this was just a last-ditch effort to bring me back into the family."

"It wasn't?" I ask.

"It was. But he also wanted something else." Asher looks to

the floor before moving his eyes up to mine. "When I left, my father disowned me. But it seems that, as he got sicker, he started looking back on his life."

I swallow tears, imagining Asher choosing a different path. The path life had planned for him. The life his father had planned for him. I can't imagine *that* man.

"Pete says, as he got closer to death, he would mutter regrets and apologies. He had me re-added to his will, Liv. He left me everything."

"What is everything?" I ask, wanting to understand every detail of this world.

"His empire. All the businesses, nine million in liquid cash, his house in Scarsdale. Every last blood-tainted cent."

I suck in a breath. "So you own all of it now?"

God, what does a man even do with all that money . . . that power? Where does that leave us—

"Fuck no," he says simply as he shakes his head. "That's why Pete was here. I just signed it all over to him." His hand comes back cautiously over mine. "I think I'm . . . fuck, I'm finally . . . free."

Asher stands, turning his body to face out the back window. His hands rest on his hips as he stares out into the dark nothingness of the snowy yard, and then the woods beyond.

"When I met you, I was drawn to you straight away. I felt protective of you and I didn't know *why*." He turns to face me and I watch him, unable to move.

"I felt drawn to you too," I admit.

"I know now it's because *you* were the sun. The light I was seeking to pull me from all the darkness of my past." He chokes on his words a little. "And you fucking did, Liv. You and little bear, you fucking saved me . . . You made me into the man I always wanted to be. The man I never thought I *deserved* to be. But you could've been hurt tonight, or worse. All I did was lead the darkness right to you."

He moves closer and drops to his knees in front of me, placing his head in my lap and his arms around my waist.

"I'm so sorry," he cries against my bulging stomach. "I'm so fuckin sorry, Liv. My baby . . . I'm so fuckin sorry. I should've told you everything. But no one's ever loved me the way you do. Because I am my own man, not James Donovan's son."

His eyes are pained, but as he looks up at me, my hands move to stroke his hair. I'm not mad, I'm settled, knowing the whole truth about him. The horrors he suffered to get here. Whatever bad he came from, *this* man is good.

"I want you to know, everything else I've told you is the truth. The moment I could leave that world, I did. I hoped that part of me would die in New York. I gave my uncle a contact in case of emergency. He promised he'd never use it, but he had no choice. My father's businesses would be at a standstill if I didn't sign all that paperwork. For what it's worth, we'll never see him or anyone from my family again."

He kisses my belly one more time and I stand, needing to stretch out my aching back.

"How do you know?"

"*Bíonn ciúin ciontach*," he says quietly and I realize those are the words inked into his forearm. My eyes drop there, and I skim my fingers over it. I noticed it the first night he took me home in his truck.

"The guilty are silent. It's our most solemn vow. Pete's word is his bond, and he's promised me a code of silence that can't be broken. He would die first."

Asher wipes his eyes with the back of his hand as he stands, moving closer to place his hands on my shoulders.

"I can't expect you to love me now, but I love you, Liv. I love you and little bear so fucking much. I'll always take care of you both, every day, whether we're together or not." I can see him breaking as he says the words. "You'll never want for anything. I promise you that. And I'll die before I let anything, or anyone, hurt you. But I won't be *him*, and I won't force you to stay if you don't feel safe."

I watch as he backs up and moves to pick up his keys from the kitchen counter.

"Freeze, Reed." I move closer to him. "You're not going anywhere. Neither of us are." I will not let this man suffer because of his past. Not when he has so much future to look forward to.

"I see the man you are shining through your father's shadow." I place my hand on his bearded jaw. "The man who was *dying* to get out, who would become someone his own child would look up to." My voice is croaky. "You think I wouldn't want you? That I would turn my back on you because of who your father is?"

"I wouldn't blame you if you did."

I take a breath, trying to order my thoughts.

"I don't remember my birth parents. I spent a long time grieving them and wondering who I was supposed to be. But I grew up in the best home. I couldn't have been more loved, felt safer or more supported than I did. If my birth parents hadn't died, who knows what life I would've lived? I've spent my whole life planning for the unexpected, because I thought if I had a plan, then nothing could go wrong like that again. But because I was constantly planning, trying to predict the future, I never felt settled in the present." I smile softly as this truth registers with me faster than I can say it. I slide my hand down into his and revel in the safety of his touch.

"But had my parents lived, I never would've met Ginger, or CeCe, or the Ashbys, who are my family too. I wouldn't have *this* life. I wouldn't love you." The lump in my throat threatens to break. "What I'm trying to say, Ash, is that I finally feel settled with you. I know now that I'm where I'm supposed to be."

He clears his throat and avoids my eyes, always trying to be strong.

"When I see you, all I see is Asher Reed. The man who escaped a life of abuse, sin, and evil. There's no one left to hurt us now; we're exactly where we're supposed to be." My eyes bore into his. "There's no guilt here, no shame, and I *choose* you. I love *you* just like I did yesterday. And now we can finally feel peace, right here at the base of this mountain." I point outside. "Just like your mama wanted."

It's at those words that Asher loses his fight to hold back the tears. His hands come up to cradle my face, and he's so damn beautiful I almost lose my breath. I love every piece of this man's tormented, loving soul.

"I fucking love you so much, Livi girl," he husks out.

"You and me," I say, just as he's said to me so many times before. A swift kick between us has both of us looking down at my belly. "See."

His arms are back around me in a blur and his face is buried in my hair. Another kick between us has him chuckling.

"I hear you, little bear, loud and clear."

Dick jumps off of the sofa and moves to nuzzle into my leg. And it's at that precise moment that I feel a slow trickle down the inside of my thigh before a little pool of liquid lands at my feet on the hardwood floor.

CHAPTER 62
Asher

Olivia looks down at the floor, her face contorting.

"What the fuck?" she bites out, cringing and gripping her belly. "It . . . feels like Braxton Hicks, but *fuck*, it's a lot worse." She's gripping onto my arm, her nails leaving little crescent moons in my skin. "I'm over three weeks from my due date. Dr. Allen said I'd probably be late, not early!"

The contraction seems to subside after a few more moments, and she takes a deep breath.

"The pain in your back today, has it been constant?" I ask, pissed at myself for not asking this before now.

"Well, no, it's been coming and going for most of the day . . . *oh.*"

"Fucking Christ, I can't believe I didn't make the connection," I mutter, scrubbing my face with my hand.

"What?"

"Your back, you've probably been in labor all day."

"But I haven't even had any contractions." Olivia grips the underside of her belly.

I calmly move toward her, running my hands down the soft

sweater covering her arms.

"Gotta read the baby books, Livi girl. Now we need to start timing these. I'm gonna call for an ambulance to Pendleton." I glance to the snow outside. "But I gotta be honest, it's not looking the best out there."

It was why I left the damn gates to my property open to begin with—the snow was just coming down too fast. Olivia sucks in a sharp breath as another contraction hits, which means they're definitely coming less than two minutes apart. Fuck sake.

"Fuck!" she snaps, squeezing her thighs together as her hand clamps down on my arm again. "Ash, they're too close together . . . That was only a minute! I'm supposed to have lots of time. Everyone says—*owwww* . . ."

You're already in hard fucking labor . . . that's what it is.

Her contraction ends and she walks over to the sofa and leans over the armrest. I rub her lower back with one hand.

"I've got you, baby. It's gonna be okay," I tell her as I look outside. Even if an ambulance can make it here, the way she's going, it's a very real possibility she's having our baby right here at home.

CHAPTER 63
Asher

I dot Olivia's forehead with kisses as I continue to rub her back. "Okay, baby, I need you to come to our room and lie down in the bed—"

"My back . . ."

"I know. I'll get some pillows to ease the pain, okay? I think we should get you changed into something with easier access."

Olivia's eyes are wide with horror.

I cup her face, "I'm trained for this, okay?"

"But I have a whole birth plan. I booked the aromatherapy room at the hospital. It was going to be so soothing for little bear . . . Oh *fuck*!" She clenches her teeth together as another contraction hits. This time, a low moan escapes her lips and even I start to worry a little. I've only assisted on two deliveries as a firefighter, but they're burned into my head. And the sort of animalistic sound Liv is making suggests she's pretty damn close to pushing. *This is too fast.*

I wait until that contraction ends, then quickly braid her hair and secure it with an elastic from her nightstand.

'Y-you know how to braid?"

"Fuck yeah. YouTube. I'm gonna need to braid my daughter's hair one day."

She wears the hint of a smile as I help her get as comfortable as possible. I've put so many pillows behind her, she's almost sitting up.

Olivia starts to shake and tips her head back as another contraction takes over, and I don't hesitate another second.

"Okay, baby, that's it, you're doing so good. Just breathe..."

She blows out a moan with her breath, long and drawn out. "It hurts too much..."

Her pained groans as the contraction fades eats away at my calm and collected demeanor. Her forehead is covered in a thin veil of sweat already, and the pair of sweats she has on are still wet from her water breaking.

"I'm gonna get these off of you," I tell her before touching her.

She nods quickly, her breath returning to normal as the contraction fades. "You better do it fast."

I work quickly, pulling her sweats off, and then her sweater, before sliding off her panties and attempting to dry her off a little to make her more comfortable. Then I get in the bed behind her.

"Oh God . . . I think another one is coming already." Her voice cracks and she leans back against me.

With her back leaning heavily into my chest, in a spoon position, I place my hand on her belly. I can feel it tighten beneath my palm. Olivia grits her molars again and, this time, a long, agonized cry escapes her.

I murmur soothingly into her ear. "That's it, baby, you're fucking incredible."

"It helps with you back there," she huffs out. "Just a little."

I kiss her head before digging into my back pocket for my cellphone. I dial emergency and turn it to speaker so Olivia can hear too, then set it down on the bedside table.

A moment passes, then a familiar voice answers. "Please state your emergency?"

"Hey, Katrina, this is Asher Reed. My wife, Olivia, is in active labor at home." I give her my address, eyeing Olivia as I call her my wife. She's close enough, even without a piece of paper saying so.

"Contractions have come fast and furious. Her water broke a few minutes ago. Can you send an ambulance our way, please?"

"I can, Chief Reed. But I have to tell you, it's going to take some time."

I wince at the reality I already knew, but another contraction starts, and I move back to make sure I'm supporting Liv again. Her shaking has grown more intense and remains even after the contraction ends. Katrina assures me she'll send an ambulance as soon as she can.

"I know you're trained for this, Chief Reed. But do you want me to stay on the line?"

"Yes," I tell her right away, because I've never done this alone and never with the woman I love. I could use all the help I can get.

"Let me know when the next contraction ends," Katrina notes.

"Done," I tell her as Olivia stops crying.

"Okay. Hi, Olivia," Katrina says calmly.

"Y-yeah," she manages.

"Okay, tell me what you're feeling when the contractions start?"

"Pressure . . ." Olivia grunts out. "It feels like the baby . . . is pressed against my back. And it feels like I need to push."

I hold her as tight as I can, whispering how amazing she is, how proud I am of her.

"Okay, don't push yet. We don't want to cause you to tear, or to push before the baby is ready."

"Well, it feels like I fucking need to push!" Olivia growls at her as she starts to move, turning to her side and gripping her belly. "I can't sit here, I have to . . . Asher, I have to move."

At least ten minutes pass like this as we stay on the line and Olivia has three more contractions. She opens her eyes as the next one ends, and it looks as though she might start climbing the walls. I've seen this before, just before a woman starts to push. Letting their body take over for their mind. It's fucking miraculous.

"I just have to get used to this pain . . . I have to get used to it . . ."

My gut clenches. Fucking hell. I hold on to her tighter, letting her lean her weight into me.

"I'm right here, baby," I whisper, my throat closing with emotion. My words aren't making her pain any less but, right now, holding and encouraging her is all I have.

A painfully desperate, clawing sound escapes through Olivia's tightly clenched teeth. Her legs tremble and then she lets out a sob. "I can't, can't wait—I need—"

I prop her up a little more, pillows under her to support her, and then I rush to the sink to wash my hands, swiping two towels from the shelf.

"Kat, do you have an ETA?" I ask toward the phone's speaker when I get back.

"They're still at least ten minutes out."

"Fuck." My voice is low. "Okay, baby, I need to have a look. I don't know if they'll make it in time. But we've got this, okay?"

She shakes her head. "I can't . . . have the baby . . . here. What if something goes wrong?"

"Look at me, Olivia—" Her icy blue pools lift to mine as I position myself between her raised knees. "It's you and me, yeah?"

She nods as I place a folded towel beneath her and another

one next to us. Then I smile at her, my breath catching in my throat, thick with emotion, as I look down between her thighs.

"I can see the baby's head, Liv." The bridge of my nose stings and I swallow down the adrenaline brimming inside me.

"We can't do this—" she cries on a whisper. Her eyes squeeze tightly shut, and tears continue to track down her cheeks before disappearing into her matted copper hair.

"Listen to me, Liv; you *can* do this. You're doing so good. We're going to deliver our baby right here, you and me. On the next contraction, I want you to push. Can you do that?"

She shakes her head no, but seconds later the next contraction is on her, and while I'm kneeling before her, she bears down on instinct.

"There you go, baby." I watch as she pushes. A little sliver of red hair grows, and I feel like I've been sucker punched. Our baby has red hair.

Another contraction begins and Olivia bears down again. Her legs shake and I move to brace them for her. "That's it. Good girl, Liv. You're doing so good."

"No, I'm not . . . I can't . . . I can't, Asher, just get him out, please . . ." she cries. "Please get him out."

"You're both doing great, deep breath," Katrina adds from the phone.

"One more! Come on, baby, you can do it."

A hoarse howl rips from Olivia's lips, and then I can see a head, eyes open, a tiny little crinkled-up heart-shaped face, and I'm fucking sobbing. Olivia pushes once more before I'm catching our squirming, tiny baby in the towel. I swipe my finger into the baby's mouth to clear the airways, then look down to see I was right all along.

"She's a girl!"

I give the baby's back a little pat and the longest heartbeat of my life passes before a gusty wail erupts from her mouth. Olivia sobs out a laugh as I wrap her tightly in the towel, cleaning her up a little before passing her to the most amazing woman I'll ever know. I set her on her mother's chest, skin to skin.

"Fuck, baby. You did it. You did so fucking good. I love you so much, Livi girl," I praise quietly, tears choking in the back of my throat. "Don't pull her too much."

I realize she hasn't birthed the placenta yet as I lean over to brush the hair away from her face.

"Oh God, that feels so much better."

Olivia is flushed and sweaty, and tears continue to fall down her cheeks, though her eyes are luminous as she stares up at me. I'm lost in those eyes. Lost . . . and completely helpless to pull my way out of them.

"You're such a fuckin' champ, baby." I kiss her. Then I peer down at the most precious little thing I've ever seen.

"I fucking knew you were a girl, little bear." I graze my thumb across the top of my sweet baby daughter's head. She's cradled in the towel, ten perfect little fingers and ten little toes, so small she seems unreal.

"Daddy wins," Olivia says, the sobs breaking on a laugh.

"Yeah, he fuckin' does," I murmur as I kiss her again.

In every fucking way.

As I watch Olivia whisper to our daughter, I know that every part of my soul now lives within the girls I'm holding close. I will be thoroughly wrapped around the finger of both of them, just like Wade said, until the day I die.

Actually, fuck that. Even death couldn't stop me from loving them. I'll be wrapped around their fingers for *eternity*.

CALLISTA MADELYN REED
....

Our sweet little bear was born tonight at home at 11:04 P.M.

Weighing in at 6 lbs. 9 oz.

Mama and Calli are so in love with each other and I am so in love with them.

CHAPTER 64
Olivia

ONE MONTH LATER

The steady rocking of the new, very comfortable chair Asher bought for the living room, along with the ice hitting the window and the little grunting sounds Calli makes as she suckles her breakfast from my breast are the sweetest melody. Duke is snoozing where he always does, right at my feet, and Dick is nuzzled under the crook of his paw. I lean over to give them both a little pat with my free hand. I may not get much sleep right now, but I am the most fulfilled and in love I've ever been.

"Here you go, mama." Asher pokes his head from around the corner, wearing his navy uniform pants and standard LCFD T-shirt, ready to head to the firehall. He's freshly showered and his damp black hair is pushed back off his face, still wet and slightly disheveled.

I'm not the only one currently getting no sleep. There isn't a moment Calli wakes that he isn't awake with me, keeping me company while I feed her. He'll change her or sometimes just stare at her as he rocks her back to sleep, and I swear this child sleeps more on his chest than anywhere else.

Watching Asher become a dad has been the most tender and beautiful thing I've ever had the privilege to witness. But the best part of all was that he confessed to me the morning after Calli was born that he was going to start talking to someone about his past, to sort through all that hurt and to become the best man he can for me and Calli. After only three sessions with a therapist Cassie recommended, he already seems lighter.

Asher sets a steaming cup of coffee down beside me now, knowing while I'm feeding her is the perfect time to drink it so she doesn't get any caffeine from me at her next feeding in a couple of hours. And God help me, without my beloved cup of coffee I wouldn't survive the day. It's a far cry from the two or three cups I drank before I was pregnant, but it's just enough to make me feel human.

"Thank you," I whisper as he bends down to kiss me, and I breathe in his delicious pine and mint scent. After a month I'm completely healed and I'm feeling almost desperate for him, though we still have to wait another few weeks until we can be together again. A few weeks I'm convinced will be torture because there is nothing sexier than the man you love stepping into his role as a dad.

Calli falls off my breast—she smells so sweet and her fluff of red hair is soft and fine—as I run the pads of my fingers over her head while she dreams. She's totally milk drunk, and a trickle of it runs down her chin. I swipe it off and she sucks in her sleep. My little bear. There's nothing in this world that could've prepared me for the love I felt the second she was placed into my arms.

"She done?" Asher asks, sitting across from me. I nod, knowing exactly what he wants.

He stands, looking like an eager puppy, and it never fails to make me smile as he bends down, his two large inked hands almost swallowing her whole as he scoops Calli up into his arms.

"How's my little bear today?" he asks a sleeping Calli as he nestles her in the crook of his arm against his strong, solid chest. "You get a good breakfast? Is your belly all full? Lots of fuel for that smile to charm the world?" She only started smiling a week or so ago, and almost all of them are for him. "You have a full day today. Nana's coming over and you have to get *at least* two poops in . . ." He prattles on to her as I watch them, and my God it's a beautiful sight.

It's not the patience he has to hold her for hours on end, patting her little bum as he rocks her to sleep, or the sweet way he whispers to her, most of the time things I can't hear, though I don't need to. It's not the sheer beauty of this big, rugged man reduced to a puddle before me for his daughter the moment she looks at him or smiles at him.

It's the beauty of watching a man who never had this with his own father, who never knew love in any way, experience it all so easily with his own child and me. It's witnessing him break the cycle, just like he said he would.

EPILOGUE
Asher

ELEVEN MONTHS LATER

"Fucking Christ, Livi, you look so damn good right now. But you need to spread these thighs, we don't have long."

Olivia moans but she doesn't hesitate as I tighten the rope around her wrists in the tack barn at Silver Pines. I look down at her, wrists tied, tethered to the thick hook on the wall of barn board in front of her. She's bent over the empty workbench. Her perfect ass is on display and she's about to be dripping down the insides of her thighs for me.

"Beg me, *Daddy*?" She looks at me over her shoulder while I start to stroke my cock at the sight of her: cheeks flushed, hair wild, and eyes hooded. I smack her ass for her sass, and her eyes flutter closed as she lets out another whimper.

"Aye," I groan. "That's more like it. Now let's make this messy cunt cry for me. Show me how needy you are."

She listens, spreading her legs wider. Only a thong stands between me and what I want because she's already stripped right down for me. Like the good fucking girl she is.

Olivia knows I'm right, that we don't have time. Her mother and Jo took Calli to the store for more paper plates, which means we have maybe an hour tops alone. We snuck out to the barn because it seemed like the most private place on the property. Especially in the winter. Plus, the door locks from the inside.

As new parents, when you have *any* time alone, you fucking take it. In a barn, on the living room floor, in the laundry room. *Any-fucking-where you can.*

Sunlight streams through the small window of the barn, giving me the perfect view of her soaked pussy as I pull the thong aside.

Christ yes. Soaked, all for me. My last thread of control snaps as I swipe her long hair off her back. Tracing the curve of her spine, I let my fingers trail down to her hips, stroking the globes of her ass and admiring the handprint I left there. Fucking hell, I'm ready to blow my load all over her just from looking at her like this.

After almost two years with Olivia, I ask myself daily when, or if, I'll ever get enough of her. I already know the answer is no. I drop my lips to her upper back, her shoulders, fisting her waves in my hand and tugging her head back.

"*Goddamn* . . . this view is perfect," I mutter, my lips returning to her skin as I slide two fingers through her pussy, then bring them to my lips, sucking them clean, just to taste her. I force her thighs open wider and hike her ass up to meet me; she's utterly helpless as I take my place behind her.

My cock presses there, and she whimpers again, rocking into me more. She's so fucking wet, there'll be no friction. But the way she clamps down around me will fucking strangle me from this angle. If that fucking smirk she throws me over her shoulder doesn't destroy me first.

"Hurry, Ash . . ."

A low growl leaves my chest as I thrust deeply, sheathing myself in her. It's hard not to get overwhelmed with the sensations rushing through me as I sink deep into *my* perfect pussy.

She cries out in the hollow space and it's fucking music to my ears. I don't take it easy on her. I can't. Olivia has shown me time and time again what she craves. My depravity fuels her just as much as it fuels me.

I grip her hips, rocking her back on my cock, with unrelenting thrusts, using her to fuck me, hard and deep. She pants and I know she wants more. But I don't give it to her, not yet. I'm taking every minute we have.

"You're driving me fucking crazy . . ." Her breaths are staggered, frantic, as I watch her flex her fists beneath the rope, then release. Every time I fill her, every time I sink my cock deep into her, I fucking hope my seed will take and another baby will come. With Olivia, I want all the babies.

"You need to learn to be patient while I breed this needy little cunt . . ." I growl as she whimpers some form of *Yes, Asher! More, Asher!*

Her legs shake and her knuckles turn white, her tits bouncing as I fuck her in punishing thrusts, never catching a full breath because the feeling of her stuns me. I never want to stop or come up for air. The dream is to just live buried deep in Olivia Sutton's, soon-to-be-Reed's, perfectly wet pussy. The moment the pad of my thick middle finger finds her needy, swollen clit, Olivia clamps down on me further and I feel her come all over my dick until she's crying my name and dripping down my shaft.

"Mmmm . . . such a good perfect little whore you are, baby." My voice is harsh as I stiffen further inside her. I untether her wrists and she falls back against me, boneless, as I slide my hand to her throat, holding there to pull air from her lungs as my orgasm threatens to chase hers.

There's no apology for the darkness between us because it has been grown from love. My lips meet hers, and as I sweep her sensitive clit, getting her there with me again, I drop kisses next to her neck before my teeth follow, biting a line down her shoulder as I picture her growing with my child again. Her arm reaches up around me and she grips tight to my hair at the roots, about to come already. That little bit of pain at my skull does me in and she fucking knows it.

"*FUCK*. Olivia . . ." I growl possessively as I come with her, so hard that a sort of buzzing fills my head when she cries out my name once more. My cock jerks long enough that she becomes relaxed and pliable in my arms before the waves end for me.

I kiss her then, as she laughs.

"I think you're lucky I brought your party clothes with me. Now, you're really gonna have to change before everyone gets here." We were both dressed casually as we helped Jo set up the living room at the big house for Calli's party. But I know Olivia brought us clothes that "match" the party.

I pull out of her fully and look down. I had barely even got my fucking pants unbuckled before I claimed her like a goddamn animal, and because of that, Christ almighty, I'm fucking covered in cum.

"There are worse problems." I chuckle, kissing her and knowing I'm the luckiest son of a bitch alive.

Olivia

"Stay still, bear. Give Daddy a fighting chance here. Mommy's a pain in the ass and she wants two piggies today."

Asher sits with Calli cradled in his lap after my mother and Jo brought her back from the store. Her first birthday party is due to start soon, and my mom has gone back home to pick up my dad.

Asher's brow is knotted in concentration as he diligently works Calli's small tuft of hair into a tiny ponytail à la Pebbles Flintstone. But she's not making it easy on him, raring to go and begging to be freed from his hold to chase the Ashbys' dog, Harley, in the yard.

"She couldn't just make it easy on us and ask for one, could she?" he rambles to her, trying a new tactic to keep her distracted. "Tell Daddy what sound a horsie makes, little cub?"

"Neighhh," Calli says, patting her hands against her thighs.

"Good girl. What sound does a . . . piggy make?"

Calli makes a funny little snorting sound, scrunching her face up. I laugh at her as I tie balloons to the back of the kitchen chairs with Jo.

"What about a cow. What sound does a cow make?" Jo continues from the sofa as she sips a glass of iced tea. It's Calli's favorite game. She's obsessed with animals.

Calli turns her head just before Asher gets the second pony secure, breaking his well-thought-out plan.

"Mooooo. . . ." she says, patting his face with her chubby little hand.

Asher looks annoyed for all of a millisecond before he melts and smiles at her, peppering kisses on her face and blowing a raspberry into her cheek.

"Smart little bear. Now . . . what sound does a bear make?" he growls, tickling her belly.

She laughs hysterically. "Da da da . . ."

"That's it, good girl."

"What about a papa? What sound does he make?" Dean asks from beside Jo, the biggest smile on his face. He's smitten with Calli, who furrows her little brow now and audibly grunts. Everyone laughs as we watch Asher finally wrangle her to secure the little bowed ponytail.

Calli started walking a week ago, seven days exactly before her first birthday. I haven't stopped chasing her since, and I feel as though I'm living in a state of constant panic every time she bumps into something or falls down. The apple truly doesn't fall too far from the tree.

"All right, get going, little cub."

Asher sets her down and she wobbles her way over to me as I move closer, meeting her and scooping her up in my arms just as the doorbell to the big house rings. I look at her and she looks at me.

"Who's here, Calli-cub?" Mama Jo tickles her belly on the way by.

"Na Na! Pa Pa!"

"I bet you're right. Let's see."

We move toward the front of the house and Jo pulls open the door to reveal my mom and dad, shaking the snow off their hair as they come through. Always the first guests for Calli.

"Good God, you went over the top, didn't you?" My dad chuckles, looking around the pink heaven that waits for them inside. There are pink cows, pigs, horses, dogs, cats, all in balloon form and scattered over the space. Homemade pink cupcakes, and cake pops, and napkins and plates—all supplied by my mom—adorn the top of a long trestle table.

"I had some help."

I side-eye Jo, who shrugs and looks at Dean sitting beside her on the sofa. "We've been the three amigos on this. Parties are our thing," she says happily, speaking of the afternoons she spent helping me plan with Dean milling about, always offering his two cents.

"Welcome to Calli's barnyard," I tell my dad as I hug him. My mom takes Calli from my arms the first chance she gets and the two of them cuddle and whisper to each other like the best of friends they are. Asher and my dad chat about the weather and the ride from town as I follow behind my little family, knowing that this is the calm before the storm. Within the hour, the Silver Pines big house will be packed with everyone we love to help Calli celebrate her first birthday.

Asher

Even fucking Olivia senseless in the tack barn didn't help me like I thought it would. I'm still nervous as hell.

Since the moment Calli was born—hell, even before that—I've planned this moment. And though I'm sure I know the answer, my palms are still sweaty, mama's spaghetti, nervous as fuck.

The big house living room and kitchen are jam-packed with everyone we know and love for my cub's first birthday.

Myself, Nash, Wade, and Haden are on the floor with Billi, Ruby, and Calli, playing with Calli's big barn set and munching on finger foods, while CeCe, Ivy, Liv, and Cassie chat in the kitchen, each of them drinking a glass of wine while Ginger stands idly by, holding her and Cole's baby, Isla. She's only ten months old and not quite able to chase the older ones yet. Little Billi is two and a half now and Ruby is eighteen months. They play like sisters and Calli just follows them around, but Mabel is the queen of all the girls, watching over all of them like a little mother badger.

"Think you can get us a boy next time?" Nash asks Cole as he joins them on the floor and takes over the role of the horse.

"Can you?" Cole chuckles. "It would be nice to add some Tonka trucks to the mix."

"Wait till this is all Barbies." Ginger nods to the pile of toys.

"We like Barbies, don't we, half pint?" Cole asks Mabel.

"Yup," Mabel says. "Even if the next baby is a boy, I'm still making him play with Barbies."

"You boys used to play with CeCe's Barbies all the time," Jo pipes up to Cole and Wade from the kitchen where she's standing with the girls.

"Yeah, we did." Wade grins. "Barbie Olympics."

"Yep." Cole huffs out a laugh. "Used to slide them down the

stair railing or toss them off the back deck to see whose could go the farthest."

"Wrecked every single one of my Barbies' hair," CeCe adds. "By the time they were done with them, they were all matted and impossible to brush through."

"Classic." Haden chuckles. "I could go for a game of that. What d'ya say, Mabes?"

"Can we make *sure* the next baby is a girl too?" Mabel asks Cole, anxious about the state of her Barbies.

Everyone laughs and I turn to watch Olivia. Her smile is so big today with everyone here to celebrate a year of Calli. Watching Liv grow as a mother has been the greatest honor of my life, and I have no fucking clue how, but it makes me love her and want her even more. This woman—who can still be so damn clumsy—has so much grace as a mom it blows my mind.

I can't get enough of her. And no matter how close I am to her, I always want to be closer. Which is why this velvet box is burning a goddamn hole in my pocket.

I clear my throat and pick up a plastic knife from the kitchen island, tapping it on my can of Pepsi. "Can I get everyone's attention for a second?"

The room immediately stops their chatter and Nash smirks at me from his side of the space. He's been my sidekick, my voice of reason, and my ride-or-die when it came to redesigning Olivia's nana's engagement ring.

Olivia looks up at me and I know this is it. Time to make her mine for eternity.

Olivia

> We don't ever say goodbye; we say see ya later.

"Thanks for coming to celebrate our little bear. Christ, I can't believe she's one."

Asher says as Mabel gives him the two-finger sign for money for swearing. He chuckles and raises his drink to her.

"This last year has been one of change for all of us. Kids, weddings, hell, I've lost family." He looks down. "Gained a family."

Asher looks to my parents and my father nods. I swear they're the best of friends and it gives me so much joy that he has my father to fill the void of his own. They're even rebuilding an old Ford Model T together in Asher's shop.

"Through all the change, I've been honored to watch Liv become a mother." My heart clunks as he looks at me. He's beaming. "It's made me fall in love with you a thousand different ways, Livi girl. And I know I'm gonna keep falling in love with you every day for the rest of my life. So . . ."

I watch with tears in my eyes as he crouches down and picks up Calli. He turns his back to me, and I hear him whisper, "Give this to Mama."

Then he kisses her chubby cheek as he comes closer, opening the box. The second I see the ring in the open box in Calli's chubby hand, everyone in the room disappears and I see only the three of us.

"Waking up to you two every day feels like the kind of dream I never thought I was worthy of," Asher says in a low voice. I swallow down the lump in my throat. "I don't know how I got this lucky, how fate found us the way it did. But I want you to know, Liv, I'll never take what we have for granted. Not for one second. Because every time I look at you it's like the first moment I fell in love with you all over again. Marry me, Livi girl."

The first tear falls down my cheek and my whisper is so quiet. "Yes . . ."

I don't even get the words out before he's kissing me.

"What was that?" CeCe calls out, laughing with the rest of the group.

"Yes!" I exclaim louder so the room can hear before jumping into his arms. Our friends and family explode into loud cheers and applause. Calli giggles and squirms, so Asher sets her down and she goes running off to my mom as Asher takes me properly into his arms.

"You and me, yeah?" he whispers so only I can hear as he pulls the ring from the box and places it on my finger. "Forever."

"It's my nana's ring," I gasp, looking down at the two-carat marquise diamond with a new white gold band and two blue diamonds flanking the original.

"It is, redone," he confirms. "The blue diamonds I added to make it yours. They're almost the color of Calli's and your eyes, don't you think?"

I nod, too overwhelmed by emotion as I kiss him. "I love you so much, Ash."

"Aye." He grins. "And me you, Livi girl."

Chatter continues around us as we kiss and our friends mumble things like "get a room" and "this is a family event." We laugh with them and I look deep into the eyes of my future. To the man who gives me everything without hesitation, even though he never knew love.

I see our whole future before us. I see us getting old together, on holiday, at baseball games, watching our kids play in the yard. I see loving him, laughing with him, and all the things in between. Good or bad, we've got this together. Always.

And it seems the man who thought he'd always be in the shadows, who thought being loved was a curse, has found a sense of peace and harmony. Somewhere out there, I know his mother is smiling down on us. Because she got her wish after all.

We're pulled apart by our friends hugging us as CeCe and Ginger take turns fawning over my ring.

As I look around, I see a family that once seemed small but now takes up almost the entire main floor of the big house at Silver Pines.

We're loud, we laugh like crazy, and hell, we're certainly not perfect. But one thing no one could ever doubt is how hard we all love each other, how we've been there for each other through thick and thin, and always will be. The Ashbys are as much mine and Asher's family as my own mom and dad, and it proves to me over and over that family doesn't have to be bound by blood.

My mom and dad hug me last, and I squeeze them tight, so grateful they gave their lives to me, and brought me the rest of my family: Jo, Wyatt, Dean, CeCe, Wade, Cole, Nash, and Ginger. And the ones we've added to our crew because of them: Ivy, Glenda, Haden, and Cassie, plus our giant mess of kids. This family is filled with love. So much love that will always be found at the end of a long gravel drive in southern Kentucky.

Through all the change, the love remains as steady as the silver pine trees swaying in the breeze. Ours is a place where food, dancing, and cookouts are practically religion. In this big white house overlooking the craggy peaks of Sugarland Mountain, there's a solemn promise. Love is abundant, advice is always free, everyone is family, and the porch light is always on.

Silver Pines.

Acknowledgments

How bittersweet it was to write the last Silver Pines book. I cried way too much while writing this. To my amazing husband for being my sounding board through every book, listening endlessly to ideas, character quirks, and spicy scene details, and putting up with me writing and editing in the zombie zone. You're always taking care of me and everything I need so I can do this incredible job. You are my other half, my LP, and I couldn't do this without you.

To Tabitha for the amazing character development that gets better with every single book. Once again, I could not have made this book what it is without our collaboration. Thank you for always helping me add the sprinkles to the cupcakes. To Rose for allowing me to never think about posting in my Facebook group and always being in my corner. To Jess and Alicia, the dream team. Working with both of you and the teams at Evermore and Dell is a joy and the highlight of my every day! You both help me make my books into beautiful, grammatically correct stories as opposed to just really long, confusing Word documents. To you, my ARC readers and all readers alike, thank you. I may not do it better than anyone else, but I pour my whole soul and a little piece of my heart into every single story. Every comment, like, share, edit, and mention is noticed and loved wholeheartedly. The Ashby family changed my life, and you haven't seen the last of them. Stay tuned for more Kentucky ranchers and some Ashby cameos soon!

PLAYLIST

1. "Makin' Me Look Good Again," Drake White
2. "Burning House," Cam
3. "Beautiful Things," Benson Boone
4. "Sober," Hudson Westbrook
5. "If We Were Vampires," Amanda Shires and Jason Isbell
6. "Devil in My Ear," The Red Clay Strays
7. "Gunpowder & Lead," Miranda Lambert
8. "If It Hadn't Been for Love," The SteelDrivers
9. "Folsom Prison Blues," Johnny Cash
10. "Are You Ready for the Country," Waylon Jennings
11. "The Man That Came Back," Jessie Murph
12. "The Good I'll Do," Zach Bryan

Read the *Soldiers of Bedlam* series in full

The dark motorcycle romance series from
PAISLEY HOPE

Read the *Silver Pines* series in full

The spicy cowboy romance series from
PAISLEY HOPE

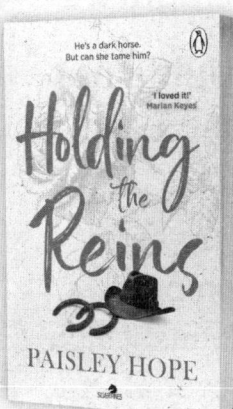

evermore

Love, spice and sleepless nights.

The hottest new romance publisher at Penguin Random House UK.

Prepare for excessive swooning, devouring love stories and dangerously high standards for your own happily-ever-afters.

Proceed with caution… and an open heart.

FOLLOW US ON SOCIALS:

  @evermorebooksuk